HAWK'S
REDEMPTION

KATHLEEN GARNSEY

Paperback-Press
an imprint of A & S Publishing
A & S Holmes, Inc.

ISBN: 0991180518
ISBN-13: 978-0-9911805-1-6

CONTENTS

DEDICATION

To Sharon Kizziah-Holmes, my best friend and critic.
Thanks for your help.

PROLOGUE

Planet Andor—2145

"𝒜rrest him!"

Hawk struggled to open his eyes as angry voices penetrated his groggy mind. He blinked several times, forcing himself to focus. Two men pulled him from the bed, jerking him to his feet, his shaky legs barely holding his weight.

"You're under arrest for murder and treason."

Pain shot up his arm when the guard on his right tightened his grip, wrenching his wrist behind him, taking something from his sticky hand. Hawk's vision began to clear. Why was the color red all he could see? He glanced down at his naked body not recognizing the red skin as his. Blood. He was covered in blood! His commanding officer, Redmon, pulled back the covers revealing Lissa's pale, naked, bloody body lying on sheets soaked with her blood. Red, everything was red.

Hawk shook his head. He vaguely remembered entering Lissa's quarters. He'd been assigned to find the traitor who was selling military secrets. Lissa called and said she had information for him if the price was right.

"What do you have to say for yourself?" Redmon stepped around the bed.

"I don't know what happened. Lissa said she had information for me. I came last moon-cycle and..."

"You killed her."

Hawk turned toward the accusing man. "No." He recognized the

1

tall, thin man as The Enforcer, the man who would take him to court and order his death for the crime. Crime? Had he committed murder? Lissa was not dead by accident. Someone killed her.

"Sir, I found this in the pocket of his pants."

Redmon took the paper from the guard's hand and read. "This is proof of treason all right." He handed the paper to The Enforcer. "Take Hawk to the holding cell."

A guard wrenched Hawk's hands behind his back and slapped restraining devices on his wrists. With a man on each arm, and one pushing at his back, he was dragged from Lissa's quarters, down the hall toward the lift. He tried to comprehend what was happening, but everything blurred. The lift doors opened and he was shoved to the back, his head hitting the hard metal wall.

Fingers of darkness closed around him, and he shivered when the door opened and he was pulled from the protection of the building into the semi-darkness of early sun-cycle. Time had no meaning, neither did his naked state. Few people were on the streets to observe his humiliation. A hovercraft arrived and he was shoved into the cage in the back. He'd seen other people in "the box" as they called it, but it was worse than it looked. His knees were against his chin, his head and neck bent as the guards crammed him into a space too small for any man.

The ride to the cell turned into the longest of his life. Uniformed men waited outside the drab, windowless cement building. Hawk took a deep breath and wondered if it might be his last. Prisoners often did not live to see their trial date, especially traitors. Relief spread through him when he was pulled from the cage, but fists pounded his ribs from the back when he tried to stand. He doubled over, gasping for breath. Restraints were placed around his ankles and he was dragged inside.

Someone hit his head with a club. A warm trickle ran down his forehead and stung his right eye, but he was beyond pain. Never had he been so helpless. As The Hawk he was a member of the Elite Operatives, Andor's most feared warriors. He'd served his planet with honor, earning the highest commendations, now he was a criminal. Something did not add up, or did it? The whole situation smacked of a set-up, and a damned good one.

The grating sound of a metal door sliding open awakened a fear every operative kept buried—the fear of being caught. He just never dreamed it would be on his home soil. The guards shoved him and he hit the cold, hard floor, the restraints making it impossible to break his fall. The door closed along with his freedom. Animals were treated better than prisoners. He rolled to his side and studied his surroundings. Nothing but impenetrable metal and concrete greeted him. There was no way out, and the thought terrified him.

***

Time-units had passed and no one had been around to check on him. The whole situation was strange. Interrogation usually commenced immediately, along with torture if the prisoner failed to spill his guts. Something was really odd about this entire situation, but he could not put his finger on what bothered him most.

The door slid open and Redmon stepped inside. He bent down and removed Hawk's restraints. "Get up."

"So they sent you to torture me." Hawk eyed his superior and thought of the friendship they shared. Duty erased all ties, he knew that as well as Redmon.

"Explain what happened. I want to help you."

"If I could, I would."

Redmon handed Hawk a flight suit.

"Thanks." He put the garment on, pulled the zipper up, grateful he no longer had to see Lissa's blood. He studied Redmon's strange expression, not sure if his friend was angry or confused. "No torture tools?"

"I came to help." Redmon removed something from his pocket. "Look."

Hawk took the palm-viewer from Redmon and watched the small screen in horror. The man stabbing Lissa was him! As impossible as it seemed, he saw himself murdering a woman. He repeatedly plunged the knife into her chest, blood splattering everywhere, her screams echoing through the cell — screams he would never forget. All he could do was shake his head. This could not be true.

"We've been together a long time, Hawk. I want to help, but I need to know what happened." Redmon scratched his head. "You must have had a good reason for killing her."

"I have no memory of last moon-cycle." Hawk shut the lid and handed the viewer to Redmon. "Nothing."

"You're to be tried later this sun-cycle, but you know as well as I do what the verdict will be."

"Death."

"Not if I can help it." Redmon glanced out the small view-port in the door. "Follow me."

Hawk would follow Redmon anywhere as long as it was out of detention. His body seemed heavy and weak, but he willed his legs to move. Hawk's bare feet made no sound on the hard floor, unlike

Redmon's military boots. His head throbbed and his vision blurred, but he kept pace. Why was Redmon risking his career, maybe even his life to save him? If they were on a mission Redmon's actions would be normal operating procedure, but this was a forbidden act, totally out of character for a superior officer.

When they reached the side door Redmon stopped. "There's a fully equipped Z-9 behind the building. I installed a special com unit so your communications can't be traced. Only I can contact you. Once you're out of Andor air space you'll be able to contact other ships, but our ships can't break the code."

"Why are you doing this?"

"Let's just say you'll owe me."

"Thanks, my friend. I'll never be able to repay you."

"You'll repay me. Now, go. And don't get caught. If you do, we'll both hang."

Hawk checked for guards then slipped out the door. He ran for the one-man fighter craft, his heart racing faster than his feet. He met no resistance. Guards should be everywhere, they always were. How had Redmon arranged this? All that mattered was getting off the planet. He would have plenty of time to sort out the last twenty-four time-units in the safety of space.

The sun sank in the north casting eerie shadows across the red desert landscape of Andor. He prayed never to see the color red again.

CHAPTER ONE

Space—2150

"I don't like it, Boss."

Hawk smiled at Jester. "We've been through a lot these past five annual-cycles."

"I still don't like it. I'm not a fish!"

"Neither am I, but we have a job to do." Hawk ran his fingers through hair that had grown past his shoulders. Haircuts for pirates were few and far between. "Redmon insisted we take over the security on SEA Lab immediately and..."

"I know, you owe him," Jester pressed buttons on the control panel, "but when will your debt be paid?"

"This assignment should do it. At least Redmon paid us well." Jester looked at him skeptically, toying with the collar of his bright purple and pink shirt. "You don't believe me?"

"I want to, Boss, I really do. But that man has a hold on your soul. And don't you think it's strange he's paying us when we usually work for nothing when he calls?"

Hawk knew Jester was right. Redmon said he would owe him, and he had made good on that statement often — too often. "Of course I think it's strange. Nothing concerning Redmon has been normal since the sun-cycle he helped me escape."

"There is no such thing as normal Boss, but I've finally found the real definition of "normal.""

"And what might that be?"

"Society's perception of acceptability."

"Then you, my friend, will never be normal."

"I'm in good company then."

Hawk grinned. "I'm glad you hold me in such high esteem."

"Normal is boring anyway. You have to do the manners thing, and the etiquette thing. No, normal will never work for me. And speaking of normal, living in a fish tank isn't normal either."

"You can live anywhere for six months."

"Six months under water is a lifetime!"

He laughed at Jester's imitation of a fish. If it wasn't for Jester's unabashed humor he would have gone insane long ago. He met Jester on DM-12, an out of the way space station he pulled into for repairs time-units after his escape from Andor. Jester hid him on his ship when Elite Operatives arrived and started asking questions about The Hawk. He left on Jester's wreck of a ship and they had been together ever since.

It had not taken long before Jester insisted he become captain of the motley crew because of his experience and training. Jester was capable in all areas, but he hated giving orders, which was why he had so willingly given up a position he never wanted. He said the only reason he was captain was because the ship belonged to him. Everyone said Jester was insane when he gave his ship to him, but he said that was what he wanted.

It only took him one annual-cycle to turn the collection of misfits into a precision team. The crew was by no means conventional, but they were good, and he trusted them with his life. The jobs they took paid well, and their reputation had become well known across the galaxy. "This job will be far easier than ending that nasty war on Metra three annual-cycles ago."

"At least we were on land." Jester leaned back in his chair. "Did you know that Neptus is 99.99 per cent water?"

"I know. We all came from there, remember?"

"How could I forget. I was only a kid when the floods came. Who would have thought the rains could last eight annual-cycles because of some freak atmospheric condition?" Jester scratched his head. "Nor could I believe my parents would choose Spectra, the religions planet. Need I tell you the story of how I was asked to leave?"

"I've heard it before—six different versions I might add."

Jester grinned. "One of them must be true."

"What do you make of Redmon's request?"

"I don't trust him, but you know that." Jester rubbed his chin. "The SEA Lab project is three fold. Estra is looking for a cure for Genesis Disorder, the debilitating brain disease that's turning their people into vegetables. Spectra is looking for lost religious artifacts, and Andor needs to cultivate a new source for food due to the abominable desert climate. Now why don't I believe Andor's intentions?"

Hawk groaned. "Because the military rules Andor and they're capable of annihilating any planet within twenty light-cycles. They've always taken what they wanted, never working cooperatively with anyone."

"Precisely."

"It's highly unusual for Andor to participate in a tri-planet project. They're up to something, and I intend to find out what it is."

"I'm worried, Boss." Jester stood and walked toward his friend. "Someone could recognize you. There's a mighty high price on your head."

"They won't as long as you don't call me Hawk."

"I always call you Boss."

"Just remember if anyone asks, my name is Bryce Saxon."

"Well it is your birth name, even if it was erased from CAM. Bryce Saxon, Chief of Security, but to me you'll always be The Hawk, the most feared man in the galaxy, the man people hire when the job requires the best warrior, the keenest mind, and..."

"Enough." He wasn't in the mood to be teased. Jester was by far the most intelligent man he knew, even if he refused to show it. The man was a virtual genius when it came to electronics, toys as he called them. "I don't give a damn about Andor's false pretenses, or Spectra's desire to recover artifacts. It's Estra that needs help, and from what I understand, Genesis Disorder could spread to other planets. I can't imagine losing my mind like that."

"Oh, Boss, you lost your mind a long time ago."

"You might be right, but it could get worse, and neither of us are ready for that." Hawk stepped toward the door.

"Is it Estra you want to help, or Andor you want to destroy?"

Hawk cringed. He would love to destroy Andor for what they had done to him. There was a time he supported everything the military did, but he realized just how evil they had become since his departure. They created wars on other planets so they could step in as saviors and demand exorbitant recompense for their help. What a scam. "Estra is a very scientific planet. If anyone can find a cure for Genesis Disorder they can. I hate to think what will happen if they don't."

"I know, I know. It's just that the crew is dying to test their abilities against Andor's best."

"Dying?" Hawk groaned. "Poor choice of words. Still, it's not a feasible plan. There are only nine of us." Hawk stepped into the hall.

"One sun-cycle we'll find a way to beat them at their own game."

"Are you sure we couldn't give it a shot before we grow scales and fins?"

"Just set course and wake me when we arrive."

***

Hawk took his seat behind the desk in his office on level four in the giant underwater pyramid. He wasn't sure if it was the close quarters and confinement that made him uneasy, or Jester's suggestion they'd turn into fish. He rubbed his temples to ease the throbbing.

"Boss? What's wrong?"

Jester's voice sounded worried. His friend may joke most of the time, but he had a serious side most men never saw. He sensed one of Jester's lectures coming on, which would not help his headache one bit. "Nothing."

"Yeah, and I'm the best looking guy in the galaxy with hordes of women following me everywhere. Now spill it before I sing you a song."

He'd do anything to keep Jester from singing. "For a project that demands tight security the set-up here stinks."

"I agree. Isn't that why we brought all my toys?"

"Yes, but I haven't decided where they're needed. We've only been here a few sun-cycles."

"So that's what's bothering you. In three sun-cycles you haven't separated the good guys from the bad guys." Jester laughed. "You're losing your touch, Boss. Must be the water pressure."

"Right." They were not that deep, it just seemed odd being underwater. SEA Lab was no different than underground cities he had visited, the main difference was the ability to escape.

"I don't like *The Redemption* so far away."

"Your ship will be fine." Hawk suppressed a smile. "The crew will be back in Neptus air space when they get bored with the women on Terra.

"Sure wish I could have gone with them, but somebody has to look out for you, Boss."

"I told you to go." Jester scowled at him. The depth of Jester's loyalty always comforted him.

"The women will wait." Jester fidgeted in the chair then flung one leg over the upholstered arm. "What's with the new researcher arriving?"

"Estra is sending Rolf Kubin. He's a Delphin expert. The Estran scientists think the Delphins may be the key to a cure so they want the best here to work with them."

"I don't like fish, but I do like those Delphins. Did you know their ancestors were brought to Neptus from planet Earth? They were called dolphins there. When they arrived they were mated with our Deltins, hence Delphins. In the crossbreeding process, their intelligence level rose significantly. I think they're probably smarter than most people I know."

"I don't know much about them, but you won't get an argument out of me on that subject." Hawk studied the stack of files in front of him on the desk.

"Why aren't there any women here, Boss?"

"There were, but for some reason when the crew exchange took place all replacements were men."

"Just my luck. I hate sharing quarters with Cook. He's big, ugly, and he snores!"

"We agreed we could learn more if we took separate quarters. I only hope Rolf is a guy since the only available bunk is in my room."

"You stand to learn more from a researcher than I will from a cook named Cook. I don't mean to complain, but this guy is off his perch to choose a name like that."

Hawk glanced at the clock on the wall. "Rolf will be here in a couple of time-units and I want to finish going over the personnel files. Redmon sent us here to find out who stole those Gwadra coins that the Spectran archeologists recovered. We need to narrow our suspects."

"Yeah, maybe we can cut the field to two-hundred out of the three-hundred here."

"Look at it this way—the sooner we do our job, the sooner we get out of here."

"I like the sound of that. Let's get to work."

Hawk wondered for the thousandth time why Jester hid his brilliant mind behind gaudy clothes and silly jokes. When Jester was ready, he would confide his secret, as if the past five annual-cycles had not offered the right opportunity. Of course, no one rushed Jester. He operated in "Jester Time". Hawk shoved a stack of files toward his friend. "You read those and I'll take these."

"Are we looking for the usual stuff?"

Hawk nodded. "Pay special attention to the money trail. Because of security, everyone's background was carefully checked, including their financial status. Right now greed is all we have to go on."

***

Kylie Beryl took a deep breath as the door to her superior's office whooshed open. She walked toward his desk, wondering why she had been summoned. Her work with the Delphins was progressing well. She loved working with the sleek mammals. In fact, she had grown extremely fond of them, which did not say much for her social life if Delphins were her best friends. Delphins responded to her without caring who, or what she was, and that was the blessing.

"Kylie," Roloc greeted. "Please, have a seat."

She made herself as comfortable as possible, considering her mind was back on the island. With Rolf going to Neptus she had been put in charge of the research project, and she was determined to make the most of her promotion.

"As you know, Researcher Kubin was to leave early this sun-cycle, however, I have some bad news." Roloc leaned back in his chair. "He didn't pass his physical. His blood test confirmed he's been infected with Genesis Disorder."

Kylie wanted to scream. Only last sun-cycle she had learned of her parents' infection. It seemed everyone was falling victim to the deadly disease. Her hands began to shake.

"In view of this development, I want you to go in his place. I know it's short notice. Your physical is set one time-unit from now, and your transportation is ready."

"I'm honored, sir, but I cannot possibly leave Estra. My parents will need my help. I can't be separated from them for such an extended period of time. and my work with the Delphins is at a critical point."

"This is not a request, Researcher, it is an order." Roloc rubbed his chin. "I've known you and your family a long time. I understand your dilemma, but hear me out."

Kylie's hands tightened on the arms of the chair. "I'm sorry, sir. Please continue."

"Professor Winn is working around the clock on a cure for Genesis Disorder on Neptus. His work in SEA Lab dictates the need for the best Delphin Researcher we have, and that's you. You're even more qualified than Researcher Kubin because of your special ability to mind-link with the mammals. Because you suspected your parents' illness, I decided to send Kubin, but as you can see, I'm left with no choice."

Roloc stood, walked around the desk and perched on the edge facing Kylie. "You can help your parents more by going to SEA Lab. Nyles Logan is the current Researcher Five in charge of the Delphin project. I don't trust him, and from what Professor Winn reports, neither do the Delphins. You know how perceptive Delphins are, you've worked with them exclusively for the past six annual-cycles. Without their cooperation, the project is at a standstill."

"I see." She leaned forward.

"I don't think you do. I need more than a Delphin Researcher. I need someone I trust to insure Winn's success. Papers have been stolen, which tells me someone is working against us. Your work with the Delphins is important, but your first priority is to the project itself."

"You mean you need a spy?"

"In a manner of speaking, yes. However, I prefer to think of you as an agent who keeps everyone honest." Roloc closed the folder in front of him. "Your parents' diagnosis was just confirmed, so they have several weeks before their minds show any signs of deterioration. I know this is difficult for you, but without a cure you know the outcome they'll face. If you go to Neptus and help Winn find a cure, they might be spared their unfortunate fate."

"I understand." Kylie took a deep breath. She had no choice in the matter. Roloc's orders must be followed. It would be painful to leave her parents, but saving their lives was far more crucial than her presence.

Roloc took her hand. "I've known you since you were a child, and I wouldn't ask this of you unless..."

"No need to explain." She watched her longtime friend and Commandant sigh in relief. He'd been like the grandfather she'd never had. She would go to the ends of the universe for him and he knew it.

"I want you to observe Nyles and his crew. I feel he's working against us, and I need you to uncover his scheme, whatever it is. It won't be easy. Nyles is a difficult man. He has a reputation with the ladies. I'm sending you as a Class Two Researcher. No one is to know you're a class five."

"You're suggesting I get close to him?"

Roloc smiled. "Not in a romantic way, I'd never suggest that, but I do want you to gain his confidence and trust. Watch, listen, and work with the Delphins. I simply want you to be aware that Nyles will be your superior officer. Don't worry if he threatens your position, you ultimately answer to me, the same as he does." He pulled a file from the desk. "Study this, but leave it on the ship when you arrive."

She glanced inside and found the complete history of SEA Lab and a brief rundown of every man stationed there. Her eyes widened and she swallowed hard. "According to this I'll be the only woman."

"For a short time. There will soon be another routine rotation bringing several women to join the crew, but yes, for now you will be the only female." Roloc returned to his seat behind the desk. "There are many Researchers capable of working with the Delphins, but none I have as much confidence in as I do you. Consider Estra's security your first priority. We cannot fail in this, because if we do," Roloc hung his head, "Estra will be destroyed." He looked up and continued, "Spectra, Estra and Andor are there for their own reasons. We've never gotten along with Andor and their staunch military ways, or Spectra, they're too involved with religion, and as scientists, well..."

Kylie grinned. "So tell me, why did we get involved in a tri-planet venture?"

"In the beginning we were only participating to research the effects the flood had on the sea life. As a community of scientists, it was tempting to learn how salt water inhabitants adapted when fresh water diluted the seawater, so it didn't take much for them to persuade us. Of course, they needed our credits. The project was too costly for one planet to undertake, so we decided to set our differences aside and work together for the benefit of all concerned. It's a good thing we did, because the answer to our crucial problem with Genesis Disorder may lie on Neptus."

"Have they found the source of the disease yet?"

Roloc shook his head. "Our efforts in creating a cure would be much easier if we had."

"I was hoping after all this time they had at least pinpointed the source."

"There are two teams working on it, one here, and one on SEA Lab. We all pray for results soon."

"You mentioned papers being stolen—who is in charge of security?"

"Spectra, Estra and Andor take turns providing security. We provided the first crew, Spectra the second, but Andor just took the rotation."

"When did the problems start?"

"On the first sun-cycle we were there, and they've continued every sun-cycle since. We still have no idea who is behind it. We thought if we rotated responsibility every half-annual-cycle, we could keep everyone honest. What a mistake. If I had my way, I'd hire The Hawk."

"You can't be serious! You'd hire a ruthless killer? A mercenary wanted for execution on Andor? He has a price on his head greater than the entire treasury of all three planets combined!" Kylie stood and began to pace."But he gets the job done, and he claims no allegiance to any planet. And for that reason, I'd hire him in an Estran minute. He may be a lot of things, but he's effective."

"Who did Andor send?"

"The Chief of Security is a man named Bryce Saxon. I hear he's good, but right now, I don't trust anyone, especially a man from Andor. However, he's only begun his rotation, so it remains to be seen how good he is."

"How much authority does Saxon have?"

"He is the law on SEA Lab, which is why I want you to work with him as closely as possible." Roloc stood, walked to Kylie and placed his hands on her shoulders to stop her pacing. "Study the reports I gave you. Memorize the layout of SEA Lab, it's a difficult facility to become familiar with. Each successive deck gets larger because of the pyramid shape, but they all look alike."

"Anything else?"

"Be careful, Kylie. Being the only woman could put you in a compromising situation."

"That's not a problem. You know I'm forbidden to form relationships with men because of my genetics."

Roloc grinned. "My dear, just because you're forbidden to life-mate doesn't mean men won't find you attractive."

"I assure you, there's nothing to worry about."

"It's not you I'm worried about. Men confined in an underwater facility can begin to act strange and do things they might not normally do."

"Then I'll let the Chief of Security take care of the problem." Kylie laughed to herself. The men on Estra never even gave her a second look. She did not expect it to be any different on SEA Lab. Even men from other planets considered the offspring of Estran scientists taboo. It was a known fact how Estran scientists experimented on themselves altering genetics, creating offspring that were considered freaks. Even Estran law forbid the children of scientists to mate, but she'd had twenty-six annual-cycles to adjust to that fact. No, she'd have no problems.

"Go say your farewells to your family. The sooner you get to Neptus, the sooner we'll find a cure."

CHAPTER TWO

Hawk ran his fingers through his hair. The coins had been missing for two weeks and he still had no clue about who was behind the theft. It was not like people had the opportunity to leave at will. The only good news was that no one recognized him. He was not used to being called by his real name. The Hawk was the operative name he had chosen when his real identity was erased from Confidentially Accessed Material, commonly referred to as CAM by those who knew of its existence.

"Boss, I've done some research on those missing Gwadra coins. They're twentieth century, valued at 2.5 million credits each, which puts the theft at..."

"I can add, Jester. Who took them?"

"Someone from Spectra, Estra, or Andor."

Hawk grinned. "Thanks for narrowing it down to three planets." There were times Jester's odd sense of humor could drive him up the wall.

"No problem, Boss." Jester glanced at his wrist. "You know that Researcher will be arriving in a few minutes. Want me to pick him up?"

"I need a break. I'll do it myself." Hawk stood and stretched his arms over his head, then bent to touch the floor. "This place is getting to me."

"Me too. Men weren't meant to live like fish."

"I agree. I'll be glad to get back into space."

"Even *The Redemption* isn't as confining as SEA Lab."

"My ship has never been confining. It's the only place I have real freedom." Hawk stepped toward the door.

"You know, Boss, we've seen a lot of action together, but this is the first time we've been stuck underwater. I don't like it. I've been studying the probabilities of a leak. The percentages bother me." Jester turned to face his friend. "There is a .00032 per-cent chance of a wall cracking. I don't like those odds."

"There's a fifty-fifty chance my true identity will be discovered. Try those odds."

"According to my calculations..."

"Save it. I'm going to meet Researcher Kubin. Try and stay out of trouble while I'm gone." Jester was still muttering facts and figures to himself as the door slid closed. It was no wonder everyone who met Jester thought him the fool. He spouted facts and fiction all in the same breath, asking himself questions and answering them as well. Of course, Jester would not be effective if people knew he was a pure genius masquerading as a simpleton.

Hawk bypassed the lift and ran the three flights of stairs to the observation deck. Running the stairs was the only exercise he'd gotten lately. At least the designers of SEA Lab planned ample escape methods should the need arise. Each level had connecting lifts, a flight of stairs, and an emergency slide pole, and he hoped he never learned why all three were necessary.

A moment alone before meeting Rolf Kubin was exactly what he needed. Since his arrival he had investigated stolen artifacts and lost papers, asked thousands of questions, and found answers to none. Not a very good start. Redmon sent him to get things under control and he was far from that accomplishment.

He stepped onto the observation deck with the same sense of awe he had the very first time he'd seen it. Beams of light from the surface penetrated the depths of the Agor Sea, glistening off brightly colored fish that swam by the clear walls in large schools. Here he did feel like one of the fish, completely surrounded by quiet water.

This was the only window in SEA Lab, but it didn't seem like a window at all, more like an air pocket in the ocean. Jester had done numerous calculations on what it would take to crack the clear walls of the pyramid peak where he stood. He didn't care, it was one of the few places he could relax.

As a warrior he hated being trapped by water. Redmon promised this would be his last obligation, and he meant to hold him to it. The only reason he appeased Redmon was to clear his name. Whether he helped his former commanding officer or not, he could not be in any more trouble. Why he thought Redmon could help clear him he wasn't sure. He still did not understand why the man had helped him escape.

Obviously Redmon wanted a man not connected to Andor he could count on to complete assignments outside the law. His sun-cycles of doing Redmon's bidding were over the minute he found dry land.

He had evaded capture for over five annual-cycles with the help of Jester and his other loyal crew. They had made a fortune as mercenaries, solving problems no one else would touch, but it could all come to an end, here in the depths of the Agor Sea. His instructions to Beggar, his first mate, were to take the men on a well-deserved leave. His men deserved some time off, yet he could never escape this watery prison if his enemies discovered his presence. For some reason the thought of ending this endless game of hide and seek held merit, it was the punishment he was unable to come to terms with...death.

For a wanted criminal he led a comfortable lifestyle. *The Redemption* was the finest ship credits could buy, fully equipped with the latest technology, conveniences, and weapons. Considering its size, *The Redemption* was fast, which served them well on many occasions. Nothing replaced freedom. Sure he roamed the galaxy doing everyone's dirty work, but it wasn't the same as being able to walk into a legitimate business and shop for himself, or share drinks with friends in a reputable tavern, not to mention the one thing he wanted most--to settle down somewhere, with a woman he could love and have children. It was a foolish dream, but the desire to be normal left an ache in his heart.

A Delphin swam by and two more followed. He admired their grace, their speed, and their freedom. They displayed concern for the family unit, a trait he had little experience with. Schools of fish skittered one way, then abruptly turned in another as if they detected an unknown enemy lying in wait. Hawk checked his wrist piece for the time. Rolf should have been here by now. All he could do was watch for the sub-shuttle.

More sea creatures casually swam by in their peaceful, quiet world. Suddenly an object plunged past the clear walls of the observation deck. Hawk strained to see through the mass of bubbles that enshrouded the object. Whatever it was he had to check it out. It could be a spy vessel, the first break in his investigation. With the luck he'd been having, it was probably space debris. Or worse, an explosive device that would turn SEA Lab into fish food. He pulled the palm-com from his pocket. "Jester, come to the ready room on level two immediately."

Hawk used the emergency slide pole to the deck below and ran to the ready room. He stripped off his clothes, pulled on a dive suit and reached for one of the clear helmets from the rack on the wall.

"Boss, what's going on?" Jester blurted, trying to catch his breath.

"Gear up. Either Rolf Kubin crashed, or we have a spy on our hands."

"Are you sure?"

"I saw a one man pod sink to the bottom." Hawk heard his palm-com squawking from the pocket of his pants on the floor. He picked it up and listened to an excited voice. "Calm down and repeat."

"We're up here with the sub waiting for the new arrival. The pod approached but didn't land on the pad, it crashed into the sea. What should we do?"

"Take the sub down to the site and wait, Jester and I are gearing up. I'll contact you with further instructions. Out." He attached his helmet and tucked another under his arm then removed a spear gun from the rack. If it was a spy, he hoped there would be a survivor to interrogate. "Jester, grab two hand-jets." Hawk jumped into the exit pool and waited for Jester to hand him the small unit that would propel him to the bottom of the sea.

The currents seemed stronger than usual which slowed their speed, but he kept his course set in the direction where he had last seen the pod. He was not sure if he wanted to find Rolf Kubin or something else that would solve the mystery of the deep and get him back on dry land. Neptus made the hot, dry deserts of Andor seem inviting. "There," Hawk said, pointing straight ahead.

"I see it, Boss."

The bottom was murky, sand still settling about the wrecked craft. Fifty more feet to the left and it would have fallen into the bottomless crevice the scientists were studying. They had yet to determine its depth, and he had no intention of being the person to do it. He turned off the hand-jet and glided the last few feet, trying not to stir up any more silt. "It must be Rolf, there's the Estran seal on the door." He glanced at Jester. "Are you all right?"

"I'm not a fish...I can't breathe."

"Calm down. Breathing in this helmet is no different than the space suits you've worn. You're fine." He put Jester's gloved hands on the hatch wheel. "Stay put, I'll be right back." Jester looked pale and scared, but he was a trooper. Hawk swam to the front and inspected the cockpit windshield. As he suspected, the outer shield was shattered and a large crack was visible on the inner glass panel. A smoky haze filled the cabin causing poor visibility, but he saw the outline of a body slumped over the console, and so far, the interior appeared dry.

With a few hard kicks of his flippers he was back beside Jester, who had not moved a muscle since he left. Jester nodded and removed his hands from the hatch. Hawk ripped a long string of kelp from the wheel then grasped it with both hands. "Jester, please tell me this model pod has a double door entry."

"It's a model RS-24, manufactured by..."

"Yes or no!"

"Yes."

Hawk used every ounce of strength to budge the wheel, but it only moved an inch. He took a deep breath and tried again, pleased when it moved a foot more. Rolf was lucky he had not been in one of the newer models with a single hatch or the man would drown before he could reach him.

"There probably isn't room for both of us between the two hatches. In fact, I'm not sure your helmet will fit," Jester said, grabbing the other side of the wheel.

"That's why you're going to wait here for me."

"It could be dangerous in there. What if it's not Rolf, but..."

"Rolf is unconscious in an Estran pod. We were expecting him, so I don't think it's a spy. Even if he were the enemy I'm more than capable of taking care of myself, remember?"

"You're the best, I know that, it's just..."

"Quit worrying and turn." Together they managed to overcome the tremendous pressure the water exerted and pulled the hatch open. Murky green seawater filled the small space so fast he wondered if it had ever been dry. Hawk picked up the spare helmet from the sandy bottom and squeezed his large body into the cramped space.

"What about the weapon?"

"You might need it to shoot a sharkus. I'll be fine." Jester closed the door from the outside and he heard the lock click into place.

The second wheel turned a bit easier, but he dropped the helmet in the process. He took a deep breath and prepared himself for a rough entry. The interior hatch swung open and an immediate gush of water shoved him face down on the metal floor. He removed the helmet and shook his head. At least the clear plastic sphere had not cracked, but he felt as if every tooth in his head had.

"Are you all right?"

Jester's voice echoed in sphere on the floor. "Fine!" He rose to his feet and turned toward the cockpit. His jaw dropped and his heart nearly stopped at the sight before him. The woman lay lifeless; her long red hair lay in a tangled, knotted mess across knobs and switches. Hawk rushed to her side, separated the curls at the side of her neck, and searched for a pulse. He moved his fingers up and down until he finally found the slow, weak sign of life.

The pod moaned and creaked, the smell of salt heavy on the unventilated air. He glanced at the crack in the front shield and prayed it would hold long enough for him to get her out. He worked quickly to untangle her auburn locks from the mangled control panel that tied her to the console.

A loud cracking noise reverberated in the small chamber and a stream of water flowed into the craft from the rip in the shield. He pulled a knife from the sheath on his weight belt and cut each tangled web of hair free. He eased her back in the pilot's seat and his breath caught in his throat.

Blood trickled from her scalp and left a thin red trail down her pallid skin. Even in disarray she was beautiful. Who was the mystery woman who crashed into his life? Questioning this little creature would prove most interesting.

Water in the cabin was rising fast, and he had to hurry if he wanted to get out before the shield gave way. He left her, moved to the back, retrieved the helmets and sloshed through the now waist deep water. First he secured the woman's breathing apparatus, then his own. He picked her up in his arms and carried her to the hatch.

A loud snap resounded through the craft, the deafening sound of the front glass shattering pierced his ears through the protective helmet. He pressed the woman against the wall and shielded her with his body from the incoming deluge of water. The rushing force pinned them for several long moments until the sea claimed the inside of the pod as its own. The water erased her weight in his arms, so he grasped her around the waist and swam toward the front.

"Boss! Are you all right?" Jester yelled, glaring into the pod.

"We're on our way out." At least he did not have to take her back through the hatches, instead he pulled her through the opening left by the missing front shield. It took little effort to pull her through the opening, but he was not prepared for the odd look on Jester's face. "Yes, it's a woman. Hand me that hand-jet so we can get out of here."

"I won't argue with that."

CHAPTER THREE

Kylie blinked several times in an effort to focus. Her head throbbed and her hand moved to her forehead. Something soft met her touch, her fingers finding some sort of a bandage. What happened? Pain pounded in her temples so hard rational thought was difficult. If she could sit up and look around, she might be able to get her bearings.

A large, shadowy figure leaned over her and hovered. Even through blurred vision she knew it had to be a man, but she could not discern his features. "Who are you?"

"Security Chief Saxon."

"Where am I?"

"SEA Lab."

"What happened?"

"You crashed."

"Could you help me up?"

"I don't think that's a good idea. You've suffered a head wound and..."

"Fine, I'll do it myself." The moment she lifted her head she felt one strong arm slip under her back and another under her knees. Before she could protest she was in his arms. His face may not be clear, but his strength was undeniable. Her arm slid over his shoulder and around his neck. He was extremely muscular, bigger than Estran men. The warmth of his body felt good, too good. "Put me down."

"As you wish, Amica."

"My name is Kylie, not Amica." He bent and set her feet on the floor, but kept one arm around her waist. A strange shiver ran down her spine. She was not used to being touched by a man, especially one with hard muscles and commanding strength. "I'm fine. You can let go."

Kylie swayed the moment he released her, and she struggled to keep her legs under control. The room began to spin and she felt faint. She refused to show weakness and willed her limp body to hold her, but she started to fall despite her efforts. He saved her from hitting the floor by pulling her to him. She could barely breathe pressed against his powerful chest.

His firm grasp made his potency palpable. He smelled of cologne and seawater. She stared at his face, startled by the brilliant blue of his eyes. Her breathing quickened, but so did his. She heard a deep, muted groan. "I'm sorry," she managed to whisper. "I guess I'm not as strong as I thought." Still gazing into the depths of his eyes, she heard the door behind them open and someone stomp inside.

"Such a pretty picture."

"Kylie," Hawk began, "I'd like you to meet Jester, my right hand man."

"Nice to meet you."

"Likewise." Jester motioned toward the door. "We need to talk, Boss."

He carried her to the bunk and laid her down. "Excuse me for a moment?"

"Sure." Kylie realized her vision had returned to normal when she caught sight of his well-defined backside as he left. He was quite a man, but she had no intention of getting that close to him again. Her eyes burned so she closed them, feeling more tired that she'd ever felt in her life. The details of the crash were returning with a vengeance. Rest was what she needed so she could begin her work with the Delphins. Tears welled as she remembered why she was here.

***

"I wish you'd get that look off your face," Jester said, plopping himself in the chair in front of Hawk's desk.

"What look?"

"The smitten look."

"I am not smitten. I simply helped her to stand and she fell, so I caught her."

Jester laughed. "Then I caught you!"

"You've got my full attention now." He wished Jester would stop his stupid grinning. "Talk. What's so important?"

"Oh that." Jester cleared his throat. "Early this sun-cycle the archaeologists found twelve Gwadra coins. They were catalogued and placed on a shelf. One time-unit later they could only find ten of them."

"Have officer Throm begin a search of the entire facility immediately. I want you to hang in the background and learn what you can. Someone now has four very valuable coins, and he's playing us for fools. Whoever it is will make a mistake, and we'll be there when he does."

Jester leaped to his feet, slapped a hand against his forehead and left. Hawk laughed. It was Jester's own peculiar salute, a joke between them. Everyone considered Jester insane, which made him a valuable tool. Hawk quickly returned to his quarters, anxious to check on Kylie.

The door opened and he stepped inside, studying the sleeping woman. Her beautiful red hair spilled seductively across the pillow. A twinge of guilt ripped through him when he noticed short, chopped off sections of hair. She might never forgive him when she saw the nasty haircut he had been forced to give her, but at least she was alive to complain.

He sat in the chair and watched her sleep, wishing she would wake so he could learn why she was here. He had never met Rolf Kubin, but he was quite sure she looked nothing like him. Kylie had to be prettier than Rolf, but that was the problem. She was the only woman currently on SEA Lab, and it was up to him to keep her safe.

She moaned softly in her sleep and he rushed to her side. The doctor had sealed the wound in her scalp, but he said he could not give her anything for pain until she was awake. He laid his hand on her forehead. She felt warm and soft. The color had returned to her skin, and she looked alluringly beautiful. No wonder he had slipped and called her Amica. Kylie obviously did not know it was a commonly used endearment between lovers on Andor. He was not sure why the term had slipped from his lips, but he would be more careful in the future.

Could Kylie be a spy? No. A woman that looked like her would stand out like a sore thumb. A spy had to blend and she could never blend, not with that perfect body and angelic face. When she had looked at him with those pleading emerald eyes all he wanted to do was hold and protect her. Silly notions did not happen to him, and if they did, Jester was usually involved.

Then again, the most ruthless spy he had ever encountered was a blonde with lavender eyes and a sumptuous body that would tempt a celibate priest. It was his first undercover assignment in the Elite Squad, and he had been perfect prey for the femme-fatal. This time he had his wits, twelve annual-cycles of warrior seasoning to draw from, and more experiences with women than he cared to remember. If she were a spy, he would know.

A swoosh made him turn. "Doctor."

"How is our patient?" he asked, sitting on the bunk next to Kylie.

"I'm still here," she answered in a whisper.

Hawk wondered if she knew he had been watching her. It did not matter, he was *only* doing his job. He watched the doctor check the bandage and take Kylie's pulse. At least he seemed pleased by her progress.

The doctor stood. "I'll give you something for the pain if you promise to stay awake."

"How could I sleep with the pounding in my head?"

"All right then." The doctor pressed a small cylinder to the left side of her neck for a second then pulled it back. "I'll leave this with Saxon and check on you in the early sun-cycle." He removed the bandage. "The seal is complete. Just take it easy. You'll be dizzy for a while." He smiled. "You're one lucky lady." He glanced at Saxon. "Keep her quiet, and do not, under any circumstances, leave her alone."

"I understand." Hawk escorted the doctor out into the hall so Kylie could not hear. "Doctor, I don't want her presence known just yet. She needs time to recover without being bothered." He pulled a small round disk from his pocket and handed it to the doctor. "If you hear it beep, come immediately. I don't want to be overheard on the com."

"I see why you're Chief of Security." The doctor gave Saxon a friendly pat on the back. "See you tomorrow."

Hawk turned on his heel, and returned to the chair, the door closing behind him. Kylie sat on the edge of the bottom bunk, a hand on each side to steady her. He noticed her feet, so small and delicate, then his gaze roamed up her bare legs to her knees where the thin fabric of the med-gown began. He took a deep breath as he continued his assessment, his gaze stopping on the firm outline of her breasts. Med-gowns should not be so revealing.

"We need to talk." Kylie pushed hair away from her face.

"That was going to be my line. Who are you?"

"Researcher," she hesitated a moment, "Second Class Kylie Beryl. I'm here instead of Rolf Kubin. He wasn't able to fulfill his assignment."

"And I'm supposed to believe you?"

"Of course." She glanced around the room. "I'm afraid my belongings are...wherever the pod landed."

"That would be at the bottom of the Agor Sea." She looked so lost he felt sorry for her. This was not going as he had planned. "Who sent you?"

"Commander Roloc of Estra assigned me to SEA Lab." Kylie stood and walked to the empty chair beside the table where he sat. "Roloc is concerned about the missing papers from the Estran research lab, and he suggested I confide in you. Considering your attitude, I'm not sure that's a wise thing to do."

"Really. Then tell me, Researcher Beryl, who should you trust?" Her green eyes bored through him. She was a tough one, he'd give her that. He was not sure what her game was, but she seemed to be telling the truth. Her silence irritated him in a way he could not explain. He met her gaze and waited.

"I've been on SEA Lab all of one time-unit, so I don't know how to answer your question."

"I am well aware of the problems here, and I assure you, I'm doing everything I can to find those responsible. It's my job to insure the success of this operation. If there is a leak in security, I will find it. You can trust me, Researcher Beryl. I take my responsibilities seriously."

"How long have you been here?"

"A month."

Kylie leaned an arm on the table. "And what have you learned?"

"I can't say."

"Won't say." Kylie shivered. "You're looking at me very strangely, and your voice, it's..." She wrapped her arms around herself. "You're interrogating me, aren't you?"

"As I said, I'm doing my job." He hated dealing with women, they were harder to read than men. With men it was simple, kill or be killed, but women played games, and he was not in the mood. "You're not being entirely honest with me, Researcher Beryl."

"What do you want me to say? That I'm a spy sent here on a secret mission?"

"Now we're getting somewhere." The look of horror on her face said he'd hit a nerve, and a mighty pretty nerve it was.

Kylie gasped. "You think I'm a spy!" She slapped her hand on the table. "If you'd put your arrogance aside for a moment, maybe you'd see the truth. Call Roloc, he'll tell you why I'm here."

"I will confirm your assignment." Hawk smiled. "Never confuse diligence with arrogance." For a moment he thought she might just smile. He wondered what kind of a smile she would have, sensual, endearing, or false like most the women he had known. If he had to wager, he would definitely put his credits on sensual.

"I'd like to go to my quarters now so I can get the salt out of my hair."

He stood and began to pace the small quarters. She was not going to like his answer, and she would have just cause to argue with him. It wasn't his fault she turned out to be a woman, but he was the one who had to break the nasty news.

"Well?"

"Ms. Beryl, you are in your quarters."

"Then why did I get the impression this cabin belonged to you?"

With a groan he stopped pacing and faced her. "It does." The stern expression on her face turned to anger. He did not have to acquaint himself with her better to know what the fire in her eyes meant. "When we received a request to house a new Researcher, we were told it would be Rolf Kubin. Currently, we are at maximum capacity."

"What are you saying, Chief Saxon?"

"This is the only available bunk in SEA Lab." Her eyes widened and he knew he was in trouble. "Didn't you know you'd be the only woman?" She looked away, but not before her emerald gaze pierced through him.

"You're playing with me, Saxon."

Now there was a thought, a very dangerous one, but most interesting. "I assure you, this is no game. And for your information, I'm no happier about this than you are." He watched her stand and walk to the bunk. She still swayed as if she were dizzy, but she held her head high. Whether it was defiance or pride, the look suited her. He smiled. Spunky women intrigued him, but he would have to keep his distance from this one. She closed her eyes and rolled to her side facing the wall.

He walked to the bunk, placed his hands on her shoulders and rolled her on her back. She raised her hand and he braced for the slap. Instead she lowered her arm, the hardness in her eyes melting, turning soft and sensual. "I'm sorry, I can't let you sleep. Doctor's orders."

"I'm so tired." Kylie blinked several times. "I need to sleep. Let me sleep."

"You promised the doctor you'd stay awake." The warmth of her skin seemed to burn the palms of his hands. He concentrated on taking long, slow breaths so she would not know how the feel of her affected him.

"I've changed my mind."

Hawk pulled his hands away then moved to the end of the room. He pressed a button and a small panel in the wall slid to the side. He ordered two cups of hot, black koffa from the recessed, personal galley computer. When the cups appeared he set one on the table and took the other to the bunk. He slid his hand behind her back and lifted her to a sitting position. Once again he felt heat from the contact and wondered how he would make it through one sun-cycle with her as a bunkmate. "Drink this," he said, holding the rim to Kylie's lips.

She took a sip, her gaze fixed on his face, her hand wrapping around his to guide the cup. Her soft skin reminded him how long it had been since he had felt the touch of a beautiful woman, and realized he could not trust himself. Kylie appealed to him in a way that scared him to the bone

"Thank you," she said, pushing the cup away. "Where can I bathe?"

"The lav is through that door." He helped her stand. "Are you sure you're up to it?"

"I'll be fine." Kylie cleared her throat. "I need some clothes."

Kylie walked to the lav like a drunken sailor. He was afraid she would fall in the shower and hit her head again. He couldn't very well bathe with her, even though the idea would be tempting in another place and time. "Here." He handed her a small circular object. "Just squeeze this if you need help, it will summon the doctor."

"You're leaving?"

"No." He took a deep breath when she entered the lav and shut the door. This was going to be a very long assignment. Hopefully Jester had made more progress with his project than he had with Kylie. It was a relief to have her in the next room where her probing green gaze could not unsettle him. As a trained military operative, he knew what a threat women could be on a mission. Warrior was the term he preferred since his escape from Andor, but the rules never changed. If he were to succeed in this mission he had to stay focused.

The past five annual-cycles had taken him to neighboring planetary systems where he worked for the highest bidder. As a mercenary, his reputation had become extremely distorted. He was paid an emperor's ransom for his skills, but the credits no longer stirred his warrior's blood, only the merit of the cause could persuade him to fight. Then there was Redmon.

Redmon's deposit to secure his services here had boosted his credit account beyond imagination. The only good thing about being a fugitive was the pay. He could never have achieved the same financial status as an Elite Operative. Operatives were well paid, led an upper-class lifestyle, but they never got rich beyond their wildest dreams. Credits meant nothing without the right person to share them with. Jester was the best pal a guy could have, but he did not want him warming his bed.

The door swished open and Jester stepped inside. "Someone shoot your pet Atew?"

"I look that bad?" Hawk glanced at his rumpled black uniform pants and shirt. "I could use a shower."

"Fine. We can talk in there."

"No we can't—it's occupied."

"Oh. Okay then, we'll talk here. Throm has completed his search, and I'm afraid there's no sign of those coins. Somebody's getting rich."

"Not yet. There's no way off this fish tank until the rotation, so we have a slight advantage." Hawk could not shake the eerie feeling that had nagged at him since his arrival. "I think we're dealing with something bigger here than someone looking to get rich. The missing papers from the Estran lab bother me more than the coins."

Jester tapped his finger on the table several times. "You think there's a connection?"

"The coins could be a diversion. The cure to Genesis Disorder will be worth far more than any stolen artifacts—priceless to the Estrans—and the galaxy if it spreads." Hawk tried to concentrate, but the sound of the shower distracted him more than he wanted to admit. Kylie could have fallen considering her shaky state. He stood, walked to the lav and opened the door. Steam poured out, but he was relieved to see the silhouette of her body standing in the shower behind the frosted partition. Her shapely curves drew his attention. She raised her arms and shampooed her hair, the outline of her breasts moving a bit higher. His invasion of her privacy sparked another twinge of guilt, and he closed the door.

"So how's cutie doing?

"Don't ask."

"That good, huh?" Jester laughed. "Well, she's in good hands."

He knew good and well what Jester was implying, and it was best to ignore it. "She doesn't share your opinion."

"Give her time, Boss. I've seen the way women fall at your feet. They always look at you with those moony eyes."

"I believe it's time you got back to work since you have nothing better to do than analyze my personal life."

Jester laughed. "Actually, your personal life sucks and we both know it. Although women do fall at your feet."

Hawk glared at his friend.

"All right, all right. But I can't spy on an empty stomach. Let's go to the galley and get something to eat."

"I can't leave Kylie right now."

"From the look on your face a minute ago, I'd say she's doing fine."

"Come on, I'll walk you to the lift. I need to make a quick trip to supply."

"Olly-dolly."

As they left and headed down the hall he could not get his mind off the woman in his shower. He checked on her out of concern for her welfare, not to get a free shot of her body. Kylie had been through quite an ordeal and he was responsible for her safety despite what anyone thought.

Jester made one last comment about The Hawk and women as he stepped into the lift. He smiled. There was some truth to Jester's words. Women did find him attractive. Whenever he wanted female companionship he usually had several to choose from, but he had never found one who interested him for more than one moon-cycle, and he had not been with a woman since Lissa. Some men were made to love a woman, destined for a life of bliss with their mate and children. Then there were men like him, who should never consider intimacy, love and commitment, especially if he cared about the woman. Fate had settled that for him long ago.

He turned the corner and headed for supply. Kylie needed something to wear until her belongings could be retrieved from the wreck. He would be glad to get her into real clothes. There was no way he could share a room with her clad in nothing but a med-gown. With luck their work schedules could be worked out so they occupied the cabin at different times. For the sake of his sanity, he hoped it was possible.

CHAPTER FOUR

Kylie dried what was left of her hair. What in the universe had happened? The doctor had no reason to chop off clumps of her hair, and certainly the esteemed Chief of Security wasn't into women's hair styling. Whoever had done the cutting sure couldn't cut straight. Well, there was nothing she could do about it now except make the best of it, and as the only woman on SEA Lab she did not want to be seen as a complainer. She wrapped the towel around her and cracked the door, relieved at the sight of an empty room. Her bare foot stepped on something soft and she glanced down.

A folded uniform and a pair of boots were piled neatly on the floor. She picked up the jumpsuit and boots and set them on the bathroom counter before closing the door. Saxon was efficient. He even managed to find her a uniform that belonged to the Estra delegation. She slipped the one-piece garment on, amazed to find a perfect fit as she zipped up the front. She smiled. Just like a man to forget underwear, but at least there were a pair of socks inside the left boot. When she bent to put a sock on a wave of dizziness engulfed her. She grabbed the counter, determined to dress so she could visit the Delphin pool.

The mission was all that mattered if Estra were to survive. Her parents' diagnosis placed a personal urgency on her shoulders. If a cure could not be found during her assignment here her parents would not know her when she returned, and that thought sent panic through her. She could not imagine the two people she loved most not knowing who she was.

Roloc said the research here could produce a cure, and she needed to believe he was right. What she could not understand was why someone would steal important research to slow the process? Greed was the only reason she could think of since a cure would be priceless to her people.

Could she trust Saxon to help her? Her past experience taught her to put faith in no one but herself. She laughed thinking of how Roloc said he would hire The Hawk if he could. It would be a mistake to put Estra's future in the hands of a mercenary warrior. Roloc held the fugitive in high regard, a fact she vehemently disagreed with. The Hawk was more of an enigma than a man. Some called him a murderer, a rapist, a thief and a traitor, a man with no conscience or morals, yet others called him "the savior of the universe". Whoever, or whatever he might be, she was glad he was not here. A man like that could never work for the good of the people, or anyone other than himself. The Hawk was evil. She prayed she would never meet him in person.

She picked up the brush. How could she ever untangle this mess? It would be impossible to look presentable with chunks of hair missing. The Delphins would not care what she looked like, and if she avoided mirrors until her hair grew out maybe she wouldn't care either.

The pulling and tugging of the brush made her head throb worse than before. Her hand shook and she felt the brush slip from her grasp. It landed in the metal sink with a loud clink. Before she could retrieve the brush Saxon burst through the door, a worried expression on his face.

"Are you all right?"

"I just dropped the brush." He stared at her for a moment, groaned and left. She thought about the cold draft that invaded the lav while she was in the shower. Had he checked on her out of concern, or had he wondered if she were a physical freak? It would not be the first time a man had spied on her to see if the scientists' offspring had any physical deformities. She was fortunate in that regard. Some of the other children she had gone to school with had not been so lucky and had to wear public brands that told the world who they were.

One last glance in the mirror made her stomach turn. She would rather look at Saxon than the massacred mess on her head. She tilted her chin up and marched into the cabin, taking a seat across from Saxon at the table. Look at Saxon? She must have been blind before not to see he was the most ruggedly handsome man she had ever seen. The memory of being held against his tall, muscular frame sent a shiver down her spine.

Not that she cared what he looked like, but his eyes were bluer than an Estran lake, and perfect was the only word that could describe the rest of him. Perfectly intimidating, she corrected. "Chief Saxon," she began, "please explain how I got here." He studied her for the longest time, making her feel like a lab specimen.

"I was on the observation deck when I saw your pod plunge into the sea. I grabbed the diving gear and..."

"You saved me?"

"Someone had to."

"Thank you. I...owe you my life."

"You owe me nothing. We all work together on SEA Lab to stay alive. Next time it could be you who saves a life."

"Sounds dangerous to live here." She thought she saw a hint of a smile tug at his lips. "Is it?"

Hawk grinned. "Not really."

"So tell me about the rescue." He seemed to be avoiding the explanation for some reason. She threaded her fingers through her hair, lingering at the large gaps in the long strands. He watched her intently, a guilty look on his face. "You're the one who cut my hair, aren't you?"

"Your hair was tangled in the control panel. The front shield was about to give way. I had no choice. I apologize for cutting your hair, but your life was more important."

"Of course." At least he had the courage to admit to making such an unruly mess. She had suspected he might have been responsible. He studied her intently which made her feel more uneasy than before. What was it about this man that made her stomach do flips and her heart to beat faster?

"Have you notified the Estran ship of what happened?"

"Your accident and condition were reported. When they were told you would recover completely, they set course for Estra."

"You are efficient, Mr. Saxon."

"Just Saxon, please."

"Do you ever go by your first name?"

"Never." He stood. "If you'll excuse me I'd like to shower and change."

Kylie watched him open a drawer, pull out some clothes then disappear into the lav. She sighed. Every time he left the room she found it easier to breathe. Was he friend or foe? He was certainly the warrior type who would welcome a fight, confident he could conquer any opponent. He was not someone she wanted for an enemy.

She stood and stretched, hearing the water in the shower turn on. It was past time she acquainted herself with SEA Lab. A trip to the Delphin pool might relax her, something she doubted she would ever do around Saxon. She walked toward the door. Before her hand could touch the lighted pad, it whooshed open. She glanced down, smiling when she found her foot on what must be an automatic door trigger.

Stepping into the sterile, windowless hall she inhaled deeply, trepidation filling her. Countless lives rested on her shoulders, including her parents', the only two people in the world who truly loved her. She walked toward the lift at the end of the hall. There was so much to do and so little time. She had not gotten off to a very good start by crashing into the sea and splitting her head open, but she was about to enter her element—working with the Delphins.

A terrifying thought crossed her mind. Had Saxon undressed her? It should not matter, after all, the man was just saving her life, but for some reason the idea of Saxon looking at her naked body made her cringe. Hopefully it had been the doctor who removed her wet clothes, not the Chief of Security. She touched the call pad and waited.

When the lift doors opened, her heart jumped to her throat. Three men stepped toward her with menacing expressions on their faces and lust in their eyes .They looked her up and down, and mumbled things she refused to think about. She felt violated, and a shiver coursed down her spine. Finally, they turned and casually sauntered down the hall, but they constantly turned their heads to ogle her over their shoulders. Disgusting. They were from Andor, which explained a lot. Military men were notorious for acting lewd around women. She had to expect that kind of behavior since she was the only woman in the facility. Hopefully the new rotation would arrive soon with enough women to take the pressure off.

She stepped into the lift and pressed three, unsure what floor she was on. The lift moved up slightly then the doors opened. Straight ahead she saw the brightly lighted pool and rushed toward the calm water. The Agor Sea was greener than on Estra, and smelled more metallic and salty. She knelt at the edge and waved her hand back and forth in the water, hoping to entice a Delphin to enter the pool.

To her left was the lab and offices up a small flight of stairs. The wall that separated the pool area was glass so the Delphin pool could be watched from inside. The lights were dim, everyone gone for the moon-cycle. At least she assumed it was moon-cycle. Her wrist-piece was lost in the crash and she had not seen a clock. The water felt cool against her hand as she swished it back and forth, desperately trying to attract the curious mammals. Delphins were naturally drawn to people, which was why it was against Universal Law to harm one of the trusting creatures.

She laid down by the belly-slide, keeping her right arm in the water. It was imperative she make contact with the Delphins. If she lay here for a while, maybe they would use the belly-slide and come to her. She tried to clear her mind to make mental contact with the Delphins, but Saxon's face was all she could see.

There would never be another moon-cycle of undisturbed sleep as long as she had to share a room with the mysterious man in black. He wore the Andor uniform well—too well. His powerful thighs, trim waist, broad shoulders and muscular arms appeared even more threatening in the body-hugging black clothes. Rumor said the men of Andor were proud of their masculine prowess in battle as well as in bed, and if they all looked like Saxon, she knew why.

She shook her head trying to erase Saxon's image. For all she knew Saxon himself might be the thief. Just because he was Chief of Security and extremely handsome did not make him immune to espionage. He was the perfect candidate—he had free reign of the entire complex, and no one would suspect the man who claimed to protect secrets. Had she become paranoid? Probably, but with just cause. Spies had been uncovered in several Estran labs where she had worked recently. She had not known the accused men personally, only by their reputations, and they all had the highest security clearances.

The water rippled and she smiled at a shadow below the surface. At least she could relate to Delphins. The games they played were simply for fun, unlike the complicated mind games people played. No wonder she preferred the calming, positive presence of Delphins.

***

Where was she? He left her alone for ten minutes, long enough to shower and change and she had disappeared. Why couldn't she rest like a normal person with a head injury that barely escaped death? He searched the galley with no luck, but he had heard three men making comments about the redhead with the sexy body and bedroom eyes. He wanted to punch them, but he could not argue with their assessment. The woman would be the death of him. How could he protect her sun-cycles and moon-cycles when his body wanted her in a most carnal way? Training. Long ago he learned the art of self-restraint, and Kylie was the ultimate test of his resolve.

Hawk pressed level three on the entry pad. The door quietly swooshed open and his heart jumped into his throat. By the Gods! She lay lifeless at the edge of the pool, one arm in the water. She must have passed out. Before he could step closer, a Delphin broke the surface and landed on the belly-slide, stopping less than an inch from her face. He heard her say, "There you are," her voice soft and inviting. Obviously the Delphin thought so too, screeching a series of high pitched clicks before nudging Kylie's hand. He watched her stroke the Delphin's bottle shaped nose and rub its back. He had seen other researchers work with the mammals, but never with the same tenderness.

A second Delphin scooted up on the slide next to the first and clicked approval as Kylie showered him with equal attention. Slowly Hawk walked up beside her and squatted. "Will I scare them?" he asked, keeping his voice as low as he could.

"Just don't make any sudden moves until you win their trust. They're very sensitive." Kylie took his hand and placed it on the Delphin's back. "It's okay, they enjoy being touched. It helps them get to know you. Look...she likes you."

"She feels like rubber!"

Kylie laughed. "Don't be fooled. They feel your physical touch and sense what's in your soul." She turned to face him. "How could you have been here for weeks without touching a Delphin?"

"I'm Chief of Security, not marine biology." Her emerald eyes moved from him to the Delphin and he suddenly felt neglected. It was not rational to be jealous of a sea creature, in fact it was not rational for him to be jealous at all.

"You've been missing a lot." Kylie patted the Delphin's back while she looked at Saxon. "I love Delphins more than people. They're never mean or vindictive, always friendly and glad to see you."

There was a seriousness to her voice that said she spoke from the heart. Someone had hurt her badly, which triggered his protective instincts. He had to stop feeling this way about her, but for some inexplicable reason he could not help himself. "Why is Estra so interested in Delphins?"

"We think they hold the key to a cure for Genesis Disorder."

"Delphins?"

"They're highly intelligent with a complex DNA. They also develop interesting RNA patterns which are passed on to their offspring and incorporated in the resulting new DNA strands—and that could be the missing link. Although, it could be one of several enzymes in their system."

Hawk shook his head. "That's a bit deep for me to follow."

"Sorry, we Researchers do tend to spout technical terms."

"I hope you find a cure." He knew what a breakthrough would mean to her people. So far, Genesis Disorder was confined on Estra, but it was only a matter of time before it spread, and this disease struck terror in the hearts of the bravest warriors. No man wanted to sit in a corner and drool, unable to control his body, with no comprehension of his surroundings, or memory of who and what he was.

Besides owing Redmon, he wanted to help Estra's search in the only way he could, by protecting their interest in SEA Lab. It was a minor part, but if their research were stopped, every man, woman and child on

Estra would eventually die. He would do everything in his power not to let that happen. He watched her stroke the Delphin and studied the upturned, happy shape of the mammal's mouth that made them look so friendly. "Why do they click like that?"

"They're talking. Look!" Kylie said, pointing below the surface. "Get ready."

"For wha..." Three Delphins broke the surface, turned in mid-air and landed on their backs, sending a flood of cold seawater washing over them.

"Aren't they gorgeous?" she asked, smiling broadly.

"Gorgeous isn't the word I had in mind." Hawk wiped water from his eyes and watched Kylie push wet hair from her face. She rolled onto her back in a fit of laughter. His gaze immediately fell to taut nipples the soggy fabric could not hide. Suddenly aware of empty lungs he took a deep breath. Gorgeous was the word he would use to describe her, but it would be difficult to stop there when sensuous, shapely and a host of other words would still be inadequate. "You must spend a lot of time wet."

"I do." Kylie straightened to a sitting position. "Do you come here often?"

"When necessary." Hawk stood, water dripping from his clothes, pooling at his feet. He should be cold, but the sight of Kylie warmed his blood and stirred his imagination. In truth, he rarely visited the Delphin pool, but he had a strong feeling his visits would be more frequent.

"Delphins have a very calming effect on people." She stood and faced him. "And from the way you look, well..."

"What's wrong with the way I look?" he asked, not meaning to sound so defensive.

"Every muscle in your body is stressed and tight. You look like you're ready to do battle. You need to relax, lighten up." She turned toward the Delphins. "You're even making them nervous."

Little did she know the battle he fought with himself. He could not afford to lose his objectivity with her, and he felt himself guilty of just that. She was a picture of feminine persuasion at its finest. Beguiling green eyes, red flowing hair that pleased his eye wet or dry, and a body that begged for his touch. If Kylie wasn't a spy she should be. She had all the right equipment to make men lose their common sense and be led to slaughter. "I'd better go, I don't want to scare the fish."

"Don't call them fish. They're..."

"I know—mammals." She smiled at him and he felt a light switch on inside his heart. He was losing his sanity faster than anticipated. She had an unnerving effect on him, and he had to work hard to keep his demeanor calm. Control of all situations was his strongest weapon. If he were to maintain complete authority here and remain effective, he would have to watch himself with the delectable Delphin trainer.

"If you don't mind, I'd like to stay."

"Suit yourself."

CHAPTER FIVE

Kylie sighed as Saxon's tall, powerful form disappeared from sight. She was relieved he was gone, but a strange sense of unease folded around her in his absence. Who was Chief Saxon? He was not like any man she had met before, and that troubled her. He seemed like a man who held deep, dark secrets that were eating him alive.

Saxon could not be evil because the Delphins responded to him, and she had never known them to be wrong. His presence made them a bit nervous, but he had the same effect on her. Maybe it was because he hid his emotions, yet his blue eyes spoke volumes. He was a hard man to read, yet she sensed a buried kindness he refused to show to anyone. Warriors viewed kindness and compassion as a weakness rather than a virtue, so she did not expect much from him.

Her work would keep her busy, and contact with Saxon would be minimal. They might be forced to share a cabin, but she was not interested in him as a man and he had not shown any interest in her as a woman. In fact she had the feeling he viewed her as one more nuisance to deal with. He was all business and that was fine since she had a job to do and no time to waste.

She returned to the edge of the pool and squatted, slapping her hand on the surface to call the Delphins back to the slide. Only one Delphin remained in the water, circling the perimeter along the bottom. She admired the graceful creature as it moved methodically closer as if following an invisible spiral toward her. Finally the female Delphin approached the slide, stopping with her nose under Kylie's hand. Water sprayed from her blowhole, the mist dampening the sleeve of her Estran uniform.

"Where's your friend?" she said softly, the Delphin's trusting eyes fixed on her. "I know, one step at a time." She patted the mammal's head, trying to discern what name belonged to the sleek female. It might take a few sun-cycles for the proper name to come to her, but it would. She preferred calling them by their name rather than their assigned number. They hated to be treated only as an object of study when they were so much more.

In a flash the Delphin pulled away from her, swam to the bottom of the pool then left for the safety of the sea through the open exit portal. It was normal to leave the portal open so the Delphins could come and go as they pleased, but what scared this mammal into a hasty retreat?

"Who are you?"

At the sound of a male voice Kylie rose and turned. A tall, well-built blond man walked toward her, confidence and male pride apparent in his stride. "I'm Researcher Two, Kylie Beryl."

"What happened to Rolf Kubin?"

"He became ill, I was sent in his place." Kylie remembered this man's face from the file Roloc had given her to study, and she was standing face to face with Nyles Logun, her superior officer. She compared Logun's size to Saxon, but size was as far as their similarities went. Nyles had a handsome face that looked almost feminine, a stark contrast to Saxon's rugged dark appeal, not that it mattered in the least. She had no interested in either of them, although she would be blind not to notice.

"I'm Researcher Fifth Class, Nyles Logun." He extended his arm.

She grasped his wrist in the cordial Estran greeting, but he held on rather than letting go as he should. There was a gleam in his eye she could only describe as sinister. With a determined effort she pulled free.

"You'll be working under me." Nyles grinned. "Our research is progressing well."

"I heard you're close to a breakthrough."

"We've had some promising results, but we're weeks, or longer, away from an actual cure."

"I see." The evasive tone of Nyles' voice and the wicked glare of his light brown eyes made her want to run and hide. She had never been a coward in her life, but something about Nyles made him seem more like the enemy than a fellow Estran.

"Do you?" He moved closer.

Kylie backed up several steps toward the wall, realizing too late it was a mistake. Nyles pressed forward until he had her pinned against the immovable steel behind her. Her heart raced when he placed his arms beside her shoulders and stared. She would be a fool not to recognize his intentions.

"Tell me more about what you see, Kylie."

"I see a man who had better learn to keep his distance," she said, pushing against his rigid chest with her hands.

Nyles laughed. "That isn't possible. We'll be working closely together—very closely."

"Back-up Researcher Logun. Now!" Why the Delphin fled was no longer a mystery, if only she could have followed.

"So...the little lady has a fiery temper to match her hair." He picked up a thick, damp lock from her shoulder and twisted it around his finger.

When she pushed harder, he jerked the hair he held, pulling her head to his chest. Her scalp hurt from the yank, but she refused to show him one ounce of weakness. "Let me go!"

"When I'm ready. First I want to..."

"You heard the lady. Let her go."

Kylie let out the breath she'd been holding when she heard Saxon's commanding voice. Nyles released her hair and stepped back. It was all she could do to suppress a satisfied smile.

"To what do I owe the honor of the Chief Security officer?" Nyles asked, turning to face Saxon.

"Your life if you touch Researcher Beryl again."

Nyles snickered. "There's no security problem here. You misinterpreted what you saw. Kylie was giving me a friendly greeting, that's all."

"You stand warned." Saxon gestured for Kylie to join him. "I'll escort you to your quarters, Miss Beryl."

She walked to the door, Saxon protectively behind her. Only minutes ago she was glad he was out of her sight, now she was overjoyed to see him. He made her feel secure, but she feared he just gained an enemy in Nyles Logun, although she doubted Saxon feared anyone.

***

From Saxon's position at the table, he studied the redhead perched on the bunk, back against the wall, legs crossed, arms folded, and wearing a scowl that promised impending battle. He might as well get it over with now so they could get a couple time-units sleep before the work-cycle began. "What happened at the Delphin pool?"

"Nothing."

"I'm not a fool. Nyles had you pinned against the bulwark about to..."

"Kiss me?"

Hawk nodded. "Or worse."

"Does that bother you?"

"You're under my protection while on SEA Lab. It's my responsibility to keep you safe." She was making this more difficult than necessary, but from the moment he saw her pod sink into the miserable Agor Sea, everything had become complicated. He hated being in SEA Lab, stuck underwater for an undetermined amount of time, and he certainly did not need the added pressure of guarding the only woman on board. "From now on, you will not leave this cabin without me. That's an order."

"Order? You have no right to order me around!"

"I do, and I will." Difficult did not define Kylie, impossible would be closer to the point. She should understand by now what she was up against. "You left these quarters without me twice, and both times you encountered problems." She gave him a disbelieving glare. "I know about the incident at the lift."

"How? I didn't mention it."

"I have my ways."

"I'm not a child who needs a sitter!"

"Definitely not a child, but you do need a sitter."

"I demand to contact Roloc on Estra. He'll set you straight. I have work to do here, and I'm not going to have an arrogant security officer interfering."

She was a spitfire, he'd give her that. He took several deep breaths to quell his impulse to toss her across his knee and give her a well-deserved spanking. Not that it would do any good. He had never hit a woman in anger, but the thought of his hand on her shapely bottom gave the idea merit. "The main com-link to Estra is protected. Nyles Logun keeps the code. If you want to go to his quarters to..."

"You made your point, Chief Saxon."

He smiled to himself when he heard his name roll off her lips like a cuss word. It was best she hated him, because he did not want to think what would happen if she used her feminine wiles on him. Women had seduced him for multitudes of reasons, but he was afraid he would let this redheaded spitfire have her way without a fight should she try.

"I'm glad you understand, Researcher Beryl." He spoke her name sarcastically in an effort to set her straight. "What do I have to do to get you to realize you're the only woman among hundreds of men, some who haven't had a taste of feminine flesh in months and are beginning to wonder if they ever will again."

"I'm not stupid. I understand."

"Good, then understand this. You are not to go anywhere without me, or an assigned guard with you."

"Fine." Kylie ran her fingers through her hair. "Now I want to make something clear. Neither you nor your assigned guard are to interfere with my work, even if I choose to work around the clock."

"Agreed." Hawk stood, hopped up on the bunk above hers and turned out the light. He heard Kylie mutter something indistinguishable as she threw herself on the mattress. She was a handful. A laugh almost escaped his lips when he thought about explaining to Jester how they would have to share watch over Kylie.

Jester would control himself, but he would like the duty all too well. At least Jester could be trusted, which was more than he could say for Nyles Logun. Thank the Gods most of the men were not like Nyles. If he had to compare the man with something, it would have to be a slime-snake. They thrived in waters full of botanical debris, covered in fungus and slime. They wiggled their way through the underground kingdom, taking their prey from behind with one lethal bite after another, injecting venom with their deadly fangs.

Nyles was a man to be watched. He disliked the man from sun-cycle one, and his tasteless display with Kylie verified his suspicions. The sight of Kylie at his mercy made his blood boil. He wanted to tear Nyles limb from limb for laying his miserable hands on her. He had no respect for any man who forced himself on a woman.

Why did it matter so? He'd protected women from unwanted advances before and never experienced the rage he had when he saw Nyles accosting Kylie. It had to be his dislike for the slime-snake. No, Nyles was not the reason, yet he was not ready to admit, even to himself, what stirred the rush of emotion he'd fought since finding the tempting Kylie Beryl. He slammed his fist into the pillow and rolled to his side. There had to be a way to get *her* out of his head.

All he could hear in the quiet darkness was Kylie's even breathing. She may be sleeping peacefully but he doubted he would find rest with her seductive body beneath his bunk. She must have superhuman strength to sustain a crash, be awake most of the sun-cycle, and nearly all moon-cycle. He closed his eyes and tried to imagine what his crew was doing on Terra to entertain themselves. A smile creased his lips. They were chasing the pink-haired vixens that made Terra the perfect recreational planet for men of all kinds.

Maybe when he shed his fins and scales, once again free to breathe real air, he himself would chase a couple of those vixens himself. It had been a long time since he'd been with a woman, and for some reason, with Kylie so close, it was all he could think about.

***

Hawk sat behind his desk, rubbing his eyes, trying to concentrate on Jester's incessant babble. Lack of sleep gave him a bigger hangover than Andorian ale.

"Boss?" Jester growled. "I don't know where your mind is, but you haven't heard a word I was saying."

"Sorry." Hawk watched Jester shake his bushy sandy-haired head and felt dizzy. Lack of sleep, lack of food, and lack of peace and quiet— it all boiled down to one hell of a headache. "I didn't get much rest."

"I know how you get when you're tired. But if it will make you feel any better, I didn't get much sleep either. Cook started the damned snoring again so I came in here and played on the computer. Decided it was time to learn my A, B, C's."

"And?"

"It seems someone on Andor is sending messages to Neptus, not only to the lab, but somewhere on the surface as well."

"That's impossible. There's no life on Neptus. The damned planet is all water!"

"Not quite correct. Thousands of tiny islands dot the Agor Sea in every direction, some larger than others. Life could very well exist on any of them. It wouldn't exactly be the preferred life style, but it's possible."

"Can you find the exact destination of the messages?"

"Negative. The communication equipment on SEA Lab is specially designed to over-ride the heavy salt content and density of Neptus' air, as well as the ring of cosmic dust in the upper atmosphere. Without technical modification, any frequency sent to normal com-links bounces and appears as if it's being received everywhere on the planet simultaneously."

"Can you make those technical modifications?"

"I'd have to modify every unit on SEA Lab. Just one unmodified unit will prevent an accurate reading."

"Work on it, and don't get caught." Hawk took several gulps of koffa, his head beginning to clear as the caffeine hit his stomach. "Run Nyles Logun through CAM again."

"Why? Did I miss something?"

"He assaulted Kylie at the Delphin pool last moon-cycle."

"Did you wipe the deck with his ugly face?"

Hawk laughed. "No, but I wanted to."

"Let me, please?"

"Just punch his name into CAM. There's something we're missing—it's got to be there." He unlocked his desk drawer and pulled out the laptop and pushed it toward Jester. He really doubted they would find anything of use, but it was worth another try.

Jester chuckled as he pressed a sequence of codes. "Did you happen to check Nyles' pockets for coins while you scuffled with him?"

"Unfortunately I didn't lay a hand on him." Hawk cleared his throat. "Because of Kylie's altercation last moon-cycle, I've ordered her not to go anywhere without a guard. There's only two people here I trust, and that's you and Throm."

"Gotcha, Boss." Jester took his eyes off the screen and studied Hawk. "She's really got you hooked, doesn't she?

Hawk scowled. "You're off base, way off. She's the only woman on SEA Lab and she's my responsibility."

"Sounds good, I almost believe you."

"She's not my type. She's temperamental, stubborn, independent, moody..."

"Are you describing Kylie, or yourself?" Jester held his hands in front of his face. "No, no, don't hit me." He laughed. "You have to admit, she sounds exactly like you. Just the kind of woman to put you through your paces, teach you patience...and a few other things as well."

"What's all this about?"

"Guess it's a warning. I'd sure hate to lose my best friend to a woman. Always thought I'd lose you out in space somewhere, you know, jumping through the wrong wormhole or something, ending up in a galaxy so distant there's no hope of return."

"You're not lucky enough to get rid of me anytime soon." Hawk stared at the screen as Nyles' file appeared, the same information glaring at him. "Nothing."

"I could try *the dump*," Jester offered, rapidly pressing keys.

"Of course." He patted Jester on the shoulder. "You're a genius. I'd forgotten you could retrieve deleted files with that special program you wrote."

"Look, here it comes." Jester bounced up and down on the couch. "My, my, my. Seems your buddy Nyles was expelled from the military academy on Andor before he could become an officer. He created a new identity and took refuge on Estra. They've treated him pretty well."

Hawk rubbed his chin. "Seems he's gained rank whether he deserved it or not. According to his qualifications, he shouldn't be more than a Researcher First Class. He doesn't have the necessary education for his rank."

"Looks like he's a fifth-class kiss-ass."

"Well put."

"Got a plan, Boss?"

"It will be easy to watch Nyles since Kylie works under him, but we'll learn more if we keep our distance. I want you to install vid-cams in all the hidden areas. Be sure to use the sound-mode models, I want to know everything."

"Gotcha." Jester jumped to his feet, walked to the metal cabinets along the wall and began to rifle through them. "We're a bit short on vid-cams, but I'll do the best I can." He straightened, a cam in each hand and wires around his neck."

Hawk laughed. He'd seen the mischievous look on Jester's face before. When he loved his job he was the happiest, and he was elated now. "You sure like your toys."

"There's no better game in the universe."

"What are you doing with those old, bulky models. Nyles is sure to spot them."

"That's the plan, Boss. I use the visible ones like a decoy, in places he has to behave anyway. We want him to think we're watching and doing our job. But the invisible ones will be in those out of the way places where he'll make his mistakes because he thinks he's safely out of the cam's range."

"I admire your devious mind. Have at it"

"Where's cutie?"

"Sleeping, with Throm outside the door." Hawk picked up the small computer and locked it in the desk drawer. "Get busy installing those cams. I want them in place before I take Kylie to the Delphin pool."

"Olly-dolly."

He followed Jester out the door and watched his friend saunter down the hall and into the lift, his sandy hair standing up in every direction. Did the man own a comb? Some things did not matter to Jester, but he took his work seriously. If any man needed a good woman to take care of him, it was Jester. The poor man had no family, no friends other than the crew of *The Redemption*—a loner by most standards.

Hawk knew why he was so close to Jester. They were kindred spirits when it came to acceptance in normal society. Everyone thought Jester insane, and regarded The Hawk as a cold-blooded killer, capable of any feat, master of impossible missions. It was indeed a lonely life for them both.

So deep in thought he was surprised to find himself outside his cabin door looking at Throm. The man snapped to attention and saluted in true military fashion. Hawk returned the formal greeting. "Anything to report?"

"No sir. I heard footsteps inside, so I know she's fine."

"Good. You can return to your duties." He studied Throm's eager expression. "How is the search going?"

"I'm sorry to report we haven't found any coins. This is a large facility with endless hiding places for something that small, but we're working on it.'

"Very well, dismissed." He pressed the palm identifier and the door slid open. His worst fear stared him in the eye.

"Where have you been? I need to get to the Delphin pool—now."

Hawk brushed past her then turned. "Give me ten minutes."

CHAPTER SIX

Kylie paced the floor, counting fourteen paces in each direction while she listened to the hum of the shower. She wanted to hate Saxon for insisting she be guarded at all times, but he made sense. Only a fool would argue the point, but she did not have to like the situation. The only thought that kept her mind focused was the Delphins.

Her parents still had a chance to survive Genesis Disorder, she had to believe that. She had vowed to do everything within her power, and beyond, to find the missing link. Time was the enemy, and she'd wasted enough already.

She turned when the lav door opened. Saxon strode into the room wearing nothing but a loosely secured towel around his waist. It didn't seem to bother him in the least to parade around nearly naked, but her heart nearly stopped beating before it began to race out of control. "Aren't you ready yet?"

He groaned, grabbed a clean uniform and returned to the lav, slamming the door behind him. He was a sight; rippled stomach muscles, a well-defined chest with a thin mat of hair in the center, powerful legs, and biceps that were as big around as her waist. She never should have noticed, especially in such detail, but she was not blind. A chill ran down her spine. What would she have done if the towel had slipped to the floor? The answer scared her.

If she had to have a guard, Saxon appeared most capable, and that was all that mattered. He was nothing more than a roommate and Chief Security Officer. She couldn't think of anyone else who could protect her better. She had a job to do, and he promised not to stand in her way. At least with Saxon around she would not have to worry about Nyles making inappropriate passes.

The door flew open and Saxon stormed by, leaving a clean musky scent on the air around her. She ran after him, the door closing behind her, but he was halfway down the hall. First he had to dilly-dally in the shower, now he was walking as if he were on his way to put out a fire!

He held the lift door for her as she jogged onto the platform. With a whoosh, the doors closed and she felt as if she left her stomach behind. Before she could catch her breath they arrived on the floor above.

"Good-sun-cycle, Miss Beryl," Saxon said as he ushered her to the pool.

She watched him turn on his heel and march to the stairs. "Where are you going? I thought you had to be with me at all times?"

"I'll not be far. Scream if you need me."

Of all the conceited, contemptuous males she'd ever encountered, he took the prize. She wouldn't scream for him if her life depended on it. Out the corner of her eye she saw Nyles approaching. Well, she'd try not to scream too soon.

Kylie sighed as Saxon's tall, powerful form disappeared from sight. She was glad he was gone, but a strange sense of unease folded around her in his absence. Who was Chief Saxon? He wasn't like any man she'd met before, and that troubled her. Being from Andor it was possible he didn't know she was the daughter of scientists and considered a freak. She glanced at Nyles. He knew good and well who and what she was, which was why the lustful look on his face bothered her so much.

"Good sun-cycle, Researcher Beryl. You look rested."

"Please, call me Kylie, but don't get the wrong idea. I simply prefer to hear my first name." Nyles grinned at her for the longest time and her empty stomach tightened. He had a sick look in his eyes, a look she did not trust.

"As you wish."

"Where are the wet suits?"

"Over there in the ready room." He pointed behind him. "Every level has a ready room in case of emergency."

"If it's all right with you, I'd like to go in the water and get acquainted with the Delphins."

"Roloc said you were unconventional."

"You spoke with him?" She watched him nod. "When?"

"Early this sun-cycle, as usual. He sends his regards."

"Well, if you'll excuse me, I'll go change." She hurried to the ready room, quickly shed her clothes and donned the knee-length rubber suit. When she returned to the pool she found Nyles, reclined on a lounger with a cup of koffa in his hand. Considering the dire situation on Estra, Nyles should have important research to do. She held her breath to keep from saying something she shouldn't to a superior officer. She actually outranked him by two ticks, but he would never know that little secret.

Roloc did not trust Nyles and she doubted anyone with a brain would, but she had to let him believe he had the upper hand, as frustrating as the thought was.

"Don't let me stop you from your work. I just thought I'd observe my newest team member in action."

"Of course." She dove into the pool, the cold water dousing her temper. She savored the weightless feeling as she sank toward the bottom then slowly floated to the surface. With a few kicks she was on the belly-slide on her knees, the water lapping around her waist. She felt Nyles' eyes on her even before she glanced in his direction. There were men who would take a woman like her to their bed out of curiosity, but she suspected Nyles Logun would bed her out of pure arrogance.

Roloc's words of warning echoed in her mind. Just because she had worked with men who never gave her a second look, she'd always known they existed. It was going to be next to impossible to gain Nyles' confidence and learn his secrets and still manage to keep her distance. She slapped the water with her hand, hoping the Delphins would arrive soon so she could get her mind off Nyles.

It was her job as trainer to get the Delphins to submit to tests they fought against. There was a drop-gate that could be used to confine the Delphins, but it could not be used until they came routinely. The Estran scientists needed samples from many Delphins to study and test, and others would not come if they knew they would be locked up, abused and separated from their families for an extended period of time.

Ripples in the pool lapped against the edges and she saw three shadowy forms circling below. She slapped the water again and they moved closer. Of all natures' creatures, she loved these graceful swimmers the best. Suddenly one broke the surface and slid to a stop in her lap.

"Hello there. And who are you?" she asked, wishing she could understand the clicks they gave for answers. A pain stabbed her temples, and she rubbed them with her fingertips. She was used to receiving mental images from the Delphins, but her head injury seemed to be interfering.

The name Mia popped in her head as if it had been planted there. She studied the Delphin who watched her, still clicking a response. "Thank you, Mia." She stroked Mia's rubbery back, trying to hone in on the mammal's unique vibration.

"You seem different from the Delphins on Estra." She watched the gray and white animal roll over and slide back into the green water. A moment later Mia reappeared with two friends, all three surrounding her and clicking wildly.

Kylie concentrated, clearing her mind to receive the images the Delphins were trying to send. Usually she could close her eyes and see through their eyes. People, places, water, fish, rocks; whatever they experienced so could she, but this sun-cycle was different. The images were garbled, and no clear pictures took form. Then everything slowly turned black, the usual symbol for danger. All three Delphins quickly left her and swam out of sight, returning to their world in the depths of the Agor Sea.

She stood and turned, finding Nyles looming over her, his feet planted at the edge of the pool, arms crossed over his chest. The reason for the Delphins' hasty retreat became emphatically clear—they hated Nyles.

"It's no use you know."

It took all she could do not to tell him what a fool he was. "I was doing fine until you..."

"Don't be stupid, woman. I've worked with those damn creatures for an annual-cycle now, you'll never gain their trust."

"I didn't think anyone stayed more than half an annual-cycle?" He grinned at her as if she were a complete idiot, and his condescending attitude forced her to grit her teeth. She swallowed the things she wanted to say and gave him a grin she hoped looked like a smile.

"I've stayed longer because I was needed, and I don't mind living here." Nyles cocked an eyebrow. "A bit claustrophobic are you?"

"No." Maybe a little, but admitting anything to a man like Nyles was out the question. "Maybe the Delphins respond better to a woman's voice."

Nyles squatted and grabbed a clump of Kylie's hair. "I know I do."

His hot breath on the back of her neck made her skin crawl and she shivered in disgust. The man was a menace. How could she ever get anything done with this woman crazy maniac drooling down her back? The roots of her hair hurt as he pulled. She had no choice but to rise at his urging. One sun-cycle she would get even with him.

Nyles grabbed her under her arms and lifted her out of the water. "You need to dry off. Let me help you." He pulled her against him and smiled.

He held her firm against his chest and crushed her face into the fabric of his uniform. He smelled of cheap cologne, mixed with chemical residue from the lab. Her stomach turned and she pushed to get away, but his hold on her hair and body was relentless.

"I'd let her go if I were you."

Saxon! Thank the stars. He had a way of showing up when needed, although he could have been a bit earlier. In a heartbeat her hair was once again her own. Nyles pushed her away roughly and she nearly fell into the pool.

"I wasn't doing anything she didn't want me to," Nyles snarled.

"You wouldn't know what a woman wants."

Nyles' hands formed fists at his sides. "And I suppose you do?"

"Kylie," Saxon called, holding out his hand.

She walked toward him but refused to accept his hand. He stared at her for a moment then turned his attention back to Nyles. The silent exchange between the two men was enough to raise the hairs on her arms. It was a good thing they were not armed or lazer beams would be flying. In fact, she was surprised they weren't using their fists in some primitive manner. Saxon grabbed her hand and pulled her into the lift.

"Where are you taking her!" Nyles shouted. "She has important work to do!"

The metal doors slid shut and he released her hand. The lift began to move. She hit the stop button, then turned toward Saxon. "What right do you have to drag me away from my work? I was doing fine until you burst in and...and..."

"Saved you?"

"Interrupted me! Oooooh." Saxon stared at her with a grin on his face she was afraid to interpret. His deep blue gaze sent a surge of warmth through her body. He studied her so intently she felt as if he were physically touching her. They were a good two feet apart, but his imposing masculine presence consumed the small space.

"I suppose you enjoy having your hair pulled and your body manhandled."

Kylie narrowed her eyes and gave him her most contemptuous glare. "That does not deserve an answer." She turned her back to him and reached for the command pad to start the lift in motion. Before she could touch the recessed numbers he grabbed her wrist and turned her to face him. Anger sparked in his eyes and she felt his hand tremble as he held her.

"I'm not looking for gratitude, Researcher Beryl. You needed protection, so I stepped in. I have no intention of interfering with your work, or your personal life. But I will not tolerate any man on this facility touching you inappropriately. Is that clear?" Saxon watched her nod. "And when I said scream if you need me, that's exactly what I meant." He released her wrist. "Instead, your misplaced sense of pride nearly got you ra—."

"It was nothing I couldn't handle."

"You think so?" He shook his head. "Are you insane woman? Nyles is a slime-snake, and twice your size—more than capable of..."

"Point taken." A wave of dizziness engulfed her and she leaned against the white metal wall. Her eyes closed and a pain shot through her stomach. Two strong hands gripped her shoulders. She opened her eyes and saw real concern staring back at her.

"When was the last time you ate?"

"I really can't remember." She stood mesmerized by his eyes, inhaling the musky masculine scent of him, finding comfort in his strength as he held her firmly yet tenderly. "A couple of sun-cycles maybe?"

"We shall remedy that immediately." He slid one arm around her waist to steady her and pressed five on the number pad.

The lift zoomed down two levels, but her stomach was a level behind. The doors opened and Saxon escorted her into the galley, his arm firmly around waist. She was grateful for his support. Her knees were weak, and her head ached. Food might help those problems, but her heart lurched to her throat when every eye in the room turned on her, their surprised expressions saying more than she wanted to think about.

She had never felt so conspicuous. A wet suit was not exactly what she should be wearing to dine in, but Saxon had not given her the opportunity to change. She glanced at his black shirt. Her wet hair had left a large wet ring on his shoulder, but he did not seem to notice. Probing looks and mumbles followed them as they walked to the beginning of the food line.

He handed her a tray and silverware. "Thank you." Saxon actually smiled at her. He looked like a different man without his usual dark foreboding expression. When he smiled he seemed human, vulnerable, and all too attractive. She moved her gaze to the food along the serving line, but her mind stayed on Saxon. He was a complicated man, who took his job seriously, a fact that should put her mind at ease, but it didn't. She doubted she would ever feel comfortable when in close proximity to the Chief of Security.

She filled her tray and walked toward a table in the far corner, trying not to be any more conspicuous than she was considering her inappropriate attire. She did not have to look over her shoulder to know Saxon was right behind her. She felt his overpowering presence, and it had nothing to do with his height or extraordinary build. It was his aura. Not that she could see it, but she could sense it. She took a seat with her back toward the onlookers she wanted to ignore. Saxon sat across from her, scowling toward the entire crowd at once. He held the warning gaze for several long moments then relaxed and began to eat. Somehow she knew it was his way of telling the diners to mind their own business, which must have been effective or he would still be staring.

"I'll see to it Nyles never touches you again."

"You get straight to the point, don't you?" She took a bite. "It would be nice to go to work without being bothered."

"Unless you welcomed his advances as he claimed."

Kylie knew he was testing her reaction. "I have no intention of seeking the attentions of any man on SEA Lab."

"Good." Saxon shifted in his chair. "I would never presume to tell you who to give your affections to, but you would be wise to keep your distance from Nyles."

"The man is a menace. I wish I didn't have to work under him, but I will do my job as ordered."

"You'll have no further worries from Nyles."

His protective nature made her want to smile and thank him, but she suspected he would not welcome her thanks, or a compliment should she offer one. "Was it necessary to threaten the man with his life?"

"Yes," he grumbled.

"What else has he done to make you hate him? Or is it all Estrans you don't like?"

"Only Nyles." Saxon laid his fork on the edge of his plate. "I have nothing against Estrans."

"I'm relieved to hear that." He studied her with an intenseness that made her cheeks burn. Wet suits molded to every curve and bump on the body, and she knew with a certainty what he was looking at. She had never felt self-conscious in one before, but then she had never been scrutinized by a man like Saxon. She concentrated on her food and hoped he would do the same.

"Hey Boss!" Jester greeted, plopping down in the empty chair between Saxon and Kylie. "And a good sun-cycle to you, Kylie."

Saxon glanced at Jester then Kylie. "I'm sure you remember Jester? You weren't feeling well when I introduced you." He grinned. "I should have told you he's a bit..."

"Strange," Jester interjected.

"That and more, however, you can trust him," Saxon said.

"I recognize your voice, but my vision wasn't good then. It's nice to finally see you."

Jester took her fingers in his, raised them to his lips and kissed the back of her hand. "Indeed it is. But the pleasure is all mine, I assure you." He winked. "I love your formal wear."

Kylie felt heat prick her cheeks and hoped she had not turned a bright shade of red. "What do you do here, Jester?"

"Whatever Saxon wants, or whatever I feel like."

"That's the truth," Saxon grumbled.

"That's a broad description of duties." Kylie pushed her tray to the empty place next to her.

"I'm a broad kind of guy, if you know what I mean."

"I think she gets the point." Saxon took both empty trays to the clean-window and pushed them through before he returned to the table. "Jester, stay with Kylie, there's something I must attend to."

"Olly-dolly, Boss. We'll be fine." Jester chuckled.

Kylie watched Saxon leave. She had the sinking feeling he was going to pay Nyles a visit. Only the Gods of the Sea could know what would happen when those two tangled.

"Be right back," Jester said. He stood and headed for the serving line.

She smiled. Jester was everything Saxon was not. They were so opposite she wondered what had brought them together in the first place. Jester was short, thin, bushy-haired, a wild dresser, a non-conformist, and from what she had seen and heard, rarely serious. He lumbered back with a tray so full that food hung over the edge. "Are you going to eat all that?"

"You betcha," Jester said, settling into his seat.

"Is Saxon always so serious?" Jester nodded as he shoved more food into his mouth. "How long have you two been friends?"

"A long time."

"How did you meet?"

"I ran into him one sun-cycle."

"How?"

"Long story," he mumbled with a full mouth."

"I've got time. Tell me about it."

"Nah, it's boring. I'd rather hear about you. How did you become a fish trainer?"

"Delphin Researcher," she corrected. "Delphins are not fish, they're..."

"Air breathing mammals, who evolved from Dolphins that were implanted on Neptus four centuries ago by our forefathers who stole them from planet Earth in the Milky Way Galaxy."

"So you know your history." She was astounded at his knowledge but did not want to insult him by saying so. Jester did not look like the kind of man who would read a book or understand complex matters. Looks were often deceiving, and in Jester's case, that would be a huge understatement.

"I dabble in history." He took several more bites. "So how did you come to work with fish?"

Kylie smiled, beginning to understand his game. "It just happened one sun-cycle. I was standing at the end of the pier when a Delphin talked to me."

"That's incredible." Jester crammed another forkful of food into his mouth. "And how do you find Saxon?"

"What?" She had not been prepared for that question. "I thought you wanted to know about my work with the Delphins."

"I do. I just wondered how you liked your roommate? Personally, I don't like mine very well at all. Wanna switch?"

"Sure." The thought had merit. "But I don't think Saxon would agree."

"I'll ask him, for all the good it will do."

"If he wasn't so...so..."

"Frustrating, overbearing and arrogant?"

She laughed. "You do know Saxon, don't you?"

"Better than you could ever imagine." Jester polished off the last two bites and pushed the tray toward the empty seat. "You should laugh more often."

"I would if I had something to laugh about."

"Well, why don't you tell old Jester what's eating at that pretty little head of yours?"

"Genesis Disorder."

"I see." Jester patted the back of her hand. "That's a mighty big worry."

Kylie wondered if it was wise to confide in Saxon's best friend, but she had to talk to someone. "My parents were diagnosed two sun-cycles before I left Estra." She leaned closer. "If a cure can be found soon, they can be saved. That's why I came."

"But you're not a scientist, Kylie. What do you expect to do?"

"I'm sure the cure is tied to the Delphins, and that's what I do best."

Jester rubbed his chin. "Interesting. Have you talked to the scientist in the Estran lab yet?"

"No, but I'm very anxious. Will you go with me?"

"Absolutely." Jester stood. "Let's do it."

***

Hawk paced the length of the deck next to the Delphin pool waiting for Nyles. He should kill him now and put everyone out of their misery, but unfortunately that was not an option. Nevertheless, if Nyles ever touched Kylie again, he would enjoy dispensing the kind of justice The Hawk was famous for.

Why he felt so protective of Kylie he could not explain, yet there was something between them that defied common sense and logic. Women. Women had caused him more pain and suffering in one lifetime than any man should have to endure. Well, no more. He'd vowed to stay clear of women, and that included on the job closeness. Now he was stuck taking care of the only woman on SEA Lab. Just his luck.

Once this assignment was over he intended to shed his Hawk identity and clear his name. It could mean a dangerous trip back to Andor, but he didn't care. He'd rather die clearing his name than continue the existence he'd been living. Jester and his crew were more than ready for a physical confrontation with Andor. He hated to disappoint them, but he planned to go alone. He would never risk their lives and their freedom.

"Well, well. What do we have here?" Nyles snickered as he approached Saxon.

"Your worst nightmare."

"I doubt that. You don't have the guts to..."

Hawk grabbed Nyles arm, twisted it behind him and threw him face first to the wet floor. He held him flat with his knee. "You were saying?"

"You're going to fail, Saxon. You don't have what it takes to stop what's going on here."

"And what might that be?" He wrenched Nyles arm tighter behind his back causing him to groan loudly.

"You're the Chief of Security--you tell me."

"Everyone knows about the missing coins. Maybe I should search your room again. Or maybe your pockets?" Hawk grabbed Nyles' hair and pulled his head up. He wanted to slam his forehead into the concrete floor, but he needed Nyles in one piece. The slime-snake had to be behind the thefts of the coins and papers, and he wanted to bring him down, but he also wanted who Nyles worked for. He released his hold and stood.

Nyles pushed to his knees then stood. "So that's how it's going to be." He brushed sand and dirt from his silky uniform. "Don't turn your back, Saxon."

"We could end it all right here," Hawk goaded, wishing the man would make a move so he could break his nose. He heard the lift door open and glanced behind him. Jester and Kylie stepped into the room while instinct warned him of Nyles' attack. Two hands wrapped around his neck to squeeze the breath from him, but he broke Nyles' hold and landed a strong punch to Nyles' gut. When the coward doubled over, he brought his fist up, connecting hard with Nyles' jaw, knocking the man flat on his back. "Like I said. Don't touch her again."

The pathetic man picked himself up and stared at him with hatred in his eyes. He expected no less from Logun. The man was trouble, but he would soon make a mistake that would provide a lead, and he was desperate enough to make it soon. Nyles lunged at him. Hawk blocked the attack with his right arm, causing Nyles to splash land on the belly-slide.

"Hey, Nyles!" Jester yelled. "If you're gonna play in the water, you'd better get yourself a wet-suit."

Hawk saw Nyles, soaked to the bone, stand and walk to the exit. He waited until the man left the room before he turned. "Jester, Kylie, what are you doing here?" He wished she hadn't seen that little altercation, but it was unavoidable.

"Kylie wants to talk to Professor Winn." Jester glanced at Kylie. "Oh yeah, and she wants to change first. Although I think she looks right smart, don't you? Boss?"

Right smart was not even close to accurate, she was devastating. Kylie filled out a wet suit like no other woman. Full breasts, small waist, and rounded hips that tapered to shapely legs well-toned from swimming. He shouldn't stare, but the sight of her mesmerized him.

"I'll be right back," Kylie said.

Hawk watched her walk to the ready-room in the corner, his gaze glued to her cute little behind. Thinking of his roommate in terms of beautiful, cute and mesmerizing was dangerous, yet he would be blind to miss her assets when she was clad in form-fitting rubber.

"Boss? Hello? Talk to me...Boss?"

"What?"

"Glad to see you're back. Kylie says that the cure for Genesis Disorder is right under our noses."

"Where?" he asked, his mind imagining Kylie in the ready room, peeling down the black rubber, exposing flawless skin, skin his fingers itched to feel.

Jester pointed to the Delphin pool. "There."

"The water?" He had no idea what Jester was babbling about, when his thoughts were obsessed with the fact that Kylie should be stark naked by now.

"The Delphins. Kylie says they hold the key. You know, she could be right. She's anxious to talk to Winn."

"Good idea. I'll take her. I want you to pump up CAM. I want to know every move Nyles has made since birth, and every person he's ever talked to."

"We know what he's done since the age of sixteen. Isn't that good enough?" Hawk glared and Jester shrugged his shoulders. "You got it. Give me a couple of time-units." Jester slapped his hand against his forehead then headed toward the lift. "See ya," he called over his shoulder.

Thank the stars Jester had finally managed to get his mind off Kylie's enticing body and back to business. If anyone could find information, it was Jester. He had the uncanny ability to discover facts others tried to bury. Nyles was not smart enough to engineer a birth-cycle party, let alone cover up his past. He had to be someone's pawn, but which of the three planets bought his loyalty?

"Let's go."

Hawk turned at the sound of Kylie's voice. She was back in Estra's official blue uniform, her hair pulled back and knotted at the nape of her neck. Green eyes stared up at him with a determined glint he could appreciate. At least she was not a woman to succumb to male domination, and she knew how to control her emotions. The last woman Nyles pawed had to be sequestered under doctor's care until her transfer flight arrived.

"I want to know if Nyles so much as looks at you the wrong way." She nodded at him, but he had the feeling she'd do whatever was necessary, and if that meant putting herself in danger to serve her planet, then that's how it would be. "Never meet him alone. For any reason. Understand?"

"You're overreacting. I can handle myself."

"Not with a man like Nyles." His hands instinctively fisted at his sides at the mention of Nyles name. The man was a coward; brave with women who could not defend themselves, and that was the worst kind of coward. "Let's go," Hawk grumbled, pointing to the stairs that led to the Estran lab offices.

CHAPTER SEVEN

Kylie entered the busy lab, amazed by the sophisticated equipment. There were rows of tables with spectroscopes, biotoscopes, microscopes, and other equipment she could not identify. Lights hung low over racks of vials which gave the sterile white room an eerie glow. It seemed surreal. Men in white lab coats were the only human touch, and they were so totally engrossed in their work they did not even notice her.

A short man with thick glasses and a scowl on his face approached them. She sensed his irritation at being interrupted. "We need to speak with Professor Winn."

"Is he expecting you?"

Saxon grabbed Kylie's hand and pushed forward. "We'll find our own way."

"Thank you," Kylie muttered to the man as Saxon escorted her down the aisle with a determined set to his jaw. "You didn't have to be so rude."

"I thought you wanted to see Winn."

"I do but..."

"Why waste time?" Saxon stopped in front of the office at the far end and knocked.

"Come in, come in."

Kylie stepped inside while Saxon held the door. "Professor Winn?"

"Just call me Professor, everyone does." The man glanced up from the high stack of papers in front of him on the desk. "And what can I do for you, little lady?"

At least he had a friendly face. His white hair, white bushy eyebrows and white beard blended with his pale skin and white coat, making him look like the mad scientist he had been called by those who had met him. "I'm Researcher Two Kylie Beryl. Roloc wanted me to discuss my work with the Delphins with you when I arrived."

"Yes, yes, sit—please. And you too, Chief Saxon." He walked around the desk and removed papers and books from the two chairs. "I know my office is a mess. It's how I work best."

She smiled. The Professor was exactly how Roloc had described him. A bit scattered, but brilliant. "Have you taken any samples from the Delphins yet?" she asked as she and Saxon took their seats.

"Yes, but we need more. Nyles said he hasn't been able to get them to cooperate lately. I can't understand the problem."

"I can." Kylie sighed. "I'll get your samples."

"Yes, yes. Good. Can I offer you a drink?"

"No, but I'd love to see the Delphin log."

"Log? We don't have a log. Should we have one?" The professor searched the drawers in his large metal desk. "No, don't see one." He glanced up. "Are you sure?"

"Researcher Nyles Logun is supposed to provide you with a daily log," Kylie said.

"Well, that explains it then. Nyles isn't the most cooperative Researcher I've ever worked with." He picked up a pen and scribbled a couple of notes. "Do you have a first name?"

"Kylie, sir."

"Please, Professor. Sir makes me feel even older than I am." He chuckled. "May I call you Kylie? It's so much better than all that formal stuff."

"I agree."

Saxon cleared his throat. "Have you noticed anything missing? Books, ledgers, equipment, test tubes, anything?"

The professor scratched his head, causing his thin hair to stand straight up on his head. "I'm not sure. I thought I misplaced some documents, but I haven't been able to find them. I'm not the neatest person, as you can see."

"I'd appreciate it, Professor, if you kept a close eye on any vital information. There have been some problems reported."

"Yes, yes. I see. You know that fella with the bushy hair and flowery shirt? Well, he said the same thing last sun-cycle." Winn stood and crossed his arms. "It's a crime, you know. Lives are at stake and all, and we've got to worry about spies and sabotage."

"Professor," Kylie began, "have you isolated the source of Genesis Disorder yet?"

"At first we assumed it originated on Estra since that was where the first cases were diagnosed, however, the first men to contract the disease were construction workers who returned from Neptus. So you see, we have a quandary." Winn scratched his head. "Personally, I suspect the origin is right here in the Agor Sea. There's experiments going on as we speak that might verify that theory."

"What does Roloc think?"

"Roloc agrees with me, because the scientists on Estra have found nothing to indicate a cause. Here we've found many irregularities in various specimens that could lead to the source."

Kylie leaned forward. "What exactly?"

"It's too early to say, and I don't want word to spread. If this leaks, we could have panic in SEA Lab."

"He's right, Kylie. It's best we leave the Professor to his work." Saxon stood and offered his hand. "Be careful, Professor, and call me the minute you even suspect something is wrong."

Winn stood and shook Saxon's hand. "I will, my boy, I will."

Kylie rose. "We'll talk again soon. Right now I'm anxious to get to work."

"Yes, yes, you are exactly the way Roloc described you. He wanted me to work closely with you. Said you could be a great asset to us."

"I hope so." Kylie left with Saxon at her heels, not quite sure if he was a help or a hindrance. The last thing she needed was a watchwort looming over her sun-cycle and moon-cycle. Her work with the Delphins was personal, private, and best accomplished alone. They wove their way back through the laboratory, out the doors and down the steps to the Delphin pool.

She stopped at the edge of the belly-slide. "We need to talk."

***

"You stupid fool!" Konar yelled over the private com-line. He was glad he could not see Nyles' face. The idiot had no idea who he was, only that he was his employer and his identity was to remain secret. Nyles would never know they had actually met in person before and that he had hated him from first sight. He only hired Nyles because he could easily be bought. "I explicitly told you not to arouse Saxon's attention. If this mission fails because of you, I'll personally end your life."

"It won't happen again." Nyles wiped beads of sweat from his forehead.

"If you keep irritating Saxon, he'll kill you. Quit making yourself so conspicuous."

"I thought it would keep him occupied so he wouldn't look for the missing..." Nyles paused, "research papers."

"You moronic imbecile! I'm not paying you to think!" You're to follow orders and nothing more. If you can't, I'll have a replacement sent immediately, and you'll disappear to work off the credits I've paid you in the mines of Andor."

"I understand, Konar. There will be no further problems, I assure you."

He was tired of dealing with Nyles, but until he achieved his goal, he had to tolerate the man. Too irritated to continue he ended the transmission. It was time to send Sira to insure success. If Nyles was cheating him in some underhanded way Sira would uncover his stupid scheme so fast he wouldn't know what hit him.

***

Kylie shifted nervously in the large domare hide chair in front of Saxon's desk. He had an inquisitive look on his face and seemed far too relaxed considering the circumstances. Just when she thought she was gaining a minuscule insight into Saxon, he fooled her by acting the opposite of what she expected. Jester stood behind him with his normally silly grin, his bushy blond hair even more unruly than usual. She had to do this, she reminded herself, but it did not feel right.

She took a deep breath. "I believe Nyles Logun is sabotaging the research here."

"We're well aware of that." Saxon leaned forward and rested his elbows on the desk. "What's your point?"

"Estra is desperate for a cure, and I...well I..."

"Get to the point."

"Hey Boss, take it easy," Jester offered, "she's trying."

"This is difficult because I have to trust you, and I haven't had enough time to decide if that's a wise choice."

"You asked for this meeting, and I assure you, what you say will go no farther than this office. Now please, proceed."

She hesitated remembering Roloc's instructions. He'd said to keep her rank a secret. She considered the wisdom of that advice, but her rank meant nothing to Saxon. Only Nyles would have a problem if he knew. "I'm a Researcher five, plus two ticks, which puts me far above Nyles, but that must remain our secret. Roloc felt I could learn more if I were under Nyles, and he thought me incompetent."

Jester grinned. "I can relate to that."

"The cure for Genesis Disorder is priceless. If it falls into the wrong hands, only the ultra rich will be able to afford it. So many will suffer. I'm here to see that doesn't happen, but I can't do it alone."

"If it's any consolation, Miss Beryl, Jester and I are here for exactly the same reason. We know the ramifications. Obviously Roloc doesn't have faith in the operation here."

"I'm afraid he doesn't. He wanted to hire The Hawk. Can you believe that? He wanted a ruthless, murdering space pirate to be in charge of security!"

"The Hawk." Jester shook his head. "He's one mean son-of-a-starfighter all right. I sure wouldn't want to work with him!"

She wondered why Saxon had nothing to say about The Hawk, although she surmised by his angry look that he did not want the man here anymore than she did. Or was he jealous of The Hawk's reputation? Men could be foolish in that regard. "Roloc said he'd still call him in if I don't succeed."

Saxon cleared his throat. "I see your concern."

"Do you? This Hawk person, whoever he is, would probably want the cure for himself. I hear he's ruthless and greedy, along with his other disreputable traits."

"Yeah, I'd guess the same thing." Jester smiled. "A man like The Hawk, well...he couldn't have a ounce of good in him. Personally, I think..." Jester groaned.

Why had Saxon kicked Jester under the desk? And why was he glaring at Jester with such an evil glint in his eye? It certainly was not the look of a friend. They were getting off the subject. "All three planets involved in this project have a great deal at stake. Which planet has your loyalty, Saxon?"

"All three."

"That's a very diplomatic answer, but I don't believe you. You're from Andor, so you must have loyalty to them."

"All that matters is my neutrality."

Evasive, she thought. Had she made a mistake, or was he what he claimed? She'd try and learn more about Saxon from Jester later, because it was clear he had no intentions of making his intentions known to her.

"It's your choice who to trust, Miss Beryl, but I suspect you'll be safer working with us than some of the others."

"I agree, but my concern isn't for myself, it's for Professor Winn. The moment he makes a breakthrough, his life could be in jeopardy."

Saxon leaned back in his chair and crossed his arms over his chest. "How close do you think he is?"

"I wish I knew for sure. I'm hoping a couple of weeks."

"Jester and I are here to assist you any way we can."

She studied Jester's compassionate expression before her gaze moved to Saxon. Why couldn't Saxon show emotion the way Jester did? It would make her decision so much easier if she had a better insight into the man Saxon claimed to be, but he sat emotionless, his blue eyes dark and brooding. "I need uninterrupted time with the Delphins, but I'm afraid that's impossible as long as Nyles is in charge."

"Does Nyles scare you?" Jester asked.

"A little...I mean he breaks my concentration," she replied.

Saxon leaned forward and leaned on the desk. "There's no room for fear. If you're to succeed, Kylie, you have to meet Nyles head on, without one ounce of fear on your face. A man like Nyles creates fear, thrives on it and uses it to his best advantage."

She took a deep breath. He just called her Kylie, and for Saxon that seemed like an intimate slip. He'd done his best to keep his distance, which she assumed was why he addressed her as Miss or Researcher. He spoke her name reverently, with respect, and it sent a warm chill down her spine. Or was it his piercing gaze that made her shiver? She scolded herself for noticing and reacting like some smitten woman who cared what a man thought of her.

"Saxon's right, ya know." Jester walked around the desk and sat on the arm of the chair next to Kylie. "You don't have to believe me, but you can trust him with your life."

"I hope that isn't necessary." Saxon gave her a look that said it could very possibly be necessary. "How many men work for you?"

"Twenty-eight. Two men patrol each of the seven levels at all times. The only area that's not monitored is the observation deck." Saxon glanced at Jester. "Did you get the information I asked for?"

"Still working on it, Boss. Could take a couple of sun-cycles. Lots of archives to search. It takes time to knock the dust off those out of the way places."

She wanted to ask what information he spoke of, but it probably did not concern her. Saxon had the entire facility to concentrate on, not just her concerns. The longer she was with him, the more she felt secure. It was hard to explain why, just a gut feeling, and she'd learned to listen to those feelings because they'd never let her down. The only time she'd had problems was when she questioned those primal messages that came from somewhere beyond.

"I want the results as soon as possible," Saxon said, reaching for his palm-com that beeped from his pocket. "Saxon here."

"Saxon! Saxon!" the voice yelled. "Come immediately to level eight. There's been an accident!"

She watched Saxon disappear so quickly she wondered if he had even been there.

Jester shut down the computer and locked it in the desk drawer. "Let's go," he said, grabbing Kylie's hand.

They were in the lift and exiting on the eighth level before she dared exhale. Jester pulled her through a maze of heavy equipment she recognized as underwater mining machinery. He guided her through a group of angry, excited men until they reached the center of their concern. She gasped at the sight of a bloody man on the floor, his agonizing screams louder than the shouting of his co-workers who were all yelling at Saxon.

"Pratt, what happened?" Saxon demanded.

Miner Pratt squatted next to Saxon. "We were working the bottom as usual when the cable snapped. It wrapped around Gavon and sucked him into the gears."

Saxon examined the man lying in front of him. "What happened to the protective casing?"

"It gave way when Gavon's body hit it." Pratt shook his head. "I think someone tampered with it."

"Here doctor!" someone shouted.

The doctor hurried to the victim and placed a tourniquet around the man's mangled right arm. "Get him to the med-room. Now!"

Pratt pulled Saxon to the far corner. "I didn't want to alarm the others, but I just got word two of my men are trapped in sector C2-east. They only have fifteen minutes of air left. When the cable broke the rigging fell and pinned them to the bottom."

"I'm on my way." Saxon wound through the crowd to Jester and Kylie. "We've got a job to do."

Jester followed Saxon, pulling Kylie behind him to the ready room. "What's up, Boss?"

"Two men are trapped." He glanced at Kylie. "I need you to pilot the sub. Your file says you're an expert. You'll be in no danger."

"Of course."

"Good, get it ready to dive." Saxon pulled his palm-com from his pocket. "Throm!" He waited until Throm's voice sounded. "I want you and four men to suit up and meet me outside level eight."

Kylie watched Jester and Saxon shed their clothes and don wet suits. They dressed so fast she had not thought to avert her gaze. Muscles tightened across Saxon's back, and she wondered how he was going to squeeze his large frame into the small suit. She should not be admiring his body at a time like this, but it was impossible not to notice since he had stripped to a skimpy pair of briefs.

Every well-toned muscle of Saxon's body bulged as he tugged and pulled, forcing the rubber up his legs. He slipped his arms into the sleeves and in a flash his bronze skin was hidden from her admiring eye. She heard Jester zip his suit, reminding her she was not alone with Saxon. They secured their helmets and walked to the exit pool. She followed behind, noticing Saxon was a good foot taller than Jester, and the size of his body dwarfed Jester in comparison.

"Get in," Saxon said, opening the hatch of the sub.

Kylie entered the sub through the round opening on the top and Saxon turned the hatch wheel securing her inside. She punched in the proper code and the sub gurgled as it sank below the surface. She cleared the exit portal and waited for instructions. Five other divers swam past the front shield and she heard Saxon tell them to hold on to the sub's side rails.

"Kylie, take her fast and steady."

"Affirmative." The green water seemed murkier than she remembered , however the sub traveled just above the bottom and stirred up sandy silt. Through the port side she caught a glimpse of her mangled spacecraft just as a large, dangerous-looking eel slithered out where the front shield had once been. It had not taken long for sea creatures to claim a new home.

As the sub moved past, she glanced inside the craft and saw clumps of red hair wave from the control panel like seaweed. Her hand instinctively moved to one of the thin, empty places on her head. Saxon had to cut her free to save her life, but she wished those waving strands were still attached to her head.

The sub turned and dove deeper into a crevice, its headlight gleaming off fish of different sizes and colors. In the distance she spotted a flashing light and knew it had to be the trapped miners. She eased back on the throttle and coasted in slowly.

"Cut power," Saxon said.

"Power off," she replied.

"We've got to get this reclamation tank off them. Jester, grab the wench on the front of the sub. Kylie?"

"Yes?"

"As soon as we connect the wench, take her up slowly until I tell you to stop."

"Affirmative." She held her breath as Jester and the other men wrapped cables around the tank, fastening them securely. Saxon double-checked each connection then reassured the trapped miners. From the sound of his voice she knew both men were lucky to be alive.

Saxon nodded at the sub. "Take her up slow."

Kylie let out the ballast, and the small craft eased upward. She felt the tug from the weight beneath her and knew the object was being lifted off the men.

"Stop. Take her twenty yards to the left and stop."

Using low power she followed Saxon's orders precisely.

"Take her down."

She held her breath as the sub descended farther into the dark water. A glance out the starboard port verified the men were free. She heard a thud just before Saxon yelled, "Stop." She waited while he freed the wench cables.

"Wind it," he ordered.

Kylie pushed the button and the long cables wound themselves slowly around the cylinders on the underside of the sub. Saxon hovered before the viewport making sure the procedure went smoothly. Beads of sweat formed on his forehead inside the clear helmet and concern filled his eyes. "How are the men?"

He looked through the portal. "I don't know. They're barely conscious."

She heard him exhale loudly, more from frustration than exertion. The cylinder stopped turning and Saxon secured the hook, pausing to look at her for a moment that seemed suspended in time. His gaze was filled with longing, and she wished she could be the woman to fill the void that held so much sadness.

"Let's pick up the men. Take it slow. We'll have to hold them. No more than half throttle."

"Affirmative." She wanted to say more, but all the divers could hear. She longed to tell him how brave he was, how well he did his job, how lucky the men were to have him as a leader. He held them together with a calm confidence she found admirable—and attractive. When Saxon was focused and intent his aura exuded power--controlled power, and she found that erotically seductive.

She maneuvered the sub back to the men and waited as they took their places on each side of the sub.

"Ready."

His voice inside the helmet sounded deeper, yet softer, filling her with a comfortable warmth. She turned the sub and began the tedious ride back to SEA Lab. Throm told Saxon the men were out of air, but the towering pyramid was in sight. She aimed the sub for the large round opening and coasted inside.

"Good job, men," Saxon said to the men exiting the water.

Through the portal she saw the injured men carried away on stretchers. She could no longer hear Saxon's voice, and that disturbed her. She liked watching and hearing him work, confirming her gut feeling to trust him. The metal wheel above her head squeaked, then opened, the filtered air of SEA Lab gushing in along with a few streams of seawater.

Saxon held his hand down toward her and she took it in hers, not surprised when he lifted her with ease out of the confining quarters. "Thanks." She met his gaze and they stood on top of the sub in the now deserted eighth level.

"You're an excellent pilot, Kylie."

"You're a pretty good rescuer."

He smiled. "I'll take that as a compliment from one who should know."

She could only imagine how he rescued her, his powerful form bent over her, cutting her hair with his knife, his strong arms lifting her from her seat, carrying her to safety. "That's three lives you've saved in two sun-cycles."

"Makes me feel heroic."

Kylie stared at Saxon, drops of moisture glistening on his lashes. Saxon was undeniably male from head to foot, and dressed in the form-fitting rubber suit he resembled the mythical Estran sea god, Ryain.

"Why are you looking at me like that?" Saxon touched her cheek. "Are you all right?"

"I...I was just thinking we should check on the men."

"Of course." Saxon jumped to the deck then lifted Kylie down.

His hands lingered on her waist long after her feet were on the ground. His eyes searched her face. She shivered, sensing his need and feeling her own. He released her with a palpable reluctance--a reluctance she shared, and that thought scared her. His touch made her feel as if she would melt, and the absence of his touch made her want more. A heated flush crept into her cheeks and she sighed in relief when he turned away.

"We'll go to the med-unit as soon as I dress."

As he entered the ready-room, she remembered how he looked dressed in nothing but a skimpy pair of briefs. Her cheeks grew hotter. She groaned and thought about her purpose, and who she was. Kylie Beryl Researcher Five, a woman who could never belong to a man, a woman forbidden to life-mate because she could never have children. Part of her resented being the offspring of scientists, but she would never trade parents, even for a normal life with a man she could love.

CHAPTER EIGHT

Hawk anxiously paced behind his desk, watching Jester search CAM, trying every conceivable category. "Isn't there anything we can use?"

"Nyles was expelled from..."

"Yeah, tell me something I don't know."

"Well, it seems naughty little Nyles has contacts on Cyron and spends time there occasionally."

He grinned. "Now what do you think he could possibly be up to on a planet full of smugglers and pirates? We have contacts there, see if any of them have been approached with Gwadra coins."

"Sending. What else?"

"Contact *The Redemption* and send them to Cyron. There must be a connection." Hawk raked his hands through his damp hair. "And make sure that motley crew of mine gets my ship back here in one piece."

Jester chuckled. "You know they wouldn't do anything to make you mad."

"While I'm with them."

"You can trust them." Jester entered a long series of numbers into the computer.

"Print up schematics on all the mining equipment. Give them to Throm and have him check every minute detail for sabotage. I want to know exactly how it happened, and if anything else has been touched."

"Got it," Jester replied while the computer ejected reams of paper. He picked up the pile of papers and stood. "I'm on my way, Boss."

Hawk slumped in his chair. Time seemed nonexistent . He could not remember the last time he slept or how long Kylie had been here. Kylie.

What was he going to do with her? He felt the need to be with her every moment, but he had other pressing matters that demanded his attention. Effon, one of his most trusted men was with Kylie now at the Delphin pool, but he wanted to be at her side. His men were capable, yet a burning desire gnawed at the pit of his stomach just thinking about Kylie doing anything without him.

He was responsible for her, worried about her, and attracted to her. There, he admitted it. Her beauty was subtle and striking, her intelligence sharp, demanding more from those around her than they were used to giving. Yet beneath that smart, self-reliant exterior lay a sensitive, caring and emotional beauty that drew him, even though he tried to ignore her unique, sensual allure.

As much as he desired her, his past prevented any hope of a relationship. She did not seem the type to be content with a passing affair, a woman who could share his bed and leave without looking back. No. Kylie would hold a man to a higher set of ideals, and he could not offer her an ounce of hope for a future. She deserved a man free to life-mate who could offer her security and children. His dream was no different than hers, however she was free to follow that dream while he remained rooted in a nightmare so cruel he wondered how he could endure it himself.

Redmon's face flashed in his mind. His check-in time passed many time-units ago, and he had put it off as long as he dared. He pulled the com from the desk drawer and pressed the transmit button. All he had to report was more bad news.

"It's about time, Hawk. What's going on?"

"Two more Gwadra coins have been stolen, Researcher Beryl arrived, Nyles has been causing his normal brand of trouble, and a mining accident has put two men in the hospital."

"What has Nyles done?"

"His usual sexual assault." That was all he felt like telling Redmon at the moment, thinking it odd, that of all the things Redmon could ask about, he chose Nyles.

"The man's a nuisance, nothing more."

"I hope you're right. What's going on at your end?"

"Andor is quiet. I'm afraid I don't have any leads for you, but I'm working on a couple."

That bit of news came as no surprise. Redmon had repeated that same sentence for five annual-cycles. The least he could do was change the words for variety. "Keep in touch," Saxon said, canceling the connection. He rested his arms on the desk, using them as a pillow, exhaustion forcing his eyes closed.

***

Kylie caressed the Delphin's back as it swam tight circles around her. She'd made good progress with nothing to distract her from her work. She had managed to get all the samples the lab required by forming a successful mind link with Mia. Needles were not her favorite part, but at least she treated the Delphins with love—an emotion they responded to well.

Mia understood why she had to take blood and fluid samples. Delphins had strong family ties themselves, and when she conveyed her parents' illness, Mia gave herself willingly. Artus had entered the pool, swimming protectively back and forth. Others joined the guard, but none interfered. The Delphins had demonstrated a major leap of faith, and she could not be more pleased about her sun-cycle's work.

Her watchwort, Effon sat like a statue, his eyes focused on everything and nothing at the same time. At least Saxon was not here interfering with her every thought and examining her every movement. He made her nervous, unsure of herself, and extremely self-conscious, yet a part of her yearned for his company.

A Delphin's nose nudged her back while two more entered the pool and joined the fun. They were overly playful now, enjoying the fun she promised when the work was completed. The Delphins on Neptus bonded quicker and deeper than on Estra. They enjoyed their play, but she felt a deep sadness in them that did not exist on Estra.

"Good boy, Artus," she said to the one Mia said was her mate. "Where's Mia?" Mia broke the surface and glided toward her. She loved working in the water with the Delphins, and they were putting her through the paces, testing, learning, and willing to communicate. The only time they hesitated was when Nyles passed through the chamber and questioned her. At the sound of his voice they had fled to the open sea, returning only when he left. Effon's presence did not bother them in the least. What had Nyles done to them to cause such fear and anxiety?

Her temples throbbed and her eyes blurred. She blinked several times and wiped seawater from her face. No matter how hard she tried to zero in on Artus' unique frequency she met failure. It took time, and she was grateful for what she had received, even if the images they relayed were disturbing. Mia was the designated spokesperson with the others adding bits and pieces.

Through Mia's eyes she had seen the rugged outline of a dark mountain. Something bright hovered over the jagged peak and Mia was scared, yet she had to enter what she feared most. It made no sense, unless she were reliving her distant past when the floodwaters changed the face of Neptus forever. She had to try harder to understand the messages, but she was too tired to think, let alone swim.

Mia nuzzled her arm and she ran her hand down the sleek back of her newest friend. There was an unnatural lump under her skin. Some of the Delphins on Estra and been implanted with various tracking devices for scientific study, and she assumed the same had been done here, yet she had not seen that in the files Roloc sent with her, or on any charts or logs she had studied. She'd inquire with the other Researchers and find out exactly what function the implant served.

Out the corner of her eye she saw Effon stand. Without looking she knew Saxon had entered the chamber. The unmistakable warmth she felt every time he stared at her consumed her, sending a chill up her spine. She glanced over her shoulder expecting to find his customary bored look, however, she met his relaxed smiling gaze. He left his hair unrestrained, the free, easy look making him appear human instead of perfect and controlled.

Effon saluted Saxon then ran down the stairs, leaving her alone with the fierce looking warrior that appealed to her more each time she saw him. Maybe it was the deep blue of his eyes, or the thin scar over his right eye, or his amused laugh—whatever it was, she felt it in her soul and cried for it with her heart.

"Working hard?" Saxon asked, stepping to the edge of the pool.

"Of course. Like to see what we accomplished?" She watched him nod. This was going to be quite a surprise for the straight-laced warrior. It was hard not to smile when she thought about her devilish plan. She clapped her hands twice and three Delphins disappeared into the depths of the green water. A few seconds later they broke the surface, jumping in unison high into the air. The wake splashed up Kylie's front and she laughed, knowing Saxon's boots were soaked.

"You take great delight in having those creatures drench me."

"I think you need to lighten up and have some fun."

"Fun?"

"Come closer and I'll show you."

Saxon squatted and leaned toward her. "What does a man like you have to be afraid of?"

"You," he grumbled.

"I just want to show you something," she said, standing on the shallow slide. Smiling she reached her hand out to him and he took the bait. With one fast, hard jerk she pulled him into the water, laughing when his head surfaced and he spit water from his mouth.

"You'll regret this woman."

"Probably, but I think it's time our Chief of Security met Mia and Artus."

"Who?"

Kylie gave Mia a hand signal and she ducked below the surface and swam between Saxon's legs. "Hang on to her dorsal fin!" she called as Mia gave Saxon a ride around the pool on her back. Mia took an extra liberty and dove down a bit too far, taking him with her, only to surface a moment later, cutting through the water as she circled the perimeter. The look on Saxon's face was priceless. Astonishment, embarrassment, fury and excitement all blended into one indescribable emotion that lit his masculine features. She could not help laughing.

"You *will* regret this!"

"Probably, but what kind of Chief would you be if you didn't meet the Delphins?"

"A dry Chief."

When Mia glided onto the slide area Saxon stood and the mammal swam off. He grabbed her arm and dragged her into the center of the aquatic arena. His touch triggered a tremble deep within and her skin tingled beneath his fingers. His eyes softened with a tenderness she had not seen before. He pulled her to his chest and she was forced to wrap her legs around him so he didn't kick her as he tread water.

His lips brushed hers and her breath caught in her throat. She wanted him to kiss her. It shocked her to admit it, but it was true. With his arm wrapped around her waist the heat of his body penetrated the cool rubber of her wet suit and she felt sinful, but safe. No, safe was not the right word for the way she felt about Saxon. The rapid beat of his heart was fast and heavy against her breast, or was that her heartbeat?

"Is there anything else you want to show me?" he asked.

She smiled at the smooth, seductive tone of his voice. "I think you've had quite enough for one sun-cycle. I don't want you to scare the Delphins."

Saxon grinned. "I think it's you who's scared."

"Never," she lied. Before she could take another breath his lips were on hers, his tongue begging for entry. Her stomach tingled as she parted her lips. He took her mouth with a hungry urgency, his hands pressing against her back, molding her breast to his chest. He tasted sweet, salty, and dangerous. She could easily lose herself in his embrace and forget what her duty demanded.

What could a kiss hurt? He stirred feelings deep within that yearned for satisfaction, yet she knew it was not possible. If Saxon knew who she really was, he would push her aside without so much as a glance and run like all the others. The pain of his rejection would be more than she could bear. She pushed her hands against his chest and felt his arm drop. He ended the kiss, leaving her lips tingling and her heart racing. He took her hand and pulled her to the slide, then helped her out of the water.

How could she have been so reckless? She did not want to see hatred in his eyes should he discover she was a freak. It was best not to let him get close. She prayed for the strength to resist. Looking up into his eyes she wanted to fall back into his arms. Saxon was the first man she'd ever wanted to kiss her, the first man who made her feel like a woman in his arms. There was no law against an affair, and the thought was overly tempting. According to Estran law she had been given a permanent birth control implant, so that aspect was not a concern. It was their inevitable separation she could not face, because she knew if she gave him her body he would take her heart.

He stared at her as if he wanted to speak, yet he remained silent, his probing eyes taking the breath from her body. They were not touching, but she still felt the imprint of his body on hers, his lips, his strength and his desire. A moment longer under his spell and she'd make a fool of herself. "I'll change and be right back."

Saxon watched Kylie jog to the ready-room. He let out the breath he'd been holding and stared at the large puddle at his feet. Cold water dripped from his clothes and hair. At least his saturated state kept a bit of a damper on the carnal lust that flowed through every vein in his body. He should be with his crew, satisfying his most basic masculine needs, but he had sworn off loveless joining's, finding them empty and cold. He wanted the hot, sweaty heat of passion that could only come from love and caring.

Kylie ignited that need. She was a woman he could care about. Love was another issue. He was not sure he had the capability to love, but if anyone could teach him it would be her. Nothing would please him more than to let her try and tame the beast within him, but he could not take that risk until that beast was dead forever, never to surface again. He had not been with a woman since that fateful moon-cycle he was found in Lissa's bed. How could he trust himself? Self-denial was not easy, but whenever temptation reared its ugly head, he thought of the color red and the nightmare returned with a vengeance, erasing all physical need.

Kissing Kylie had been irrational, unprofessional--and necessary. Thinking of her in a romantic way could be his undoing. He had to fight the hold she seemed to have over him. For her safety as well as his, he had to avoid involvement. If his true identity were discovered and Kylie was with him she could be tried along with him. Any intimacy with her was a risk. He could not set foot on any planet without the threat of arrest or death. Until he established his innocence and proved to himself he was not capable of harming a woman, he would keep his distance.

As hard as he tried, the lingering memory of Kylie's kiss remained. He'd felt her surprise, held her as shock turned to desire. Her firm breasts against his chest had nearly been his undoing. When her hands pushed against him he knew he had made a mistake, even if she wanted that kiss as much as he did. Wanting was different than having, and he could never have Kylie the way he wanted. He had to get her out of his mind.

The swoosh of a door made him turn. Nyles marched into the room, a smug grin on his face. Just what he needed, another confrontation, and more lies.

"Tired of woman-sitting yet, Saxon? I'd be more than happy to relieve you of your duties. We both know who the better man is now, don't we?"

Saxon's hands fisted at his side and he clenched his teeth. He'd like nothing better than to teach Nyles a lesson he would never forget. "What test tube did you crawl out of?"

"I could take that as an insult, Saxon, but I have better things to do."

"I doubt that." Saxon stepped closer. "You can't stand the thought that the only woman on SEA Lab is with me."

"Do you really think I'm that shallow?" Nyles snickered. "Don't answer that." He took a step back. "Haven't you heard the rumors? You're the one sleeping with her. You're the one who get his..."

"Enough!"

Nyles grinned. "What's the matter? Did I hit a nerve?" He shook his head. "Pity. We were getting along so well too."

He knew Nyles was testing his patience with this stupid little game. It rubbed him wrong for the slime-snake to use Kylie as the pawn. "Don't you have something to do? Or should I say someone to spy on?"

"I'm not a spy."

"Nor an actor." Saxon heard footsteps behind him , deciding it best to allow Nyles to return to whatever hole he crawled out of. He suspected Kylie was as tired as he was and would not welcome further upset.

"I'm ready," Kylie said.

"For what, my dear?" Nyles cooed.

"Work." Kylie turned and walked toward the lift.

Saxon followed her into the lift and pressed the down button. He glanced at Kylie, her long, wet hair caressing her shoulders, her eyes straight ahead. She looked as tired and frustrated as he felt.

CHAPTER NINE

Kylie fidgeted nervously in the chair in front of Saxon and Jester. Saxon said there was something he had to check on before they could go to dinner. She was starving after a sun-cycle in the Delphin pool, but before she could relax she had to tell them what she had learned. "Saxon, Jester, there's something you need to know about the Delphins."

"More than you've already showed me?" Saxon grinned.

"Nyles has done something evil to the Delphins."

Saxon leaned forward. "What gives you that idea?"

"Kylie talks to 'em, Boss. I'll bet she's darn good at it too. What did they tell you?"

She smiled at Jester's eager manner. "They don't tell me in the way you think. They send me mental pictures that project their thoughts."

"Telepathy?" Saxon inquired.

"A form of it, yes. However, the images they sent this sun-cycle were evil, and they involved Nyles."

"Tell us something we don't know," Saxon grumbled.

"I believe he's using them for more than research."

"How?" Jester asked.

"I don't know."

Saxon cleared his throat. "We've been keeping an eye on Nyles for some time. He's our number one suspect, capable of anything."

Jester walked to the vid screen on the wall and pushed several buttons. "Watch this, kids."

Nyles' form appeared by the Delphin pool. He was alone with a syringe in his hand and Mia was locked in the pool. When she swam up to Nyles he injected her. Kylie instantly felt sick watching Mia's movements still. Then he tied something around her tail and pushed her toward the center of the pool. The drugged Delphin sluggishly moved about until Nyles opened the gate. Mia languidly swam into the open sea, and Kylie felt her heart break.

"What do you make of that?" Saxon asked.

"It's obvious he drugged her. I don't know what he tied around her tail, but he's using her to..."

"Smuggle," Jester and Saxon simultaneously mumbled.

"That's very possible." Kylie crossed her legs. "They hate Nyles, and I know they wouldn't do anything for him voluntarily."

Saxon frowned. "What kind of drug did he use?"

"We've developed several drugs to make them more cooperative. But we usually only use them on difficult cases, and only in the beginning. These Delphins have been acquainted with human contact for quite some time, long enough not to need drugs. Personally, I never use chemicals on them to gain their trust."

"I trust you," Jester began, "and I'm not even a fish!"

She almost laughed when Saxon growled at Jester. It was obvious the two men had a very close, intimate bond, the kind of relationship that did not require words. She'd lost count how many times she wished to find a friendship like theirs, but men and women both were afraid to get too close to a genetic freak.

Saxon turned his eyes on her and she immediately felt the intensity of his stare. He looked exhausted, but that did not diminish his intense potency, or his ability to peer into her soul. Well, he could look as hard as he wanted, but she would never give him access. She should be ashamed of herself for trying to read something into a simple kiss that was not there. He was only doing his job, and she was a fool to think otherwise.

"How much information can you get from the Delphins?" Saxon asked.

"They're learning to trust me. I made progress with Mia this sun-cycle." Both men gave her a skeptical look. "The Delphin Nyles drugged is Mia. She was the first to make contact with me, and seems the most cooperative."

"Isn't Kylie something, Boss? Not your average fish trainer, that's for sure. No sir, she's special, don't ya think?"

Kylie noticed the irritated look Saxon gave Jester, the kind one friend gave to another when they stepped over the line. If Jester were like Saxon, that look would bring them to blows. However these two men together were comically amusing. She knew all too well how surly Saxon could be without Jester. She thanked her lucky stars Jester was here, because she was in no mood to tangle with him alone.

"Jester, I want you to stay here and monitor the Delphin pool. Beep me if you see Nyles do anything else with the Delphins."

"Olly-dolly, Boss."

Saxon rose, walked around the desk and grabbed her hand. He pulled her to her feet and out the door before she could utter a word in protest. His long strides made her jog to keep pace. She took a deep, composing breath as she stepped into the lift. "Where are we going in such a hurry?"

"To see Professor Winn. I have a pretty good idea what's going on."

The lift doors opened and they hurried across the large area in front of the Delphin pool , then up the steps into the main lab room. Saxon pulled her past the handful of scientists at work, not stopping until he reached the professor's office. Without knocking he shoved the door open, quickly closing it behind them. Winn looked up at them quite startled, but he smiled.

"Saxon, what a coincidence. I was about to call you," Winn said, shuffling papers back and forth on his desk.

"How many documents are missing?"

"Best I can tell, three. Results of DNA and RNA testing we just completed on the Jelpta fish."

"What were the conclusions?" Kylie asked, sinking onto the chair.

"Results? Oh...yes. Well, they were most interesting. Seems we're finding the sea life here has altered genetics from their counterparts on Estra. Our theory is that when Neptus flooded and the sea mixed with the land, many contaminants and diseases entered the systems of all marine life. The strong survived and created RNA which they passed on to their offspring, and as a result, those offspring developed new DNA."

"And you think this new DNA can cure Genesis Disorder?"

"Very possibly, child. I think we're close to isolating it, of course we're still looking for the source as well."

"Professor," Saxon began, "is there any way you can keep your records and notes in another language, or some cryptic code?"

"Well, I do know an ancient language from a distant planet. I used to love to study foreign cultures and languages."

"Good. Use it. We can't afford your results to fall into the wrong hands."

"But no one else will be able to read it without me, Saxon."

"Precisely. I need to insure your safety."

The seriousness of Saxon's words settled over Kylie. She had not thought the Professor's life, Saxon's life, or her own could be in jeopardy. Greed. It all came down to credits and greed. She'd always known there were people who would do anything for wealth, but it made her sick to think they would sacrifice so many lives to achieve a financial goal.

She studied the dark-haired warrior with a critical eye and realized he was proving his loyalty to the cause. If he had wanted Professor Winn's data, he certainly would not have suggested he record his finding secretly so no one could decipher them. Whoever was behind the conspiracy to steal the cure for Genesis Disorder would not hesitate to kill the one man who could stop them. Thank the stars she could trust Saxon, but who would protect him?

***

Saxon had not been able to take his eyes off Kylie for more than a minute during dinner. Her tousled red hair spilled past her shoulders, hair he wanted to run his fingers through and feel on his chest as she lay beside him. Hair he regretted cutting the way he had, but the shorter curls around her face made her look even more alluring in the subdued light of the dining room.

It was difficult to concentrate on business while her green eyes studied him so intently. She had been unusually quiet through the entire meal, and he wondered how she felt about the kiss they had shared. Just thinking about it sent sparks of heat to parts of his body he would rather not acknowledge at the moment.

He was drawn to her, and for some inexplicable reason, he trusted her. He had spent the last five annual-cycles trusting only Jester and his small crew of misfits. He loved Jester like a brother, but it felt wonderful to share a woman's company and admire a feminine face.

Kylie was everything a man could ask for in a woman. Intelligent, gorgeous, playful, and elusive. Playful. He laughed to himself thinking of his Delphin ride. He knew she was going to pull him into the water, and he purposely used the opportunity to get close to her. And he would do it again for another kiss. So much for putting her out of his mind.

"Kylie?" She glanced up at him seductively, even though she had not meant to. She was not the kind of woman to recklessly flirt. In fact, she usually did her best to hide any amorous tendencies, which is why her look caught him off guard. "How do you link with the Delphins?"

"I tune into their wavelength by picking up their vibrational frequency. Once I do that, I can sense their moods and see the images they send. I put the pictures together like pieces of a puzzle. Sometimes I hear words, like when Mia told me her name, and the name of her mate."

"If we go back to the pool, can Mia tell you more?"

She nodded. "You want to know what Nyles did, don't you?"

"The sooner the better." She silently contemplated his request while he silently contemplated her. He knew why the men on SEA Lab lusted after her. By the Gods, he did too. He had tried not to be so obvious, but when she decided he should swim with her he lost all self-control.

"I'll try. What about Nyles? What if he interrupts us?"

"Jester will take care of Nyles." Jester would take care of *him* if he knew what he was thinking about Kylie.

"Then let's do it."

***

Kylie heard Saxon's boots echoing a steady cadence as he paced outside the ready-room while she changed. He had seemed different at dinner, overly quiet and reserved. She had to admit her feelings toward him were changing rapidly. At first she could not wait to get away from him, now she wanted him with her. Had one kiss changed so much? She should not read so much into a kiss, but then it wasn't the kiss, it was Saxon the man. He was the first person in a long time to look at her as if she were normal. He made her feel safe, and spoke the truth, whether she wanted to hear it or not.

Her mind wandered to Nyles and his repulsive advances. She shivered at the thought of ever having him touch her again. The man was a monster, a real menace, and she could not believe he had attained such a high position all on his own merits. Most Researchers were diligent, devoted to their work and approached a crisis like this one with a passion only success could satisfy, but Nyles was smug and self-serving, and that made her stomach turn.

"Saxon?" she called, stepping out of the ready-room.

"Over here."

He was leaning against the wall, arms crossed over his chest, one leg cocked to the side, and the hint of a smile tugging at the corners of his lips, giving his handsome face an erotic charm. If she looked at him any longer she would forget why they were here. "I'm ready."

She walked to the edge of the pool and he followed, his body so close behind her she could almost feel him against her. If she were to successfully complete six months with Saxon, she would have to stop these wayward thoughts.

"What do you want me to do?" he asked.

"Just listen. I'll repeat what I'm seeing." She watched him nod. "Are you sure Nyles won't interrupt?"

"I talked to Jester, and he was more than happy to keep Nyles busy."

Kylie laughed. "Jester is very inventive. I'm not sure I want to know how he's doing it though."

"Wise choice."

She eased into the water and stood on the belly-slide. "Saxon?" He knelt down at the edge of the pool. "What if I fail to make contact?"

"We'll find another way."

After slapping the water several times, she felt Saxon's hand on her shoulder. She turned to find his dark blue eyes filled with concern.

"Relax, Kylie. Whatever you can do will be a help."

His expression held her spellbound. He actually cared! It should not come as a shock, but she never expected to hear such compassion in his voice. "I'll try, but..."

"You'll do fine."

He said those simple words in a way that made her heart melt. She was not used to a man speaking to her in a caring tone. She was scared. Scared to care, afraid to hope, foolish to even wonder what it would be like to share his bed. Water churned behind her and without warning she was pushed forward from behind, falling into his arms. "Sorry," she whispered, "Mia..."

"I'm not sorry."

His lips brushed hers so softly she shuddered. He did not kiss her deeply, yet he took her breath away. Water lapped at her waist while Saxon pulled at her heart. She wanted to be a woman, to experience every desire and fulfillment women found in the arms of a man, yet she lacked the courage to put her emotions at risk. No matter how well they got along, or how badly they wanted each other, there could be no real relationship—only heartache and disappointment. Her hands pressed against the fabric of his shirt, her fingertips grazing the solid muscle of his chest, delighting the feel of him, wanting more.

She pulled back and turned toward the pool, but he did not release her. "We'd better do this before Nyles shows up. Even Jester isn't a miracle worker." But you are, she added silently. Saxon tapped into the essence of her womanhood and stirred desires she never thought possible.

"You're right."

Saxon's voice was husky and low. She swallowed hard, feeling his embrace loosen. An energy sparked between them and penetrated her body. Cold salty water showered over them when Mia's tail slapped the water. "That's enough, Mia." She turned to look at Saxon and could not hold back laughter as she watched water drip from his hair and face.

"Why do your Delphins insist on trying to drown me every time I get close?"

She reigned in her laughter. "I don't know." Kylie's hands flew to her temples where a violent pain suddenly erupted. An image of two Delphins mating danced past her inner eye. They were happy, in love, and as her mind saw them swim away, the Delphins magically turned to images of her and Saxon. "Mia!"

"What's wrong, Kylie? What did you see?"

"Ah...Mia sent me an image of...us."

"What does it mean?"

"She ah...sees us as friends. People she can trust."

Saxon released her and stood. "She's right. Keep talking to her."

It was difficult, but she forced her attention on Mia as she swam to the center of the pool. Mia eased up beside her and offered her a ride, which she gladly accepted. She held Mia's dorsal fin while Mia pulled her through the water with great speed, taking her deep, then surfacing. The cold water was exactly what she needed to get Saxon off her mind. She'd been so obvious even the Delphins knew she lusted after him!

"Saxon," she called, swimming to where he stood. "Please, bring me an air helmet."

"I'll be right back."

Vivid pictures cascaded in and out of her mind so fast she felt dizzy. "Mia, slow down. It's too jumbled. Easy, baby. Send me one at a time." The pain subsided. She tapped into Mia's unique frequency with ease. The images lingered and changed. Mia swam toward the exit portal.

"Here," Saxon said, handing her a helmet.

"Thanks." When she reached for it, she saw Saxon suited to dive. "What are you doing?"

"If those fish are going to drag you off into the depths of the sea, I have to go with you."

"They're not..."

"Fish. I know. Guess I've been hanging around Jester too long."

Three Delphins broke the surface, arched high into the air, then disappeared. "They seem a bit nervous." She glanced back in time to see Saxon jump off the edge. His bubbles tickled her legs as they drifted to the surface. When Saxon protected a person, he went all the way. She secured the breathing apparatus, pushed off the ledge and sank toward the bottom.

"Nice moon-cycle for a swim."

Saxon's soothing masculine voice drifted melodically in her helmet, but she did not see him.

"By the exit. Come on."

She swam toward his outstretched hand. He grasped her firmly and pulled her into open waters. Kylie gasped. "Dear Stars! I've never seen so many Delphins in one place."

"Is it unusual?"

"They congregate in groups, or families, but I've never seen hundreds in the same place at the same time."

"Get to work then and find the answer."

Mia swam close to her and gently nudged her arm. A sensation like an electrical buzz coursed through her body, and she knew they were well linked. Mia sent mental pictures at a rapid pace. She desperately returned thoughts to slow and clarify the images. Mia complied as she swam tight circles around her and Saxon while the other Delphins kept a safer distance.

"I see a small island. A black cone protruding above the surface. A lone Delphin in pain. War, peace, suffering, death, revolt." She paused and glanced at Saxon. "They're angry, and I hear the word 'help'."

"Are they recalling the past, present, or predicting the future?"

Icons flashed before her eyes, the bright lights from SEA Lab illuminating the green water. Everything turned blurry, her head pounded from information overload. She felt like a computer headed for a data-crash. Saxon's arm circled her waist.

"Are you all right?"

"I don't know. They're sending too much information too fast. My head," she said, her hands moving to the sides of her helmet.

"I'm taking you back. We'll try again tomorrow."

"No, I'll be fine, it's just..."

"You will not argue with me."

"Wait. They're...telling me they're being used, and they don't like it. I don't know how it's being done, but..." She gasped for air.

Saxon started swimming toward the open portal, his arm firmly around her, taking her to safety. She floated helplessly by his side as he guided her back, unable to free herself from his magnetic presence. It wasn't his physical hold that kept her from protesting his overprotective nature, it was her own mind and body that wanted the tenderness she found in his arms. Besides her parents, no one had shown this kind of real concern for her, and it felt good—too good to be true. This was behavior she knew would be dangerous if left to continue, but she floated alongside him in quiet acquiescence, enjoying the moment. She closed her eyes and blackness swallowed her.

***

Konar waited impatiently for Nyles to answer his private com. If he were anywhere near Neptus he would kill the fool. Nyles was a weak link in his plan, but the man was already in place and it was too late for a change. Too many people were involved to suit him, but this operation required more help than usual. But then, if he was successful, it would be his last caper.

"Konar?" Nyles answered.

"Of course it is, you idiot!"

"I'm no idiot," he protested.

"You're worse than that. You're a thief! Did you really think you could steal those Gwadra coins without me finding out?"

"I...aah, I..."

"Don't try to cover up your stupidity. I have contacts on Cyron who intercepted your botched attempt to sell the coins."

"I was doing it for you, Konar."

"Don't insult my intelligence, you greedy son-of-a-bitch! We both know what you were doing, and if you try it again, I'll kill you myself!"

"I just thought..."

"Don't think!" Konar crumpled the paper in his hand and threw it across the room. "And quit underestimating Saxon." He hated to think what mistakes Nyles would make if he knew Saxon was The Hawk. "The coins were tracked to a slimy dealer on Cyron. Don't try that again." Thank the Gods the only connection they made was to Nyles, and he was expendable.

"You told me to create diversions for Saxon, and that's what I did."

"Your stupidity amazes me, Nyles. You have the brain of an ameba and the backbone of a jellyfish. Know this, I have an operative arriving tomorrow who will keep her eye on you, so don't fail again, or she'll take you out."

"I...I...understand, sir."

"Just stick to the original plan and don't deviate. Is that understood?"

Konar listened to Nyles beg forgiveness, swearing his undying loyalty. It was sickening. "At least the mining accident went well." He had to give Nyles a few positive strokes to feed the man's frail ego.

"Thank you sir. It did go well, even if I say so myself."

"Watch yourself around Saxon." He terminated the connection. At least he could trust Sira. She would never betray him. The slut believed he loved her. She was definitely in for a surprise when she finished her part.

He settled back in the chair. There was nothing more satisfying than seeing a plan come together. The worst part was patience. It had been close to six annual-cycles since he framed Hawk for murder and turned him into a fugitive, but he had to have him in place early. Hawk was no fool, yet his search for proof of his innocence had failed. Neither Nyles nor Saxon knew that he, Konar, had loyalty for no one but himself.

***

"Kylie? Can you hear me? Open your eyes." Saxon stroked her cheek and pushed stray hairs from her face as he knelt beside the bottom bunk. "Kylie?" Relief flooded through him when her lashes fluttered and her emerald eyes opened. "Glad you're back."

"What happened?"

Hawk helped her sit up. "You passed out before we entered the Delphin pool."

"I think every Delphin in the Agor Sea tried to send me a message all at once. I got dizzy. That's all I remember." She glanced up at Saxon. "Did anything I say make sense to you?"

"It's going to take some thought, but it might." How could he think while she stared at him like that? It was hard to remember he was a mercenary, a wanted man who was off limits to decent women when she gazed into his eyes. It was as if she saw into his soul and knew he wanted her.

Kylie rubbed her eyes. "At least we found out they want to help."

"Yeah, Mia wants to turn me into a fish. She can't stand to see me dry."

"She likes you." Kylie smiled.

Kylie smiled at him in her usual sensual way that he had come to adore. If only he could tell her how he felt. "How can you tell?"

"She told me in a very direct way."

"You didn't share that with me."

"I told you she liked you." She averted her gaze. "The Delphins are scared. The images they sent were terrifying. I just can't tell if it's the past or the future they're conveying."

"My guess is the black, cone-shaped island is the present. I believe Nyles smuggles information and artifacts by securing them to a Delphin, who takes it to this island where Nyles has it picked up." Hawk rubbed his chin. "When you saw the vid Jester showed us, you said it was Mia. We need her to tell us more. There's thousands of black, cone-shaped islands dotting the waters of Neptus. Mia needs to be more specific."

"Why don't we follow her the next time Nyles sends her out?"

"We will, but you'll need to plant a tracking device on her. Can you do that?"

"I might be able to procure one from the lab."

"No. Don't do anything to arouse suspicion. Jester has one in his bag of toys." Hawk watched her lips for a smile and he wanted to kiss her in the worst way, the impulse growing stronger as he remembered the taste of her, the scent of her and the feel of her. She licked her lips and he felt a quickening in his groin, a firm reminder to behave himself before he created problems he was not ready to handle.

"Jester's quite a guy. I can honestly say, I've never met anyone like him."

Hawk moved to the chair, desperately needing to put a little distance between them. "He grows on you." The same as you have, Amica, he added silently. Her smile was like the sunshine he had not seen in over a month. The thought of going to an island, breathing real air and feeling the warmth of the sun on his skin excited him, but not as much as spending time alone with Kylie.

"Jester's very loyal. You're lucky to have such a friend."

"You say that like you have no friends."

"I don't. It's the nature of my job." She stood and walked into the lav.

She sounded serious and sad, and he understood all too well. True friendship did not come often. He thanked his lucky stars every sun-cycle for Jester. They had a quiet understanding, one that never required words. He was close to every member of his crew, but the bond he shared with Jester superseded all others, except for his only brother, Tynon.

If he had one regret about his forced exile, it was not being able to see Tynon. He would contact him in a second but it would put both of their lives in jeopardy. His baby brother had a promising career in the military and certainly did not need a reminder that a member of his family was a traitor. Knowing Andor, they would arrest Tynon for even talking to him, and he refused to live with that on his conscience.

Kylie walked back into the room and every muscle in his body went on alert, her distinct scent filling the room. She paid no attention to him. Instead she was looking in drawers, slamming them shut in frustration. He knew she was frustrated when she threw her hands in the air. "What's wrong?"

"I need a pair of scissors."

Hawk stood and stepped to the drawers built into the wall next to the bed. He opened the bottom drawer, pulled out a pair of stainless steel shears and handed them to Kylie. "Need help?"

"You've done enough already," she said, returning to the lav and shutting the door.

Women. Who could understand them? What a woman did in front of a mirror had always been a mystery to him. Why he even wondered what she was doing he didn't know. He heard the shower start and decided it would be a good time to check in with Redmon since his moments alone were rare. Hopefully Redmon would have some news. Hawk grabbed the private com from its hiding place and initiated the call.

"Hawk?" the voice inquired.

"It's me. Have you come up with anything I can use?"

"Not yet. I've got the feeling the sabotage starts and ends on SEA Lab."

"I wouldn't be so sure of that." Hawk waited for Redmon's response, but all he heard was heavy breathing. Redmon seemed nervous. "What about those leads you were working on?"

"They went nowhere. Sorry. What's new on your end?"

Redmon was overly evasive. It would not be the first time, but it always set off his built-in alarm system. The edge in Redmon's voice told him the man knew something of importance he refused to disclose. Of course he'd had that feeling since the sun-cycle Redmon helped him escape. His ex-superior officer was famous for testing his men, playing mind games to suck information from them, and he had no intention of playing. "Things have been quiet."

"That will change tomorrow when the replacements arrive."

"Why wasn't I informed of this?"

"You were sent a memo last sun-cycle. What have you been doing?"

"My job." The connection went dead. He was too tired to talk anyway, but the sound of Redmon's voice bothered him deeply. He knew the man well and he was up to something. Hawk replaced the private com inside his pillow, then climbed onto the upper bunk.

CHAPTER TEN

Kylie stared into the mirror, scissors in hand, poised for cutting. She really hated to do it, but she could no longer stand the chopped up mess. A snip here and there had to make it better. Hair as long as hers was not practical anyway, she decided, taking a deep, fortifying breath.

Chop. Several inches of hair fell into the sink along with her heart. It was necessary. Chop. More hair gone. It was too late to turn back now. She pulled the longer back area toward the front and cut, adding to the pile in the sink. A few more cuts should do it, she thought, cringing at her reflection.

Her arms grew tired holding them at strange angles, trying to shape the mess on her head into some semblance of order. One last snip and that would be it. She studied her new style, barely recognizing the woman who looked back. She shook her head from side to side, marveling at the light and free feeling it gave her.

Maybe the new style would have positive merits. It certainly would dry faster. Yes, there must be benefits to short, bouncy hair. She slipped on her robe and opened the door. The moment she stepped into the room Saxon's gaze zeroed in on her hair. His eyes widened and he almost fell out of the bunk. She watched him jump down and walk toward her. Warmth crept into her cheeks and she suddenly felt naked.

"By the Gods, woman! What have you done?"

"I had to finish what you started."

He touched the bottom edge of her hair. "It barely touches your shoulders."

She studied his disapproving expression. "Do I look that bad?"

"I just..." His fingers threaded through the silky strands. "No, Amica. You're beautiful."

His hand slipped behind her head and he pulled her toward him. Before she could speak, his lips were on hers, brushing lightly, their noses touching, his breath coming faster. He had called her by that pet name, and he called her beautiful! She felt her body warming all over and an aching need settled between her legs. What this man could do with a kiss was beyond words, and she hoped he would never stop. Her mind was a blur and her legs might not hold her if he kept this up much longer. No sooner had that thought crossed her mind when he pulled back, leaving her lips bereft of his.

"I regret cutting your hair, but I had no choice," he whispered in her ear.

Saxon's warm breath sent chills down her spine. She should push him away and stop the insanity between them, but she did not have the strength or resolve. His hand moved to the center of her back coaxing her closer. His mouth closed over hers again. This was reckless, dangerous and wonderful. Her heart raced, or was it his? She felt light-headed and it had nothing to do with her haircut. Surges of emotion pulsed through her awakening desires buried long ago, never expecting to surface again.

When his tongue probed deeper she met his search with her own, lost in his masculine power. It was as if time stopped and nothing mattered except Saxon. Doubts and worries melted from her mind and her body demanded more. His other arm slipped around her and he pulled her even tighter to his chest. How could anything so wrong feel so right? That burning need at the juncture of her thighs throbbed faster and she knew it was time to stop. She could never give her love to Saxon, or any man, and she had no desire for empty sex. Men wanted commitment, a woman who could give them children, and she could provide neither.

Saxon tempted her with his tender kiss and strong arms, but when he left her mouth to trail kisses down her neck she pushed away and turned her back. She felt his hands rest on her shoulders, glad he could not see the tears welling in her eyes.

"I'm sorry, Kylie. I thought you wanted me to kiss you."

"I did, but..."

She blinked several times then turned to face him. His expression seemed pained and she knew she'd hurt him in a way she could not understand. She had no experience with men to draw from, but she was sure she had insulted his male ego in some primal way. "Where are you going?"

"I need to see Jester." He glanced back at Kylie. "I'll make sure Throm guards your door. You'll be safe."

Kylie nodded. When the automatic lock clicked her heart sank. "Damn you!" He had no right to kiss her or hold her. It was his fault, she had not done anything to entice his advances. She may have kissed him back, but he was the one who pursued her. Roloc warned her men here might act different, and she should have believed him, but then, she had not planned on a man like Saxon.

Twice she had tried to have a relationship, only to be left in misery. She'd known better than to open her heart to them, but it was impossible for her to have intimacy without involvement. Of course they had lied, saying they wanted her, not just her body. When she insisted they get to know each other better before becoming physical, they took that as an opportunity to run to the far reaches of the planet to hide from her. She refused to allow the same thing to happen again. Saxon was stronger, more self-assured and in control, but he was a man, and all men wanted a son to carry on the family name, and a life-mate to be proud of. A lone tear trickled down her cheek. She threw herself on the bed and curled around her pillow, hugging it to her chest, knowing it was the only comfort she would ever find in her bed.

***

"Hey Boss, we've got a problem," Jester said as Hawk walked into the office. "Seems there's been a valuable find this sun-cycle. A gold, jewel encrusted ceremonial chalice. The archaeologists say it's worth millions, and they're nervous."

"How many people know about it?"

"Word spread fast. I suppose everyone."

Hawk pressed the com link on his desk. "Harris? This is Saxon. Jester will be right there with instructions for you. Do as he says. Good. Saxon out."

Jester punched a few more keys to put CAM on hold. "What's up, Boss?"

"I want you to take that old bag of mine from the closet and pick up the chalice. Tell Harris we're locking it in the safe in my office. Say it loud enough for everyone to hear."

"And the fun begins! I like it. What else?"

"Just bring it here for now."

"Olly-dolly."

Hawk watched Jester rummage through the closet, pick up the bag and skip like a child out of the office. He laughed. Jester would never grow up, and he knew he would not want to see Jester as a sullen adult. He had never known a man as brilliant or childlike as Jester. He was a breath of fresh air in a galaxy full of stuffy people—people who wanted The Hawk's head on a platter. At least there was one man he could trust, even if that man was unconventional, goofy, and at times, insecure, although Jester would never admit that to anyone, including himself.

A blinking light on the computer screen caught his eye. Someone was tapping into CAM. He watched, amazed how Jester's ingenious program was working. Jester had installed some intricate system that detected anyone's request to the master CAM system on Andor--the system Andor swore did not exist.

Kylie's name appeared along with every statistic ever collected about her. He had seen her file before, but he read it again with renewed interest. Her parents were top level scientists on Estra, she had no brothers or sisters, and no family except an aunt who lived on Spectra. Everything in her file was exemplary to a fault. Who wanted to know more about Researcher Beryl? If he had one guess it would be Nyles.

He pondered Kylie's future. The Estrans just passed a new law forbidding the offspring of scientists to life-mate because of all the deformities. How could a woman like Kylie live the rest of her life without a man? Hawk laughed to himself. She would accept it the same as he had—with great difficulty.

Her safety was his main concern, yet he could not shake the memory of her body against his. Thinking about her was intoxicating and stirred his blood, and other parts, to life. She had a definite effect on him he seemed helpless to control. His conscience said, "Stay away from her." The last woman he shared his bed with was dead, and he still wondered if he'd killed Lissa. As bizarre as it seemed, he was guilty. He could not allow himself to get close to Kylie. If he had made love to a woman he barely knew and rewarded her by taking her life, what would happen to a woman he felt passionate about?

The whole Lissa episode was a blur. The only memory of that fateful moon-cycle was him walking through the door and seeing Lissa dressed in that transparent pink gown. He had gotten quite an eyeful, yet she had not excited him. In fact his every instinct screamed, "Set-up." How he wished he had listened to that inner voice that begged him to leave immediately. Of course he ignored the urge to run. He'd gone to Lissa to uncover a traitor selling military secrets. How ironic he was the one judged a traitor.

He had to believe he was innocent, yet in the past five annual-cycles he had not found one shred of evidence to support his belief. Redmon swore the vid-disk was the real thing even though it was common knowledge they could be altered. He'd seen it himself in the cell, his own eyes unable to deny what he saw. If he were ever to take a breath as a free man, he had to get his hands on that disk. And until he was free, he could not offer his heart to any woman. His dreams of a life-mate and children remained, even if the reality could never come to pass.

Why he thought of Kylie every waking moment was difficult to explain. She deserved better than he could offer, which was nothing but life on the run. No woman in her right mind would scour the galaxy with him in search of a safe haven, which could only be found among thieves, murderers and scoundrels. Yet her red hair begged for his fingers to stroke the strands, and her green eyes beckoned to him with a primal need so overpowering he lost himself in their depths.

"You've got that look again, Boss," Jester greeted, bouncing into the office.

Hawk's head jerked to attention as he pushed his wayward thoughts of Kylie from his mind. "Let's see it."

Jester pulled a red velvet pouch from the duffel bag, set it on the table, freed the tie and let the fabric fall. "Wow! Have you ever seen anything like it?"

"Can't say I have."

"Shall I put it in the safe?"

"No. I'll take it back to my room. Just make sure the vid-cam is focused on the safe and my desk. I have a feeling we're going to have company."

"I do like guests." Jester stood and began to dance a jig. "I could stay and entertain them. What d'ya think?"

"You've lost your mind."

"Maybe, but I think I'll let one of those women coming tomorrow look for it. Yes, one of them has the cure I need."

"A curse would be more like it. But if you'd like, I'll put you in charge of checking them in and assigning cabins." Hawk scowled. "How many women are coming?"

"All twenty-two arrivals are women and, it would be my pleasure to assist the ladies. But it's going to be hard to decide which one should be my roommate.

"Jester!"

"Well, you have Kylie! Just thought I'd even things up a bit."

"Having Kylie as a roommate is no picnic."

"Trouble in paradise?" Jester watched Hawk stand and pace behind his desk. "She really gets to you, doesn't she?" He laughed when Hawk growled and sneered. "Okay, okay, I'll drop it. But I think she's good for you."

"So are vegetables, but I don't want too many of them."

"Strange analogy, Boss."

"Have you heard from *The Redemption*?"

"I almost forgot. Beggar called. He has the missing coins. Said he sort of 'appropriated' them from an unsavory dealer."

"That's the best news I've heard in a long time. What did you tell him to do?"

"Keep them on *The Redemption* and hover close, just like you requested, Boss."

"I'm beginning to miss the crew."

"Yeah. It'll be good to fly like the birds rather than swim with the fish."

Hawk grinned. "I couldn't agree more. Soon, Jester." He walked to the door. "How fast can you make a replica of the chalice?"

"Couple of time-units if I have the right materials." Jester smiled. "I like it, Boss."

"As soon as it's done, put it in the safe, and make sure the cameras are set."

"Got it. Anything else?"

"You'd better get some rest so you'll be ready for the women tomorrow."

Jester checked his wrist. "It's already tomorrow."

***

Kylie stood beside Hawk and Jester as they greeted the new arrivals and assigned quarters. Saxon acted like a drill captain, but Jester was as goofy as ever. If she didn't know better she'd swear she saw Jester drool. She felt sorry for Jester, knowing all too well what it was like being alone, unable to share intimate time with the opposite sex. Some sun-cycle Jester would find what he was looking for, but she never could.

When the last woman stepped from the shuttle-sub, even Kylie's mouth dropped open. A dark-haired woman with exotic eyes, a perfect body, and a face that would tempt any man walked toward them. She eyed Hawk and Jester eyed her. What a combination.

"You must be my new roommate," Jester said to the woman.

"And you are delusional, sir."

"Don't take Jester serious," Saxon replied. "He meant no harm." He took the list from Jester's hand and scanned the names. "You must be Researcher Sira Modin."

"Researcher Fourth Class," she stated. "I'm to be Researcher Logun's new assistant."

Saxon stared at the woman and Kylie was not sure if his expression conveyed male curiosity or anger. He'd given her the same look when she'd first arrived.

"You're assigned to cabin 325."

"Thank you." Sira turned and walked away.

Jester shuffled his feet. "Sorry, Boss. Thought she'd have a sense of humor."

"It wasn't your fault," Kylie interjected, feeling sympathy for Jester.

"Yes it was," Saxon corrected. "We're to maintain professionalism at all times. Especially with new arrivals."

Kylie laughed to herself. Had Saxon's kisses been professional? She certainly did not think so, but who was she to remind him of professional indiscretion?

"Watch yourself, Jester. We don't need problems," Saxon said.

"I guess I'm better off with Cook."

"She was rude, Jester," Kylie said, giving him a friendly pat on the back. "You could hear it in her voice."

Saxon cleared his throat. "We have work to do."

Kylie followed Saxon and Jester back to the office, wondering what it was about Sira that made her uneasy. Had she been jealous when Sira eyed Saxon? A little, but that had nothing to do with the eerie feeling in the pit of her stomach.

She was probably making too much out of it, although Sira could have been more cordial. The rest of the women had seemed friendly enough, eager to settle in, and every woman without a mate's bracelet was interested in Saxon. Okay, it was jealousy. She had no designs on Saxon, yet she did not want him with another woman. Selfish as it was, the thought of sharing him made her angry. It was foolish to even acknowledge such an emotion, yet she couldn't help herself.

If she were honest, she'd be ashamed. Saxon was a free man, doing his job. He could look at, or be with, whomever he chooses, it was not her concern. She had important work to do, and she was not free to give herself to Saxon even if he wanted her to. She followed him to his office in silence. He paused at the door to let her enter first. He was a gentleman, and the best kisser she'd ever known. That's it. She'd let his arduous kisses change their relationship and it was time to get her mind back where it belonged.

"Jester, run Sira through CAM, " Saxon ordered, taking his seat behind the desk.

Jester punched buttons and made faces while he waited for the information to appear. She wondered if Saxon appreciated Jester for the sweetheart he was, and for his unwavering loyalty. She still felt angry for the way Sira treated him. Maybe she should have a talk with the snippety woman.

"Wow! I've never seen any woman make rank as fast as Sira," Jester said, scrolling the screen. "Seems she's been handed promotions without proper credentials."

Saxon leaned over Jester's shoulder and studied the vid-screen. "Seems Sira isn't as qualified as her rank would have us believe. Reminds me of Nyles."

"Think she's a spy?" Jester clapped his hands. "I love finding spies."

"Use caution. I don't want her to know we're wise to her," Saxon said to Jester before turning his attention to Kylie. "You'll be working with her, don't let her know what we suspect."

"Of course not," Kylie replied. "Who do you think she's working for?"

"Since she's from Estra, I thought you might have an idea."

"Boss," Jester interjected. "Her place of birth is listed as Andor, but everything else in her file indicates she was born on Estra. I think someone altered this file, but was a bit careless."

"So it seems." Saxon raked his fingers through his hair. "I wonder how many other files have been tampered with."

"Since CAM is Andor's creation we know..." Jester's eyes widened when Saxon's boot made contact with his shin under the table. "What I mean is, there's no way to know."

Kylie watched an annoyed grin pull at the corners of Saxon's mouth, and she had not missed his kick either. What were they trying to hide from her? She hated being treated like a stupid woman, and it was time they knew. "Why don't the two of you say what you mean. CAM has been tampered with and it was done by someone on Andor, someone who planted Sira on SEA Lab. There could be others as well."

Saxon and Jester turned toward her, their mouths half-open. She felt warmth in her cheeks, but it was satisfying to let them know exactly what was on her mind. "Don't look at me like that. Roloc wouldn't have sent me here if I wasn't qualified. Why should that come as a shock?"

"We ahh...ahh..." Jester looked at Saxon.

Kylie smiled. "Besides, the existence of CAM isn't quite the secret you'd like to think it is."

"You're right, I apologize," Saxon began, "I'm not used to working with..."

"Women?"

"Outsiders." Saxon walked around the table to face her. "It's a matter of trust."

"And you can't trust me?" Her hands fisted at her side. "What have I done to betray your trust?"

"It's not that, Kylie," Jester added. "Saxon's careful. He waits for a person to prove loyalty, and he..."

Saxon held up his hand. "Tell you what, Researcher Beryl. I'll trust you, but if you betray me, I'll kill you myself."

This time it was Kylie's jaw that dropped. She couldn't believe he just threatened her! A man who kissed her passionately, who protected her and saved her life? She let his words settle. His blue gaze was unrelenting as he waited for her response. She would not give him the satisfaction of letting him think he intimidated her. She took a deep breath and summoned every ounce of courage she could find. "I'd expect no less."

"I'm glad we understand each other."

"Well, now that we have that settled," Jester said as he walked toward the door, "why don't we have lunch? You know I can't catch spies on an empty stomach."

"You go ahead," Saxon said.

"Gotcha, Boss."

Kylie couldn't help notice Jester's sly, knowing wink as he left the room, nor could she ignore Saxon's blue eyes. "Is there something you want to tell me?"

"I don't want to hurt you, but I meant what I said."

"Is that some sort of apology, Chief Saxon?"

"Just business."

"Business? Like your kisses?" She hadn't meant to let that slip. Saxon's eyes darkened and she could not decide if he wanted to kiss her or beat her to death. "Sorry," she mumbled, looking at the floor.

His finger tilted her head up. "I deserved that, but I won't apologize for kissing you." He slipped his arm around her waist and pulled her to his chest. "I promised myself I'd never kiss you again."

"I promised myself never to let you."

"Then stop me, Amica, before it's too late."

"I can't," she mumbled, tilting her head back, parting her lips. She had no intention of stopping him, no matter what her conscience argued. He excited her and she wanted his lips on her, his arms around her, his body pressed to hers. Wrong as it may be, she could not lie to herself, or Saxon. Desire flickered in the depths of his eyes as he bent his head and brushed her lips with his. Her stomach fluttered and her heart raced. Saxon had an undeniable effect she had no control over. Should she take a chance? Should she give herself to him, or spend the rest of her lifetime wondering what it would have been like?

He left her no more time to decide, his tongue finding hers, searching, asking and demanding. Every argument dissolved. She could not fight the attraction any more than she could fight her body's need. His hand inched up her back and pressed her tighter to him. His warm breath tenderly caressed her ear, and she knew in her heart she could deny him nothing.

His mouth worked magic on hers and her body ached for more. He tasted sweet, exciting, dangerous and provocative. She never wanted him to stop. Thoughts of another man's kisses on a different planet reminded her that first came the joy, then the pain. She prayed Saxon would be different, that he wanted more than empty sex, that he would not run when he learned the truth about her. She wanted him in a way she'd wanted no other man. She would take the risk.

With every move he stirred desires she had never felt with such intensity. His kiss was fire, his touch loving torture. Her mind spun, her body ached. How could he make her want him so badly?

Bzzzzzzzzzzz.

Saxon's fingers threaded through her hair until he cupped the back of her head, guiding her movements. Whatever that horrible buzz was, she hoped it went away. This was no time to be interrupted.

Bzzzzzzzzzzz.

Saxon groaned. She felt his hands move to her shoulders and he ended the kiss as delicately as he'd begun.

Bzzzzzzzzzzz.

He took her hand and led her to the vid-screen. He turned it on and they watched. A sick feeling assaulted her stomach, her forehead broke into a sweat. Her throat went dry and she felt dizzy. She swayed, her knees buckled.

Saxon grabbed her around the waist. "What's wrong, Kylie?"

"It's Mia. I'm sensing her fear and anxiety. She's being forced to do something...she's angry...she can't help herself...she's in pain...she's crying for help."

"You're sure?"

Kylie nodded, unable to speak. If it weren't for Saxon's support she would have collapsed on the floor. "We have to help her. Hurry!"

CHAPTER ELEVEN

Hawk eased Kylie to the edge of the Delphin pool. He might never fully understand how she communicated with the Delphins, but whatever connection she had worried him because of the obvious toll it took on her. "Call Mia."

He eased her to her knees so she could slap the water. Nothing. She slapped again, but there was still no sign of the Delphin. "Try again." She tried in vain to draw the mammal's attention, but for some reason Mia didn't respond.

"My, my. Aren't you the diligent ones, working so well together. Such dedication." Nyles laughed. "I do like loyalty in my Researchers, but you do keep strange time-units."

Hawk stood and helped Kylie to her feet.

"Have you met my new assistant, Researcher Sira?"

"We've met." Hawk tried not to cringe when Sira took Nyles' arm and smiled admiringly at him. It made his stomach turn. He did not need CAM to confirm these two were working together. Sira was slick, just the kind of woman to be a double agent—he'd seen the type before. Her long dark hair hung down the front of her uniform that she had purposely not zipped high enough to conceal her ample cleavage.

"Chief Saxon, Researcher Beryl. Good to see you again." Sira blinked several times. "Would the two of you join us for dinner?"

Kylie stepped forward. "I really don't think..."

"We'd love to. Seven?" Hawk offered.

"I look forward to it. See you then." Sira took Nyles' hand. "Come Nyles, we have work to do."

KATHLEEN GARNSEY

Hawk studied the couple as they sauntered out of the open pool area and into the offices above. Such a perfect couple. The only question was which one would betray the other first? An interesting thought to be sure. He turned his gaze to Kylie and smiled at the fire in her green eyes.

"Have you lost your mind? Have dinner with Nyles and that...that barracuda!"

"I thought you liked fish." He grabbed her hand and pulled her toward the lift.

"What are you doing? I have work to do. Let me go."

"Not here." He almost laughed when she pouted. She had a lot to learn about spying. The doors opened and he guided her to his office, her body shaking beneath his touch. Once inside he eased her into a chair and took the seat next to her.

"Are you going to explain?"

"Rule number one—never discuss anything of import outside of this office, or our quarters. Those are the only two secure places."

"I'm not having dinner with..."

"You are, and you'll be a gracious dinner companion, speaking only when necessary. Understood?"

"No. I will not have you telling me how to behave and what to say."

"I thought Roloc sent you to find the security leak."

"He did, but..."

"Then you'd better listen to me. I've had more experience in matters like these."

"Really? Care to discuss your credentials?"

"My past has nothing to do with this assignment."

Kylie cleared her throat. "I think it does."

"I'm here to stop the leak, same as you. And if you want my help, you'd better listen."

"Don't use the word leak while we're living here, please."

"Worried?"

"I'm not used to being closed in."

"This place affects everyone like that. I prefer not to think of what could happen."

She sighed. "I almost met one watery grave, and I have no intention of meeting another."

"I'm glad to hear it. Now can we get down to business?"

"Dinner with Nyles and Sira is business?"

"Absolutely. Why else would I accept?" Hawk saw a look of relief replace her anger. She was beautiful, but when she was angry she tempted him even more.

"Because Sira was batting her lashes at you."

"Jealous?" He smiled when she blushed and looked away. "I suggest you put all personal feelings aside and think with your mind, not your heart. Nyles and Sira are up to something, and it's our job to find out what. Can you do that?" She bristled at his words and he knew she was about to unleash on him, and he couldn't wait.

"Personal feelings? Are you insinuating that I have feelings for you?" She stood. "Of all the arrogant, self-indulgent..."

Hawk stood and pulled her into his arms, ending her speech with a kiss so hot he wanted nothing more than to take her to their cabin and make love to her. Instead, he would have to settle for a kiss and the feel of her breasts pressing into his chest. She began to relax, kissing him back with such passion he felt his need press tightly against his pants. He heard Kylie take a sharp intake of breath and he knew she'd felt it too. With regret, he ended the kiss and took a step back.

"You do have a way of making your point without using words. But don't think for one minute that I'm some foolish woman who can't keep her hormones under control, because I...." Kylie blinked heavily. "I always have."

"I have the greatest respect for you. Your work with the Delphins is phenomenal." He picked up her hand and brought her fingers to his lips, kissing then lightly. "I'm good at what I do, and I need you to trust me. Work with me." Kylie looked confused, as if she were fighting her feelings as much as he was. "Let's have lunch with Jester, then we'll go back to the pool and make contact with Mia."

***

Nyles paced the length of his quarters. "What are you up to, Sira?"

"Konar sent me to help you." She stopped him and ran her hands up his chest.

"You're a beautiful woman, but you don't fool me."

"I'm not trying to fool you." Her arms threaded around his neck. "I thought we could help each other. Aren't you lonely?"

He pulled her to him forcing her breasts into his chest. He liked her body. He'd thought he'd wanted Kylie, but Sira was better endowed and far more willing. "I could use a woman in my bed."

"I thought so." Sira unzipped his uniform and let it slip to the floor, making quick work of his underwear. She studied his nude body and smiled. "You have much to offer a woman."

"Take your clothes off." Nyles turned on some music and watched Sira undress in a most seductive manner. She was a master enchantress, her every move erotic, her hips swaying rhythmically to the music. Sira peeled her clothes off so slowly he thought he might die, but she finally danced toward him in all her naked splendor. She rubbed her body up and down his. This moon-cycle he would enjoy. Her ring pricked against his neck and everything faded to black.

***

After one time-unit of extensive questioning, Sira made contact with Konar using Nyles' personal-link. "Konar, my love. I have found out everything you wanted to know. The drug worked like a charm. Nyles will wake up thinking we made love, with no knowledge of my interrogation."

"Don't keep me waiting."

"Nyles took the coins as you suspected. He uses the Delphins to smuggle out information and anything else of value he decides he wants. He said you'd never find out he was getting rich off stolen artifacts."

"Nyles will pay for betraying me. Watch him for now. Do whatever is necessary."

"I understand, Konar. What about Saxon?"

"He's dangerous. Hawk is the best Elite Operative Andor ever trained. Learn what you can, but be discrete. Take no chance with him. He's not dim-witted like Nyles. You must always call him Saxon, but never forget he is The Hawk."

The link went dead.

***

Hawk knocked on the lav door. "I've brought you something to wear to dinner." He hoped she liked his choice. There wasn't much available in the SEA Lab provisions shop, but he knew she'd look wonderful. The door opened a crack and he smiled when he saw her dressed in nothing but a towel.

"I have a clean uniform."

"This dinner requires more. Here," he said, handing her a large box and a smaller one.

"Are you sure it's necessary?"

"Positive. Trust me, Amica." She opened the smaller box and scowled.

"Make-up?"

"Not that I think you need it, but it will impress Nyles, or should I say distract him." She took the boxes, set them on the lav counter, then closed the door. He'd love to see her reaction when she put on the rather seductive gown he'd chosen. Kylie was definitely the woman for the job. Of course Nyles would take any woman that was breathing. He'd heard Nyles brag about his bedroom exploits more than once.

He'd have to make sure Kylie was never alone with Nyles because he suspected he'd rape her in the blink of an eye. Kylie could never be put in that position. His plans for the slime-snake had nothing to do with women. Showing Nyles what a warrior could do with a primitive sword was more his style, but he doubted the coward would give him the chance.

Hawk checked his appearance in the mirror. He was not used to the full dress uniform, but he had to admit the royal blue with gold buttons and trim was flashy next to his usual black attire. He'd showered and changed in Jester's room to give Kylie her privacy.

They'd had a busy late sun-cycle with the Delphins. She was amazing with the creatures, and they adored her. Mia had been very upset, but Kylie managed to calm her by conveying they were going to help them. How the woman did it was a mystery, but she'd performed miracles. Luckily Nyles had not reared his ugly head and Kylie had made some real progress. She managed to implant Mia with the tracking device Jester gave them at lunch. Mia put up a fuss at first, but Kylie swam with her, calming her, gaining her trust in some magical way.

He heard the door open behind him, and her delicate floral scent tickled his senses. He turned and his jaw dropped. She was radiant. Her bouncy curls hung just above her bare shoulders, and she did more for the short, emerald green gown than he dreamed possible, and the heels made her legs look shapely and long. "You're absolutely stunning, Amica."

"Thank you." She stared at Saxon. "And you...I've never seen you look so...elegantly official."

"Please, have a seat." She sat and crossed her legs, but his gaze was drawn to the top of her dress, settling on her all too tempting cleavage. He decided he might have trouble concentrating on business when she looked so alluring—the exact effect he wanted her to have on Nyles.

"Saxon, I really don't think this dinner is a good idea."

"It's a great idea. I know how you feel about Nyles and Sira, but we need to plant some seeds, and find answers."

"This dress is too revealing. I don't feel comfortable."

If she knew how uncomfortable he felt she would run and lock herself in the lav. "The dress is perfect."

"Perfect for a moon-cycle of seduction, but not dinner."

"Think of this as seduction. I want you to give Nyles the eye. Pretend you're more than casually interested in him. Humor him, make him believe he's..."

"Repulsive?" Kylie laughed. "I get the idea."

"Follow my lead, and don't be surprised at anything I say or do. Just agree, or say nothing." She looked at him very hesitantly, her hand moving to the deep vee of her dress, her fingers trying to pull the fabric closed. "Don't worry, I won't leave you alone with him."

Kylie nodded. "Let's do it before I change my mind."

***

Kylie seated herself on the pale blue, velvet covered chair Saxon held for her. She hadn't seen the officer's private dining room before and was amazed by the elaborate intimacy. "Do you dine here often?"

He smiled. "No."

"Too refined for you?" He scowled at her comment and took a seat next to her. "Just teasing. Actually it suits you well." A realistic mural of trees, mountains and birds wrapped around the room. The artwork was so perfect she could have sworn they were in a jungle setting. The soothing sounds of a rock waterfall in the center of the room blended with the soft music, complete with faint animal sounds. "I never expected anything like this. It makes me homesick."

"It's a bit of Estra and Spectra combined, however, I prefer..." Saxon stopped short and stood. "Sira, Nyles."

Kylie cringed at the appreciative smile Saxon gave Sira. The front of the woman's dress plunged to her navel and hugged her hips so tight she wondered how Sira would be able to sit. Sira's gown made the one Saxon gave her seem prim and proper. A woman owned a dress like that for only one reason, and she was no match for the dark-haired vixen.

"Kylie," Sira began, "I'm looking forward to working with you. Nyles has had nothing but praise for your abilities with the Delphins."

"I'm sure you can teach me the finer arts of Delphin training, Sira. It's obvious, with your rank, you're more qualified than I am." Kylie crossed her legs and smiled at Sira.

"I'll be happy to, Kylie." Sira turned her attention to Saxon. "Chief Saxon, I'd love you to give me a tour of SEA Lab. I'm sure you could show me things Nyles can't."

"I certainly could."

A nauseous feeling roiled in the pit of Kylie's stomach. It would be hard to eat with all this false admiration floating around the room.

"You look stunning, Kylie." Nyles picked up her hand and kissed her fingers.

Kylie had the urge to pull back and slap Nyles' pretty boy face, but she'd promised Saxon she would behave. "Thank you." She dropped her gaze to the pale blue tablecloth, thinking it far more appealing than Nyles.

"I do like your gown, Sira," Saxon said. "You wear it well."

Sira smiled and leaned closer to Saxon. "I look even better without it," she whispered in his ear.

The vixen was a barracuda! Sira did not fool her, she had meant for her comment to be heard—a comment that brought a devilish smile to Saxon's lips. There was a time she wished she had Sira's effect on men, but after the brazen display she just witnessed, she was glad she abandoned the idea annual-cycles ago.

The waiter brought wine and filled all four glasses, then set the decanter on the table.

"A toast to new friends," Sira said, touching glasses only with Saxon.

Nyles bumped Kylie's glass and it was all she could do not to cringe at him. She pretended to be interested in Nyles as Saxon requested, but it was a strain. After a sip of wine and batting her eyelashes at Nyles a few more times, she turned toward Saxon. Did he have to ogle Sira's breasts like that? He said he wanted to sew some seeds, but if he wasn't careful, he'd be sewing the wrong kind.

The salad arrived and Kylie was grateful to have something to keep Nyles' hands occupied. He'd touched her arm, her shoulder and her hand too many times already. Thank the stars she did not have to dine alone with the monster. The small round table put them all shoulder to shoulder—too close for comfort.

"We seem to have the dining room all to ourselves this moon-cycle," Kylie remarked to break the silence, and distract Saxon's roving eyes from Sira's ample attributes.

"I reserved every table...for privacy." Nyles picked up his glass and drank. "That accident was certainly a tragedy, wasn't it, Saxon? What have you learned?"

"It was an accident." He glanced at Nyles. "My men haven't found anything to prove otherwise."

Saxon was a convincing liar. Kylie wiggled in her chair and re-crossed her legs. He was so cool and collected. Where had he acquired such skills? He seemed at home in this strained social situation, far more at ease than she was. The whole moon-cycle made her so nervous she prayed she would not be sick before it was over.

"You have me at a disadvantage," Sira cooed. "What happened, Saxon?"

Saxon, Saxon. According to Sira he was the only one at the table, and it was far more irritating than she dreamed possible. Sira made bedroom eyes at Saxon while he explained what happened to the miners; his story quite different than she remembered. The woman was shameless. Sira didn't think anyone noticed her slip off her shoe and rub Saxon's leg with her foot while he talked. Either the woman was not as slick as she thought, or she did not care who noticed. It wasn't hard to guess which. How Saxon could continue his conversation as if nothing were going on, she'd never know. Saxon was not just good at what he did, he was excellent.

"Have you found the missing coins?" Nyles interrupted.

"I'm beginning to think the archaeologists miscounted. If the coins were here, they would have been found."

The satisfied look Nyles gave Saxon almost made Kylie laugh. Did Nyles really think Saxon such a fool? She studied Nyles gloating expression. Yes, he did. The only thing visible on Sira's face was pure lust, and from Saxon's response, she was quite effective in her pursuit.

Course after course was served, and the conversation politely dulled. Kylie pushed food around with her fork and wondered if this moon-cycle would ever end.

"Nyles," Saxon began, "did you hear about the priceless artifact that was found late this sun-cycle?"

"No. Do tell," Nyles replied.

Saxon cleared his throat. "The divers unearthed a jewel encrusted ceremonial chalice worth millions. It's the best find to date."

Nyles grinned from ear to ear and Kylie knew Saxon was setting some kind of trap for him. "You didn't mention it to me," Kylie said in a low, throaty voice, trying to imitate Sira's sticky sweet approach to men. Saxon turned to face her, a sexy smile still tugging at his lips. Why did he have to be so desirably handsome? Why couldn't he be old, fat and fatherly? At least then her heart would not leap into her throat every time he looked at her.

"I wanted to make sure the chalice was secure before anyone knew of its existence." Saxon turned back to face Sira.

Nyles groaned. "I hope you guard it better than the coins, or it will end up missing."

"It's locked in the safe in my office."

"Glad to see you're doing your job, Chief." Nyles chuckled.

"Nyles, don't insinuate our handsome chief isn't doing his job. He looks very capable to me." Sira reached across the table and took Saxon's hand.

Kylie wanted to wipe that sexy grin off her face with her fist! Behave, she reminded herself. She let the napkin fall from her lap so she could pick it up and see where Sira's foot was now. When she bent down and reached for the cloth she gasped. Sira's foot was in the chair between Saxon's legs, rubbing his..."

As Kylie straightened she made sure her elbow knocked a full glass of wine into Saxon's lap. She jumped up and dabbed the stain with her napkin. "I'm so sorry," she managed, barely able to stifle a laugh.

"Please, let me," Saxon said, taking the cloth from her hand. He wiped the front of his pants then laid the cloth on the table. "I think we'd better go."

"Must you? What about my tour?" Sira whined.

"Another time." Saxon held Kylie's chair as she rose. "Good moon-cycle."

Kylie felt his hand grasp her elbow as he guided her to the door. His "Good moon-cycle" sounded a bit short, and she knew it was meant for her. Oh well, at least she'd put an end to Sira's plans. Watching Jester drool over the women arrivals had made her laugh, watching Sira salivate over Saxon made her feel like losing her dinner.

***

Hawk stepped from the shower, pulled on a clean pair of pants and marched into the main cabin, still drying his hair from his second shower of the sun-cycle, not counting the wine bath and the Delphin drenching. He stared at Kylie as he draped the towel around his neck. "What did you think you were doing?"

"It was an accident, my..."

"Accident my..."

"All right. I did it on purpose, and I'm not sorry. You were drooling!"

She's jealous! The thought had crossed his mind, but he'd dismissed it as foolish. "I was doing nothing of the sort. Information was all I was after."

"You looked like a bigger love-sick fool than Jester did greeting the new women arrivals!"

"Leave Jester out of this. We were having dinner for a purpose."

"I saw your purpose. If you want Sira, go. Don't let me stop you. There's still time to show her SEA Lab's most intimate corners. I'm nothing more than your roommate." Kylie took a deep breath. "I'll be fine here in the cabin alone."

"Jealousy becomes you, Amica." Hawk wanted to be mad, but he was too flattered. She pursed her lips and squinted. "You're beautiful when you're angry." He couldn't remember the last time a woman cared enough to throw a fit, if there even was a last time.

"I told you not to be surprised by anything I said or did." She turned away from him and all he saw was the luscious skin of her back. The halter style gown had fabric only from the waist down in the back, revealing more than he imagined it would. His hand reached to caress her bare shoulder.

She twisted from his touch. "Don't."

"You're being a bit sensitive, Amica."

"Don't give me that Amica stuff. I'm not your sweetheart."

He had been remiss to believe she did not know what Amica meant. "Are you sure?" He grasped her shoulders and turned her to face him. Her eyes were watery, reminding him of the Agor Sea. His heart beat faster. Oh hell. He bent his head and pressed his lips to hers, easing his tongue inside, amused by her half-hearted attempt to stop him. She tasted of sweet wine, her delicate perfume invading his senses like a cosmic storm. She would never believe him if he told her she was far more beautiful and desirable than Sira could ever hope to be. Sira did not excite him the way Kylie did—no woman had. His hand roamed the silky flesh of her back and he pulled her tighter to his chest. Kylie was all he wanted. Sira may have lit the flame, but only Kylie could put out the fire.

This should not be happening. He had told himself a thousand times that he would keep his distance, act professional and refrain from touching her. May the Gods help him. He ended the kiss and released her. "You did well this moon-cycle—until the wine." Hawk sat in the chair by the table. "I think we accomplished our goal, although I was hoping Nyles would slip and tell you something important."

"All Nyles did was look down the front of my dress the same as you were..."

"Looking down Sira's?" He grinned. "There wasn't anything to look down, it was all there, right in front of me." He chuckled to himself when she sank on the chair across from him, anger growing wildly in her emerald eyes. "It was business, Kylie. Not that it should matter to you one way or the other."

"Fine. Let's get down to business. What exactly did that stupid charade accomplish?"

"With a little luck, Nyles will break into my office and steal the chalice."

"And you're going to let him?"

"Of course. How else can we follow Mia."

"I hate diving in the dark."

"In the sub, Kylie."

"Oh."

She looked so kissable he needed a diversion. If he followed his male urges he'd create more trouble than he bargained for. He walked to the personal galley for a cup of koffa. "Want a drink?"

"I want some sleep." Kylie threw herself on the bunk. "Spying makes Jester hungry, but it makes me tired." She closed her eyes.

"I'll wake you when it's time to..." He was wasting his breath, she'd already dozed off. She deserved a rest. Life on SEA Lab was difficult and she had not had the usual adjustment time due to extenuating circumstances.

Most new arrivals did not work for the first three sun-cycles until they became acclimated to the living conditions, and knew their way around the complex. It took a while to adjust to the rigorous schedule, and separate sun-cycle from moon-cycle, since both looked the same. He admired her work ethic, her determination to make a difference, and her strength. Kylie had the will of a warrior and the body of a seductress, a combination he found irresistible.

He regretted getting her mixed up in his job, but it was her job as well, and he needed her ability to communicate with the Delphins. Mia was the key to Nyles' little scam of getting stolen artifacts and documents off the planet. He had to know the entire process in order to stop it. He could arrest Nyles now, but someone else could take over. This operation went far beyond Nyles, and he wanted them all.

Hawk climbed into the top bunk and closed his eyes. He needed some shut-eye himself. Jester promised to page him the moment Nyles made his move. Even with his eyes closed, all he could see was Kylie in that revealing dress. It had been worth the exorbitant credits he'd spent to see her wear the gown. He would gladly buy her more if she would wear them for him. She was a naturally beautiful woman, but make-up had given her a sophisticated, exotic allure.

Lack of sleep was making him delusional. Just because she'd reacted with jealousy did not mean she wanted him. Stuck with him was more like it. He had not given her a chance to make a choice of her own. Insisting she bunk with him, kissing her every chance he got. Not very professional on his part. It was a wonder she hadn't slapped him across the face. He'd acted like a new recruit on his first leave, starved for the touch of a woman. Maybe he was starved, but he had to get a grip on himself and resist temptation before he ruined everything.

CHAPTER TWELVE

"Saxon? Saxon wake up." Kylie shook his arm. "Saxon!"

Hawk opened his eyes when his hands closed around something soft. Immediately he removed his hands from Kylie's neck and cursed his trained reflexes. "I'm sorry, Kylie. I should have warned you never to touch me while I'm sleeping."

"Good thing you sleep alone." She stepped off the bunk ladder and rushed to the lav.

Beeeeeep.

He jumped from the bunk, pulled on his shirt, slipped into this boots and opened the door. "Hurry," he called. Kylie burst out of the lav still zipping the front of her uniform. She rushed past him and ran to the lift."

"The pole." He grabbed Kylie around the waist and slid down the emergency slide, her perfume teasing his senses. "Head for the sub."

Kylie ran to the platform, opened the hatch and stopped. "It's a one man sub."

"I'll get in first, you'll have to sit on my lap."

She stepped aside as he entered the close quarters of the small sub. "I'll ease your feet down." She lowered herself slowly and he guided her feet between his legs to rest on the seat. "Secure the hatch before you sit, I can't reach it."

"Got it," she said, pulling the round metal door closed and spinning the wheel to lock it tightly. She eased herself down. "Who's driving?"

"I am. Don't let me crash." Hawk submerged the craft and headed out to sea from the exit pool. She reached for the light switch and he grabbed her hand. "No, we'll draw attention."

"Right." Kylie sighed. "But how will we know where to go?"

"Why do you think I brought you along?"

"You don't need me, look. There's Mia's signal on sonar."

"That won't tell us everything, and she could get out of range. Now concentrate. Mia's life could depend on it."

"I'll try."

She was quiet, her fingers pressed to her temples, her red hair teasing his nose, her exotic perfume driving him wild. Could this job get any more difficult? He doubted it. Fighting physical battles was far easier than resisting Kylie's charms.

"Which way, her signal's fading."

"I can't find her. There's no link."

Hawk maneuvered the sub farther away from the lab, but the going was dangerous. Tall rock formations dotted the sea and he knew their sub didn't stand a chance if they tangled with one of the sharp protrusions. He prayed Kylie could make contact with Mia. The only thing he was sure of was that Nyles had taken the bait.

The real chalice was safe in his quarters, and the fake Jester made would fool the best thief, but tracking a Delphin in dark seas was another story.

"It's no use, Saxon."

"Relax. Maybe Nyles hasn't turned her loose yet. We'll wait." Not too long he hoped, fighting his body's reaction as her backside squirmed on his lap. This was torture, but he wouldn't want it any other way. He liked Kylie close, he liked touching her, yet it was agony. He was sure his growing need would become more than evident to her if he did not bring himself under instant control. He swallowed hard, returning his thoughts to the difficult task at hand.

"I feel her! Her mind is blurry. She's swimming out of SEA Lab. She's heading north. I see an island in her mind. She's dying...we have to help her."

"We will." Hawk steered the sub northward at a steady pace. He would need more than luck not to run into something. "Can you see the terrain the way she sees it?"

"No. Yes. I don't know. It's hard to tell where she is compared to us. Can't you see on sonar?"

"Not clearly."

"Then push up the knots, we have to get closer before I lose her."

"How fast can she swim?"

"Close to thirty knots, so get this buggy going!"

It was against his better judgment, but he pushed the throttle full speed ahead, forty-five knots. Jester would call it suicide, and he would be right. He turned on the high power running lights now that they were far enough from SEA Lab not to be seen, yet it was not enough.

The sub leaned to the side, barely missing a sharp protrusion. He settled into a small valley and followed between the rough walls of the chasm. The light glowed eerily off the rocks as he maneuvered the crooked passage, fish darting out of the way.

"I'm getting something. Mia's not far. She's very distressed. She's swimming with all her strength. If she doesn't arrive, they'll kill her family. Mia's terrified for Artus."

"Artus?"

"Her mate."

Kylie leaned her head back against his chest and he felt her shake. "Are you all right?"

"I'm better than Mia. Hurry."

Silence fell between them. He knew Kylie was suffering along with Mia. She was sensitive to their thoughts and feelings, as if she became a Delphin herself. He did not fully understand, but he knew it took a heavy toll on her physical strength.

The sea stretched on and on. Hawk checked the instruments. They had traveled over seventy-three kilometers which put them in uncharted waters. Only a sixty kilometer radius around SEA Lab had been extensively charted. The rest of the Agor Sea was anyone's guess. There were buried mountains and cities, either of which could be the end of their life should they unexpectedly hit one.

As long as the valley held out he could maintain his speed. It was clear running, except for fish. Kylie sat up, her fingers returning to her temples.

"We're getting close, I can feel it."

He pushed the little mini-sub to the limit, hoping to cut speed soon.

"Look out!" Kylie screamed.

Hawk pulled up and swerved to the right. He had not seen the jutting rock. Subs did not respond like starfighters, and he found their slowness irritating. How he itched to fly *The Redemption*. He missed his ship, and his men. They may be a group of outcasts, but they were loyal friends, and he longed to explore space with them again.

"I'm picking her up. Do you see her on sonar yet?"

"Yes. Two kilometers ahead, skimming the surface."

"Take us up, it's easier to read Mia's thoughts if we're closer."

He knew it would slow them down, but he did as she requested. Suddenly she stiffened against him.

"Cut the light, we're distracting her."

He didn't like the idea, but he shut off the running lights and prayed they would not hit anything. Being so close to the surface was safer than on the bottom, but they could still hit a coral reef or run amok in the shallow waters off one of the many islands.

"Stop the sub."

"Power cut," he mumbled.

"Someone's touching Mia."

"How?"

"A man is removing something tied to her tail. She's staying still, but she wants to escape...wants to hurt him. She's mad." Kylie bent her head and held it in her hands.

Saxon threaded his fingers through her hair and massaged her neck. "Easy, Amica."

"It's just that Mia's emotions are so strong they're overwhelming. Her cries for help are agonizing."

"We are helping her."

"She sees the man leaving into the sky."

Hawk surfaced. "Pop the hatch." She turned the squeaky wheel and he reached around her to push it open. They managed to make it topside in time to see a spacecraft zoom across the moon-lit sky. At least part of the mystery was confirmed. He eased his body back into the cramped space then helped Kylie inside.

"I need to find her," she said, fastening the hatch.

"All right." Before he could start the engine, the sub began to move. He feared they'd fallen into one of the swift currents that could carry away the largest of ships. "Hang on, Kylie."

"Saxon, what's wrong?"

As hard as he tried, he could not start the engine. All power was dead, no instruments. The sub moved faster and faster toward an unknown destination. Steering was useless against the determined waters. The craft shook violently, then he heard rocks scraping the bottom.

"What's happening?"

"We're in a current." The sound of metal ripping and water gushing spurred him into action. "Open the hatch." He held her while she turned the wheel. "Hurry." He lifted Kylie out then followed. He grabbed her hand as the sea consumed the interior of the sub, churning water pulling them down. He held her wrist tightly while the sea tried to tear her from him. Saxon swam toward the surface With every ounce of power he could summon, hoping it would be enough. There was no way to tell how deep they were, or what progress he was making. The Agor Sea swallowed them in silent darkness. Just as he thought his lungs might explode he broke the surface.

"Sa...Sa...axon," Kylie managed, spitting water from her mouth.

Hawk swam with all his strength, still holding her tight. Jester told him about these killer currents before they ever arrived on Neptus. He said some people believed the mystery currents were nothing but legend because no one had ever experienced them and lived to tell their story. Drowning was a possibility he refused to consider. "Hang on, don't let go!"

"I can't, it's pulling me...awa..."

The raging current pulled Kylie from his grasp. His heart raced. He reached, but the current was too strong. Over the gushing sea he heard her gasp for air, screaming his name. He prayed he could reach her in time. Hawk's heart pounded heavily. He desperately groped for her in the dark water. "Kylie!" By the Gods, he could not lose her.

The churning flow pushed and pulled, tossing his body like an insignificant leaf in the wind. He swam with it, knowing the angry sea clutched Kylie's life, intending to pull her to her death. He screamed her name in his mind. With every stroke, emptiness consumed his soul, guilt eating him alive. He'd brought her here, and only he could save her.

He cursed the water and the deafening sound it created. His hand brushed something and he grabbed hold, feeling Kylie's ankle as the water tried to pull her to her death. Hand over hand he worked his way toward her arms, fighting the current that was determined to claim them both.

Hawk found her shoulders and grasped her firmly under the arms. He pulled her to the surface, fighting to keep her head above water. "Breathe, Kylie, breathe!" He wrapped both arms around her and squeezed, forcing her to spit up water and gasp for air. "That's it—breathe!" She had swallowed too much water. The pounding and churning of the water was so loud it was impossible to hear or feel anything else.

Suddenly he was pulled down. The current spun him and twisted his body, but he refused to let go of Kylie. With every ounce of strength he scrambled for the surface, kicking and pulling. He would not go to a watery grave, yet the unrelenting sea insisted otherwise. His lungs were empty. Water flooded his nose and trickled down his throat. The current spun him in circles under the water making it impossible to know which was up and which was down.

They were going to die.

Just when Hawk felt the last of his air leave his lungs and all hope had fled, something pushed at his back. He held Kylie tight in his arms and they were rapidly propelled to the surface. The current pulled at him as he gasped for air. A large rubbery creature brushed his side. Mia. He grabbed her dorsal fin, and the powerful mammal pulled him and Kylie from the swirling vortex of death.

Mia swam faster, as if she knew Kylie was in trouble. He wished he had her ability to communicate with Mia. Minutes dragged on until he felt something beneath his feet. Coral? No, he saw an island in the moonlight. They were almost there.

"Swim, Mia." He heard her familiar clicking noise. What was she trying to say? Then he knew. With one quick flick of her tail, Mia dove beneath the surface. The water was so dark he had no idea where she was taking them, but he had to trust her. It seemed like an eternity before he realized they were in a tunnel. He hoped it wasn't too long because he was running out of air, and he wasn't sure Kylie had even taken a breath before the dive.

In a flash Mia surfaced and slid to a stop on a smooth, shallow ledge that reminded him of the belly-slide in SEA Lab. He let go of Mia. "Thanks, girl." He carried Kylie to the sandy shore.

He pinched Kylie's nose, tilted her head back and placed his mouth over hers, desperately breathing life into her. Again and again he blew his breath into her. Finally she sputtered water. He rolled her to her side and she wretched several times, holding her stomach, coughing, still gasping for breath.

"Kylie?" She moaned. Relief spread through him as he helped her sit on the soft beach.

"I'll be all right." She looked into his eyes. "Seems I owe you my life once again."

"It's Mia you need to thank."

"Where is she?"

"I don't know." Just then Mia broke the surface, spun in the air and landed with a victory splash.

Kylie smiled. "Seems she's feeling better."

"So are you." He wanted to tell her how worried he'd been, instead he stroked her cheek with the palm of his hand. "Why is it every time I'm with you I end up wet?"

"Lucky, I guess." She pushed soggy hair from his forehead. "Where are we?"

"On some uncharted island. The sub is destroyed, and no one knows we're here." Hawk groaned. "By the Gods, I don't even know where here is."

"Look on the bright side—we didn't drown."

"No, we'll just starve to death." Kylie shivered and Hawk wrapped his arms around her. The moon-cycle was cool, but bearable. He glanced at their surroundings. "There's nothing here." They were totally encased in a secluded, private world by high cliffs that circled the lagoon. There was not a single plant or animal in sight on the sharp protruding rocks. The only refuge was the black sand where they sat. They were trapped in an island within an island, the only route of escape through the underwater tunnel Mia had used to bring them inside.

"How are we going to get out of here?" she asked, easing away from him.

Hawk shook his head, wishing he had the answer. With one finger he tilted up her chin. "We *will* survive this." Her skeptical grin did little for his confidence. "I've been in worse scrapes."

"Like what?"

"Now isn't the time to discuss disasters."

"You never talk about your past. Why?"

"Because it's the past."

"I think you're hiding from something."

"Aren't we all?" Hawk stood. Kylie's questioning look turned to sadness and regret.

Kylie rose and walked the sandy beach to the water's edge. He wanted to go to her, but he sensed she needed a moment alone. Alone. He was used to life threatening situations, but not with a woman. His men relied on him, but they were capable of defending themselves and knew the risks involved. Kylie had no idea what she'd become involved in, and he doubted Roloc had warned her how dangerous this mission would be.

Now that they were safe on shore, he feared he was about to face the worst danger of all—Kylie. She had the power to melt his resolve and see into his soul. The problem was, he wanted her to do that, and more. He wished he could share his anguish with her and take comfort in her body and her love. The only thing holding him back was her. He cared too much to put her in more danger or cause her more pain.

"Kylie," he called, running to catch up. "You'd better stay with me, we don't know what's here."

"What could be lurking in rocks and sand in the middle of nowhere?"

"Knowing this planet, anything."

They walked in silence around the small ocean that was trapped within the mighty cliffs. Hawk grabbed her hand and pulled her to a stop.

"What?"

He knelt and ran his hand along a deep impression in the wide expanse of sand. "It's still warm."

"You saw them leave, didn't you?"

"I couldn't identify the craft, it was too dark. All I saw was the glare of their thrusters. It was a small shuttle headed back to a larger ship."

"So we're no closer to finding the truth than we were three sun-cycles ago."

"I'll find them."

"How? We're stuck in uncharted waters on an island no on knows exists with no transportation. Sure you'll find them."

"Have faith." Hawk inhaled deeply. "It's good to breathe real air and walk on land."

"It's good to breathe. I thought we were going to drown." Kylie groaned. "You call this land?" She glanced at Saxon. "Shall I pray for divine intervention?"

"Couldn't hurt." Hawk laughed when her fists flew to her hips and she gave him a disgruntled look, wrinkling her pert, little nose.

"Be serious and tell me what you're thinking. It's obvious you know something, so tell me what it is."

"Jester will come for us. I just don't know when."

"How can you be sure?"

"After five annual-cycles together, I know."

Kylie dug the toe of her boot into the moist sand. "I admire your friendship with Jester."

"A man is lucky if there is one person in a lifetime he can call friend. The sad look returned to her face. "Did I say something wrong?"

"I've never had a friendship like yours and Jester's. My work makes for a solitary existence, and when I'm in the city, I'm always in a laboratory with scientists who see nothing but their research."

"Sounds dull."

"I don't know anything else." She dropped to her knees next to him. "You mean my life's dull compared to yours."

How could he answer her? He could not reveal his past, and risk her learning his identity. If he said nothing, she would become more suspicious. He hated to lie, so he decided to stick with his habit of stretching the truth to suit his needs.

"Well?" she prodded.

"I just can't imagine doing your job."

"So what do you do that's more exciting?"

Saxon smiled as he began the deception that rolled from his lips so easily it scared even him. "I run a trade ship. Importing and exporting goods between planets." It was the closest explanation to the truth and satisfied all that heard the tale. He had transported goods before, even if The Hawk was what drew the highest price.

"You're a trader?"

"You sound surprised." He took special note of the way moonlight glistened in her emerald eyes and highlighted the golden strands in her red hair. Pure beauty. "What's so odd about being a trader?"

"Traders don't become security chiefs." Kylie picked up a handful of sand and let the granules sift through her fingers. "You must have some special training that qualified you for such a position."

"I worked security until I saved enough to buy my ship."

"Security credits could never buy a ship the size you'd need. Tell me the truth, Saxon. What do you really do? Run contraband?" She stared into his eyes. "You're a smuggler, aren't you?"

"Not exactly."

"You are!"

He shook his head and stood. It was probably the kindest thing she could think about him. He started to walk away, guilt ripping through every pore.

"How did you get this job?" she asked, following behind.

"All that matters is the quality of the job I do, not how I got it."

"It does if I'm to trust you."

Hawk took a deep breath. "I took this job to repay a favor to a friend."

Kylie laughed.

"You find that amusing?"

"You're not the kind of man who owes favors."

"And you know what kind of man I am?"

"You're the kind of man others owe, not the one who owes."

He grasped her hand and pulled her to him. "I have a past I'd rather forget." With one finger he traced the outline of her jaw. "If you knew more about me you wouldn't have a thing to do with me. So let's just leave the past where it belongs." He released her and walked away, a difficult move when he wanted to make love to her and forget he was one of the most wanted men in the galaxy.

How could she know what kind of man he was when he didn't know himself? He could never hurt or dishonor her. It was best he stay clear of her temptations.

"Saxon!"

CHAPTER THIRTEEN

A piercing scream rent the placid air of the moon-cycle. He turned. Kylie stood frozen in her tracks, a large creature emerging out of the sand in front of her. "Don't move." He approached the mutant from behind, surprised when it twisted toward him and showed long, sharp fangs. It appeared snake-like, but it was too big for a snake. Then scaly arms popped out of the sand and hooked claws reached for him with a deadly sounding hiss from its throat.

It grew in size as it pulled its entire length from the underground hole. A putrid smell engulfed him as the creature lunged. He jumped to the side, and the malodorous miscreant of nature landed beside him. It rose on large, flat webbed feet using its short reptile-like legs to spring at him.

Hawk fell on his back, the creature's claws digging into his flesh. He wrapped his hands around its neck and squeezed, but his strength was no match for the reptilois that was twice the size of a human and ten times as strong. Sharp fangs pressed at his throat. The muscles in his arms shook as he and the creature struggled for power.

Then he heard a thwack, and the slimy creature released him and gave a blood-curdling roar. Hawk jumped to his feet. Kylie stood on a large boulder with a bloody rock in her hand. The monster was angry and grabbed Kylie, throwing her to the ground like a rag doll. His heart nearly stopped. In a flash he grabbed a rock of his own and mounted the creature's back, beating its head from behind while it aimed its new assault toward Kylie, anguished animal wails piercing his ears. The grotesque life-form began to weaken, then stumbled to the sand giving

Hawk his only opportunity.

Hawk bolted free, grabbed Kylie and carried her up the rocky slope, easing her to stand on the boulder next to him. He picked up a rock with a sharp point and grasped it firmly. "I'm going to draw his attention." He glanced at her, terror dulling her eyes. "Run up the mountain, and don't look back."

"But..."

"Go," he commanded, then let out a war cry loud enough to wake the dead. The beast rose up to its full height and moved toward him. When it got close enough, he drove the rock between the reptile's eyes repeatedly until it fell, yellowish goo pulsing from the wound in its skull.

He rushed to Kylie and pulled her into his arms. "Amica, are you all right?" He felt her body shake against him as they both stared at the still form of the grotesque creature.

"I thought it was going to kill you!" she cried.

Hawk looked into her teary eyes. "I'd never let anything that ugly kill me." He grinned when a smile tugged at her cheeks. His hand rested on her shoulder and his fingers found ripped material. Instantly he ripped the fabric away to inspect her injuries. "You are lucky."

Her hand went to his neck. "His fangs left puncture marks." She gasped, her touch moving to his stomach. "You're bleeding."

"I'm fine, it's just a scratch." Kylie unbuttoned his shirt and inspected his stomach, her gentle touch igniting a fire deep within. Little did she know how excited a warrior became after a battle. He felt nothing from the injury, but if she kept caressing his chest and stomach in that manner he would have to demonstrate how warriors celebrated their success. "Can you walk?"

"If my legs will stop shaking."

"I'll help you. We need to move higher. That foul-smelling thing could have friends." He took her hand and helped her climb to a ledge high above the beach where they sat and stared at the sight below.

"What was that thing?" she asked.

"I'm not sure, and I really don't want to know."

"Look!" Kylie screeched, pointing to the dead creature.

Several clawed, scaly arms slowly emerged from the sand. They encompassed the dead body and pulled it under. "I was afraid of that."

"Great. We're not only stuck on this God forsaken island, we're banished to the rocks as well."

"Beats a watery grave."

"Not by much." Kylie pulled her knees to her chest and wrapped her arms around them. "Now what?"

"We wait. Get some sleep," he said leaning back against the

pumice-stone wall.

"How can you sleep with those...those...things on the loose?"

"I've encountered worse." Worse was Kylie's tempting body so close when he felt so aroused, but then, she'd had that effect on him all moon-cycle, or had it been since he found her in the pod, sprawled across the console? It was a good thing he was tired. He laughed. He was never too tired for Kylie.

"It's not funny. Don't you laugh at me!"

"I was not laughing at you." He perused her body all huddled protectively in the moonlight. She looked lost and scared, and he wanted so badly to show her how safe she would be in his arms.

"You were too."

"Have I not demonstrated a rock will kill them?"

"I hit him first."

"So you did." My little warrior, he added silently. He'd known it from the start, she did have a warrior's heart, which attracted him all the more. "Rest, Amica."

"Where did you encounter worse creatures?"

"I fought an eighty foot dragon on Practa once."

"Dragons are nothing but myth," she said. "You're kidding, aren't you?"

He smiled. "Myths are born of reality." This was going to be a long moon-cycle, he decided as he tried to get comfortable on the cold, hard rocks.

"What's your reality, Saxon?" She turned her gaze on him. "Who are you?"

"Bryce Saxon, Chief of Security."

"Bryce? Why doesn't anyone ever call you that?"

"Don't know."

"You don't tell anyone your first name, just like you don't tell anyone who you are. I'm sure Jester knows. I'll find out from him, if he ever shows up."

"Good luck." Kylie scooted farther back, keeping a safe distance between them as if she knew he wanted her.

"I'll bribe him."

He met her heated gaze with one of his own. "That might work if you can fix him up with a woman."

"That could be arranged." She sighed. "He will come, won't he?"

"I'd bet my life on it."

"I think you already have." Kylie pushed wet hair off her cheek. "I miss Estra."

"Someone special waiting for you there?"

"Just my parents. I promised them I'd bring back a cure in time to save them." She wiped a stray tear. "If I don't, I'll never forgive myself. I have to..." More tears fell.

Hawk inched closer and put his arm around her shoulders. She buried her face in his chest. He'd never seen her cry, and it tore at his heart. "You will."

"I...I have to." She pushed away. "Don't you understand? Every man, woman and child on Estra will die if Genesis Disorder isn't stopped. We're not sure where it comes from, how it's contracted, or how to stop it!"

"Calm down." He cleared his throat. "That's a mighty big load for one woman's shoulders." Tilting up her chin with his finger he kissed her cheek. "I understand what being responsible for another's life is like, but you alone cannot do anything, no matter how badly you want to. Your scientists are working on it as we speak.

"We don't know the origin, how it's transmitted, or how to cure it. It seems to be everywhere, yet only certain people become infected. They've tried to isolate why select people are stricken, but as yet, they've had no success."

"Is it airborne?"

"At one time they believed it was. An entire city became stricken all at once. There was dead spore in the air, so they made their assumption. Further testing in other affected areas showed no spore in the air, yet entire villages were infected."

"That makes no sense. Either it is, or it isn't."

"I wish it were that simple. Our scientists are the best in the galaxy, and this disease has them stumped."

"So what is this theory of yours concerning the Delphins?"

"It's not just my theory. The scientists on SEA Lab have reported the Delphins may carry an antibody for Genesis Disorder."

"You're saying they survived the disease?"

Kylie nodded.

"If that's true, the disease must have started here."

She sighed. "We think so, but that theory hasn't been proven either."

"I'm no scientist, but this sounds more confusing than it should be. When I was an El..." He'd almost said Elite Operative. Never had he come so close to divulging his identity as he had this very moment. Kylie had a way of pulling things out of him and he fought the urge to confide in her. It would be so easy, especially when she looked at him with love and compassion in her beautiful green eyes.

"When you were what?" she asked.

Hawk shook his head, knowing he could not answer without revealing his past. His suspicions that Andor was behind this mysterious plague to her people still nagged at him. He knew Andor possessed many mind-altering drugs which they used on unsuspecting people so they could gain information. Those drugs often mimicked the worst mental disorders known to man. If that were the case on Estra, the cure would be simple. The Andorian military, and their leaders, did not care who they destroyed to attain their goals.

"Saxon?" Kylie straightened her legs. "Level with me. You're keeping valuable information from me, aren't you?"

"I only have suspicions with no proof."

Kylie laughed. "You must be a scientist after all. That's their usual mode of operation."

"Do you trust Roloc?"

"Completely. Why?"

"I have a hunch this disease is no accident."

"By the Gods, Saxon. Do you know what you're saying?"

How could he tell her of the atrocities he'd witnessed during his military career, and after? Unfortunately, war and suffering had always been a lucrative business, next to spying and thievery. It was all part of war.

"Saxon."

"I'm sorry. I'm tired and I don't know what I'm saying."

"Oh, I think you do."

"Rest, Kylie."

***

Kylie scooted as far away from Saxon as she could. She wanted to read his mind, like she did the Delphins. He had many secrets. She didn't give a damn about women in his life, or what past sins he may have committed; all she wanted was information that would lead to a cure of Genesis Disorder. Saxon knew more than he was telling, and she had no idea how to coax it out of him.

Would the man fall for seduction? She knew he was attracted to her, his kisses did not lie. He'd probably see through her scheme in a flat minute, but it was still worth a try. She moved closer, careful not to be too obvious. He pretended to sleep, but his rapid breathing indicated he was all too awake.

Did she want to play this little game for the good of her people, or because she wanted his touch on her again? The idea of touching and kissing him was appealing, but she feared she would like it too much, a response she doubted she could hide.

Inch by inch she eased her head closer to his chest. She shivered, more from his closeness than the cold. If he stirred, she would simply say she was freezing to death, which was not far from the truth. Her head met his chest and she felt instant warmth through the dampness of his shirt.

He moaned and wrapped his arm around her, but she'd left him no choice. It was best to do this without words. Her hand moved up the wet fabric, and she marveled at the hard contoured planes that rose and fell with a comforting rhythm. She could only imagine what it would feel like to have her bare hand on his skin. What was she thinking?

One lousy job and she lacked the courage to do it right. It was more difficult to be close to Saxon than she had anticipated. Every time she touched him her desire became more intense. What was it about him that sent her into a tailspin? He was just a man, she reminded herself, as her hand moved toward his neck.

"Kylie..."

"Is something wrong?"

"Yes." He removed her hand from his neck and placed it in her lap. "We can't..."

"Are you afraid of me?" His answer was a disgruntled look. "You are afraid, aren't you?"

"You don't understand," he grumbled.

"Then explain."

"It's best if you keep your distance."

"Like you did when you kissed me?" She ran her fingers through her hair. "I'm trying to understand. Let's see. If you deem a kiss or a touch appropriate, it's all right, otherwise, you're off limits. Is that about it?" Turning her head she scooted away, feeling like a failure as a researcher and a woman.

"I won't deny I find you attractive." With one finger, he turned her head toward him. "We have a job to do, Kylie, and it's best we remain professional."

"It's because of who I am, isn't it? You can't stand to touch me—a genetic freak who never should have been born." She barely got the words out before he grabbed her and pulled her onto his lap. His hands holding her head in front of him, forcing her to look into his eyes.

"You couldn't be more wrong, Researcher Beryl. If that were the case I never would have kissed you, nor would I touch you now."

"But..." His gaze bored into her and he held her firmly, knowing she wanted to turn away from him. "I've been kissed before and the result was always the same—he ran from me as fast and as far as he could."

Saxon groaned. "And you think I'll do the same?"

His lips closed over hers, and his arms wrapped around her in an embrace so tender it brought tears to her eyes. He was trying to prove something to her, and was doing a most thorough job. His tongue dueled with hers while he pulled her so tight she could barely breathe. A moan she did not recognize came from her, and she knew he was like no other man she had ever met. He tasted and took, reveled and enjoyed, and the effects tickled her all the way to her toes. Her cold body turned to heated flesh, while doubt of his intentions fled.

Ever so slowly he ended the kiss and loosened his embrace. She stared into the depths of his deep-blue eyes and saw flames of desire. No, Saxon could never be called an ordinary man.

"Now do you understand?"

She nodded.

"Do you? I think not."

"You find me attractive, but..."

"No buts. I want you, which is why I've kept my distance. A union between us is dangerous."

"Because of who I am," she muttered in a voice so husky it surprised her.

"No Amica, because of who I am." Saxon picked up her hand in his. "You are perfect to me. Your genetics are meaningless." He exhaled loudly. "You deserve a better man than I can ever be."

Kylie blinked back tears, all too aware of warmth in her cheeks. "Tell me why you can't be that man."

"Some things are better left unsaid."

"I want to understand. When are you going to trust me? Haven't I proven myself to you?"

"It's not a matter of trust, my sweet."

His endearment was spoken in a soft velvety voice that sent tremors of desire rippling through her body. May the Gods forgive her for wanting him. "Please, tell me."

"If I tell you, your life would be in danger, and I cannot allow that."

"Who, why?"

"Whoever is responsible for stealing secrets and artifacts will stop at nothing to succeed. If they suspect you know what they're up to, they'll kill you. And I *will not* have your blood on my conscience."

She considered his words. "Don't you think *they'll* naturally assume I already know since we room together, and you won't let me out of your sight?"

"Nyles isn't the only threat. He's working for someone, I just don't know who yet. Until I do, you will remain under my protection."

"Then let's work together and quit playing games. I've been honest with you, why can't you do the same?"

"It's not that simple. There's things about me you're safer not knowing."

"Fine, I accept that. We'll keep it to the assignment." Even as she said the words she didn't mean them. She needed to know everything about Saxon, professionally and as a man. Whatever the reason, she was hopelessly drawn to him.

"Let's start at the beginning." She clasped her hands in her lap before she made matters worse. "Spectra, Estra, and Andor built SEA Lab as a joint project to satisfy each of their needs. Spectra is primarily interested in artifacts, Estra wanted to research the sea life on Neptus originally, but it has turned into a race for a cure for Genesis Disorder, and Andor is seeking a food source."

"True." Saxon rubbed his chin. "When was the first person diagnosed with Genesis Disorder?"

"Six months after the first construction crew returned to Estra from Neptus. That's why we think they brought it back with them. We had nothing like it before." Kylie sighed. "Which brings us back to the question, which planet has the most to gain from stealing information or artifacts?"

"It may not be a planetary thing." He rubbed the back of his neck. "It could be the efforts of a small group of men merely to gain immeasurable credits."

"Okay." She considered his theory. "Which planet are these men, or women, from?"

"Based on the knowledge that Nyles is involved, I would narrow it down to Estra or Andor."

"It must be Estra since that's where he's from." She may have said it, but she did not want to believe it.

"But he was born and trained on Andor."

"How do you know?"

"Trust me, Nyles' affiliation with Andor is correct."

"So who is he working for?"

"If I knew that we wouldn't be sitting here." He eased Kylie off his lap, then stood. "If I could have seen the ship that landed here, I'd have a better idea."

"We could set up surveillance. They're bound to try again."

"I'll put Jester on it as soon as we get back."

"He has to show up first." Kylie stood and stretched her back.

"Jester has rescued me from worse scrapes than this."

"I'll bet he has. Care to tell me about them?"

Saxon smiled. "You are persistent, Researcher Beryl."

"How do you think I ended up here?"

"You may wish you never saw SEA Lab."

Kylie looked directly into his eyes. "I'd do anything to save my parents, and my planet."

"Be careful who you say that to." He smiled.

There was a mischievous twinkle in his eye. "Should I be careful of you?"

"Especially me." He slipped his arm around her waist and pulled her to him. "Don't you see?"

Kylie fought for breath. The feel of his body against hers was intoxicating and extremely disconcerting. His closeness chased all rational thought from her mind, replacing it with pure desire. His effect was devastating and dangerous. Why she was so drawn to a man with such a dark side she would never understand, but she wanted to know everything about him.

She raised on her tiptoes. "I'm trying to see."

"And I'm trying to warn you."

"Don't. Kiss me."

His mouth was on hers in a flash, searching and pressing for dominance. He tasted salty and masculine. A shiver coursed down her spine and settled in her stomach as he devoured her with a passion she'd never felt before in a kiss, but this was no simple kiss. He was a raging tempest and a calm sea all rolled into one.

Large, strong, hands roamed her back, easing lower until they cupped her bottom. He pressed her tight against his arousal and groaned. She knew he wanted her as much as she wanted him, yet he abruptly stopped. Why couldn't he let himself enjoy the moment?

He released his hold, and she suddenly felt empty. Every man she'd tried to get close to pulled away. He said her genetics did not bother him, but she still doubted his words were true. Why else would he refuse to take their relationship further? He was right. Some things were better left unsaid.

A rustling noise in the sand pulled her attention to the beach, and she was glad Saxon's arm was still around her. Her breath caught in her throat when she saw three creatures rise from beneath the small beach area. The creatures groaned and loudly sent a piercing screams from their tooth infested mouths.

Saxon leaned his mouth to her ear. "Don't move."

She could not move if she tried. A putrid odor wafted on the slight breeze, sea gulls squawked overhead, time stood still. She wanted to scream...run...bury her face in Saxon's warm chest. The last option was all she could do. His arms closed protectively around her back. He made her feel safe, and she wished the secure feeling could last forever.

A loud, sharp, angry wail caused her to cover her ears. She watched in horror while the creatures lumbered toward them. Their front claws dug into the rocks below, but when they tried to pull their back legs up, they fell gasping and shrieking to the beach.

Saxon laughed. "They can't climb!"

"Thank the Gods!" Kylie took a deep breath.

"We should be safe on this ledge for the moon-cycle." He helped Kylie sit. "Get some sleep."

She nodded, too afraid to speak, and too embarrassed to let Saxon know she was scared to her very soul. It had been one traumatic moon-cycle. First the dinner with Nyles and Sira, which had been like eating with a sharkus and a barracuda! She still could not believe the audacity of that woman putting her foot in Saxon's...lap!

Sira was cunning, and she knew how to use her feminine assets to get what she wanted. She'd almost forgotten that she was angry with Saxon for looking at Sira with lust in his yes. Or had he been acting, like he said? Dear stars, she was jealous. Not a good sign considering she would have to work with the woman.

Professional. That's what Saxon suggested, and he was right. If they made love, the only result would be losing her heart and finding more pain. Her life did not permit intimacy. She'd dealt with that issue long ago, but then, she had not met Saxon. Her past experiences taught her that no man wanted a genetic experiment, spawned by two scientists who were themselves genetic outcasts.

Estra even passed a law eight annual-cycles ago that forbids her kind from life-mating. Their reason was based on the amount of deformed babies born to mated scientists. Her parents were lucky, she seemed to be normal, but she would never have the chance to find out what her genes would produce.

Casual sexual encounters were permitted, but somehow she knew intimacy with Saxon, no matter how brief, could never be casual. Her feelings for him already ran too deep for that, and her body betrayed her every chance it got.

Settling back against the rock wall behind her, she closed her eyes. It had been quite a moon-cycle, and she was tired. Tired of worrying about her patents and her planet, and tired of wondering what Saxon would do next. Would he kiss her, or push her away? Nothing would matter if they never got off this remote, desolate piece of pumice.

CHAPTER FOURTEEN

Hawk's eyes flew open at the screech of a gull, and he blinked several times at the sun that peaked over the mountain wall. Every muscle in his body was stiff, and the beautiful reason still slept cradled against him while he held her tight.

During the moon-cycle she cuddled against him, and he'd lain awake for time-units enjoying the steady rhythm of her heart, and every breath of her delicate scent. Her arms were around his waist, and his around her shoulders, her head against his chest.

Even sleeping, she aroused him. He thought about the kisses they'd shared last moon-cycle and blood surged to his groin. She was a delight and a curse. He had to learn to control his primal urges when he was around her, yet he lacked the honor and desire to let her go. Making love to Kylie was all he thought about, no matter what he said to the contrary in his vain effort to convince himself otherwise.

She began to move and slowly lifted her head while rubbing her eyes. He smiled at the confused look on her face. It was obvious she had no memory of seeking solace in his embrace. "Good sun-cycle to you, Amica."

"I wasn't sure we'd live to see the sunrise."

"We have, and it's time to make our move."

"Move?"

"We need to swim out of here so Jester will see us if he surfaces."

Kylie stood and stretched. "Oh, no...we can't...the creatures."

"I have a suspicion they're nocturnal."

"You'd better be right. I'd hate to think we spent a miserable moon-cycle on rocks just to be eaten for breakfast!"

Saxon rose and stretched tight muscles. Kylie looked even more tempting in the light of the early sun-cycle, her hair mussed provocatively around her face. "Give me your hand." She placed her hand in his and he felt her tremble, but she had a courageous tilt to her chin. Kylie had the heart of a warrior, she just had not realized her strength.

He led the way to the beach where he paused to examine the sand. There were concave depressions where the creatures had disappeared and he thought it best to avoid those areas. It was too early for another battle, but he'd be prepared just in case they liked the sun as much as the moon. He picked up a good size rock and glanced at Kylie."

"I thought you said..."

"Insurance," he mumbled, jumping from the rocks. He turned, grasped her waist and lifted her down to the warm, dark sand. He released her, but she immediately grabbed his hand. He smiled inwardly at the death grip she had on him. He helped her around the depressions toward the water's edge. Once in the gentle lapping of the tide, he faced her. "Wait here."

"Oh no you don't. I'm going with you."

He laughed to himself as he guided her back to examine the rings of sand where the craft had landed, hoping to find some clue he'd missed in the moonlight. As they approached the definable tracks, he spurred his pace. There it was, plain as sun-cycle, and he wondered why he hadn't noticed before. "The ship was from Andor."

"How do you know?"

"See the indentation?" She nodded. "That was made by an exit ramp which has the Andorian insignia stamped on the bottom that left a depression on his hand. See?" He pointed to a large 'A' with a lightning bolt blazing through it.

"Is it a military or a private craft?"

"Military."

"Are you sure?"

Saxon held his temper. When would she learn to trust his judgment? Although, he couldn't fault her for her reasoning since she had no idea of his past affiliation with the Andorian military.

"Are you going to tell me how you know?"

"Let's just say I've been to Andor and have seen their craft." She looked at him with a thousand questions on her lips, but she bit them back. Kylie was too astute for him to keep lying to her, yet this was not exactly a lie, only a half-truth.

"That means the military of Andor is responsible." She knelt beside

Saxon. "Any ideas?"

"It would be someone of considerable rank who has command of ships and men."

"That narrows it down."

He dropped the rock he'd carried and smiled. They both knew how many men held high enough rank to pull off a job like this. "Ready for a swim?"

"You don't think those creatures could be in there, do you?"

Her eyes were zeroed in on the lagoon in the direction they had to swim. He wanted to ease her fears, but he was not confident himself. "As busy as they were last moon-cycle, I'm quite sure they're resting. Let's go." He walked into the cold, salty water with Kylie at his side, the sun glistening off the green surface. Not far from shore the shallow shelf ended and they were swimming over the depths of the sea.

"Which way?" Kylie asked.

Hawk pointed to the left and began to swim, hoping he was right. When he saw streaks of sunlight below he was sure it was the undersea tunnel. "Take a deep breath and follow me."

The water was clear, but his ears hurt at the twenty foot depth. He had not remembered feeling the pressure last moon-cycle, but then he had been consumed with Kylie. He remembered the terrifying thoughts of losing her and the panic that engulfed him. His feelings for her had progressed to a dangerous level.

Seaweed swayed in the current and fish darted in and out of verdant stalks. With long, hard strokes, they made their way through, then surfaced together on the other side.

Kylie wiped water from her eyes with her hands. "Wow! It's beautiful down there!"

"Only a Researcher would think so." Hawk swam toward the lowest rock formation he could find. He listened to Kylie splashing behind him and laughed. She was right, but it was not the sea he'd found beautiful.

He braced himself against the submerged rocks and lifted Kylie out of the water, then used his arms to pull himself up onto the rocks. When he stood next to her his gaze focused on her one-piece uniform plastered to her shapely body, and the outline of her breasts pulled his gaze to taut nipples. He fought the will of his hands to reach out and touch what did not belong to him. He turned around and looked toward the watery horizon, but it did little to stop visions of Kylie in his bed.

"Now what?" she asked.

"We wait." He heard her settle on the rocks behind him.

"Do you have any family?"

"Where did that come from?"

"We have to do something to pass the time. Surely it's safe to talk about family."

"My parents were killed in a space accident when I was young. I have a couple of uncles and one brother."

"What's his name?"

"Tynon. He's two annual-cycles younger. We're often mistaken for twins."

"When was the last time you saw him?"

"Too many annual-cycles ago." He missed his brother. As soon as he cleared his name, he'd be able to make contact with Tynon again. Tynon was a Martial in the military, and he'd be forced to make an emotional decision about The Hawk. Of course Tynon would not have the chance to choose between his brother and the law since the military had his com monitored. Tynon would be under a magnifying glass. He regretted putting his brother in that unfortunate position. If he ever saw Tynon again he had numerous amends to make.

"Where does he live?"

"Andor." He stared into her eyes and found compassion, along with longing. No matter how well intentioned Kylie might be, he could not reveal any more about himself.

"Andor's a large planet."

"So it is." Her irritation showed on her face, her lips drawn tight— lips he longed to taste. "What of your family?"

"My parents are both scientists, and I'm an only child." She took a deep breath. "Do you know much about Estran scientists?"

"They dedicate themselves completely to their work, and use their own bodies for experimentation, usually resulting in the inability to have children because of gene damage."

"So how is it your parents were able to have you?"

"The law against life-mating and child bearing was passed eight annual-cycles ago."

"That's not what I meant."

"My mother says she was lucky, my father says they only experimented with safe drugs before I was born, but they both agree it was a tremendous risk to have me. Their biggest fear was deformity."

"Their fears were unfounded." He turned and walked to her side and squatted. With one finger he traced the curve of her perfect jaw line. "You're flawless."

"You're wrong."

The sadness in her voice said he'd never be able to convince her she was perfect to him, or that he did not care about genetics and laws. Was she afraid he could not love her because she could never give him a child? Or did she fear he would leave her later because he could not accept her after all? If he were a free man, he would take her with him. He had never cared much for rules, and the Estran law forbidding her to life-mate seemed very unfair.

***

Kylie cringed. She'd told him, even though she was sure he knew of her planet and their laws. He'd said her genetics did not matter to him, but he would change his mind when he wanted to have a child.

She studied his quiet demeanor and wondered what he was thinking. Why should she care? Saxon himself said they had no future together, or had he? All he referred to was remaining professional during the mission, he had not said a word about after. Fool. She had to be a fool to think he cared enough to consider any relationship with her.

It was obvious how he felt. He stood in front of her, staring out to sea as if he were alone. Well, life would be easier if she did not have to fight her feelings for him, taste his kisses, or feel his warm embrace. Then she heard him mumble, "I was thinking." Her heart sank and her mind raced. She could just imagine what was on his mind. "What?" she managed, not surprised her voice shook when she spoke.

"We should go to Andor. It's the only way to find the mastermind of this operation."

Shock struck Kylie all the way to her soggy toes inside her wet boots. He had not been thinking about anything she said. She wasn't sure if that was good or bad, but it quieted her overactive imagination for the moment. "Who would protect SEA Lab?"

"I've trained Officer Throm well. He's more than capable."

"But how could you uncover anything on Andor? The military complex is impenetrable. They wouldn't let you near it."

"You have no faith in me, Amica. I can easily get in. It's getting out I worry about."

"It won't do much good to go in if you can't get out."

"Maybe not, but if I go down, I will take the guilty party with me."

Dear stars! He was talking about murder and sacrificing his own life to stop the thieves. "You can't mean that."

"Oh, but I do." He turned and focused on Kylie. "I've told you before, you don't know me. And if you have to ask if I mean what I say with shock on your face, you don't want to know me."

"I'm sorry, Saxon." She lowered her head. "I don't know what to think or who to believe."

"Think what you want, but believe me." He pulled her to her feet. "I *will* stop the secrets and artifacts from disappearing. I promise you."

She stared into his eyes. Truth mixed with desire, and she found her body longing for his touch. "I believe you." His arm circled her waist, and she felt his gentle pressure pull her closer. She tilted her chin up and parted her lips, a move she knew he could not refuse.

Saxon gently brushed her lips with his. She heard a low groan before he took her with a ferocity that made him seem like a savage, yet he had the gentle touch of a practiced lover. How could everything about him be so contradictory? She didn't care. His arms around her were enough for now, and the salty taste of his skin a firm reminder of his solid masculinity, a strength she craved.

If this moment could last an eternity, it would be all she ever wanted. Or would it? She wanted him to make love to her, to feel him deep inside her, to know him completely. It was irrational under the circumstances, but desire knew no bounds. His hands roamed her back, while that part of him that was all male pressed hard against her abdomen. She may be a fool, but she could not deny the strong physical longing that threatened to consume her into a misty vortex, where only the sensation of his touch was real.

Stars twinkled in her mind while her body prickled with heat. She wanted to shed her clothes and feel his bare skin against hers, to kiss every inch of his magnificent body and explore regions she'd only dreamed about. Then his hand suddenly closed over her breast, and she could not stop the moan that formed in her throat.

Birds squawked overhead and the sea lapped at the rocks, but all she heard was the unmistakable click of each zipper tooth as he eased the slide down, click by agonizing click. The slide hit bottom, and her breath caught in her throat when his hand made contact with her bare skin.

His fingers toyed in her cleavage before finding their way to her nipple. He leisurely circled before capturing the sensitive tip between two fingers. She wanted to scream from the delirious torture he inflicted, but all she could do was release her grip on his shoulders so she could run her fingers through his long, silky hair. Saxon's hand may be rough, but his touch felt like velvet. Her heart raced, and she was not sure how much more she could take before she begged him to finish what he started.

"Quite a sight!"

Hawk jerked his head back and pulled his hand from Kylie's uniform. "Jester!"

She was so glad to see Jester the embarrassment of being caught in a compromising position quickly faded. She hated to think what Jester would have seen if he had arrived a few moments later. Or would she wonder for the rest of her life what could have been? At least Jester was far enough away that he might not have seen where Saxon's hand had been, but since Jester knew Saxon, he'd probably guess.

"You two weren't easy to find. I spent all last moon-cycle feeding coordinates into the computer and having it chart the surrounding area, combining that with possible directions, tides, currents, obstacles, the pull of the moon..."

"How did you find us?" Saxon asked a moment before Mia broke the surface and did her famous victory twist.

"Through good scientific calculations, of course." Jester climbed out the hatch and stood on the deck of the four-man sub. "If you two are finished with the mouth to mouth, swim on out and I'll take you back."

Saxon turned to Kylie. "Ready?"

She dove into the sea and swam toward the sub. When she lifted her arm and reached for the side rail two strong arms grasped her waist. When Saxon lifted her from behind Jester winked. Her cheeks warmed with embarrassment she felt to the tips of her ears. She accepted Jester's hand and he pulled her up so she could stand on the deck. In a flash she stepped over to the ladder and quickly descended to the interior below where she took the seat in the back.

Saxon pulled himself up onto the deck and stood. "Thanks, old buddy."

"Please don't tell me my timing was off again. I had no way of knowing what you were up to."

"Your timing is perfect."

"Olly-dolly. Hop in and let's get this buggy back before someone gets suspicious. I told the mining crew I had to work on the computer system, and I'd have to take the sub on a spin to complete the job. They bought it." Jester chuckled. "I think they're still a bit squeamish since the accident. Can't say I blame them."

"Let's go. We've got plans to make."

***

Hawk paced the length of his office, glancing at Kylie on the way up and Jester on the way back. Both of them watched him. He knew they were waiting for him to come up with the perfect plan, and he could not afford to make a mistake. Every life on Estra was in jeopardy, not to mention his own, which seemed quite insignificant at the moment.

Most of his missions involved the lives of others, every decision crucial, and even more dependent upon the congruity of the plan. He'd never get used to the pressure and anxiety of making life and death decisions, but he also knew if he did, he'd no longer value the very lives he fought to save.

"Jester," he said, not missing a step, "did anything show on the grid when the craft landed?"

"No. They were cloaked. All I caught was Nyles on the vid-cam breaking into Professor Winn's office."

"I wish Winn knew what papers were missing."

"Well Boss, you know how he is, but he's working on it. He assured me that all his research was coded in that weird language he knows."

"Thank the Gods for that." Hawk raked his fingers through his hair. "I see no way around it, we must go to Andor." He noted the scowl on Kylie's face. If she knew what a risk he was taking, she'd fly out of her chair. It might be insane, but he felt sure the information was headed there.

"Boss, you know what's at stake as well as I do, but it's still suicide." Jester chuckled. "It might work, since that's the last place they'd expect you to be."

"Saxon," Kylie interrupted, "I don't like it. Something doesn't feel right. SEA Lab can't afford for you and Jester to be gone, and I can't leave either."

"There's no way I'd take you anyway. I won't put your life in danger." Hawk stopped pacing and leaned on the desk. "I have capable people here to protect you and SEA Lab. I'll stay in touch."

She was visibly upset by his plan. Was it the mission, or could she actually be concerned for his safety? Their last kiss flashed through his mind. He could still feel the warm impression of her breast in the palm of his hand, and taste her sweetness on his lips.

He'd sworn not to become involved, but it was too late. The woman was in his blood, but he could allow nothing to stand in the way of a successful mission. Yet, it bothered him to leave Kylie on SEA Lab. He told himself it was for her safety, but he knew in his heart he could not bear to be separated from her.

By the Gods! He was thinking like a love-sick fool instead of the highly trained military Operative he was. What would his men think when they learned he was sweet on a woman? They knew him as The Hawk, fearless fighter, mercenary, man without a heart. His reputation was his best weapon, and it could also be the tool of his destruction where Kylie was concerned.

"Chief Saxon!" the voice yelled over the com. "Come to level seven immediately."

"Let's go," he said sternly, rushing toward the door.

***

Kylie listened while the delegation of archaeologists babbled simultaneously about a missing scepter that once belonged to a High Priest. She'd never seen a group of men so worked up, but they made the religious connotations clear, then stressed how the object was priceless.

Would the duplicity never end? No matter what they did, someone was always one step ahead of them. Maybe Saxon was right. A trip to Andor might reveal the source of the conspiracy, but she feared it could cost Saxon his life. It was a well-known fact the military rule on Andor was shoot first and ask questions later. Their regard for life was close to non-existent. She could not bear to think what she would do when he left her, even though his departure was a foregone conclusion. He was nothing more to her than a co-worker, yet she knew that too was a lie.

His commanding presence calmed the archaeologists, and it made her realize how he'd become a significant part of her life, a part she was not prepared to relinquish. Saxon was the one man she trusted to help her—she needed him.

"I will find it and return it to you," Saxon reassured the angry men.

"This is an outrage!" one of the men yelled.

Saxon held up his hand and silence fell over the group. "I couldn't agree more. It will be returned, you have my word."

"If you were doing your job, this would never have happened!" the spokesman said.

Kylie watched Saxon grimace and draw his dark eyebrows tightly together. He struggled for control of his emotions, and she sensed how difficult it was for him to maintain control of his temper. A feeling of pride coursed through her when he squared his shoulders and tilted his chin up with a confident air and reassured the group once again.

"He's good, isn't he?" Jester whispered to Kylie.

She nodded. He was better than good, he was magnificent, from his flowing black hair to the tips of his boots, but it was also his leadership ability that made him so attractive. The men began to walk away, satisfied Saxon would take appropriate action.

Saxon approached her with a serious expression on his face, but there was a glow of rage in his eyes. He was a proud man, and she knew he was doing the best job he could. They should not blame him for the evil of others, but they couldn't very well blame an unknown entity.

"Jester, take Kylie to the dining room. I'll meet you there in a few minutes."

"Olly-dolly. Come on, Kylie." Jester took her hand and led her toward the door.

***

Hawk hurried to his office and made contact with *The Redemption*. He prayed his men had tracked the ship. "Beggar?"

"Hawk, it's good to hear from you."

"Were you able to detect a landing last moon-cycle?"

"Yes sir, a ship came from the east and hovered in the north-east quadrant, it launched a small shuttle to the surface which landed on an island our computer shows as grid thirty-seven."

"And its destination?"

"The mother ship was cloaked so our sensors couldn't track it very far, but from the coordinates, it appears to be destined for Andor."

"Ready *The Redemption* and put the men on alert. We will be heading for Andor within a sun-cycle or two. I don't want to follow too soon and alert our target. I'll be in touch." Hawk closed the link.

CHAPTER FIFTEEN

Sira entered Nyles' cabin and made herself at home on the bed while she waited for him to finish in the lav. A moment later he stepped out, half-dressed, his bare chest exposed to her view. He was well built, younger, and stronger than Konar. Would he make a better lover than Konar? It was only natural to wonder. Konar seemed to be losing some of his passion lately, and she missed that.

"Nyles, darling. Join me?" Sira threw open her robe to let his eyes feast on her naked body, and he did not disappoint her. He was interested, and she'd do her best to keep him that way. She smiled when his masculine bulge pressed against the fabric of his pants.

"Well? Don't keep me waiting." She laughed. "Take your pants off. Show me what you're so proud of." He did as she instructed, and he should be proud.

"To what do I owe this honor, Sira?"

"Just call it a fringe benefit for a job well done."

"What do you mean?" He knelt on the bed, then laid down beside her.

"The scepter you stole. You *are* going to cut me in for a share, aren't you?"

"I might consider it." He reached out and cupped her cheek in his hand. "If you please me."

"Have no doubt." She touched his shoulder, then moved to the nape of his neck, and slowly slid her hand down the bare skin of his chest, then inched lower until she gripped his swollen manhood.

"You do have a way of persuading a man, my sweet."

Sira laughed. Nyles was as gullible as they came, but he'd serve her needs this moon-cycle. "First, I want your promise to share the profits of all stolen artifacts."

"All?" Nyles chuckled. "You drive a hard bargain." He traced the outline of her breasts with his fingers. "What makes you think your favors are so valuable?"

"What makes you think I won't turn you over to Konar if you don't cooperate?"

"You would, wouldn't you?"

"Of course, Nyles. We both know what kind of woman I am."

Nyles pushed away from her and got out of bed. "I don't think sex is worth the price you're asking." He put his pants on and pulled the zipper closed.

Sira snickered. "Neither is your life, I assume."

"You have no intention of turning me over to Konar's wrath. Besides, what makes you think Konar isn't involved in the thefts?"

"You're a bigger fool than I thought." Sira closed her robe and rose from the bed. "Nothing escapes Konar. He has eyes and ears everywhere."

"Then let him try and stop me."

"Of that you can be sure." Sira smiled. "If you cut me in on the profits, I'll see what I can do to convince our leader you had nothing to do with the stolen artifacts that belong to the Spectra delegation."

"I don't."

She rose from the bed and stood right in front of Nyles. Getting right into someone's face usually had the desired effect. "And next you're going to tell me you don't want my body!"

Nyles slapped Sira's cheek. "You bitch!"

Sira regained her composure and punched Nyles in the gut. She quickly stepped back to avoid his retaliation.

He lunged toward her and delivered an uppercut to her jaw with his right fist. She fell backward against the wall, and slowly sank to the floor. She touched her lip and found a trickle of blood that oozed from the corner of her mouth.

"It's time someone gave you a proper lesson in bedroom behavior." Nyles jerked her to her feet.

"You're not man enough, you bastard!"

In an instant, his fist connected with her jaw once more and she moaned. He grabbed her shoulders before she fell, stripped off her robe and threw her to the bed. "We'll see who's man enough."

"I swear to the Gods, Nyles, you *will* pay for this!"

Nyles threw himself on her, taking her mouth by force while he groped her breasts. When he reached for his zipper, Sira stabbed him in the neck with her ring that instantly injected him with a tranquilizer. Konar had insisted she wear the concealed weapon at all times, the only weapon she had. Nyles would pay dearly for his transgressions.

Once Konar learned of Nyles' behavior with her, he'd wish he were dead. Of course, her story would include how he seduced her, and how he planned to betray Konar. She knew how to make it sound convincing. Yes, he would pay.

Sira went to the desk, pressed the call button on the com-link and waited to hear Konar's voice. She missed the man, in a perverted sort of way. He was old enough to be her father, but that never bothered her. It was his power, and how he would use it against her if he even suspected she'd betrayed him.

"Yes," the commanding voice answered.

"Konar, it's good to hear your voice, my pet."

"Get to the point, Sira."

"Nyles is out of control. He has stolen another artifact, and he tried to rape me."

"Which are you angry about?"

"Your concern is..." she stopped before she made him mad. This was not the time to make a move against Konar.

"Is welcome?" he said. "That is what you meant, isn't it, my dear?"

"Of course." Her stomach knotted and she gritted her teeth. "What do you want me to do with Nyles?"

"We can't afford trouble. Find the artifact he stole. Leave it in plain sight, then call security. Saxon will arrest him, which will get him out of the picture for a while."

"Are you sure you don't want the valuable find for yourself?"

"Don't be stupid woman! I want nothing that will lead anyone to me. Now, do as I ordered!"

The connection was severed.

At least Konar thought the worst about Nyles and had not questioned her. That meant he bought the story. Sira began a fast and furious search of Nyles' quarters. The scepter had to be here somewhere. She checked drawers, closets and cabinets. Nothing. Where had he put it? The only place left was the lav, and she quickly entered the small space. Pulling open the cupboard doors beneath the sink, she saw a maze of pipes, but one stood out among the rest, as if it were not attached to anything. She grabbed it and scooted it to the front.

Holding the cylinder in her hand, she unscrewed the end, not surprised to find the treasure she sought. It was beautiful. A two foot golden rod with a jeweled ball at the top. It had to be worth a fortune, one she'd love to keep, but Konar would not let her live long enough to reap the rewards.

She replaced the pipe as she found it then walked back to the bed where Nyles, the eternal fool, lay unconscious. She tucked the scepter under the pillow beneath his head and carefully placed his hand around the golden rod. She tidied the room as if she'd never been then, then went in search of Saxon.

***

Hawk jumped when he heard the door chime. He was not expecting anyone, nor was he in the mood for another problem. He pressed the button and the metal slid open. Sira! Just what he needed.

"Chief Saxon, I'm so glad I caught you in...especially alone." She chuckled. "What a treat. I was afraid I'd never see you without that Delphin woman."

Sira was baiting him, but he hated to let her nasty comment about Kylie pass. "To what do I owe this visit, Sira?"

He stood and held his breath as she walked toward him. She was definitely up to something. Warnings flashed in his mind when she ran her hands up his chest to circle around his neck. Her perfume was strong, her intentions clear. Why did women think seduction was the only way to get information?

"There is something you should be aware of, but it can wait a few minutes." She smiled. "I think we should get better acquainted, if you know what I mean."

With great effort Hawk grinned at her while he touched the control pad on the wall beside him, turning on soft, seductive music. He'd learned long ago the fine art of the sexual games spies made famous. He had no doubt Sira was one of the best at her profession. "How's this?" He slipped his arm around her waist, his other hand behind her neck.

"I'm glad you're a sensible man who knows what he wants. I like that." Her hands roamed his chest.

Hawk cringed at her touch, but hid it behind a practiced smile. Instead of the warmth Kylie elicited through his body, Sira's touch felt like a cold shower, and he had to think fast to get out of her grasp before he was forced to kiss her. She was smart enough to recognize a half-hearted kiss, and he knew he could not bring himself to kiss her the same as Kylie.

"How about a drink?" she asked, tickling his ear with her finger.

"Of course." He moved away from her and took a deep, cleansing breath. Something about Sira made his skin crawl. He ordered her the strongest alcoholic drink the fabricator could produce and handed it to her.

"Aren't you going to join me?" I hate drinking alone." Sira turned up the volume of the music.

With a quick hand he ordered a drink that matched the pink one in her hand, but without alcohol. He needed a clear head to deal with this diva. With glass in hand, he led her to the small couch against the wall and sat on one end, not surprised when she snuggled so close she was nearly on his lap.

"Now, what was this matter you wanted to discuss?"

Sira sipped her drink then fluttered her lashes at Saxon. "Don't be in such a rush." Her free hand rubbed Saxon's thigh. "There's many things I want you to know."

He winced when her fingers began to work the buttons of his shirt free one by one. This was not going well. If he allowed this charade to go any further, he'd be forced to have sex with her, and that was definitely *not* on his agenda. He'd been in this position too many times in the past and knew the expected outcome. He wasn't proud of what he'd done in the line of duty, but since his escape from Andor, he'd never used sex as a weapon again. He was determined *not* to fall into Sira's trap. Pride was all he had left.

Sira pushed aside the fabric of his shirt and threaded her fingers through the mat of hair on his chest. "This is much better, isn't it? A little relaxation never hurt anyone. You work too hard." She set her drink on the floor, then hopped onto his lap. She straddled his legs, unzipped the front of her jumpsuit and slid it from her shoulders.

The woman was trouble. No, *disaster* would be closer to the truth. Sira was cunning, and if he wanted to learn who she worked for, he had to react to her. He pressed his hand against her stomach and slowly moved toward her breast. She was a beautiful woman, very well endowed for the job. If she were Kylie, he'd devour her in a second and enjoy every minute of it, but Sira was as poisonous as the most deadly serpent.

She took the drink from his hand and set it on the table beside the couch, then stared into his eyes, giving him an icy chill. Picking up his free hand she placed it on her breast. She was warm to the touch, but the softness of her skin only served to remind him she was as hard as they came. He knew she'd kill him without remorse if given the order and opportunity, and he was not sure what her orders were, or who gave them.

"Kiss me," she demanded, pressing her lips to his.

She leaned toward him, pressed her lips to his and thrust her tongue into his mouth. He pretended she was Kylie to keep from getting sick. He felt her hands slide to his belt, and she wasted no time opening his pants. The loud music drowned out Sira's moans, but he could take no more. There was no way he was going to...

A loud gasp caught his attention, and he knew he was in trouble when he realized it wasn't Sira who made the sound. He jerked his head free and saw two emerald green eyes blazing with fire brighter than the red hair that framed her beautiful, angry face.

No explanation would convince Kylie what she saw was business, and at the moment, he could not undo what he had just done. He needed Sira to believe his interest was real, even though Kylie would be deeply hurt. He prayed when he was finally alone with Kylie once again she would understand.

He pushed the vixen off his lap and fastened his pants. "I think you'd better go."

Hawk's eyes widened when Sira turned to face Kylie and Jester, her shoulders thrown back, her bare breasts jutting proudly in front of her. She had nerve, he'd give her that, but nothing more.

"Aah...Boss...we...aah...wondered what was taking you so long," Jester muttered.

"I was distracted." He glanced at Sira and forced a smile, purposefully avoiding Kylie's heated gaze.

"I can see that." Kylie brushed past Saxon.

Sira slid her arms into her suit and zipped the front. "I thought you should know, Saxon, that Nyles is in his cabin, asleep, and he has the missing scepter."

"Thank you, Sira. I appreciate all you've done." He used his most accommodating voice, allowing Sira to believe he was interested. He might need her later. When Sira smiled seductively, he became acutely aware of Kylie's gaze burning into his back.

"I haven't done near enough, Chief Saxon."

He cleared his throat. "We'll discuss that later." He walked her to the door. She stopped and threw her arms around him in a farewell hug that forced him to hang on before she knocked him over. Without warning, her mouth covered his. He'd never get Kylie to understand what she'd just seen was not real, and he was not kissing her back. Finally she ended her assault, released him, and exited through the open doorway. His heart sank when the door swished closed behind her.

Hawk returned to his desk and took a seat. Jester had an impish smirk on his face, but Kylie's expression bordered on murder. "Sorry for the delay. It was...unavoidable."

"Yeah, Boss, I could see that. She had you pinned to the couch, and you were trying to push her away with your hands on her..."

"Jester!" Hawk warned.

"Sorry." Jester took a seat across from Kylie. "We decided to have dinner sent to the office. If we'd known Sira was here we would have ordered four dinners."

"Dinner will have to wait." He stood and walked to the door. "I need to check out Sira's story about Nyles." He watched Kylie frown when he spoke the woman's name. "Are you two coming?"

***

Kylie refused to acknowledge Hawk during their walk to Nyles' quarters. She turned away every time he turned his gaze on her. Jester tried to ease the tension, but that was impossible. How could she ever forgive such a betrayal.

Saxon used his security key to enter Nyles' room. She followed him inside and gasped when she saw Nyles lying still in the center of the bed. He certainly didn't look threatening dressed only in a pair of pants, curled up like a baby, his hand grasping the stolen scepter even as he slept. Saxon called for two of his men to come and take Nyles to the holding cell. He turned and stared at her in silence. She wanted to strangle him for touching Sira, but she had no right. It was insane to be jealous, and she fought against the unwanted emotion as if her life depended on it.

The handsome, beguiling Chief of Security could become intimate with anyone he chose—he was a free man, but it would no longer be with her. She would never allow his traitorous hands to touch her again, or his deceitful lips to kiss her. It was a foolish notion in the first place to believe he cared about her.

"What about the scepter, Boss?"

"I'll take care if it." Saxon stepped over to the bed. Jester nodded.

"Do you think Nyles took it? Or was it Sira? She was way too accommodating."

"I know." Saxon picked up the artifact.

"So you do." Jester covered his mouth as he snickered.

"Jester," Kylie began, "you know Saxon doesn't want to be reminded of how we interrupted him. I'm sure he's quite disappointed since he didn't get to finish what he started." Saxon's penetrating blue gaze bore into her, and she hoped the truth hurt.

Officer Throm entered the room and saluted Saxon. "You called?"

"Lock Researcher Nyles Logun in the holding cell. He's to have no visitors, is that clear?" Saxon focused on his first officer.

"Yes, sir." Throm waved the two men behind him toward Nyles. They picked him up and carried him out. "Anything else, sir?"

"Just see he doesn't escape."

"Of course." Throm saluted, turned on his heel and left.

"Well, let's get back to our dinner," Jester suggested, slapping Saxon on the back.

"I'm going to my quarters." Kylie walked toward the door. "If that's all right with you, Chief Saxon?" Before he could answer she was out of the room and half-way down the hall.

How could she ever have trusted Saxon? She knew all too well why she had, but it would never happen again. If he thought he could kiss her and she'd forgive him, he was wrong. She was through with him and his stupid games. All her good sense had vanished with his first kiss, but it had suddenly returned with a vengeance.

For all she knew, Saxon was a major player in this clever charade. It was hard to tell the good guys from the bad. Maybe she wasn't cut out for the spy game. Why had Roloc chosen her for this assignment? She hated this undersea prison.

She entered Saxon's private quarters. A prison it was. Not because she lived in the sea, but because she had to share a room with *him*. It was as clear as ice. Saxon was in this for whatever he could get. He and Sira probably cooked up this little scheme to protect their own behinds.

She walked into the lav, ripped off her clothes and stepped into the shower. She felt dirty. Betrayal had that effect on her. She cringed. In her own way she had betrayed Roloc when she'd allowed herself to get too close to Saxon. She had the feeling he'd used her to gain information. She had not told him anything useful—or had she?

The steamy spray of water warmed the icy chill of her skin. She felt cold all the way to her heart. This time her mistake of having feelings for a man hurt worse than she ever imagined it would. The pain was so strong it felt physical.

All the soap in the universe could not wash Saxon from her mind. As much as she tried to deny it, she still craved his touch. She missed him. Not his physical presence, but the place she'd given him in her heart, the place that ached so badly now.

He'd saved her life, more than once. He'd kissed her like no other man had, and stirred her emotions to the brink of disaster. Now it was over. The looks, the kisses, the caresses, and everything else that made her want him. Never would he touch her again. This vow was for her people and Estra as much as for her.

***

The moment the door closed behind Jester he began to babble, but Hawk was not in the mood for questions, or answers. He needed time alone, mistakenly thinking his office would provide the opportunity. Since Kylie arrived they had been together constantly. Not that he objected to her company, he just preferred quiet time once in a while, and Jester obviously decided to take up where she left off.

"You're not listening to me, Boss. What am I going to do with you?" Jester slumped in the chair and stared at Hawk, and the scepter that rested in the center of the desk. "If you want to keep Kylie, you're going to have to tell her you're The Hawk so she'll understand what you were doing with Sira. It's the only way you can..."

"Kylie isn't mine to keep, and she isn't my concern."

"She's not? You could have fooled me." Jester crossed his legs and bounced his foot in the air until one sandal flew at Saxon. He laughed when Hawk caught his shoe inches from his face. "She's important to you, I can see that, so can everyone else."

Hawk threw the sandal at Jester, hitting him in the chest. "Who in the universe is everyone else?"

"Anyone who sees the two of you together. But that's not the point. I'm worried about you, and I care about Kylie. If I have to lose my number one friend to a woman, she's the best candidate I've ever seen. And I think she cares about you as well. The Gods only know why, but she does."

"I have no intentions where Kylie is concerned, and I don't give a damn what anyone thinks. We're here to do a job, and when it's done, we're gone. Now, if you're through?"

"Actually, no. I still want to tell you that you're behaving like a ..."

"Stop while you're ahead." Hawk drummed his fingers on the desk. "Let's get down to business." He watched Jester smile and roll his eyes. "The only way we're going to find the man behind all this is to go to Andor."

"I don't' like it, Boss. We haven't been back there since they chased you off with a death warrant, and now is not the time to see if they've changed their minds. Which we both know they haven't."

"We'll go undercover. Redmon will help. He's the one who sent me here in the first place to find the culprit."

"Do you hear what you just said?"

"I'm beginning to, and it scares the living hell out of me."

Jester laughed. "It should. He's one of the most powerful men on Andor. Redmon has the authority to issue a ship to Neptus without question. He also craves wealth. The only good thing he's done in his life is save your miserable neck, and for that minor deed, he's kept you indebted to him. I think he's in on this mess."

"No one is beyond suspicion."

"Have you ever asked yourself why he saved your life?" Jester groaned. "I have...and I've yet to come up with an appropriate answer."

"Redmon's motives always bothered me. He does enjoy having me 'owe' him."

"So why would he call in a favor for a mission like this one? You'd think he'd use you for something more dangerous like he usually does."

"Danger aside, this mission is of grave importance. Whoever gets their hands on the cure for Genesis Disorder can name his price."

"Yeah, I see. I just don't like any of it." Jester stood and walked to the personal galley to get a drink. "And what was that *thing* with Sira?"

"Don't remind me."

"That's my job, you know? However, I can't help you with Kylie if you aren't willing to help yourself."

"That *thing*, as you put it, was the usual bait trick. I'm not sure what she wanted from me, but she was here to set Nyles up."

"I've seen the ladies with you before, and I know what she wanted. I just don't know why she's setting Nyles up."

"Sira is smart. She knew we suspected Nyles was the thief, but for some reason she, or whoever she works for, wanted Nyles out of the picture for a while." Hawk ran his fingers up and down the gold rod. "Why else would Sira drug Nyles and provide us with the secptor?"

A soft beep signaled a call on his private line. "Yes?"

"Chief Saxon? This is Professor Winn. I have some very good news and wondered if you and Kylie could come to my office straight away?"

"Certainly. We'll be there in a few minutes." He closed the line and stared at Jester. "This could be the break we've been waiting for."

"Yeah, and Kylie may break your neck when she sees you."

"I'll take my chances."

Jester laughed. "You're a brave man."

"Be sure you hide the scepter with the other items."

"Gotcha, Boss. Now, get out of here!"

CHAPTER SIXTEEN

Kylie finished dressing, ran the brush through her hair one last time, then opened the lav door. Her heart stopped when she saw Saxon sitting at the table, his eyes fixed on her. She was not about to let him intimidate her. He was the one who flaunted himself with no morals or remorse.

"Kylie, please, sit down."

She'd sit, and she'd listen, but she would never believe him.

"What you saw was innocent...part of the game."

"You should go into the theater with your acting abilities."

"I might consider it when this mission is over."

"Why wait till then? I think you and Sira should take your show on the road while it's still fresh and exciting. I know how quickly you become bored."

Saxon stood. "I came to apologize, but since you're of no mind to accept anything I say, I'll get to the point. Professor Winn requested our presence as soon as possible and I came to escort you to his office."

"Fine." She stood and walked to the door.

"I wasn't sure you'd go with me," he said, walking down the hall behind her.

"Duty comes first. In case you forgot, that's why I'm here." She turned to glance at him. His groan echoed through the empty hall, and she felt a twinge of satisfaction at his reaction. She really should not enjoy revenge, but it felt good watching him squirm. He could use a heavy dose of humility.

Saxon brushed ahead of her as they stepped off the lift and headed to the back of the busy lab where the light in Winn's office shone like a beacon. He opened the door for her and she stepped inside.

"Kylie! I'm so glad you could come. And Saxon...please, have a seat. I'm delighted to say...we've found the cure!"

Kylie let out a shriek. "Are you sure? I mean will it really work?"

"Yes, yes, my dear, it will really work. You see, we discovered the Jelpta fish is the source of the virus." Winn searched a pile of papers and removed one. "The Jelpta is a scavenger fish, which has a biological make-up that is extremely resistant to viruses and bacteria. It became a carrier which passed the virus to other fish and mammals when they were eaten by them."

"How old is this virus?" Kylie asked.

"When the floods consumed Neptus, toxins, bacteria and viruses were released into the sea, which evolved and found new homes. It's a case of only the strong survive, and one particular virus evolved and changed to adapt to its new environment, becoming one of the strongest."

Saxon leaned an arm on the desk. "So how did this virus get to Estra?"

"The construction crew ate Jelpta fish, thereby becoming infected. However, because of the gestation period the virus requires before it can take root in the host, none of the men knew they were sick until the first symptoms occurred, which took about six months."

Kylie sighed. "How is the virus passed?"

"We haven't explored every possible means because we've been so busy looking for a cure, but we do know that ingesting the virus through eating an infected Jelpta is one way. It is also sexually transmitted, and we believe that any body fluid that comes in contact with another individual can carry the virus."

"Are you saying that sneezing, coughing, blood transfusions and transplants can carry the virus?" Saxon asked.

"Yes, all that."

"It's worse than we thought," Kylie added, "but at least Estra doesn't have any Jelpta fish in the sea."

"Not quite so. The construction crew took living specimens of the Jelpta back to Estra to be checked out by the scientists, but a freak accident on the docks broke the transport case and the fish fell into the sea."

"Dear stars!" Kylie felt her body begin to shake.

"But the good news is that we have developed a vaccine that can stop the spread."

"What about the people who have already been infected?" Kylie feared the answer, knowing her parents' time was limited before the virus took them.

"Until the virus reaches the brain, we can save them. Unfortunately, we can do nothing for those who have already sustained brain damage. As you both know, brain damage is irreversible."

"Can you explain the cure?" Saxon asked.

"I'll try. Genesis is a retrovirus because of its unique mode of replication with the cells of their hosts. Retroviruses contain a core of the nucleic acid RNA instead of the usual DNA. Unlike other RNA viruses, retroviruses replicate as DNA rather than RNA genomes inside their hosts by means of an enzyme they carry, called reverse transcriptase."

"You've lost me," Saxon mumbled.

"I'm sorry. I'll try and simplify. Since the Delphins eat one-third their weight in fish every sun-cycle, they were the first to be infected. Because they have twice the chromosomes as humans, they incorporated into their DNA a code to produce an antibody which we can duplicate from the samples we took from the Delphins."

"How long does this duplication take?" Saxon inquired.

"Only a few sun-cycles in a laboratory."

"How soon can you get started?" Kylie asked.

"As soon as I complete my notes. I should be finished in a few time-units."

Saxon cleared his throat. "How many people are aware of this discovery?"

"At the moment, only I am. However, several of my top men know I was close to this discovery, but they don't know the final outcome of my last experiments which led to the vaccine."

"For your own safety, keep it that way." Saxon stood and pressed the com button on the wall. "Throm, I want a guard posted immediately at Professor Winn's door. He's not to be left unguarded." He glanced back at Winn. "Call me the moment you're finished. We don't want anyone getting your papers." His hand reached for the door. "Did you ever discover what papers were taken in the last theft?"

"Yes...I...ah...made a list for you." Winn shuffled through the loose papers in front of him. "Oh yes, here it is. Actually, there's nothing crucial that isn't documented in my new findings."

"Remember, call me the minute you're through, and tell no one you've found the cure."

"Fine, fine," Winn said as he began writing in his journal.

"Let's go." Saxon waited at the open door for Kylie.

They walked past the long rows of tables covered with test tubes and microscopes on the walk to the lift. The moon-cycle crew had taken over and were busy at work, glancing at them as they passed.

It was impossible to avoid the intensity of Saxon's gaze, or smell his musky, manly scent as he moved next to her. Heat from his body radiated toward her. She tried to ignore him, but escape was impossible.

The door slid open and Saxon stepped off, but she refused to move. She would no longer allow him to dictate everything she did. Saxon had no more excuses to smother her with his protection.

"Kylie, come with me."

"No."

"Don't make me force you."

"You have no right. Nyles is locked in a cell and there are other women to distract the men. Your presence is no longer nee..." Her words were cut short when he grabbed her hand and pulled her from the lift. "Let me go!"

"We're having dinner, then we'll go back to see Winn."

"I'm not eating with you. Go find Sira. I'm sure you'll enjoy her company more than mine."

"If you don't walk into that dining room with me, I'll carry you in." Saxon crossed his arms over his chest. "Well, which shall it be?"

"You wouldn't dare."

"Wouldn't I?"

Kylie stomped her foot, wishing she could punch him. Without a word she brushed past him into the main galley and headed for the serving line. She turned when his hand touched her elbow. "Take your hands off me."

"Then head for the private dining room. What I have to say is for your ears only."

Kylie did as he requested, only because she did not want to make a scene. Enough diners were staring and she did not want to be on public display.

***

The waiter removed the remaining dishes and Hawk settled back in his chair, sipping his koffa. "You haven't said a word. I allowed you this time to calm down, but..."

"Calm down? Like an unruly child?"

He was not doing very well at his attempt to soothe her ruffled feelings. When he was with Sira, he had annual-cycles of training and experience to guide him. Dealing with a woman on a personal basis was another matter entirely, one he was not prepared for. "Can we call a truce?"

"Why? We don't need to be together anymore. Nyles is out of the way, there's other women in SEA Lab. In fact, we need each other for absolutely nothing now."

"Are you sure?" Hawk grinned when doubt crept into her eyes. "The last time we kissed, I felt you needed me for something." She looked beautiful in the candlelight even though her angry expression kept her sensual smile from lighting her face.

Kylie leaned forward and rested her elbows on the table. "Don't flatter yourself, Chief Saxon. It was just a kiss, nothing more."

"It meant more to me." Her eyebrows raised and he took the gesture as a sign of hope. "I'm trying to say I care about you, and I never meant to hurt you. Believe what you want, but I'm not attracted to Sira in any way." He held up his hand when she opened her mouth. If he didn't finish now, he never would. "Sira is a spy, I'm sure you gathered that. I've been trained to deal with such matters."

"Oh? When and where did this training take place? Is it standard procedure for all traders? That is what you claim to be, isn't it?"

Hawk nodded. There wasn't much more he could tell her without revealing his identity as The Hawk. If he told her who he was, she'd run even faster, or worse—she'd turn him over to the authorities. There were enough credits on his head to insure she'd never have to work again.

"You can't answer me, can you? Who are you, Bryce Saxon?"

"I'm a man who cares about you, whether you believe it or not. I won't deny I've done things I'm not proud of, but I did them to survive."

"I didn't know it was so hard for a trader to survive."

"There are many bandits and pirates in space. I've learned to protect myself."

"You still haven't told me where a trader would acquire spy training?"

"Have you ever been off Estra?" She shook her head. "It's a big galaxy with much to offer—and much to learn."

"Why is it so important I believe you?"

Hawk leaned toward her and took her hand in his. "Because what we have between us is special." He stroked her fingers. "We might not have a future together, and I wouldn't presume you wanted one, but I'd like to consider you a friend at least."

Kylie glanced at the three other couples in the dining room and pulled her hand back. He immediately felt the loss. Friends. Lovers was what he wanted them to be, but he'd settle for friends as a start. He'd mishandled himself from the moment they met, and he wasn't doing much better now. One thing had become undeniably clear, he wanted her. It may be selfish and dangerous, but he couldn't help himself. "Well?"

"I need time to think. With Professor Winn's news, and all that's happened, I'm exhausted." She pulled the linen napkin from her lap and laid it on the table. "I'd really like to get some sleep, if you don't mind."

"Certainly." Hawk minded, however, he'd give her the time she needed. He stood and moved behind Kylie to hold her chair while she rose. "I'll meet with Winn and fill you in later."

"Fine."

Kylie left the dining room, and she took his heart with her. Soft. He'd become soft over a woman. He never suspected he could be capable of such an emotion. Annual-cycles of military training should have hardened his attitude towards women. The military viewed them as objects to use, either for sex or information. He might have looked at Kylie in that manner when he first saw her, but the moment she looked at him with big green eyes he felt something change.

How did he view her? She was an excellent Researcher, who proved her worth, and he respected her abilities, but that wasn't all. It was her smile, her eyes, her hair, her mind, her laugh, and her body. Everything about her pulled him to her. Now she was pulling away.

If he was any kind of man, he'd allow her to do so with dignity, yet some primal need deep within would not permit him to be so honorable. The Hawk may not always act with honor, but Bryce Saxon had never regretted his past more than at this moment. A past he could not erase. Or could he?

As soon as he wrapped up his assignment on SEA Lab, he was determined to clear his name. Someone had worked long and hard to convince him he was a murderer and a traitor, a fact he refused to believe. Whoever set him up had done a thorough job. They said he was guilty, they had the proof. The only salvation he could hold on to was a gut feeling he did *not* kill Lissa five annual-cycles ago, nor did he pass classified information to Andor's enemies.

Hawk headed toward Winn's office. Surely he'd completed his transcriptions by now. All this reminiscing about his past made him uneasy, reminding him how vulnerable he was. On every planet in the galaxy he was a wanted man who risked capture and execution every time he landed. However, he had no time to think about that now. Estra's future hung in the balance of one man's knowledge.

The moment he stepped into the empty lab he had the uneasy feeling something was wrong. The moon-cycle crew should be working, yet the place was deserted. The guard should be standing at attention in front of Winn's door, but he saw no one. When he cleared the last table he found the guard on the floor. He knelt and checked for a pulse—he was dead.

Hawk rushed into Winn's office, his steps halted by the sight before him. Papers were strewn all over the floor, and it wasn't Winn's usual carelessness. The office had been ruthlessly searched. A small table lay on its side by two overturned chairs. Winn was nowhere in sight. Hawk carefully stepped toward the closet in the back, but he froze in his tracks.

Winn lay lifeless on the floor behind his desk, face down, arms and legs sprawled in an unnatural position. He squatted next to the body and felt for signs of life, but found none. By the Gods! Where would it end? All he could do now was pray he could find Winn's completed journal.

Hawk examined Winn's ransacked office, afraid the murderer had taken the notes that cost the professor his life. He'd found a few papers in code, but nothing complete enough to be the cure. A sinking feeling assailed his senses. Had he totally failed, or was this feeling a premonition of things to come?

Damn! He'd liked the scatter-brained professor, and knew what an asset he was to the scientific community, and Kylie. She was desperate to save her parents. She'd never forgive him. It was his responsibility to keep Winn safe. He'd failed miserably. If he could find Winn's journal, at least the man would not have died in vain.

Out of desperation he returned to the body to see what it could tell him. A trickle of dried blood ran from his lip, down his neck and toward his chest. His lip had been split by a blow to the mouth, and he had two broken fingers on his left hand. Someone had tried to get him to talk, but from the looks of it, had not succeeded.

Careful not to disturb any evidence, Hawk slid his hand under Winn's chest in an effort to roll him to the side. He wanted to see if Winn had been shot, stabbed, or...his hand touched something hard under Winn's shirt. Evidence be damned! He rolled Winn onto his back and pulled up the fabric.

Dear Professor Winn! He had slipped his journal under his shirt. Thank the Gods. Hawk removed the book and hid it under his own shirt. He pressed the com to call his first officer.

"Officer Throm," the man answered.

"Send an investigative team to Professor Winn's office immediately. He's been murdered, and I'm afraid Alton is also dead." He heard Throm give a grievous sigh, and he shared his sentiment. It always hurt to lose a good man.

"Right away, sir."

Hawk returned to Winn and rolled his body back to the original position. Sira. She had to be responsible since Nyles was still in lock-up. He knew she was capable of murder, but something told him Winn had died of a heart attack induced by stress and Sira's torture. She'd been after the journal, he had no doubt. Winn's death was provoked, but accidental. He was too valuable to kill. If Sira couldn't find the book she would have taken the man, however, Winn himself prevented that.

"Saxon?"

Hawk turned at the sound of Throm's voice and found shock on his face. "You know what to do. Keep this investigation quiet." He put his hand on Throm's shoulder and walked him to the far corner of the room, away from the four men who accompanied him. "Arrest Sira. I'm sure you'll find evidence she was here. Put her in a cell as far away from Nyles as possible."

"You know word of Winn's death will spread fast, regardless of what we do. SEA Lab is big, but not big enough."

"True. Stall as long as you can. And if I'm unavailable, I want you to take control of all security."

"I don't understand, Chief."

"You will. I trust you, but I can say no more."

"I appreciate your confidence."

"Where are all the scientists?" Hawk asked.

"A meeting was called in the conference room. Every scientist attended."

"How convenient for our killer."

"Indeed."

"Post guards at the conference room, and assign one guard for every scientist, sun-cycle and moon-cycle." Hawk headed for his quarters. He hadn't left Kylie alone this long since she arrived and it bothered him. She was furious with him, and she had a right to be.

He knew Kylie felt betrayed, especially since she'd exposed her hereditary lineage to him in good faith. She believed he had turned to Sira because she was beautiful, and seductive. Truth was, she repulsed him. He'd love to kiss the truth into Kylie until she believed him.

By the stars, he was little more than a freak himself, so he understood how people could turn hostile in a heartbeat. Somehow he had to make her understand, but the only way possible would be to confide in her and take the risk. He'd lived his life taking calculated risks. What was one more? If she betrayed his trust, he would pay with his life.

The moment the lift stopped and the door opened, his heart jumped into his throat. He ran toward his cabin and prayed he'd find Kylie safe. The same fear he'd experienced before entering Winn's office once again took hold.

Hawk rushed into the room and found Kylie on the floor, her back against the bed, her head slumped down. He knelt beside her, and every muscle in his body went rigid when he touched her neck in search of a pulse. She was alive. He picked her up and laid her on the bottom bunk.

Her breathing was shallow, and he could barely find her pale skin under all her hair that had fallen in disarray, covering her face. He stroked long, tangled strands away from her eyes and tucked them behind her ears.

There it was, a tiny spot of blood slightly below her ear. He'd seen the mark before. Diabolus, he'd used the same weapon himself on certain occasions. He took a deep breath of relief now that he knew she'd only been drugged. Kylie would be fine in a few time-units when the chemical effects wore off.

Winn was dead, but he'd found the journal. His mind was made up. He would leave for Andor immediately, and he would take Kylie with him. A vision of Kylie walking the halls of *The Redemption* passed through his mind and made him smile. Due to her current mood, he'd be lucky if she didn't try to kill him.

"Boss?"

Hawk glanced at Jester who appeared in the open doorway.

"Let your housekeeping slip a bit I see." Jester stepped over drawers strewn on the floor with their contents hanging over the edges. "Didn't know you had so much stuff."

"I didn't either."

Jester eyed Kylie on the bunk. "Is she all right? What did you do to her?"

"Sira drugged her." Hawk stood and stepped toward his friend. "Have Beggar send a transport to pick us up within the time-unit."

"Us...as in three of us?"

"Yes."

"This ought to be interesting." Jester shook his head. "Pack the usual?"

He nodded. "Meet me on the observation deck when you're ready. Tell Beggar to use the regular signal."

"Olly-dolly." Jester saluted, then rushed from the room.

Hawk closed the door and picked up his duffel bag from the middle of the floor where it had been dumped. He began to cram his and Kylie's clothes into the canvas bag, but what she owned did not take much space. She was probably the only woman he knew who had so little. Of course, he had no idea what she'd brought with her that stayed on the ocean floor.

He checked his timepiece. By thirteen-hundred time-units they would be free of Neptus aboard the shuttle Beggar would send. He'd thought about checking with Redmon, but decided a surprise visit was in order. Right now, he was not sure who his enemies were. They could be anyone, or everyone, especially if word spread he held the cure to Genesis Disorder in his hands.

Doctor Winn's notebook was still in his shirt. He walked to the private galley and opened a small cabinet next to the control panel that contained watertight bags. Taking the journal from his shirt, he slipped it into the plastic, ran the end under the sealing light, then dropped it in the duffel bag.

A quick glance around the room said he'd packed about everything he had intentions of taking. He slung the bag over his right shoulder and crossed the room to where Kylie lay in innocent slumber. She would not remember a thing if Sira used the drug he thought she had.

He grabbed her hands and pulled her to a sitting position, then lowered his left shoulder positioning her over him before he stood. Her breasts pressed against his back, and his arm felt warm where it wrapped around her thighs. The feel of her awakened his senses to her femininity, while her delicate perfume teased his better judgment. He pushed aside those thoughts.

When the door slid open he checked the hall before he stepped outside the cabin. It would look strange if anyone found him carrying Kylie like a sack of grain. Due to the late time-unit, he did not expect to run into anyone.

The way remained clear until he reached the observation deck. He dropped the duffel bag and it hit the floor with a thud. He lowered his shoulder and guided Kylie to a prone position, propping her head against the canvas bag. The subdued lighting around the base of the floor where the clear walls met with metal, illuminated her red hair to a golden hue. He folded her hands over her stomach.

Would she hate him even more when he told her who he was? It didn't matter. He paced back and forth, staring into the darkness of the Agor Sea that pressed ominously against the clear walls. When one stood in the tip of the pyramid, one felt small and insignificant, like a tiny speck in the universe. If only he were insignificant, then he might have a future with Kylie.

Thoughts of the indifferent ocean made him realize what had been missing in his life, and why he was so drawn to Kylie. Emotion. She stirred feelings and raw emotions he had repressed since his parents' death. She made him care about something other than himself, or a meaningless mission. Not that his missions were of so little value, but they were in contrast to caring about another human being.

The thoughts that swam through his mind were foreign and made him embrace life in a different light. He could not be falling in love, yet how else could he describe the sensation? No. It was not possible, and could never be.

A rustling in the background made him turn. He smiled as Jester ambled up the last two stairs, dragging several bags behind him. With a laugh he walked over to give him a hand. "Did you get everything?"

"Doesn't it look like it?"

"You know what I'm asking about." He almost laughed when his friend straightened his yellow flowered shirt and fluffed out his baggy red pants. Only Jester could get away with dressing in such a manner.

"If it's missing items you want, then I've got them. Oh, I brought a watertight bag for you. Here."

Hawk took the slick covering from Jester and enclosed his duffel bag. "I'll get the diving helmets."

"No, let me."

Kylie moaned slightly. Hawk laid his hand on her forehead, and she moved her head from side to side. He checked his timepiece, relieved it was nearly time for the pick-up. He missed his men, and his ship. When Kylie woke, she'd see him for what he really was. No more games, no more lies. By the Gods, he hoped she could accept him.

Red hair lay in wild curls against the canvas. His breathing quickened just looking at her. He ran a finger down the bridge of her nose and counted the faint freckles on the tip. She never looked more beautiful, and he never desired her more. Would he ever taste her lips again? Hope was all he had.

"Here you go, Boss." Jester walked to Hawk and handed him two helmets. "I still don't like this idea of going to Andor. It's too risky."

Hawk chuckled. "When have we done anything safe lately?"

"It's not the normal risk, it's your life we're talking about."

"There's no other way. We have to finish this."

"A lot of good that will do if you're dead!"

CHAPTER SEVENTEEN

"I'm willing to take that risk." Hawk fastened a helmet on Kylie. "We have no choice."

"I just...well..." Jester hung his head. "What I'm trying to say is that we've been together a long time, and I don't want..."

Hawk gave Jester a friendly slap on the back. "Nothing will happen to me. We've survived bad scrapes before. This is no different."

From the distant darkness a beam of light pierced the sea and both men turned toward the muted illumination.

"Beggar's right on time. Let's go."

Hawk picked up Kylie and secured her over his shoulder, then slid down the pole to the level below. He no sooner landed when a bag landed half on his foot with a loud thud. "Jester!"

"Sorry, Boss. Watch out, the rest are on their way."

He held Kylie to him with one arm and tried to catch the bags with the other as they fell through the opening one by one. He reached for the last bag, but his hand grabbed Jester's ankle instead as he slid down the pole.

Jester smiled and batted his lashes. "Didn't know you cared."

"You didn't have to dive-bomb me with the luggage."

"Time is short." Jester secured his helmet then dropped one over Hawk's head.

With a nod, Hawk fastened his breathing apparatus, checked Kylie's one more time, then carried her to the exit pool. The moment he stepped into the water, he heard a splash in the semidarkness. He smiled when Mia popped her head above the water and clicked a greeting. "Jester, float the bags in the water."

"Okay." Jester dropped all four bundles into the pool.

Hawk was amused to see Mia slip her nose through the rope tie and pull them under. "Looks like we've found a porter for our luggage."

"I hope you told Mia where we're going." Jester glanced at the glass wall that separated them from the scientists working in the lab. "We'd better follow her before they see us." He tipped his head toward the window. "And before our stuff ends up on a distant shore." Jester jumped in, sank below the surface and swam toward the exit.

Shaking his head, Hawk followed, his arm tightly around Kylie. Memories of her rescue consumed his thoughts. She had been unconscious then as well, and he'd been extremely worried about her, but this was worse. When he first touched her he'd felt an unforeseen, unwanted tug on his heart, now everything had changed. That little tug had turned into a full out war on his senses and better judgment. As a warrior, this was bad news indeed. To feel was to become vulnerable, and when he had to put other lives in danger for a mission, regret rang clear. All he really wanted to do was protect Kylie and his men.

The sea appeared eerie and foreboding in the darkness as they swam toward the periodic flashes of light from the surface platform. The cold water made him shiver, but it was prudent they not use diving suits, or the sub. He did not want their escape to be discovered any sooner than necessary.

SEA Lab would be in good hands with Throm in charge. Before Kylie had appeared on the scene, he had spent considerable time tutoring Throm as his first officer. The man had no military training, but he caught on fast and had a sense of duty Hawk could appreciate. Throm could maintain order on SEA Lab as long as he kept Nyles and Sira locked away.

The surface was only a few strokes away, and Hawk had never been so happy to see the light from the sky. Finally, he would be able to function normally. He would not have to maintain a false façade every waking moment, not with *his* men, on *his* ship. They knew him and respected him instead of condemning him. They all had a price on their heads for one crime or another, but none had attained the notoriety he had. Then again, their crimes were insignificant, it was The Hawk's crimes they would be executed for.

"Hawk!" Beggar yelled. "Good to see you, Captain."

Hawk opened the front of his helmet. "I couldn't agree more." He lifted Kylie so Beggar could pull her through the side door into the small shuttle. Once Kylie was safely secured he hopped up, then climbed inside. Jester nearly stepped on his feet when he hopped on board.

"Sorry, Boss. Guess I'm more anxious to leave than I thought."

Securing the hatch he turned to Jester. "I take it you feel better about going to Andor?"

Jester pulled off his helmet. "No, I miss *The Redemption*'s computer and my other 'toys' as you call them."

Beggar took the shuttle up, heading toward the stars, and Hawk sighed in relief, removing his helmet, then Kylie's. "I certainly wouldn't want to stand in the way of you and your 'toys'."

"Good, because I'm looking forward to lots of playtime."

Hawk wrung out his shirttail. "Ever since Kylie arrived I've been wet! What is it about that woman?" He looked at Jester, who scowled at him. "What?"

"Are you complaining, Boss?" Jester shook his head. "Here you are, with the most beautiful woman in three galaxies, a woman who has eyes for you as well, and you're complaining? I wish I had such a problem."

He heard Beggar join Jester in a laugh at his expense. His friend did have an excellent point, even if her eyes looked at him a bit different right now.

"Captain, if I may speak freely?"

"What is it, Beggar?"

"The men and I...well...we're concerned about having a woman on board, and..."

"You're questioning my judgment?"

"No sir, we've never had a woman on *The Redemption*, and frankly..."

"You'll be happy to welcome her?" Hawk cleared his throat. "That is what you were going to say, isn't it?"

"Yes, sir." Beggar hung his head. "Docking in a few moments."

One look at Kylie and he knew it wouldn't be long before she woke. Explanations did not come easy to him, and she would have nothing but questions, which he would try to answer if she could manage to listen.

He never thought his men would balk at a woman. They all shared a strong bond as a crew of men, a bond each of them had earned by numerous acts of heroics. It would be an adjustment, but he had confidence they would behave themselves and accept Kylie's presence.

"Boss, before we dock, do you want to tell me why we left so abruptly?"

Winn and his guard were murdered. He found the cure, and I have it."

"Wow, I'm beginning to see. But shouldn't we be taking it straight to Estra?"

"Not until I'm sure it will be safe there. Whoever wants it won't stop with killing Winn, and I don't think Estra can afford more of their best scientists to be murdered."

"See what you mean." Jester glanced at Kylie. "Does she know?"

"Not yet. When I went back to find her she was unconscious." The shuttle rocked slightly when it settled in the docking bay of *The Redemption*. "I'll fill you in later."

Six men pulled the hatch open and cheered when Hawk stepped out of the shuttle, Kylie in his arms.

"It's about time!" one shouted.

"Wait till you see what we have for you," another said.

"I'm glad to be back." Hawk walked past his men and paused in the hall. "As soon as I secure our guest, I'll join you in the conference room. Beggar, make way for Andor immediately."

Beggar nodded, Jester shook his head and the rest of his crew mumbled as they returned to their stations. He walked toward his cabin, glancing at Kylie. Kylie a guest? It sounded strange since *The Redemption* had never had a guest. Cargo, and an occasional passenger, but never a guest. He laughed to himself. She would probably view herself a hostage, and he had to agree that assessment would be fair since she had no choice in the matter. He had a lot to answer for, and he was not looking forward to facing those green eyes for fear he would kiss her instead of talking. It might be safer. At least he had another time-unit or so before she was conscious.

He took Kylie to his cabin and laid her on the bed, the realization that she was soaked to her gills evident as the top cover began to absorb moisture. He had to undress her, one more thing that would put her in shock, especially since she'd made it clear he was never to touch her again.

What choice did he have? He pulled off her boots and socks then moved to the head of the bed. His hand shook as he reached for the zipper of her blue, one-piece uniform. He'd seen women naked before, including a brief glimpse of Kylie through frosted shower glass, yet this was very different.

There was nothing to be afraid of, he reassured himself, pulling the zipper lower. Carefully he eased the top from her shoulders and peeled the wet uniform down her body until it was free. She was clad in a pink camisole with matching panties. He paused to catch his breath. The undergarments clung to her body in a way that made her look naked, yet he hesitated to remove them.

His heart thumped wildly in his chest and he was breathing as if he'd run a mile. This was ridiculous. He eased her arms over her head then pulled the top garment off, baring her breasts. She was beautiful, and his fingers burned from her soft skin.

Without further thought he peeled her panties off and dropped them on the floor, his eyes drawn to the curly patch of red hair between her thighs. By the Gods! Perfection was the only word that came to mind, and he knew from his wayward thoughts he had to walk away quickly.

He strode into the lav, picked up a towel, pulled a blanket from the closet then returned to Kylie. Gently he rubbed the towel over her skin, wishing it were his bare hands on her nakedness. "I vow to you, I will never touch you unless you want me to," he whispered. Would it ever be safe to touch this woman who he wanted with every fiber of his being?

After wrapping the towel around her hair, he took one last long, admiring look at her shapely body before covering her with the blanket. He had hardened just carrying her in to the cabin, now his body was in anguish. Lust, duty and honor warred inside him as he stepped away from the bed. Hawk reminded himself he had remained celibate since Lissa, and this was no time to test himself. Kylie was safe under the Downey softness now, but her image was forever etched in his mind. Would this memory be all he would ever have of her? An empty ache surged through his body.

Soon he would reveal himself to her, and she would be lost to him forever. It was the price he had to pay, even though she was the first woman he'd wanted by his side…and in his bed. Not for casual fun, but to share feelings and emotions he'd never admitted to anyone. She was special. It would hurt to let her go, yet he had to prepare himself for that eventuality.

He stepped toward the door. There was no more he could do for her, and it was past time to take control of his ship and get reacquainted with his men.

***

Konar nervously paced the length of his sleeping quarters. Sira had not answered his calls, and Nyles, the fool, had not checked in as usual. What was going on? Had Nyles failed again? No. He'd sent Sira to insure success.

They could be busy stealing the cure and smuggling it out, but his instincts screamed there were problems. He did not trust Nyles any farther than he could throw him, and Sira was not far behind. Betrayal remained his biggest concern.

Had The Hawk interfered? Or had Sira turned traitor along with Nyles? The cure was too valuable to put trust in anyone holding it since it had become more priceless than any antiquity in the universe. At least to those who put value on human life.

Konar laughed. His plan would succeed, and when it did, he could buy and sell anything, or anyone he chose. Power was an intoxicating tool, one he'd wielded his entire life. The greater the power, the greater the man.

Where was that whore, Sira? In her absence, he'd had to find satisfaction with several other women. As much as he hated to admit, Sira was the best he'd ever had. It would be a shame if he had to kill her, but there were more like her waiting to pleasure him.

This *Konar identity* served him well. In fact, he liked it better than who he really was. The name Konar brought fear to all who heard it, and he reveled in the power. He laughed at the operations he'd engineered as Konar over the past ten annual-cycles. Once The Hawk was dead, Konar would become the most feared man in the galaxy.

He picked up the com-link and called Sira one more time, impatiently waiting for an answer. When no response came, he slammed his fist on the table sending a crystal goblet crashing to the floor. "I'll kill you, bitch!"

***

"Thanks for the meal," Hawk said, patting his stomach. "I haven't had roasted porcenia since we left Practa two annual-cycles ago."

"We knew you'd like it," Beggar said, pouring Hawk another glass of Belise wine.

"Tell us, Hawk, what's the plan for Andor?" Dylor asked.

"We have no secrets between us, we've been together too long for that, and I won't start now. Whoever comes on this mission with me will do so voluntarily, and I'll understand if..." Hawk smiled when all eight of his men stood. It was their private signal of willingness, and it felt good to see such loyalty.

"I never had a doubt, but I had to ask." Hawk gave each man a proud nod of thanks. "Be seated. The purpose is to find who's behind the plot to steal the cure for Genesis Disorder. The missing artifacts, priceless as they are, aren't the main concern. The man who holds the cure to a disease that could annihilate worlds holds the power."

"Was a cure found?" Russa asked.

"Yes, but Professor Winn is dead. I have his journal, however, it's written in some ancient language." Hawk glanced at Jester. "I want you to work on a translation. Beggar, you will remain on *The Redemption*, as usual, when we take the shuttle to Andor. Jester, Kamito, Ogar and Rusa will go with me."

"What about Kylie, Boss?"

"She could be a problem, but I'm sure Beggar, Dylor, Mikos and Chase can handle her while we're gone." Hawk watched four sets of eyebrows raise. "She is to remain sequestered in my quarters. Make her comfortable, but keep your hands off her. Is that clear?"

"Sounds a bit possessive to me," Mikos said.

Jester giggled. "You don't know the half of it!"

"Enough! Kylie is not a topic for discussion." Hawk glared at his men. "Kylie is part of this mission, nothing more. Understood?"

"Perfectly, sir. I'll keep them in line, as usual," Beggar stated firmly.

Kamito smiled. "It's good to have you back, Hawk, even if you did bring a woman with you. We can handle it."

"I know, that's why you're all here." Hawk stood and pushed his chair toward the round table. "Jester will fill you in on all the details. I have some business to attend to."

CHAPTER EIGHTEEN

Kylie sat up and surveyed the room that had no resemblance to SEA Lab. Judging from the metal walls, lack of windows, and the faint hum of engines; she surmised it was some type of space craft. The air had the same filtered smell as her ship, and lacked the salty aroma so evident in SEA Lab. How had she gotten aboard? She searched her brain for her last memory, but at the moment, it escaped her. All she felt was a dull ache in her temples, as if she had a hangover.

Dear Stars! She was naked with no memory of how she got that way. Who undressed her? The answer scared her as much as not having anything to wear. She did not feel any effects of being raped or abused, yet she felt violated all the same.

She stood on shaky legs, wrapped the blanket securely around her, then slowly made her way to the door. The moment she stepped on a small rug by the opening, the door slid open. Once in the hall, she followed the sound of muted voices until she could hear them clearly.

From the laugher, it sounded like there were several men, but she could not tell how many. She tucked the end of the blanket securely in the wrapped portion in front of her then hugged the wall behind her, the metal cold against her back. She concentrated on the voices, sure two of them were familiar. Her breath caught in her throat when one of the men called another Hawk. Her mouth suddenly went dry with the metallic taste of fear.

One of the voices was unmistakably Jester's, and then she heard the deep, resonating quality she knew so well...Saxon. She could not believe her ears when he said she could be a problem! When had she become a problem, and why would Saxon say other men could handle her?

She shivered. Who had been called The Hawk? Had they all been kidnapped by the maniacal fugitive? Somehow she doubted Saxon could be taken by any man. She heard the scrape of chair legs, then Saxon said something about attending to business. Footsteps caused her to turn and run back to the room she'd come from.

Throwing herself on the bed, she closed her eyes and waited, her body trembling involuntarily, her heart racing. Thoughts flew through her mind in a blur while the door slid closed. There was nowhere to run, and hiding would prove futile on a ship. The best she could hope for was Saxon's protection, if he hadn't turned traitor. Nothing made sense, but she had to believe Saxon would not harm her.

Heavy boots sounded on the metal floor outside moments before the door whooshed open. She was now wrapped in the blanket instead of covered by it. Too late now. She wasn't very good at the spy game. If she lived through this ordeal, she vowed never to attempt it again. When she looked at the entrance a large figure appeared, the light from the hall concealing his identity.

"Kylie?"

The voice was definitely Saxon's, and her eyes confirmed it when she focused on his powerful form that stood at the foot of the bed. He looked like a different person. His shiny mane was tied back, and his usual uniform was replaced by tight black leather pants, knee-high black boots, and a white shirt with blousy sleeves that laced up the front. Attached to the wide black leather belt was a holster containing a fazer. She'd never seen him carry a weapon. The change was remarkable. He always appeared formidable, but he'd never looked so dangerously attractive. Her cheeks turned hot, and there was that unmistakable tickle in her stomach.

"Are you all right?"

"Never been better," she said as sarcastically as she could. "It may be an every sun-cycle occurrence to you, but I'm not used to being drugged, kidnapped from the bottom of the sea to wake up in space— naked!"

"I'm glad you're taking it so well." He walked to the side of the bed.

"Don't you dare lay a hand on me. Nothing has changed between us."

"Nothing?" Saxon laughed. "Everything has changed."

"You and Jester are spies, that's a different twist." She sat up, swung her legs off the bed, and crossed her arms over her chest, clutching the blanket. "Aren't you going to deny it? Surely you have a good cover-up story. Chief of Security was a cleaver disguise. Did you kill the real Chief in order to assume his identity?"

"Kylie, please. I came to explain, if you'll give me the chance."

"Chance? You've had plenty of chances, but all you've done is lie to me."

Saxon sat in the chair facing the side of the bed. "Not everything was a lie."

She shook her head at his stoic expression. Was the man made of stone? "Go ahead, tell me more lies. You aren't the man I thought you were."

"I am Bryce Saxon, but my men call me Hawk."

"As in The Hawk?" When he nodded a numb feeling consumed every ounce of her body. One hand fell to her side to steady herself on the bed so she didn't fall over. She knew he had a secret, but never once suspected this.

Hawk grinned. "I see I've rendered you speechless."

Roloc's words gnawed at her. He had insisted The Hawk was the man for the job, but was nowhere to be found. Little did Roloc know The Hawk was already on SEA Lab. Betrayal and anger ate at her empty stomach. Never would she have suspected that the most wanted, most feared man in the galaxy would also turn out to be the most handsome man she had ever laid eyes on, and the first man to ever stir her sexual desires. She should be ashamed considering the circumstances, but she remembered his every tender kiss and gentle touch.

"I won't hurt you, Kylie. You're in no danger."

"No danger? I'm flying around the Maraf Galaxy with a known murderer, pirate, mercenary, thief...and..."

"Spy," he added.

"And spy, yet you say I'm in no danger?"

"The danger was on SEA Lab. My ship is secure. It's well armed, and I have a very capable crew. I assure you, you're safe on *The Redemption*."

"Such a fitting name for something you'll never attain." He scowled at her and her stomach tightened. "What danger is on SEA Lab?"

"When I went back to Professor Winn's office, he and his guard were dead."

Kylie's hand flew to her mouth. Tears burned at her lids, and she didn't have the strength or will to stop them. Crying would solve nothing, but she'd kept her emotions locked away for so long it was like a dam breaking. She closed her eyes, but hot tears rolled down her cheeks despite her will to show this space pirate her strength.

The bed dipped next to her, and she felt Saxon's warmth even before his arm wrapped around her shoulder. She vowed never to let him touch her again, yet she needed his strength more than she wanted to admit. "Wha...wha...what about the cure?"

"I found his journal."

"Did he have time to finish his notes? Is the cure completely doc...doc...documented?" She wiped her eyes with the back of her hand and took a deep breath.

"I'm not sure. Winn wrote in a language we haven't been able to decipher. Jester is working on it. Hopefully we'll know soon."

"Who killed them?"

"It had to be Sira. Nyles was locked up."

"We both knew Sira was working with Nyles, but I had no idea she was capable of murder."

"She tortured him to get him to talk, but Winn had a weak heart and..."

"She's still responsible." Kylie sighed. "Who is she working for?"

"I don't know. Why do you think you found us together?"

"I...I...assumed you two were ah..."

"The first thing women spies are taught is how to use their powers of seduction. She was trying to learn something from me, and I was doing the same. It was a draw." Hawk smiled. "I welcomed your interruption. Sira never tempted me for a moment. I've known her kind before and...well, let's just say I despise women like her and was glad you ended her little game."

"Do all spies do their best work in the bedroom?"

Hawk laughed and wiped a tear from her cheek. "No, Amica. Just spies like Sira."

"Have you ever...?"

"I came to explain, not confess." He took her hand and kissed her fingers. "I've done things I'm not proud of, to answer your question. But I've also completed missions of great importance that have saved lives. Not everything I do is dishonorable."

"You're proud of murder?" she asked, pulling away from him.

"I thought you knew me better than that. I've never murdered anyone." He watched her eyes widen. "I've killed in the line of duty, but never needlessly."

"What about the woman on Andor? Everyone knows the story."

"That's where you're wrong. I don't even know the story."

"You expect me to believe that?"

Hawk groaned. "Tell me how you got on this ship and what happened to your clothes."

"I ah..." Kylie pulled the blanket up to her chin, Saxon's point well made.

"I believe I was drugged and framed. At first, I believed I did it, but deep in my soul, I know I didn't. And when this is over, I intend to prove my innocence."

"Why now?"

"I'm tired of living like this. I'd like to settle down, have a family, live like a normal person."

Kylie felt her heart sink to depths she never knew possible. He said the one word that struck terror in her heart—family. She could give no man a child, a painful reminder of her genetics, and a dismal prophecy of her future.

"Did I say something to upset you?"

"Everything. But why should you care?"

Hawk tilted her chin toward him with one finger. "I'm the same man who pulled you from the sea, who kissed you, and who wants to see the cure in the right hands. I care about *you*. That will never change." He pulled the towel from her head and tossed in on the floor.

His fingers threaded through her hair and her stomach fluttered nervously. His eyes filled with desire, and his lower lip quivered. Suddenly he pulled his hand back and stood.

Kylie immediately felt the loss of his closeness. "If you mean that, why are you pulling away?"

"I have no right to touch you, you've made that quite clear. I'm sorry." He walked toward the door.

"Wait." She stood, tucked the blanket securely around her and walked to him. "What if I asked you to stay?"

"I can't." Hawk caressed her bare shoulders. "I don't trust myself with you."

"Why? You've never hurt me, and just swore to me you never would." Her hands found his chest and she felt his heart race.

"Don't be naïve. You know I want you as a woman. No, I can't stay." He dropped his hands and groaned.

Kylie pressed closer and threaded her arms around his neck. "May the Gods forgive me, but I want *you*." She watched shock play across his masculine features. Before he could utter another word she placed her fingers on his lips. "Don't ask me to explain, I just know it's right."

"I want you to be sure, Amica. I cannot change who I am." He trailed one finger down the nape of her neck. "I swore I'd never touch you unless you asked me to. And if you do, there's no going back." He brushed her lips with his. "I've always wanted you."

"Even though you know what I am?"

"Perfect?" He smiled, then touched his nose to hers. "You are.

Never doubt that." He swept her into his arms and carried her to the bed. "And if you ask, I shall kiss every perfect inch of your body."

"Every inch?"

"Mmmm, every inch."

Fire spread from her cheeks to her stomach then lower, settling between her thighs while his heated gaze bore into her. Deep in her heart, she knew it would be impossible not to love him. She couldn't stop him anymore than she could stop the beat of her heart. He reached for the blanket, and her hands instinctively grabbed the edge.

"How am I to kiss every delectable inch if I cannot even see you?"

His mouth covered hers possessively, and his tongue teased. The passion in his kiss sent shivers down her spine. Her stomach tingled while his sensuous seduction pushed away her fears. His hands caressed her bare shoulders, then moved upward and twined through her hair. He settled down beside her ever so carefully, insuring his gentle, caring lips never left hers.

Her heart told her this man who held her was incapable of brutally murdering an innocent woman. If he were that kind of man, she'd know. He was right, he hadn't changed, only his name was different.

When he tugged at the top of the blanket, she knew exactly where it would lead. Could she love a man she barely knew? Or did she know him better than he knew himself? It was insane to get close to him. They could never have a future together. He wanted a family she couldn't give, and duty would tear them apart no matter what they wanted. She pushed against his chest and he pulled back, a surprised look on his face.

"I'm sorry." Hawk rolled off the bed to stand next to it. "I am sorry."

"Sorry you kissed me?"

"I've never been sorry for holding you, feeling you against me, or tasting your sweet kisses. I'm only sorry if I've done something you didn't want me to do."

The sadness in the depths of his blue eyes brought tears she could not hold back. He truly meant what he said, and she felt ashamed for the way she'd acted toward him, especially concerning Sira. "Saxon...or should I call you Hawk?" He grinned at her, but she was not sure if it was remorse, or desire.

"Use the name you're comfortable with."

"I owe you an apology for..." His fingers touched her lips so softly she could barely feel them, but the effect was intoxicating.

"You owe me nothing, Amica. I know how it looked to you, and I don't blame you for assuming I was interested in Sira. I never meant to hurt you. I care about you more than you realize."

"I have to know what you intend to do with Winn's journal. It belongs to Estra, and it's my job to deliver it to Roloc."

"That's my goal as well. But not until we learn who tried to steal it."

"You can't be serious!" She sat up on the bed and stared, his anxiety evident in every tensed muscle. "We could be saving lives while you play more of your spy games."

Hawk sat next to her, running the back of his hand down her arm. "How long do you think the cure will remain in Roloc's hands if the man behind this isn't stopped? He could end up dead, along with anyone who has knowledge of the cure." He kissed her shoulder. "Plus we have to have the journal translated or it will be of no use to anyone." He kissed his way up her shoulder to the base of her neck. "I think we should discuss this later."

"I believe you're right, Captain." He chuckled deep in his throat, but he did not stop his exploration. He kissed her neck and slipped his arms around her and eased her down on the bed. He then began to caress every inch of her with his lips. He then took his assault lower, easing his way to her nipple, causing waves of delight to surge through her as he loved the tender tip. A slight moan escaped. He groaned as if he knew what pleasure he brought.

Only once had a man touched her before, but he had only kissed her and fondled her breast through her clothes. The coward ran away when she told him who she was, as if she'd had an incurable disease.

She let her fingers explore the long strands of his hair. He made a deep purring sound, and she knew loving him could never be a mistake. Nothing this special could be wrong. For once in her life she would throw caution to the wind, follow her heart, and cherish the physical sensations only Hawk could create.

His mouth meandered to the other breast, giving it equal attention. With a determined hand he jerked the blanket free and tossed it to the floor. He raised his head, and his gaze raked her from head to foot. Her body burned with a desperate heat so foreign it scared her. She'd heard women speak of the fire a man could cause, but she never dreamed it would be so intense, so intimate, so wonderful.

A shiver coursed down her spine. She trembled. He smiled. Not the smile of a friendly greeting, rather the smile of a knowing lover ready to give ultimate pleasure.

"You're blushing."

"You're staring." She met his gaze, unsure how to handle this intimacy. He knew exactly what he was doing to her, and it was an unfair advantage since she had no idea what she was supposed to do to him.

"As I have wanted to for so long."

His head bent and he scooted his body lower so his tongue could find the indentation of her bellybutton. That part of her body had never been of much interest to her, but now that he was exploring it, she realized it could be a sensual area. She placed a hand on each side of his head and forced him to look up at her face. "You are not playing fair."

"Aah, but I am."

"You are not, Bryce Saxon Hawk."

He chuckled. "And which one of me is not playing fair?"

"The one wearing clothes."

"I see." His grin widened when Kylie pulled the lace from his shirt. "Are you anxious?"

"Doesn't the first time make a woman anxious?"

"Indeed." Hawk rolled off the bed and stood before her. "Maybe I should appease your curiosity?"

Hawk ripped the front of his shirt and it fell in a torn heap to the floor. He removed his belt, then bent and pulled off his boots. When he straightened he placed a hand on each side of the waistband of his pants and began to push them down. She took a deep breath when she really wanted to scream at him for taking so long to lower his pants.

Hawk made undressing into an art form, which made her squirm in anticipation. Without a shirt he looked amazing, bulging biceps, strong forearms, and a muscle-rippled stomach. He was indeed a warrior, the most perfect one she'd ever seen.

She watched his pants slide down his well-shaped legs, and in the blink of an eye he stood tall in all his masculine glory while her eyes feasted on his naked body. She could not bring herself to meet his gaze, especially when her eyes focused below his waist, wanton desire pulsing through her veins.

The sculpted planes of his chest rose and fell. His powerful arm muscles flexed when he rested his fists on trim hips above sturdy thighs slightly apart. There were battle scars across his stomach, chest, shoulders, right upper arm and the inside of his left thigh. He didn't blink while she took in the awesome splendor of his potent male physique, including the part that was hard and ready. It was the part of him she wanted to feel inside her that sent tremors of anticipation through her body.

Kylie cleared her throat. "I believe my curiosity is...is satisfied," she said in a husky voice, her mind reeling with the reality of what she was about to do. He was so overpowering she feared she might faint from the new, heady sensations that poured unrestrained, and he had yet to even touch her.

"Hardly." He positioned himself on the bed next to her. "You have no idea of what I am capable."

Hawk bent his head to resume his promise of kissing every inch of her, beginning at her neck, lower to her breasts, then her stomach, and even lower to the juncture of her thighs. She gasped when his fingers explored the feminine region that ached for him. He touched her carefully, erotically, until she thought she'd go mad. Hawk made all other men seem like boys with his obvious experience. He knew all the right places to entice unbridled desire.

The moment his mouth nuzzled into her womanly curls and his tongue found the sensitive nub her breath caught in her throat. He expertly worked his magic and sent surges of pleasure that spiraled through her. Saxon had always made her stomach flutter by merely walking into a room, but as The Hawk, he added a dark, mysterious excitement she found irresistible.

She tilted her head back and inhaled deeply to stifle a scream of ecstasy as he brought her closer and closer to release. She held her breath when a tremble began deep within, causing one glorious spasm after another to grip her very core.

With a sigh she wondered if she would ever get enough of this fearless man. He lifted his head and kissed his way to her lips, her scent still on him. Hawk slipped between her legs and his manhood pressed for entry, his eyes glassy with need. For the first time in her life she realized what the power of a woman felt like. His fierceness had melted, his icy nature stripped by fire—the fire that burned between them, the fire she prayed would never die.

"Make love to me Hawk," she whispered, startled when he thrust into her without hesitation. Her legs twined around his, and she grabbed his shoulders as a fast stab of pain took her breath.

Hawk stilled. "My sweet Amica, why didn't you tell me this was your first time?"

"I tried. Did I not ask if the first time should make a woman nervous?"

"I assumed you meant the first time with me." He buried his face in her hair. "I'm sorry. I never would have..."

"Made love to me? That's what I was afraid of." Tears welled in her eyes.

"I never would have hurt you." He kissed the wetness from her lashes. "I would have been more gentle."

"Gentle will not do, my handsome warrior." He grinned wickedly and began to move slowly. He filled her so fully she thought she'd burst, but her body, as well as her heart, was consumed by him as if he were a part of her—the part that had been missing her entire life.

Hawk moaned. "Kylie, my sweet Amica." Her tightness held him, then loosened, then held him again. She sent liquid fire through his veins, and it took great restraint to prolong the release he so desperately wanted. He wished this joining could last forever; pure, simple and filled with love.

Yes, he loved Kylie with all his heart, but he could not tell her. He had nothing to offer except this moment, his body, and his heart. She writhed beneath him and tested his control, but also filled him with emotions he never dreamed he could have. He covered her ripe breast with his mouth to taste her once again, to revel in her innocent sensuality.

Kylie was all woman, more than he could have hoped for, and far too good and innocent for a fugitive. He moved faster and his heart pounded in his chest. He lifted his head, licked his lips, and savored the salty taste of her skin while her unique scent found a permanent place in his memory. He took one deep breath and brought himself under control. He slowed his movements. This had to be special for Kylie.

He wanted to make this a moon-cycle she'd remember for the rest of her life. Even if he could not be with her, he wanted her to cherish this moment of becoming a woman, and to think of him when she recalled their joining.

"Hawk, please...you're driving me mad."

Her husky, needy voice told him he had the same effect on her that she had on him. From the instant he first touched her he'd felt a magical fire between them, a passion only love could cure. He groaned and gazed into her eyes. "I love it when you beg." With renewed strength he moved his hips in a circular motion. "And I love driving you mad."

He kissed her softly, but she returned his kiss as if they were lovers reunited after a long absence. Kylie had given him a most precious gift, and he prayed he was worthy. He sensed her trust, and he vowed never to betray what he had worked so hard to gain.

Primal need drove his movements, love drove his desire. He possessed her as his own. Could she ever accept the man he was? Would she regret giving her virginity to a wanted criminal? It was up to him to insure that did not happen. He would shower her with love and take what she offered for as long as it lasted. Love. It had been only a word until the red-haired beauty crashed into his life.

She moaned, and he moved faster to possess the woman who now owned his heart. His mind became dazed, his body responded, his thrusts quickly building to a frenzy of movement and emotion. She gripped his arms, her nails digging into his skin. Stars danced and the floodgate opened as he spilled his seed into the woman he loved.

He kissed her softly as he slowed, finally stopping, but not withdrawing. Her hands caressed his arms. Pride and happiness soared through him, along with a satisfaction he never dreamed possible. Kylie had given him the one thing he had longed for, yet never experienced. Rolling to lay by her side, he cradled her head against his chest, willing his pounding heart to slow down so he could catch his breath.

Words seemed meaningless at a time like this. It was a moment of perfection they may never find again. She looked at him and wiped beads of sweat from his forehead with her fingers, her green eyes full of love and wonder. He wanted to tell her how much he adored her, but it would only hurt her in the end.

Too much lay between them. Her duty to her people, and his need to clear his name. He studied her face and took solace in her contentment. She was warm, giving, and trusting. He wished he could keep her by his side forever. "Kylie?"

"Hmmm…?"

He sat up and pulled her with him.

"What are you doing?"

"I'm going to show you my shower."

"I've seen showers before. I just want to sleep."

Hawk laughed while he pulled her off the bed and walked her into the lav. "I guarantee you'll never view a shower the same when I'm through with you."

She giggled. "Pretty sure of yourself, aren't you?"

He opened the door and pulled her inside, turning on a warm, steamy spray of water. "Positive." With soap in hand, he massaged every inch of her body. He rubbed himself against her, and slid back and forth, skin to skin in the slick lather.

"This is nice." Kylie ran her hands over Hawk's shoulders as his chest glided across her breasts.

"No, this is nice." He picked her up and positioned her over his swollen manhood and entered her quickly, and a groan escaped him at the feel of her. He savored her heated response, and enjoyed her ardent attention. "This is where you belong." Kylie began to laugh, and he stopped his movements. "What's so funny, Amica?"

"I just remembered that you said you haven't had a dry moment since you met me. Look at us!"

"Indeed." He suckled a rosy tipped nipple for a moment, then looked up into her beautiful green eyes. "Look at us." He pressed her back against the wall and let the water trickle over them, their bodies even hotter than the water. "I like the sound of *us*."

CHAPTER NINETEEN

"Konar?"

"Sira, it's about time. What's happened?"

"I've been evading the entire security force. They're going to arrest me for Winn's death. Nyles is already behind bars."

"By the Gods woman! What have you done?" The bitch was infuriating him, and he had no patience left.

"I was trying to make him talk. I hit him a few times and broke a couple of fingers, but I swear, Konar, I didn't kill him. He grabbed his chest and fell to the floor."

"Be glad you're out of my reach or you'd join Winn in the great beyond. How could you let this happen? I wanted him alive!"

"How was I to know he had a weak heart?"

"What's Hawk planning to do with Nyles?"

Sira sighed. "I don't know, he's gone."

"What do you mean, gone?" Konar slammed his fist on the table in front of him. If he angered Sira to the breaking point, she wouldn't speak to him at all, and he needed her. "Well?"

"I've been evading guards for several time-units. They will arrest me. I'm running out of hiding places and..."

"Just tell me where Hawk is!"

"I...I...don't know. He doesn't seem to be on SEA Lab. No one has seen him since he found Winn." Sira stared at her shaking hands. "Wherever he is, I think he took Kylie Beryl with him. I was forced to drug her when I searched his room for the journal. I managed to get out before he returned. Later, I saw him carry Kylie down the hall over his shoulder."

"You stupid bitch! Why didn't you just leave a note!"

"I'm sorry, Konar."

"You'll pay for your mistakes." He closed the link and began to pace his bedchamber. He knew Hawk well, and he'd head for Andor to find Redmon. Laughing, he shook his head. If Hawk only knew, but he would not live long enough to learn Konar's true identity. Too bad, it would be most satisfying to see the look on his face.

If he were lucky, he'd be able to dispose of Hawk, Sira and Nyles, all at the same time. However, that would require proper planning, but not until he was finished with them. The cure had to be in his hands first.

He would set The Hawk up to take the blame for murdering Nyles and Sira before he allowed the military to execute him. His plan five annual-cycles ago had been a stroke of genius. The Hawk's only downfall had been trusting the wrong people, a trait that would be his downfall again. Even the best Elite Operative the corps ever had could not escape this time.

The fool would bring him the journal and take the fall for every crime on SEA Lab, of that he was certain.

***

"Good sun-cycle, Jester," Kylie said as she took a seat. "I'm starving."

"And good sun-cycle to you." Jester stood still and stared first at Kylie then Hawk. "I must say you're both beaming. I take it things are going well?"

Hawk cleared his throat and laid a hand on Kylie's shoulder. "Very well. Kylie's recovered from the drugs."

He stepped to the computer operated galley and ordered two breakfast plates. "She knows who I am."

"Really." Jester smiled. "I always knew Kylie was a smart woman, but I never thought she'd guess."

"I told her."

"And she's still speaking to you?" Jester shook his head. "Miracles do happen!"

"We need a miracle." Kylie took a sip from the cup of koffa Hawk handed her. "Jester, have you been able to decipher the journal yet?"

"I've tried every known language with no success. It's not one of the thousands of languages in the computer." Jester propped his foot on the seat of the chair in front of him. "It's got me stumped."

"Jester the great—stumped?" Hawk laughed.

"You two seem in an awfully good mood. Is there something I should know?"

"Definitely *not*, my friend."

"I see…well ah…I've got work to do. Have a good breakfast." Jester removed his foot from the chair and left the galley.

Hawk carried two plates to the table and set one in front of her. Hawk. It seemed strange to think of Saxon as Hawk, but it flowed more naturally from her tongue. The Hawk fit his personality and his moods. She loved his new look. His usual black uniform was nice, but the lace-up white shirt made his skin look more bronze and his eyes more blue.

"What are you thinking, Amica?"

"How your name fits you." She took a bite of sweet Kalar fruit and stared at him. His eyes narrowed, his lips turned down and he groaned deeply. "What's wrong?"

"I'm not sure how to take that."

"It was a compliment, I assure you." She smiled. "And I like your new attire. It makes you look…desirable." His concerned look faded into the masculine sensuality she found hard to ignore.

"Then I shall always wear it."

He grinned so seductively her heart beat faster and her stomach lurched with the familiar tickle only Hawk could produce by his very presence. Kylie glanced around to insure they were alone. "Maybe you shouldn't."

"So, the Delphin lover has found something else that tickles her fancy."

"You tickle more than my fancy."

"Indeed." Hawk cleared his throat. "Maybe we should retire to the cabin and find out just what that might be."

"I think we should discuss business."

"It would be safer, but not as much fun." He took a long drink of koffa then set the cup down. "We'll reach Andor in three sun-cycles. You'll stay aboard *The Redemption* while I go with a handful of men to the surface."

"You don't trust me to go with you?"

Hawk laid his hand on hers. "It's too dangerous."

"Then you shouldn't go either."

"I'm trained for battle."

"And you're targeted for execution!"

"I've remained a free man for over five annual-cycles, and I don't intend to be caught now."

"True, but you haven't set foot back on Andor, have you?"

"I know Andor like the back of my hand. There's no problem."

He was convincing, but she didn't believe him for a moment. It was like walking into a serpent's den and expecting not to be bitten. "I'm worried about you."

"I'm flattered."

"I'm serious! You could be killed, then what would happen?"

"Jester and my men would take care of you and see to it the cure arrives safely on Estra. You have my word."

"I want you...not your word."

Hawk leaned toward her and kissed the tip of her nose. "Knowing you want me is enough to keep me safe." He smiled. "There's still two sun-cycles until we arrive. Any suggestions on how to pass the time?"

"I might have a few."

"Hawk!" Beggar called over the com. "Come to the bridge."

He stood and rushed out of the room. Kylie experienced the same loneliness she felt every time he left, but in order to be with Hawk she had to accept his work. He was a man of many talents, the man everyone called when something went wrong. She took one last bite then decided to find Hawk. After all, he did not tell her to stay in the galley.

The Redemption was an amazing craft. She didn't know much about ships, but this one was far larger than anything owned by one person. It was relatively new, and from the looks of the equipment and amenities, exorbitantly expensive. In fact, it put to shame a large, Estran military battleship she once toured. Dear stars, Hawk owned his own battleship!

It was the classiest warship in any galaxy, which is why she had not recognized it for what it was when she first woke. She rushed toward the voices. When she entered the control room she listened to the ongoing conversation.

"Three fighters, and one mother ship are all I see right now, but it doesn't mean there aren't more coming."

"Did you set the cloak-field?"

"Yes, and all weapons are ready."

"Everyone, strap in. It could be a rough ride. When the fighters get within striking distance, execute 'the drop'."

"Gotcha, Boss."

Kylie stood in the entrance, mesmerized by the way Hawk and his crew meshed together. It was as if they read each other's minds, reacting as a well-oiled unit. Hawk turned his penetrating blue gaze on her and she shivered. True to form, her stomach fluttered as he approached.

"Here." He took her hand and led her to a flight seat. "Strap in."

She pulled the harness over her shoulders and buckled it in the slot between her legs. Hawk recited commands to his men so rapidly she had trouble comprehending them all, but she heard enough to know they were going to execute a difficult maneuver for a large craft. From what she could surmise, they were about to do a panic dive, straight down at warp speed.

It was an extremely dangerous thing to do, but the crew operated like it was business as usual, nothing they hadn't done many times before. She should be scared, but Hawk's authoritative presence had a calming effect. Obviously he was used to tight scrapes because he acted like this was just a walk in the park.

"Fighters approaching starboard side, impact in twenty-seven seconds."

Hawk pressed a series of buttons. "Dive in ten."

The men gripped the arms of their seats, knuckles white, expressions tense. Kylie glanced at her hands, her own fingers wrapped so tightly around the arms of her seat they'd turned white. She began to shake like she always did when she was nervous.

"Five, four, three, two, one..."

Kylie's stomach lurched into her throat, and her heart raced so fast she thought she might die. An incredible sense of falling assailed her and a nauseous feeling rose in her dry throat. Then as quickly as it began, it was over. The crew cheered, clapped, and a couple of the men burst into song. Every muscle in her body was paralyzed, and if she looked in the mirror she knew she'd see green. She stared at her feet and gasped for breath.

"Are you all right?" Hawk freed her harness. "Kylie?"

Two blue, probing eyes stared at her, waiting for a reply, but she failed to find her voice.

"I think she's got a bad case of space inertia, Boss. Better get her to bed before she...you know."

Hawk lifted her into his arms and carried her from the control room to his quarters and laid her on the bed. She stared at the grin on his face. "Why are you smiling like that?"

"I was thinking how I felt riding on a Delphin for the first time."

"I see. Pay-back time, huh? You'll be sorry!"

"So punish me."

"I would if I weren't so sick."

Hawk disappeared into the lav and returned with a small pill and a glass of water. "Take this. You'll feel better in a time-unit."

She popped the tablet in her mouth and took a drink. Hawk turned his back on her and walked toward the exit. "Where are you going?"

He paused at the door. "Rest. I have a ship to run."

"But..."

"You'll get no rest if I stay, and you're in no condition for what I have in mind."

"Don't threaten me, warrior."

"I make promises, not threats."

***

"What did you do to her, Boss? She's been out for twelve time-units."

"I gave her an air-sickness pill, nothing more."

"You can't fool me, I saw the look on your face this sun-cycle, and you gave her more than a pill!"

"Never could fool you."

"You know what they say, 'you can't fool a fool'."

"True, and I'd be lost without a fool like you."

"Aah, Boss. I think you're getting soft now that you're in love."

"Don't count on it." Hawk cleared his throat. The impulse to argue with Jester's statement about love tried to surface, but it was an argument he could not win since it was the truth. He was desperately in love with Kylie. He was also in lust with her, which he had to admit was easier than the love part of the equation, but he planned to have fun getting used to both. "We're getting close to Andor."

"Yeah, and I'm beginning to feel as sick as Kylie."

"You'll get over it. I have to meet with Redmon."

"The usual disguise?"

Hawk nodded.

"Can I be the Chieftain this time? I'm tired of being just another desert nomad."

"If you're not careful, I'll dress you as a member of the Chieftain's harem. You'd look great in a woman's caftan and headdress. Of course you couldn't remove your face-veil or they'd arrest you for being ugly!"

Jester punched Hawk in the upper arm. "Funny. Okay. I won't complain. Maybe you should take Kylie as your number one wife?"

"I won't put her in danger."

"She's in danger just being on *The Redemption*, or have you forgotten how many enemies would love to blow you out of space and turn you into galaxy dust?"

"You're giving me a headache." Hawk rubbed his temples. "Have you updated all the men?"

"As you instructed." Jester studied his friend's face. "Did you sleep at all last moon-cycle?"

"No. And don't ask."

"Well, you'd better get some rest. We'll be fine without you."

Hawk stood. "Call me if..."

"Yeah, yeah. Now go, and get some sleep this time."

"Right." He turned and walked down the long corridor toward his cabin, but he had to laugh to himself. As long as Kylie was willing to make love to him, he doubted he would ever sleep again. The time they had together was precious, a once in a lifetime opportunity, and he did not plan to waste one precious minute.

The door swished open and he saw her sitting up on the bed, rubbing her eyes. "Feel better?"

"How long have I been sleeping?"

"Thirteen time-units or so."

Hawk took off his boots then removed his shirt. He laid on the bed and rested his right forearm over his forehead.

"You look exhausted." Kylie snuggled down next to him and placed her head in the crook of his raised arm. She traced the scar on his stomach with her fingers. "How did you get this?"

"My opponent's sword was longer than mine."

"You were fighting with swords? What happened to laser weapons?"

"I've fought and defended many primitive civilizations."

"But you have sophisticated weapons. Why didn't you use them?"

"Amica, no matter what you think of me, I believe in a fair fight. Besides, there is a challenge to using a sword."

"And what about this one?" she asked, running her finger over a long jagged scar on his left shoulder.

"Do you remember when we were on the island and I mentioned a dragon?" She nodded. "I'm afraid he was a better opponent than I'd planned on. They have very sharp claws."

"And the one on your thigh?"

"I crash landed a one-man scout." He laughed. "I'm glad you can't see all the scars on my head."

Kylie sat up. "What happened on Andor?"

"You mean the murder charge?" He lowered his arm and pulled her close, and her emerald eyes took on a dark, serious glint. He hoped she was ready to hear his version, but the apprehension on her face made him wonder. However she took the news, she deserved the truth. "I went to Lissa's apartment. I knew she was a spy with information to sell, and I was sent as the buyer. As usual, she started with the sexual games, but I refused her, at least I think I did."

"You think?"

"The next thing I remember was waking up next to Lissa, both of us naked. She was lying in a pool of blood, my dagger in her heart. There was blood on my hands, blood everywhere."

"And?"

"Before I could get up, soldiers rushed into the room and arrested me for murder and treason."

"Treason, why?"

"The authorities found highly-classified information in Lissa's room that could only have come from me. Therefore, they logically assumed I sold it to her."

"How did you get away if they arrested you?"

"Redmon arranged my escape from prison and provided me with a two man scout. Only a man with Redmon's position could have pulled it off. He jammed all the tracking devices and communications systems until I was clear. I owe him my life."

"Tell me about Redmon."

"He's an extraordinary man. Tall, dark hair with gray hair at the temples, immaculate dresser, and he has a fondness for the ladies."

"Do they have a fondness for him?"

"He's sophisticated and quite rich for a career military man. I suppose you could call him handsome, if you're a woman who likes older men."

"I like my men about your age."

He groaned. "There is more to my arrest, and I want you to know everything." She shivered in his embrace. "There is a vid-disk that shows me making love to Lissa, then killing her."

"You've seen this disk?"

"Redmon played it for me." Hawk turned her chin with his finger, not surprised at the doubt that clouded her eyes. "What they say about me could be true. Why do you think I hesitated to make love to you? I wanted you desperately on the island, and before, but I didn't trust myself. Until we made love, I hadn't been with a woman since Lissa."

"Feared you'd hurt me?" Kylie shook her head. "I'm beginning to see."

"Are you? I don't understand how you could see when I don't. I'm not sure I understand. I have no memory of being with Lissa in bed. The last thing I remember was her putting her arms around me when she greeted me at the door that fateful moon-cycle."

"Someone framed you, Hawk."

"I've held on to that belief all these annual-cycles, but there's times I doubt myself. I don't know what happened." The painful memories exhausted him. He closed his eyes to block out the world for a little while.

***

Kylie eased out of bed and walked into the lav to dress. While she brushed her hair, Hawk's story about Lissa rolled around in her mind. She could not explain why, but she knew he was telling the truth. Was it instinct, or wishful thinking? Whatever it was, she refused to believe she'd made love to a cold-blooded murderer, nor could a cold blooded killer be so tender and loving. He could not be guilty.

She'd met and desired Bryce Saxon, but she'd fallen in love with The Hawk. There had to be a way he could learn the truth, and if there was, she would help him. Once the cure was safe on Estra, she would take a leave of absence from her work and go with him. Convincing him of her plan was another matter.

Why did life have to be so complicated? She wished she could contact Estra and talk to her parents. Although they still had a few months before Genesis Disorder began eating away their memories, she still felt panicked. Without a translation, the cure would be useless, and that would cost more precious time.

Hawk and Jester had to find a way. She laid down the brush and walked back into the bedchamber. Hawk still slept peacefully on the bed, and she did not have the heart to wake him. She picked up the blanket and slowly pulled it up to cover his bare chest. When her hands neared his neck two arms wrapped around her and pulled her down onto the mattress. "Hawk!"

He released her. "I'm sorry, Amica, it's reflex. I warned you about my sleeping habits. I'm not used to having anyone in my bed."

"Based on the stories you told, that's not true."

"No one has ever *slept* with me."

"Shall I find another cabin then?"

Hawk smothered her with his body and kissed her with a passion that made her melt in his arms. The man could excite her so fast it made her head swim. Waves of desire coursed through every inch of her body. It took great resolve, but she pushed him back and ended the kiss.

"What?"

"You're exhausted and you need to…"

"I need you."

Kylie laughed. "I doubt you have the strength. Besides, I need food right now." She stood and covered Hawk. "I'll be back."

"I shall hold you to your promise."

She walked to the door and threw him a kiss before she stepped out into the corridor. Her stomach still fluttered from the hungry look in his eyes and the sexy grin on his lips. Incorrigible! And she loved it, but the man had to rest.

CHAPTER TWENTY

"Jester," Kylie began when they'd finished lunch, "how much danger will Hawk be in on Andor?"

"No more than he's faced every sun-cycle for over five annual-cycles, I suppose."

"Please, Jester, be honest." She knew from the tense look on Jester's usually smiling face that he feared for his friend's life. "Hawk told me everything. There's no more secrets."

"I'm worried, but I also know him well enough to realize he's capable of taking care of himself." Jester chuckled. "With my help, of course."

"What's your opinion of Redmon?" She watched him shrug, the fabric of his wildly colored shirt bunching around his neck.

"He's an important man with a lot of power."

"You don't trust him, do you?"

"Hawk taught me to trust no one."

"That must be a terrible way to live."

"It's the safest way." Jester smiled. "Don't worry your pretty little head. I've watched over Hawk for a long time, and I'll watch over him on Andor as well."

Kylie stared at Jester, unable to shake the feeling of impending doom. She'd never seen Jester remain serious for so long, which meant he was more concerned than he wanted to admit. Worry never kept anyone safe.

"Trust him, Kylie. You won't regret it."

Trust him. The words seemed so simple. Her mind reeled with

questions she could not ask, questions with no answers. She had to believe he had Estra's best interest at heart. He said he did, but she still questioned his motives for going to Andor. It all came back to trust. She'd given him her body and her love, as well as her admission of trust. She would stick by her vow.

Jester stood and began to bounce around the galley. "Hawk's happier since he met you, even though he says you've complicated his life. Don't listen to him, he tells me the same thing."

"I hardly think so. I've seen the way you two work together. You read each other's minds."

"Really? Everyone tells me my mind is too scrambled to read."

"Have you ever had a woman in your life, Jester?"

"You wouldn't be getting personal, would you?" He laughed while he pushed buttons on the food fabricator.

She was amazed how much Jester could eat since his thin, wiry build offered no clue to his insatiable appetite. "No, just curious."

Jester grinned. "There's been a few women, but nothing serious. We don't stay in one place long enough to become attached to anything." He dropped his gaze. "I wouldn't mind finding a woman who could appreciate me. I'd love to have someone look at me the way you look at Hawk."

"I had no idea I was so obvious."

He laughed loudly. "I'm sure you didn't, but it's there. You both have it."

"It?"

"You know, that special spark—the one you have to have if you love someone."

"One sun-cycle you'll have that spark. I'm sure you will." She decided to change the subject because it was Jester who had suddenly gotten personal with his remark. She'd have to work on being less obvious where Hawk was concerned. "Tell me about your 'toys'."

Jester talked and talked and talked. Hawk was absolutely right, he did love his toys. She checked her wrist-piece as Jester droned on for over a time-unit. He'd set up his portable com-unit on the galley dining table and explained every intricate function he tried in the process to decipher Winn's journal.

She prayed he'd be successful. Time-unit after time-unit passed while Jester tirelessly labored in front of the green screen. Six time-units later, looking exhausted, Jester groaned and ran his hands through his disheveled hair. She'd learned more about his 'toys' than she ever wanted to know.

"What's going on here?"

Kylie turned toward the deep, demanding voice she knew belonged to Hawk. He was dressed once again in the black uniform he'd worn on SEA Lab, and he looked more dangerous than ever. "Jester's been educating me on his toys, and I've watched him eat nearly everything in the galley."

"That I believe." Hawk sat on the chair next to Kylie and leaned his arm on the table. "Is everything ready for our excursion to Andor?"

"You betcha."

"Good. We should be in the safety zone in less than a time-unit."

Kylie felt her heartbeat quicken along with her breathing. Just the thought of Hawk on the planet that wanted him dead sent chills up her spine. "Safety zone?"

Jester nodded. "That's what we call the invisible line between free space and Andorian territory. Their tracking equipment monitors farther than any other planet in the galaxy, so we'll have a greater distance in the shuttle."

"Won't they detect the shuttle in their air space?" Kylie asked.

"Hawk knows how to evade detection by coming in from the dead zone."

She winced at the word 'dead'. "I don't like the sound of that."

Hawk smiled. "It refers to the desert sector that is uninhabitable. Not even insects or snaktors can survive there. The temperature exceeds one-hundred-fifty degrees at the peak of the sun-cycle."

Jester laughed. "Sure hope the old shuttle doesn't break down."

"That's not funny, Jester." For the first time his humor rubbed her the wrong way. Then again, she'd never had a man to worry about before.

"We'll be fine." Hawk rubbed Kylie's forearm and looked into her eyes.

"I have a strong feeling you shouldn't go, Hawk." Kylie stared into the depths of his radiant blue eyes. How could any man look this good? Would she ever get used to the way he made her feel? She hoped not because she liked the feelings he stirred.

"Is this a psychic premonition?"

"Oh Boss, she's just worried about you. Which is something you're not used to—a woman fussing over you." Jester laughed. "You can't remember the last time someone worried about you, can you?"

"I don't think Kylie's interested in your gibberish."

"Oh, yes I am. In fact I'd love an answer to that." She loved watching him squirm. He was a very private person and this was as new for him as it was for her. However, Jester started it, so she might as well play along. "Well, when was the last time a woman worried about you?"

"My mother when I was a baby. Now, can we get back to work here?"

She and Jester laughed together, but she could tell they'd pushed Hawk as far as they dared for the moment. The last thing she wanted was for him to get mad at her. "Okay. I'm worried about you and I don't think you should go. It's too dangerous, and I don't like it. Maybe if you took me with you."

"Absolutely not. You will stay here with the crew. Only Jester and I will set foot on Andor. Kylie, going to Andor is a necessity. If anyone knows who can translate Winn's journal it's Redmon. He may also know who's after it."

"He's right, Kylie," Jester offered. "Redmon is as good a place to start as any, especially since it was an Andorian craft that landed on that island you two were so fond of."

"I was not *fond* of that place." Her words were full of defiance and fear, and she shuddered at the thought of the smelly sand creatures.

"Can't fool a fool." Jester chuckled. "You two looked pretty happy when I found you. But not quite as happy as you've looked since you've been roommates on *The Redemption*."

Hawk glanced at Kylie. "Remind me to find Jester a roommate that will keep him occupied."

Jester rubbed his hands together. "Oh goody!"

"Captain," a voice called over the com.

Abruptly, Hawk jumped from the chair and pressed a button on the wall. "Yes, Beggar."

"It's time for your departure, sir."

Kylie felt tears well in her eyes and desperately blinked them back. The last thing Hawk needed was to see her emotional. He was about to risk his life, and she did not want to add to his worry.

"We're on our way."

Jester pulled several bundles from a cabinet and threw one at Hawk. "It's time to show Kylie a new identity, Boss."

"As if he doesn't have enough of them already." She forced a laugh to hide the pain while she watched the two men put on dusty colored robes they secured at the waist with wide, black sashes. They donned matching turban headdresses that hung nearly to their knees in the back, and the top was secured with a black band. "Wow, you two look...very native."

Hawk grinned. "That's the point." He slid his arm around Kylie's waist and pulled her to his chest. "Do you like natives?"

"Only tall, dark-haired ones."

Jester cleared his throat.

"It's time, Amica." He lowered his head and kissed her. She felt his urgency, as well as reluctance. She was surprised he'd kiss her so passionately in front of Jester, the reluctance showed. Slowly he brought the kiss to an end and she immediately missed him, even though he stood in front of her. "Come back to me, Hawk."

***

Hawk landed the shuttle outside the city of Potestas, the first civilization that bordered Andor's dead zone. He opened the hatch and stepped into the stifling heat of the quiet desert sunset. He took a deep breath and the hot, dry air seared his lungs. The desert of Andor made him miss the salty moistness of SEA Lab.

"Boss?" Jester waited a moment. "Are Rusa and Ogar staying here with the shuttle?"

"They'll stay here since we may need a quick exit." Jester nodded at him, then picked up four canteens of water. He then grabbed his canteens and backpack from the open shutter doorway, then started walking across the burning red sands of the dead zone.

"He sure is preoccupied these sun-cycles," Kamito said, following his captain.

"Maybe," Jester said, "but if you know what's good for you, you won't say anything about it to Hawk. He's been a bit sensitive recently."

"The woman?"

"Afraid so, but he'll never admit it."

"He doesn't have to," Kamito remarked. "I've never seen Hawk so moody and off balance."

"I'm the one who's supposed to be off balance!" Jester laughed. "Look at him, he's walking like he's on his way to a fire!"

Hawk stopped and turned. "Are you two coming, or are you going to persist in useless gossip?" He shook his head and picked up the pace. If he were to meet with Redmon and return to the ship before dawn, they had to hurry.

The band of his headpiece absorbed the sweat on his forehead, but the heavy desert costume over his uniform gave little relief to the sweltering heat. He glanced at the mountains in the north where the sun sank slowly. The dead zone was barely tolerable in the dark.

Fine, dry, red sand billowed around his boots with each step. It was no accident this area was not patrolled, it could not sustain life if it tried. Andor was the most formidable planet in the galaxy, the perfect outpost for a military installation, but it had little to offer other inhabitants.

Time-units dragged, but the light of Potestas loomed before them.

The military compound Redmon had once called home was directly adjacent to the small city. Soon he'd have to kick into gear. His mind and reflexes had to be sharp and focused. He thought of Kylie and all they'd shared. If he died this moon-cycle, at least he'd die happy.

"Hey, Boss," Jester called, jogging up to Hawk. "What entrance are we going to use?"

"I'm going in alone."

"You can't!" Kamito protested.

Hawk glared at his friend. "I want you both to scour the pubs and learn all you can. You know the routine."

"A drink does sound good," both men said with a smile.

"You know the rules."

"Have we ever let you down?" Jester asked.

"Should I remind you about that little incident on Cryon an annual-cycle ago?"

"Captain, Jester and I had no idea that pretty little woman belonged to that hulk!"

"No women! That hulk damned near killed you both." He shook his head. "Women are nothing but trouble," Hawk reminded them, even though they were well aware of his number one rule. He decided to throw out number two, just in case. "No intoxicating drinks, and no fights."

"Olly-dolly."

"I mean it!"

"Lighten up, Boss. We know our job."

He knew they did, he was just on edge. Kylie was counting on him, as well as every inhabitant of Estra, and they could not get caught...for any reason. "One more thing." Hawk laughed to himself as Jester and Kamito both groaned and rolled their eyes. "I'll meet you out back of *The Liar's Den* in exactly two time-units from the time we part. If I'm not there, you're to leave without me."

"No!" Jester yelled.

Hawk silently walked toward his men. "That's an order."

"If you think for one instant that I'm going to face Kylie without you, you're crazier than I thought!"

Kamito held his hands up in front of his chest. "Don't look at me."

"You will obey my orders. I want your word on it." He stared at Jester's worried expression. "Well?"

"All right, but I don't like it."

"Good." Hawk checked his timer. "It's exactly nine-thirty. Two time-units, not a moment more. Understood?" He glanced at a building fifty yards ahead as two locals exited and strolled up the dusty path.

"Two time-units." Jester verified, glancing at his wrist.

Before Jester could offer his last protest, Hawk disappeared into the moon-cycle before they could complain any more. He ran toward the back wall of the official Andorian Military Compound. He knew the patrol schedule well, and every area where guards were present. Overhead the faint hum of a security vessel caught his attention. He ran for the stone wall that surrounded the compound. In a flash, he removed his desert garb, pulled a knit mask from his back uniform pocket and pulled it over his head.

After burying the nomad disguise in the sand, he reached in his pack for the gaff-rope, threw it over the twenty-foot wall and began to scale the stone barrier. The monotonous drone of the security vessel drew closer, pushing his ascent faster. If he were caught on the wall, the heat-seeking lazer weapon would literally cut him in half.

Inches from the top, he paused to pull the frequency-diffuser from his pocket. He tossed the small, flat round disk on top of the wall to temporarily disrupt the invisible light beam that would sound an alarm. Quickly, he threw his leg over the top, knowing the interruption of security would only be effective for ten seconds.

Immediately he pulled the rope to the other side, grabbed the disk and slid to the ground. A quick jerk and the rope fell into his hands. He tossed it in the pack and ran toward the dormitory. He reached the safety of dark shadows an instant before the security craft cruised over the well-lit courtyard.

The adrenaline rush spurred his instincts and honed his abilities, as only a narrow escape could. He was a well-trained operative and would use all his knowledge against the very men who trained him. No man would stop him. He turned the corner and paused to wait for three patrol officers to enter the building they had to check. He'd done it himself long...long ago.

Kylie's face flashed in his mind's eye and he smiled. He would do anything for her, including sacrificing his own life to save her and her people. She was the woman of his dreams and had found a place in his heart he never thought could be filled.

A blunt object pressed hard against his back. He knew the feel of an eradicator. It was not the first time a weapon had been pointed at his back, he prayed it was not the last.

***

"Drop the bag and put your hands up!"

Hawk heard the man's voice shake and that was all he needed. He spun on his heel, lifted his leg, then thrust his foot toward the man, kicking him in the head, knocking him to the dirt. Before the young soldier could rise, Hawk applied a pressure hold to his neck that rendered him unconscious.

He dragged the man behind a nearby storage shed. To insure he stayed out of the way, Hawk took a tiny tablet from his shirt pocket and placed it under the man's tongue. The rookie would not rejoin the world until the heat of the sun hit his face.

Redmon's quarters were in the officers' wing, two buildings away. He had no choice but to walk the distance in plain view as if he belonged on the compound. There were no walls, no shadows, and no vegetation...nowhere to hide. He glanced at the unconscious man at his feet. Damn. Even the uniforms had changed since he'd been gone. Instead of the old stark black, the pants and shirt were now dark green, the only black was the belt.

Swiftly he stripped the man of his uniform, wishing he'd been stopped by someone more his size. It would be a tight fit, but there was little choice. He changed clothes and laughed to himself. The waist was too large and the shirt too small. He cinched the belt tighter than it had ever been, and jammed the buckle prong into the last hole. When he reached to pick up his clothes, he felt the fabric strain across his shoulders, then he heard the tear.

A torn sleeve was the least of his problems. He crammed his black clothes and mask into his backpack. The sound of approaching laughter put him on alert. He straightened and walked straight toward the group of men.

"You there, halt!"

Hawk wanted to laugh, but that would be a mistake. "Yes, sir," he replied in a high, meek tone as he gave the men the appropriate salute. He assessed the four entry-level officers who had obviously come from tipping a few too many mugs of dema ale. Too bad the uniform he appropriated was of a much lower rank.

"What's in that bag?" the tallest man inquired.

"Laundry, sir. Hawk impatiently waited while the man had a lengthy laugh.

"I should hope so, look at you! You look like you've been rolling in the dirt!"

The loud, pudgy officer grinned at him, and Hawk had to dig deep to remember what it was like to be an entry-level soldier. "Sorry, sir. I just returned from field maneuvers and haven't had time to change, sir."

"Well, be gone. Get yourself cleaned up. You're a poor example for others."

"Yes sir." Hawk saluted then marched toward the dormitory as the drunks stared. It wasn't the direction he'd intended to go, but the rank his uniform indicated could not be found anywhere near the officer's dorm. He hoped the idiots would leave before he reached the door.

"That one couldn't shine my boots!" the tall man yelled.

"Definitely not officer material. He's barely qualified for infantry."

Hawk's right hand turned into a fist. He'd love to give the smart-mouths the lesson of their lives, but he had far more to worry about. They certainly were not worth the sacrifice. The three men turned a corner of the building behind him. Finally.

In a mad dash he ran straight for the officer's quarters, stopping under Redmon's locked window. No security beams were visible, so breaking in should not be a problem. Redmon usually left his alarm off because no one dared break into *his* room.

He rummaged through his bag and found the palm-code that could decipher the digital lock so fast it always amazed him. When he heard the click, he pushed the window up, tossed his bag inside, then crawled through the narrow opening. Now all he had to do was wait.

CHAPTER TWENTY-ONE

Kylie paced, wringing her hands. Where was he? How long would it take before they returned? Her patience had become nonexistent. She fought the foreboding feeling that settled inside her the moment Hawk left her sight, a feeling she could not stop every few minutes. Beggar said Hawk would not return until the sun dawned on Andor, which was a good six time-units away.

The thought of his arms around her, his body pressed to hers, and the taste of his kisses were the only things that helped dispel her worry. Making love to Hawk was the most beautiful experience she'd ever had, one she wanted repeated over and over again.

There were times she still thought of him as Saxon, staunch Chief of Security. The Hawk had grown on her. He was wild and dangerous, sensual and caring, always the contradiction. She'd seen his softer side, the part of him he never showed. Jester knew better, so he was not surprised by their newfound togetherness. Her lover and protector had become captain of her destiny, and the man who held her heart in his hands.

"Kylie?"

"I'm sorry, Beggar. I didn't hear you come in."

"Just thought I'd get a cup of koffa."

"Have you made contact with Hawk?"

"Rusa and Ogar confirmed landing. Hawk, Jester and Kamito are on their way into the city. They expect to return to *The Redemption* before dawn, if all goes well."

Kylie stopped pacing and sat across from Beggar who settled in with his koffa. "If all goes well? I don't like the sound of that. We have to do something. We could..."

"Whoa, little lady. We will *not* disobey the Captain's orders."

"What will happen if he doesn't make it back?"

"We go to Estra with Winn's journal."

"Without Hawk and his men?" A grim look took over Beggar's face as he nodded. "You can't be serious. You wouldn't leave them to die down there!"

"It's not my choice. Hawk's orders."

"Then he's a fool!" Kylie slammed her fist on the table. "I'll take a shuttle and rescue him myself!"

"I can't let you do that." Beggar took a drink.

"You can't stop me." How could Beggar sit there, calmly drinking koffa while Hawk's life was in danger? He looked so composed he made her angry. He finished his drink, then rose and walked toward her. She stood, hands on her hips, and glared at the large, fierce looking man.

Beggar grabbed her arm just as Dylor rushed into the galley. "Take your hands off me!"

"What's going on?" Dylor asked.

"Seems like an appropriate time to lock her up."

Dylor winced. "The Captain isn't going to like this."

"He wouldn't like seeing her on Andor either."

"I'll carry her, you open the door." Dylor scooped Kylie off the floor and carried her down the hall.

She beat on Dylor's chest, but he was like a rock, stubborn and immovable. She jerked on his shaggy brown hair and screamed. He only smiled. The familiar swoosh of a door caught her attention.

"No!" she yelled. Dylor deposited her on a small cot and abruptly left. Interior bars slid into position first, then the solid metal door closed. "Hawk will make you pay for this!" Her words echoed in the cell that contained little more than the cot she sat on.

Tears welled, then gushed down her cheeks. She'd held back for as long as she could, now there was no stopping herself. What did it matter, there was no one to witness her emotional breakdown, or hear her anguished cries.

She was helpless, and there was nothing she could do behind bars. Hawk had told her many times how loyal his crew was. If this was loyalty she'd hate to see deceit! She took a deep breath, desperately trying to calm the storm of emotions that ripped through her. She had reacted with her heart, not her head, but then, she'd never been in love before. She'd always heard that love made people do crazy, stupid things. Hawk taking a shuttle to Andor certainly qualified.

Her body shook and her heart ached. Love was painful, but she would not trade it for anything in the universe. Hawk promised he would come back to her, and she planned to hold him to his promise.

***

Time moved slowly while Hawk sat in the darkness and waited for Redmon. It was nearly time for his rendezvous with Jester and Kamito, but he would not leave without seeing the one man who could lead him to a translator. Or would Redmon send him to his execution? No, he had the feeling the man was definitely not done with him yet.

He hoped Jester and Kamito were behaving themselves. If they got arrested, he doubted he could spring them from an Andorian holding center the way he had on other planets. He'd found humor in his men's misbehavior in the past; however, this mission could not afford any delays or unnecessary risks.

Time was the biggest enemy, but it usually was. He hoped Kylie was getting some rest while he was gone, because he had plans for her when he got back. They may not have had many sun-cycles together, but what time remained, he planned to make memorable.

The door opened, lights came on, and Redmon stepped into the room.

"Hawk?"

Redmon feigned astonishment at his presence, but they both knew better. He stood and accepted the man's outstretched hand.

"The uniform doesn't do you justice." Redmon grinned. "You were never fond of lower ranks." He raised one eyebrow. "Why have you come?"

"Professor Winn is dead. I have the journal, but it needs to be translated. You're the language expert." He handed Redmon a copy of one journal page.

"Where's the rest?"

"It's safe." He studied Redmon's suspicious countenance. He didn't trust the man, but he could provide the necessary contact.

"Good." Redmon examined the page. "I don't know the language myself, but I've seen it before."

"And?" Redmon hesitated too long. He had not been around his former commanding officer since his escape, but he knew the man well, and his behavior was suspicious.

"It's the ancient language of the psychics of Vanefca."

"That planet died fifty annual-cycles ago." Hawk walked to the crystal and gem star chart Redmon used as a room divider and traced his finger around the area Vanefca once occupied.

"As you see, Spectra is the closest planet, and that's where most survivors settled."

"Do you know of anyone who can translate the journal?" Hawk watched a gamut of emotions play across Redmon's face, unsure how to read his peculiar reaction to a simple question. Had the man changed so much, or did he know more than he claimed? Either way, caution was required.

"There is a woman who lives in the mountains on Spectra."

"Do you know her?" Hawk noticed all color drain from Redmon's face.

"No."

Redmon's denial was too curt. He knew her all right, but why did he want to hide the fact? "Will she help?"

"Couldn't say."

He'd seen Redmon act this way when he tried to hide pertinent information about a mission. "How do you know of her?"

"Many annual-cycles ago, an ancient scroll was found here on Andor. It was written in Vanefca. This woman was the only person we could locate who could decipher it. Redmon scratched his head. "She wasn't cooperative, but we persuaded her."

"You tortured her?"

"Not exactly."

Hawk knew all too well the various methods operatives used to get what they wanted. He had his work cut out for him. The woman would never help him if she knew he was from Andor. He would be lucky if she didn't shoot him on sight. "How do I find her?"

"Land as close to the mountains in the Northern Sector as possible. The jungle is dense. It's no easy task to navigate. There are no roads or landing sites. Once you're clear of the jungle, it's a three time-unit hike up the mountain. The coordinates are N5-24 by 36-29 of sector nine."

"How do you remember so well?"

"Some things you never forget."

It was all too conveniently strange. Winn kept his journal in the most obscure language in the universe, yet Redmon knew exactly where to find a translator? He knew better than to question Redmon. Some things had to be accepted on faith, especially when there was no other choice.

"I hope for Estra's sake the woman still lives. For all I know she's moved to another planet." Redmon pointed to Spectra on the chart. "But I'd bet my credits she's still there."

"Have you heard from SEA Lab since I left?"

"No."

Another obvious lie. Everyone had a giveaway habit when they lied, and Redmon had a barely detectable shake to his hand when he poured himself a drink.

"Join me?" Redmon held a glass toward Hawk.

"I have to go." Hawk grabbed his bag and moved to the window.

"By the way, who's in charge of security on SEA Lab?"

"Officer Throm. He's a good man."

"Yes, I've heard of him." Redmon took a long drink. "Does he know your suspicions about Nyles?"

"Nyles is under arrest." Hawk thought he heard Redmon groan.

"Really. For what?"

"He stole artifacts."

"Have you recovered them?"

Hawk nodded. Redmon still seemed more concerned with Nyles than he should be, even if protecting artifacts was part of the assignment.

"And what of the women that arrived? Any problems?"

What was Redmon fishing for? Hawk glanced at his wrist piece. Jester and Kamito should be on their way to the shuttle. He'd have to hurry or he'd be stuck on Andor indefinitely. "I think one of the women is working with Nyles."

"What proof do you have?"

"No proof, just a suspicion," he said withholding Sira's escapades. Hawk opened the window and tossed the backpack to the ground.

"Keep me informed."

"Of course." Hawk slipped out, fastened the pack over his shoulders and headed for the back wall.

The wind picked up and dust blew in his face as he ran toward the enlisted men's dormitory. Muffled voices came from the building when the front door opened. He hugged the cold cement wall and restrained a cough. Damn dust!

He monitored the men's conversation while they exited the dorm, and he cringed at what he heard. They were talking about a fierce sand squall heading toward them from the dead zone. When the men hurried out of sight to escape the increasing wind, he ran for the darkest area of the stone wall.

He removed the rope from his bag and tossed it over the wall, then quickly scaled the twenty foot barrier, never happier to be free of the military compound. Thanks to the dust storm, the security cruiser was no longer in the sky, and the walking patrols had also stopped to take cover. He followed the wall to where he buried his disguise and unearthed the garment, quickly securing it in place. It was full of sand, but it would protect him from the cutting wind he would fight every step of his way back to the shuttle.

Once the headpiece was in place, he wrapped the long tail over his nose and mouth, securing the end through the band. He walked toward *The Liar's Den* just to be sure Jester and Kamito hadn't decided to wait against his orders.

Visibility was zero, the twin moons obscured by tons of swirling sand. If he were lucky, it would rain to settle the dust, if not, he'd be damned lucky to locate the shuttle. Countless men had disappeared in Andor's sand squalls over the sun-cycles, never to be seen again.

Thank the Gods for security lights or he never would have found the back of the pub. He walked several feet in each direction. At least Jester and Kamito had a head start. As far as escapes go, nothing shielded a man better than blowing sand, but it slowed progress and erased all sense of direction. Tracking and surveillance devices failed in the unrelenting wind that blew enough sand to bury a man alive. In fact, nothing worked in a sand-squall...nothing.

It would be ironic to escape capture for all these annual-cycles only to lose his life to nature's cruelty in the dead zone on the planet he despised. He lowered his head and pulled the material over his eyes. There was nothing to see anyway, and he needed his tears to wash the dust from his eyes. He'd known men to be permanently blinded by the sharp tiny grains that cut eyes like razors.

Step by step he fought the force of the howling wind, leaning into it to remain upright. He hoped Kamito hung on to Jester, or his skinny little friend might well blow away. Kamito had more than his share of weight to anchor him to the ground, but Jester did not weigh much more than Kylie, even though he was taller.

Kylie.

The thought of her spurred his momentum and pushed him to endure the storm. Her last words were, "Come back to me, Hawk." It was an intoxicating feeling to have a woman worry about him. She may not have said the words anymore than he had, but he'd seen love in her beautiful green eyes.

Gusts of grit rocked his body, cutting the thick robe to shreds. He could not even see his own feet, but he knew they were dragging their way through the rapidly changing drifts. At least there was nothing to run into. Over the centuries, these squalls had reduced mountains to boulders, then to sand.

He spurred his pace, muscles straining against nature's assault. The storm could last for several sun-cycles, even weeks, but he could not. No man could. He prayed Jester and Kamito were safe in the shuttle, yet he knew the rapid onset of the squall had not afforded them the necessary time.

In a flash, he found himself face down on the desert floor unable to breathe. What had he tripped over? He rose to hands and knees and crawled toward a lump half buried in the sand. He turned his back to the wind and lowered the cloth from his eyes. By the Gods

"Jester?" He rolled the familiar body over and peeked under the headdress. His eyes were closed, but he was breathing. "Talk to me!" he screamed, grit invading his dry mouth.

"Boss? That you?"

"Who else were you expecting?"

"Kamito, I lost him, but I think he's close."

Hawk removed the pack from his back, pulled out the rope and tied it around Jester's waist. "Don't move." He walked straight out from Jester until the fifty-foot rope stopped him. All he could do was walk circles around Jester and pray he'd find Kamito. After each revolution he reeled the rope in one arm's length.

With cloth over his face he walked, searching with his feet for anything buried in the sand. Sand, the only thing he could smell, taste or feel. It was next to useless, he thought, as drifts formed and dispersed in the blink of an eye. On the eighth time around, he kicked something and stopped.

"Kamito?" He heard a groan and followed the sound a few feet to his left. Bracing against the wind, he ventured a look and was relieved to find his ship-mate. "Can you stand?"

"Jester, I lost him. A gust knocked me down. I lost my grip and..."

"He's fine." Hawk helped Kamito to his feet and tied his end of the rope around Kamito's waist. "Stay close." Hawk wound the rope as he led the way back to Jester. Finally he reached Jester's prone body. He grabbed Jester under the arms and pulled him to his feet. He draped Jester's arm over his shoulder and steadied him with an arm around his waist.

"Is he all right?"

The wind and sand had nearly absorbed Kamito's voice, but he did hear him. "Yeah." He adjusted his hold. "Tie the rope around your waist and I'll tie this end around mine. We can't afford to lose each other. I'll hang on to Jester." He waited while Kamito took the rope from Jester's waist and tied it around his. "Let's go."

Hawk secured the fabric over Jester's face, then his. He clamped his teeth together, took a deep breath and started walking. Was he heading in the right direction? He had no way to tell. Not even a primitive compass could work in the squall, and certainly not a tracking device. He had to rely on instinct and prayer.

Time wore on as he led his two crewmen aimlessly, the velocity of the storm worsening, if that were possible. Jester groaned from time to time while he dragged his feet in the sand. He was barely conscious, but still moving. Half carrying Jester took its toll on his strength. The walk from the shuttle to town had taken a little over two time-units. He paused, moved his wrist to his face and tried to focus on the glowing numbers. Four time-units! They should have found the shuttle by now. He lowered Jester to the ground and caught Kamito's shoulders as he walked into him.

"We've missed our mark." Hawk groaned and sank to the ground along with his men, all three of them too exhausted from fighting the wind to continue. "We'll rest." Hawk lay next to his men and hoped they would not be buried alive if he fell asleep. Fatigue gripped his muscles and his mind. He closed his eyes, seeing the same darkness he saw with them open. Their only hope was rain.

***

Kylie heard the door open and rushed to the bars that remained unmovable.

"Have you calmed down?" Beggar asked.

"Yes. Let me out...please,"

The restraining iron bars rolled to the side and she stepped into the hall. "Why do you look so worried?" Beggar averted his eyes, but didn't answer. A chill ran down her spine. "Dear stars, they haven't returned, have they?"

"No." Beggar turned and walked back toward the control room.

Kylie hurried behind, wishing she could stop her heart from racing out of control. It pounded against her chest so fast she had to stop to catch her breath. The tears she held back stung her eyes. She stopped abruptly in the entrance at the sight of Beggar, Dylor, Mikos and Chase all quiet in their seats, their heads bowed, their hands clenched in their laps, knuckles white. "Is anyone going to tell me what happened? Beggar?"

"There's been no word from the shuttle. Our scanners indicate empty space."

"They're dead?" She rushed toward the port view window and stared out over the star studded darkness for some sign of life.

"I didn't say that. We just haven't heard from them."

"That's it. We have to go after them. They're in trouble, I can feel it." She turned toward the men behind her. "Please, help me save your

Captain!"

"We would all go if we thought it would do any good." Beggar escorted Kylie to a flight chair and eased her trembling body down. "There is one thing we know."

"Then for heavens sake, tell me!" She meant to yell, but her voice was a mere whisper, full of trepidation.

"There's a desert squall in the dead zone. The winds carry so much sand they disable all communication equipment. Nothing can function during one of those storms."

"Including Hawk." Her head began to throb. She'd heard about those killer storms, but never gave them a second thought since they did not happen on Estra. "What are you going to do?"

Beggar shook his head and stared at the floor. "I've decided to give them four time-units from the time the storm abates. If they haven't returned by then, we're heading for Estra."

"Agreed." At least it was a reprieve, even though she wished he'd given them more time. Were they hurt? Lost? Captured? She refused to think of all the possibilities. Hawk was alive, she was sure of it. If anything happened to him she would know. They shared a new, unexplainable connection since they made love. As silly as it sounded, she felt linked to him.

"I'm going to my room. Call me if there's any word?"

Beggar nodded. "I will."

She hurried down the hall to Hawk's cabin, secured the door and threw herself on the bed, wiping tears that had escaped on the way. It might be useless, but she decided to try and make contact with Hawk's mind. If it worked with the Delphins, there was a chance it would work with Hawk.

He did not have to be close for her to remember his frequency, her entire body remembered him. She had never attempted communication like this before, but suddenly the impulse was overwhelming. Rolling to her back, she closed her eyes and concentrated, calling his name in her mind, screaming for him to answer.

It was all she could do.

***

"Sira?" Konar was surprised to hear from her since he thought she'd been arrested. She was good.

"Konar, where have you been? I've tried to reach you for several time-units."

"I had a meeting. What's going on there?"

"You've got to get me out of here before Throm puts me away for good! Hawk's gone. No one seems to know where, or how he came up missing."

"I've seen him and he has Winn's journal." Konar took a deep breath. "Can you break Nyles out of the holding cell?"

"I think so, why?"

"I'll send a ship to pick both of you up. Follow Hawk to Spectra. I want that journal."

"Fine. Just hurry before Throm feeds both of us to a sharkus!"

Konar shut down the link and paced the length of his quarters, glancing at the star chart. Sira was clever, but could she intercept Hawk? He had to put his faith in her. Soon the cure would be his, and his alone. Only then would he possess the true power of the galaxy.

***

Hawk's eyes flew open and he coughed. He could have sworn Kylie called his name. Dreams certainly could be real. Judging from the amount of sand accumulated on his back he had not slept long, otherwise he would have been buried alive. He shook Kamito and Jester. "Get up, we need to keep moving." He barely heard their groans above the howling wind. He stood and helped both men to their feet.

"Keep the ropes on." Hawk's gaze was drawn to the skies when he saw a flash of light through the fabric covering his face. Could it be? A loud crack of thunder was music to his ears. "Come on, guys. Luck just fell in our laps." Welcome rain pelted his back.

The thought of water brought Kylie to mind, the woman who delighted in keeping him wet. How he missed her smile, her sweet scent, and her body. Everything about her was perfect, and he planned to tell her just that when he saw her again. Had she worried about him? He laughed. She'd probably driven Beggar out of his mind, which would not be hard. Jester had been doing it for more annual-cycles than he wanted to count.

Wind driven rain settled the sand and soaked them to the bone. The heavy robes grew burdensome, hindering every step, dragging in the mushy ground. Hawk hated the God-forsaken desert. A bolt of lightning cut through the dark sky ahead, and he saw something shiny in the distance.

He thanked every deity he'd ever heard of as he ran toward the shuttle, pulling Jester and Kamito behind him, ignoring their protests. Luck had smiled on him once again.

The moment they reached the shuttle he pulled the hatch open, climbed in, and settled into the pilot's seat. "Strap in." He prepared for departure as quickly as humanly possible. He glanced at Jester and Kamito to be sure they were ready, then pressed the ignition button. Nothing. He pushed it again, pelting rain the only audible sound. "Damn!" He unbuckled the safety harness and headed for the hatch. "Stay put."

Jester and Kamito nodded as he opened the door and stepped outside into the storm. He knew sand had blocked the thrusters intake, which meant the engines would not come to life until they could breathe. Inching his way to the back of the craft in the driving rain, he found the problem. It was no longer sand. He stuck both arms into the blocked opening and pulled handfuls of thick mud toward him, the heavy, wet gritty gunk stuck to his skin. One more reminder of why he hated Andor.

Why he'd been angry for his imposed exile from this desolate, antagonistic pile of dust he'd never know. He should consider it a favor, and he would if it wasn't for the murder and treason charges against him. He moved to the other side and cleaned away the obstructions as best he could.

Lightning struck close by and temporarily turned the moon-cycle to a sun-cycle, blinding him as he followed the contour of the ship back to the hatch, fighting the wind driven rain that stung his face. Actually, the sun-cycle had begun, but the clouds were so dark and thick it appeared to be the height of a moon-cycle. He couldn't curse the rain that saved their lives. A few more time-units of inhaling dust, even through the filter effect of the material would have killed them.

The hatch sprang open and Jester grabbed his hand and pulled him inside. "Thanks." He returned to his seat and buckled in.

"Boss?" Jester stared at Hawk as he removed the rain-soaked headdress. "Do you think they waited?"

"Probably." He smiled. "But I bet there was one horrendous clash between Beggar and Kylie."

Jester laughed. "Sure hope Cutie won."

"So do I." Hawk pressed the ignition button. Jester and Kamito's jubilation sounded louder than the engines winding up.

"Thank the Gods!" Kamito yelled. "Good job, Captain."

"Congratulate me when we're safely docked in *The Redemption*."

***

"No!" Kylie screamed. "You can't leave now. You promised to wait four time-units!"

It's already been five. We can't wait any longer. Hawk would be furious if he knew we'd waited this long. Now strap yourself in, or I'll do it for you," Beggar ordered."

She didn't like the tone of his voice. This was Hawk's ship and he had no right leaving him behind. Beggar glared at her and her fists clenched. "I will not sit here and let you abandon Hawk and his men." Hawk and Jester needed her. She had no idea where the shuttle bay was, but she intended to find it. The moment Beggar turned his head, she jumped from her seat and ran down the hall. Two strong arms grabbed her from behind.

"Oh no you don't!"

"Let me go!" Kylie kicked and screamed, but Beggar did not budge. He carried her down the passage she recognized all too well. "No! You will not put me back in that cell!" She bent her head and bit his arm.

"Why you little..."

She felt his fist connect with her jaw and her head swam, a nauseous, faint feeling numbed her body. "You'll pay for that." She tried to yell a few choice words, but her voice failed as he tossed her into the bleak room with bars across the front.

Hawk. She silently screamed his name, searching the black void she felt in his absence. Still, she knew he was alive. How could Beggar be so cold and uncaring as to leave him behind? Did he want *The Redemption* for himself? Was he working for, or against Hawk? Betrayal was not out of the question, especially since the cure was aboard ship.

She was thinking crazy thoughts again. Beggar was following Hawk's orders, which meant he was loyal. She had seen true pain in his eyes. As far as locking her up, well, she had not given him much choice. She would have taken a shuttle and gone to look for Hawk. It might be suicide, but what other option was left?

Tears rolled down her cheeks. "I love you, Hawk," she screamed in her mind. It was useless to think he heard her, but she could offer little else. Reclining on the cot, she closed her eyes. If she concentrated on Hawk long enough, maybe she could guide him back to her.

Engines roared and the ship lurched into movement. Beggar was really leaving! Her heart sank and she gasped for breath as if she were being suffocated by lack of air. She had allowed Hawk into her heart, and the pain of losing him viciously ripped through her. Why hadn't he come back? By the galaxy, why?

***

"Beggar, slow this buggy down. I've got a blip on the scanner," Mikos said.

"Power down." Beggar approached the screen. "Could it be Hawk, or a patrol?"

"Can't tell yet. There's one ship, and it's small. Has to be him."

Beggar pressed the com. "Open the docking bay."

"Yes, sir," Dylor replied.

"How long?" Beggar asked Mikos.

"Three minutes." Mikos studied the screen and pointed. "It must be Hawk. There's four larger craft hot on the tail of the first small one."

"Prepare to jump as soon as he's aboard."

"Yes, sir."

Beggar called Dylor in docking bay. "The instant he's inside, close and prepare to jump."

"Yes, sir." Dylor stood with his hand on the button, staring through the observation window into space. He tapped his foot and craned his neck. "Here he comes. Contact in fifteen seconds."

CHAPTER TWENTY-TWO

Hawk smiled when he saw *The Redemption*. She never looked sweeter. The four attack vessels on his tail were too close for comfort. They had already fired several shots and it was impossible to out-run them in the shuttle. He headed for the docking bay, approaching faster than he should.

The shuttle hit the inside wall of the bay with a jarring crash. Before he could catch his breath, he felt the unmistakable thrust of *'the drop'*. Thank the stars Beggar had been ready. Suddenly everything rattled right down to his teeth. The fighters would have hit their mark if *The Redemption*'s maneuver had failed to remove them from their location instantly.

"Is it safe?" Jester inquired, reaching for the buckle on his harness.

"Yeah." Hawk released his restraint, stood, and followed his men out the side hatch.

"Thank the Gods!" Dylor yelled, running toward his companions.

"You should have been gone by now," Hawk grumbled, silently relieved his men had disobeyed his orders.

Dylor slapped Hawk on the back. "But you're glad we're not. Right, Captain?"

"I'd better have a word with Beggar." With confident strides he walked to the control room, not surprised at the contrite look on Beggar's face when he entered.

"Captain," Beggar greeted with a salute. "It wasn't entirely my fault. The woman, sir, she, aah..."

"She what?" Hawk growled.

"She insisted we wait. I appeased her as long as I could before I...aah..."

"What?" Hawk stared at Beggar's shifting eyes, knowing he was not going to like the answer. "Where is she?"

"In the holding cell, sir."

"You'd better have a good reason, or I swear, I'll tear you apart with my bare hands!"

"When I tried to make way, she ran toward the bay. She was going to take a shuttle and go after you. She fought hard."

Beggar held out his forearm and pulled up the sleeve to expose teeth marks in his skin. The bite location was black and blue, and had welted up pretty good. He probably would have done the same as Beggar under the same circumstances.

"She attacked like a wild, feline-monster, sir. I didn't mean to strike her, but..."

Hawk abruptly turned and ran toward the cell. He'd deal with Beggar later. All he wanted to do was hold Kylie in his arms. He reached the door, his heart racing as he impatiently waited for the door to open. His breath caught in his throat when he saw her sprawled on the floor, hair tousled, eyes red, one cheek bruised and swollen. She also looked green around the gills from *'the drop'*. He punched in the bar release code and rushed to her side. He knelt on the floor and scooped her into his arms and cradled her against his chest. "What have they done to you, my sweet Amica?

"Oh, Hawk." She flung her arms around his neck. "I never thought I'd see you again!"

Before he could answer her mouth was on his, and she instantly brought his burning need to life. He returned her kiss, which caused her to melt in his arms. Every movement of her tongue sent surges of blood to his groin. If he did not end the kiss now he would have her right here in the holding cell. That would not be good since this room was always under surveillance. He pulled his head back. "You missed me." She nodded. "For a kiss like that I'd gladly leave again."

"No. I will not allow it."

"You're being a bit possessive, but it stirs my blood." He stood and carried her out of the cell and out the corridor. She nestled against him while he carried her to his quarters, and he knew how right it felt. He'd missed her, and the unmistakable desire to keep her with him forever played through his mind, no matter how futile a thought it might be.

He laid her on the bed as the door swooshed closed. "Sweet Amica." He knelt beside the bed and stroked her hair. "I missed your smile, your scent," he sniffed her hair, "your touch...I...missed you." A smile lit her face and he noticed a naughty little twinkle in her eyes. "Yes, that's the smile I missed."

"If I'd known what effect a separation would have, I might have sent you away myself, fearless warrior."

"Would you now?" He kissed the side of her neck, then nibbled on her earlobe. His hair fell forward and grains of sand fell on the blue fabric of her jumpsuit. He raised his head. "During the storm, when I wasn't sure we'd make it back, I could have sworn I heard you call my name."

"Really?" She chuckled. "You're more like the Delphins than I thought."

"You would compare me to a fish?" He watched laughter dance in her emerald eyes. She was a beauty to be treasured, a rare gem to be cherished.

"No silly. I did call you." Kylie stroked his cheek. "I used the same technique I use with the Delphins to send messages to their minds."

Hawk grinned. "I *was* soaked to the bone, but I didn't turn into a fish."

She ran her fingers through his hair and sand trickled onto her neck. "A fish no, a snaketor or lizard maybe." She grinned. "Don't question it, just believe."

"With you, Amica, anything is possible." He pressed his lips to hers, tasting her sweetness, reveling in her sensuality. She offered something he'd never had. Love. The urge to tell her he loved her consumed him. Yet to tell her would mean a promise he could not keep, and a struggle for existence he could not let her endure. He would settle for the moment, and every moment they had left together.

When he pulled back her expression puzzled him. He gently touched her bruised cheek. "What happened to your face?" With one finger he traced the outline of her jaw.

"It's nothing."

"Tell me. I'll see to it Beggar pays for..."

"No, Hawk. He did what he had to do." She averted her gaze. "I was sick with worry, and I'm afraid I acted unprofessional." She looked into his eyes. "Childish actually. I should have had more faith in you. Please, don't punish Beggar for doing his job. I really did give him a hard time."

"But he hit you, and there's no excuse for that."

"He only hit me after I bit him." She dropped her eyes. "Please, tell Beggar I'm sorry." She looked up again. "But I'd do it again if it meant saving your life."

"He never should have laid a hand on you!"

She pressed two fingers against his lips. "I fought him. He knew how determined I was to come after you, and even I knew how foolish it was. He simply stopped me from risking the mission. He was following your orders, Hawk. He is devoted to you, you know that. It was my fault. Really."

"Be that as it may, he will still feel my wrath. No man touches my woman!"

"Your woman?"

"Yes, Amica." He slid the zipper of her jumpsuit half-way down. Her hands pressed against him and sand fell to the bare skin between her breasts. "I think my woman needs to take me to the shower before I bury her in sand." The need in her eyes made his heart pound faster. "You don't object to being *my woman*, do you?"

Kylie rose from the bed and took Hawk's hand. She led him into the lav. "I'm honored." She untied the sash around the tattered remains of the desert robe. "There isn't much left of this." When she pulled the tattered disguise over his head, sand poured to the floor. "I'm afraid to ask what happened." She found the buttons of a green shirt. "Nor will I ask where this odd fitting uniform came from."

"Let's just say the soldier I ran into didn't need it as much as I did." He grasped her hands when she reached for his belt. "You're what saved me. If it hadn't been for your voice in my mind I might not be here."

"My sweet, fearsome warrior." She unbuckled the pants and they fell to the floor. "I would have done more, but..."

"Do more now." Hawk reached in the shower and turned on the water then pulled Kylie to him. He brushed his lips across hers and she moaned seductively. Steam from the shower billowed in the small room. He kissed her and lifted her to him. Without further thought he pulled her into the shower.

"Hawk, I still have my clothes on!"

"That--I can fix." He finished unzipping the jumpsuit and peeled it slowly down her body, then kissed his way back up from her ankles to her throat. "First you get the sand off me, then I will ease the tension in your body."

"I'm not tense." Kylie raised her eyebrows.

Hawk ran his hands down her arms, then up from her waist, testing every muscle beneath his fingertips. "You need to relax, and I'm just the man to teach you." She flashed him a smile that sent a rush of blood to his groin. He was more than ready for her, but he wanted this to be a long, slow moon-cycle to remember.

She pumped liquid soap into the palms of her hands and began to massage his body from the neck down. She lingered on his shoulders before running her soft hands over his biceps and forearms. The spicy, soapy scent tickled his nose as bubbles floated up with the steam. "Be sure to give the same care to every muscle." He groaned when she slapped his bare butt.

He closed his eyes and savored the velvety-touch of her hands on him. She was all he ever wanted. Why she offered herself so willingly to a wanted man he might never understand, but he relished what she gave. The distinct aroma of flowers made him open his eyes an instant before she covered his head in lather. He closed his eyes again while shampoo slid down his forehead. "That isn't my shampoo."

"It's mine. I thought you could use a little sweetening up."

She giggled when he made a face at her, but it was worth it to hear the enchanting sound of her laughter. Her fingers massaged his scalp like a professional, the effect pure heaven after his bout with the desert. Even with his eyes closed, his mouth found the taut nipple that had teased his chest while she worked. Now it was his turn. His tongue circled and tempted, while he waited for her response. Then she moaned deep inside her throat. He took suds from his hair and rubbed them over her stomach while he explored her other breast.

He would cherish her till the sun-cycle he died. She represented all that was good about life, and he would hold her in his heart forever. His hands roamed down her hips until he found the mat of hair between her thighs. His fingers toyed with her until her moans drove him to the edge. He could stand the luscious agony no longer. He rinsed the soap from his hair, his mouth still on her firm breast.

Slowly he released her and stepped back to admire her perfection. Her flawless skin was rosy pink from the heat of the spray, but he intended to make her hotter still. He knelt in front of her and his mouth explored the womanhood he craved. Only she could extinguish the fire that burned deep in his soul.

How could he ever let her go? Even when she was away from him she was a part of him. She would be with him always. Suddenly he thought he heard her say, "I love you, Hawk." He found her delicate nub and she rewarded him with a loud purr. Then her mouth opened and he felt her spasm. Her head fell back and she gripped his shoulders tightly.

"What did I hear you say?" He eased her down onto his lap as he sat on the shower floor. Her eyes widened when his swollen manhood pressed for entry and gently slid into her. He didn't move.

"I said...I love you, Hawk."

"I heard you in my mind."

"The same as I called you when you were lost."

"My sweet Amica. I've been lost my whole life, but no longer." He kissed her gently, sucking in her lower lip then releasing it. "I love you,

Kylie." This time she kissed him with more passion than he dreamed possible, and more feeling than he could have hoped for. He moved inside her, first slowly, then faster. This was not sex. It was sharing, soul to soul, heart to heart.

The love he felt for her could never die or be broken. She was his now and forever. She might be ripped from his life, but never from his heart. In his mind he screamed, *"I love you, Kylie."* He never wanted to hurt her. Yes, love could hurt, of that he was certain, but the love between them, this moment, was special and enduring. If only they could stay this close for eternity.

***

"What did you do to her, Boss? No one sleeps that long!"

Hawk stared at the satirical smile on Jester's face. "I'm going to ignore that question."

"All right." Jester continued punching keys on the computer-board. "How's Beggar's black eye?"

"Another stupid question."

"I didn't think your conversation would be so physical." Jester cringed at Hawk's glare. "I'll try to find a safer subject." Jester propped his feet on the desk. "What's the plan for Spectra?" We'll be there in less than a time-unit." He stared at Hawk. "Or have you been too busy the past two sun-cycles to think about it?" His hands flew up to shield his face. "Okay, okay! Take it easy." Jester covered his nose as Hawk's fist moved closer. "I'll quit."

"I'm only taking you and Kylie with me. I don't want to bring any more attention to our expedition than necessary. I've already instructed the crew. They're only to interfere if Kylie's life is in danger should anything happen to us."

"Glad to know I'm expendable!"

"Have you packed everything we'll need?"

"Yup. All's ready, if you are." Jester rubbed his forehead. "I'm still surprised you're taking Kylie with you."

"So am I." He half groaned and half growled at Jester. It was out of character for him to include Kylie in anything that could be dangerous, but considering what happened between her and Beggar the last time, he had little choice. Plus, there was his selfish need as well. He could not bear to be separated from her, but he'd never tell his crew about that reason. "I'll wake Kylie. Meet you in the shuttle bay in one time-unit."

"Olly-dolly!"

Hawk laughed to himself as he walked toward his cabin. Even

though Jester annoyed him at times, he never ceased to be amusing.

***

Kylie paced the length of the cabin. Hawk had said next to nothing about their quest on Spectra, and she was getting nervous. Something about finding an old psychic woman who knew how to translate Professor Winn's journal. Hawk promised they would take the cure to Estra as soon as it was translated, and she was more than anxious to make that trip.

There had been little time to think about her parents. All she could do was pray the disease had not yet progressed to their minds. There should still be a quarter-annual-cycle window left before the situation became critical, however, some people showed signs of brain deterioration quicker than the normal half-annual-cycle incubation period.

The door slid open with a whoosh, and she turned in time to see Hawk stride in, a serious look etched on his handsome face. She smiled. They'd spent nearly all their travel time from Andor to Spectra in bed.

"Glad to see you're ready." Hawk stepped toward her and kissed the tip of her nose. "Here." He handed her a small round disk. "Keep this in your pocket at all times. It's a transmitter. If you should be in serious danger, squeeze it twice to activate a distress signal."

She took the small object from his hand and dropped it in her zippered pocket. "Why the somber expression?"

"I don't like putting you in jeopardy, and I'm not sure what we'll encounter. I've steered clear of Spectra for five annual-cycles."

"Do you think someone will recognize you?"

"That's always a possibility. I'm never safe." He took her hand. "I'm worried because Redmon made this too easy. Something isn't right. It feels like a trap, and I don't want anything to happen to you because of me."

"I can handle myself. Besides, no one wants *me*."

"Don't be so sure. You could easily become a weapon to capture me." He shook his head. "Why do you think I've lived the way I have for so long? No one is safe with me."

"You make me feel safe." She slid her hand up his arm and across his shoulder to thread her fingers in his long, dark hair.

"I'll protect you with my life."

"That's what bothers me." She smiled. "Let's go. I'm afraid if we stay here any longer, we'll be back in that bed. It could be embarrassing when Jester comes looking for us."

"You do tempt me." He brushed his lips across her cheek. "You're right. We'd better go before my thoughts turn to action."

***

Hawk opened the shuttle hatch and stepped outside into the thick, oppressive humid air of the Spectran jungle. He offered Kylie his hand and helped her out of the craft. Jester followed so close he almost stepped on her heels.

"Wish we could have used the port like other humans." Jester juggled three backpacks, but stumbled on the soft, damp ground.

"You know Cyron is the only planet where we're warmly received." Hawk took his pack from Jester and slipped his arms through the straps.

"But there's guys there that make you look small, and docile, Boss, and that's no easy feat!" Jester grinned.

Kylie cleared her throat. "Are you two finished?"

"Quite." He secured Kylie's pack on her back. "It's a long hike to the mountains."

"According to my calculations," Jester began, "it will take approximately twelve time-units by foot if we average fifteen miles per time-unit. If we fall behind the prescribed speed, we will lengthen our trip by..."

"Jester!"

"Sorry, Boss. Thought you wanted precise information."

Hawk led the way out of the clearing to the edge of the thick vegetation that surrounded them. "Where's the machete?" He took the weapon from Jester. "So much for your average speed. We'll be lucky to make five miles before dark."

He began to hack a path through the over-vegetated terrain. Even the sun had difficulty penetrating through the dense foliage, which offered a slight reprieve from the heat of the sun. Sweat ran down his face. With every few steps, his clothes became wetter, his skin stickier. This mission had run the gambit of extremes. From underwater, to a dry desolate desert, and now an overly humid tropical maze that refused human passage.

Time-units dragged, and every muscle in his body screamed while he hacked a path through strange looking plants, leaves, small trees and vines, all the while constantly swatting insects that stung with a vengeance and left big, red welts on his skin. He should have left his shirt on, but it had become uncomfortably sweat-soaked and obstructed his movements.

A quick glance back at Kylie confirmed the heat and humidity were

216

taking their toll on her. She'd been a trooper, not one complaint had escaped her lips, which was more than he could say for Jester.

It was difficult enough to make headway when he could see, and now that the sun-cycle was nearly gone, he had to find a place to camp. The faint sound of water made him pause. He listened intently for a few seconds then proceeded in the direction of the trickling sound, hacking faster, pressing harder. A waterfall? The thought of diving in a cool pond drove him faster.

"Hawk, you'd better slow down before you drop," Kylie warned.

"A few more feet." He swung the machete back and forth, cutting away vines and branches. Kylie's gasp made him turn. "Are you all right?"

"Look!"

Hawk felt her hands on his wet shoulders and looked up. Relief coursed through him at the sight of the cascading waterfall. He rushed to the water's edge and knelt, scooping a handful of water. It smelled good. "Jester!" He turned to look for his partner. "Run a check."

Jester took off his pack, removed a small vial and knelt beside Hawk. He immersed the tube into the water, then held it high and swirled the contents. "It's good, Boss."

"Just watch out for snakes and..."

"Don't remind me what could live here."

With a laugh, Hawk stood, stripped off his remaining clothes and boots, then jumped into the cool water. When he surfaced, he saw a white flash sail by him and land a few feet away. Jester surfaced, pushing hair from his face. "You undressed in front of Kylie?"

"I'm too hot to be modest." Jester glared at his friend. "It didn't bother you to strip in front of her."

"That's different."

"No it's not."

Hawk groaned when Jester's hand skimmed the surface, shoving water into his face. "You'll pay for that!" He lunged for Jester. With his hands on Jester's shoulders, he shoved him to the bottom of the small pool.

CHAPTER TWENTY-THREE

Kylie watched in amusement while the two men frolicked in the pond, playing silly games only men would play. They were quite a sight. Jester's white skin pressed against Hawk's sun-kissed bronzed color as the two men wrestled like boys. Hawk's strong, well-defined muscles glistened. Jester did not stand a prayer against Hawk's overwhelming strength. Jester was no slouch, but he was no match for the massive warrior.

A chill ran down her spine at the thought of those brawny arms around her, pulling her close, and guiding her movements while they made love. The heat of a blush burned her cheeks. Hawk turned his gaze on her and smiled, as if he'd read her mind.

Hawk extended his hand. "Join us, Amica."

"Yeah, the water's great," Jester added.

"Turn your back, Jester. The lady wishes to undress."

"Only if you turn yours."

Kylie laughed at Jester, especially when Hawk scowled, but he turned his back along with his friend. She quickly disposed of her pack, then her clothes before diving in and surfacing next to Hawk's naked body. The sensation sent butterflies dancing through her stomach. Knowing they could not act on their desires made every movement, every touch, and every glance even more erotic.

Hawk swam close and whispered, "You're driving me mad."

She leaned toward his ear. "I want you."

Jester thrashed his way toward the waterfall. When he was a safe distance away, she felt Hawk's arm snake around her waist and pull her close, her nipples rubbing against the rough hair of his chest.

"I should have left Jester on the ship."

"We need him." Her finger traced the firm set of his jaw, the stubble of his beard tickling her skin.

"Not right now."

His arousal pressed against her abdomen and his breathing quickened. "I'm glad Jester's here. I wouldn't want you to get bored with me." His lips met hers with a ferocious hunger that sent waves of desire coursing through her. Memories of him inside her burned in her mind.

His hands found her buttocks and he pulled her tighter against him. "Do I feel like a man who is bored with you?"

"Actually, you feel quite..."

"I see you!" Jester yelled.

"Damn," Hawk grumbled, releasing Kylie.

"You two should take a look behind the falls." Jester laughed as he swam closer. "Just don't forget to come back. I'll set up camp."

She opened her mouth to answer, but Hawk pulled her the short distance across the pool toward the falling water. The fine mist filled her lungs. Her heart swelled with love as he guided her behind the thick curtain and kissed her with so much passion she thought she might drown.

Her legs wrapped around him, and she gasped when his hard warmth entered her. "Hawk!"

"He sent us here to be alone, and I don't plan to miss the opportunity." His hips rotated as his movements quickened.

"You're bad!" She tilted her head back and a slight groan escaped, only to be muffled by the roaring cascade. "Whatever you do, don't stop."

"Now who's bad?" He growled before covering her lips with his.

Kylie held on to the moss covered rocks behind her and reveled in Hawk's masculinity. Yes, she was behaving badly, but where Hawk was concerned, she had no will to stop herself. All that mattered was making love to the one man who possessed her heart and soul.

***

"Thought you two drowned!" Jester greeted. "Dinner's ready. Such as it is. Can't say much for these HS-packs."

"What's an HS-pack?" Kylie took the unusual looking bag from Jester.

"Hot survival-pack." Hawk grinned at the look on her face which was accentuated by the green glow of the luma-stone. "Here," he ripped off the seal and laughed as she let out a squeal at the instant heat generated inside the bag.

"That's amazing."

"Not when you've eaten them as much as we have," Jester complained.

"You have wonderful food on your ship," she replied.

"We usually spend more time off the ship than on. But Jester likes to complain, don't you, buddy?"

Kylie slapped her neck, removed a blood-sucking insect and tossed in on the ground. "I hate bugs!"

"Estra, your planet of origin," Jester began, "has 6,985,482 varieties of insects, a mere 651 less than Spectra."

"Bugs are bugs. I don't care how many varieties there are, I don't like them."

"Neither do I," Jester agreed. "Just thought you'd like to know Spectra has even more."

"I'd like to know when we can get back to Estra." She smiled and glanced at Hawk, as if he had an answer.

"Amica, I wish I could tell you, but you cannot time a mission such as ours. There are too many variables. Even ones Jester hasn't taken into consideration with all his careful planning and analysis."

"Are you saying I've fallen down on my job?" Jester groaned.

"No, but you always forget to factor in human nature. We have no idea if this woman we seek will agree to cooperate. Friendly persuasion can take time."

"Never thought of that," Jester admitted.

Kylie swallowed the last bite of food from her pouch. "Hawk's right, Jester. We know nothing about this woman, except that she knows the language Professor Winn used." She stuffed the empty bag into her backpack. "How did Winn know this language?"

"Vanefca?" Hawk watched her nod. "I don't know, but I'm sure he didn't plan to die with the secret." Kylie's eyes begged for his touch, or was he reading more into an expression than he should? No. He'd seen that look too many times over the last few sun-cycles. That was the look of a woman in love, who needed the touch of her man.

"We'd better turn in if we're going to get an early start," Jester suggested.

Three metallic fabric sleep packs all in a row glowed in the light of the luma-stone. He wished he was alone with Kylie, but he did need a rest after the exhausting sun-cycle he'd spent manicuring the jungle. Of course, he always had energy for her.

Kylie leaned toward Hawk. "Will we run into any settlements or cities?"

"None that I know of." Hawk handed Kylie a drink pack. "Those who collect bounties on men like me hang out in every city, hoping for a lead." He smiled. "My life commands an extremely high price."

"Don't make light of it, Hawk. I worry about you."

He wanted to tell her he was not worth her worry. If he could not clear himself, sooner or later, he would be caught, and his execution would take place. It had been a mistake to love Kylie, yet he could not help himself. The troubled look on her face was a minor reflection of the pain he was sure to cause her before this was over. He prayed loving her would not destroy them both.

***

Kylie woke before the sun fully rose. She eased out of the silver, metallic fabric quietly, then walked to the waterfall and sat on the rocks by the edge of the pool. Sleep evaded her, knowing Hawk lay inches away, untouchable. She'd heard him toss and turn most of the moon-cycle. Had he wanted her as much as she wanted him? From his behavior in the water last sun-cycle, she had no reason to question his desire.

She bent and splashed water on her face. Images of her parents played in her mind's eye. Were they becoming forgetful yet? If not, how soon? Could she return with the cure in time to spare them the agonizing degradation of Genesis Disorder?

Hawk was the only reason this ordeal remained tolerable. He'd been there for her since her crash, helping in every way he could, loving her every available moment they had together. How could their relationship progress past what was here and now? Hawk constantly reminded her of the precarious circumstances of his survival, and she'd pushed the problem of her genetics to the darkest recesses of her mind. It had been stupid to think that forgetting who she was could erase the inevitable. She could never life-mate, or have children.

Casual. She had been taught since her teenage annual-cycles to keep all relationships casual. She had failed miserably this time. If she had it all to do over again, she would still choose to lose her heart to Hawk. Better to have experienced love with Hawk, than never to know love at all.

Could they let each other go their separate ways when this was over? She had to let him go. If he ever cleared his name, he would want a family, a family he deserved; a family he could only have without her.

Her parents had told her she was lucky to be alive. Women scientists who became pregnant had to abort, for the good of the unborn child. Her mother had been a rare case that beat the one in a thousand odds.

Was she lucky? She was alive, but she feared she might die the sun-cycle she said good-by to Hawk. Were the fates really that cruel? Had they sent her a man to love only to take him away? Hawk would remain in her heart forever, but it would not stop the loneliness for the rest of her life. Nothing could.

"There you are."

She turned toward Hawk's handsome, smiling face so vibrant in the rays of early dawn. His blue eyes were inviting and sensual. She wanted to kiss him and spend the sun-cycle wrapped in his arms.

Hawk squatted and began to fill the empty canteens. "You're quiet this sun-cycle."

"Sorry. I was thinking about my parents."

"What are they like?"

Kylie smiled. "My mother's a worrier, constantly trying to make things better for everyone. My father spends most of his time calming her down. They're a perfect couple really."

"Like us?"

"We're far from the perfect couple, Hawk."

He capped the canteens, stood, then embraced Kylie. "I think you're perfect."

"Sure, that's why you were so nice to me when we first met."

"I thought you were a spy."

"From what you tell me, if I were a spy, I would have made moves on you that first moon-cycle."

"Instead, you wanted to kill me." He laughed. "I wasn't nice, and I apologize. It's just that I wanted to kiss you the moment you opened your eyes." His hand cupped her cheek. "I couldn't very well have done that, now could I?"

"I might have killed you if you had."

"What about now?"

"I'll kill you if you don't!"

He pulled her close and she closed her eyes as his lips gently closed over hers. Every time he kissed her, her stomach fluttered and she felt herself melt in his arms.

"Lighten up, Boss! The poor woman can't breathe."

Kylie smiled when Hawk groaned and released his hold. "Good sun-cycle, Jester."

Jester chuckled. "I sent you to fill the canteens." He glanced at the empty containers on the shore. "Did you think they'd fill themselves?"

Hawk mumbled under his breath as he shoved the canteens below the surface and waited while the air bubbled out.

Jester clapped his hands. "I've got everything packed and ready to go."

"Good." Hawk glared at his friend.

"Not so good. I contacted the ship and they reported a storm heading our direction. High winds and heavy rains."

"I'm glad I have bad luck or I wouldn't have any at all. How long before it hits?"

"A couple of time-units. At least it's not a sand-squall."

"Don't remind me." Hawk glanced at Kylie. "Ready?"

"Let's do it."

***

Hawk hacked away at the overgrowth of vegetation. Would the jungle never end? Big leaves, little leaves and vines fell beneath the wide, sharp blade of the machete. Surely the foothills were close. Hawk's arms ached from the time-units of whacking a path through the impermeable jungle. Even the weather worked against them.

The rain had started over two time-units ago, and it was taking its soggy toll on them all. The driving winds cooled the temperature, and every time he glanced back at Kylie, he could see her lips chatter. One sun-cycle he'd like to settle on a planet without too much water, or too many deserts, or severe weather. Was there such a place? No, he decided while he wrestled with an obstinate tree branch.

"Boss!"

He turned at the sound of Jester's worried cry. By the Gods! A giant snaktor hung from a thick branch over Kylie's head. The slimy creature slithered its body down so it now stared her in the eye. If she moved, she was dead. He eased his way toward the giant serpent that probably outweighed him by three-hundred weight-units. The scaly reptilians were hard to kill. For every part of their body that was severed, they could reproduce, and the head could still deliver a lethal, venomous bite even if he had no body left.

The only way to stop the creature was to remove its front fang so it would drown in its own poison. Thank the heavens Kylie played her part of a statue to perfection while he approached the snaketor's back. Its head moved from side to side, while its long, forked-tongue struck and recoiled in a rhythm that hypnotized the unsuspecting victim.

Kylie had to be the bravest woman he'd ever seen to stand still and not scream. He'd seen warriors make the deadly mistake she seemed determined to avoid. The reptile pulled back, a sure sign it was about to strike. In one giant leap, he threw himself at the snaketor and grabbed it just below the head with both hands.

The creature rotated in his grasp and bit down on his arm, one fang piercing his right forearm. The snaketor pulled back to ready itself for a second strike. Pain stabbed up his arm. Hawk gritted his teeth and swung the machete, nearly severing the head from the long, heavy body. With careful deliberation, he brought the weapon down over the fangs and heard them snap.

"Hawk!" Kylie screamed, rushing to his side as he dropped to his knees beside the wiggling body that slowly slithered into the dense greenery. She picked up his arm. "What should we do?"

"I'll help him," Jester said, pulling a first-aid kit from his backpack. He removed a cylinder and pressed it against Hawk's arm. "I hope this works, my friend."

"So do I." Hawk stared into Jester's eyes as he began to wind a bandage tightly over his arm.

Kylie knelt beside him and brushed wet hair from his face. "You saved my life again, warrior."

"I'm afraid it's becoming a habit." He grimaced as Jester tied the bandage. "And I'm still wet. Do you always attract water?"

She smiled and ran her hand across his forehead. "I must." She glanced at Jester. "What did you give him?" Hawk opened his mouth and she touched her fingers to his lips.

"It's a generic anti-toxin serum. It's effective, but I don't know about a snaktor that size. It may not be enough." Jester looked at Kylie. "It may not work at all."

Hawk shoved Kylie's hand away. "Will you two quit talking like I'm not here." Rain had already soaked the bandage. "Let's move. I'm sick of being wet." He stood, not quite as steady on his feet as he would have liked. With his left hand he picked up the machete.

"Oh no you don't," Jester protested. "You can't move that much unless you want to kill yourself. You shouldn't even be walking, but we have no choice."

"I'll be fine."

"Sure, tough guy." Jester took the machete from Hawk and started hacking a path. "Come on."

"Hawk," Kylie whispered. "Are you..."

"I'm fine, Amica." With his fingers he traced the contour of her jaw.
 "Kiss me."

Her wet, red curls hung close to her head and water trickled over her face. Or was some of it tears? She was one tough Researcher, but she was also human, and the stress of the last few weeks was bound to take its toll. "We have to go. Follow Jester. I'll be right behind you."

"No, I'll be right behind *you*." She pushed her hand against his back. "And don't argue with me."

With a groan Hawk fell in line behind Jester. He did not have the energy to argue with Kylie. For once she might even be right. The way he felt he could collapse, and if he were last they might not notice. That was a laugh. He doubted there was anything he could do that went unnoticed. Abruptly he stopped and turned. As planned, Kylie ran into his chest and he threw his arms around her and kissed her. Her body shook and he felt the instant response in his groin and he knew, even in the middle of a jungle, in pouring rain, his arm throbbing from a poisonous snaktor bite, he wanted her desperately. With easy pressure, he deepened the kiss until he heard Jester clear his throat.

"Boss, I really hate to break this up, but if we don't find you shelter and medical help, you may not live to kiss another sun-cycle."

Kylie laid a hand on Hawk's cheek. "He's right."

Her hand was cool on his face. Fever already burned in his body, and it was not his desire for the woman he loved, it was the snaktor's invading venom. He would not alarm Kylie and Jester, they would learn soon enough that the anti-venom serum was not working. "Let's find the woman." He brushed water from Kylie's face. "There's no time to waste."

It took great effort to place one foot in front of the other, but he trudged on. Time blurred. Pain soared through every pore of his being. He had to fight the worsening fatigue, dizziness and nausea as long as he could. The steady rain hid the sweat on his brow, but he doubted he could fool them much longer. He was responsible for Kylie and Jester, and would not stop until he found a safe haven where they could rest.

Darkness engulfed the jungle as they slopped through mud and gushing torrents that tore deep trenches in the wet earth beneath the vegetation. Wind whipped through the trees, the sound vibrating through Hawk's aching head. He struggled and stumbled clumsily. He could no longer feel his legs or feet. His entire body was losing its ability to function.

Jester hacked a path in front of him while Kylie's footsteps sloshed behind. All he wanted was to find a dry place and hold her in his arms. In all his annual-cycles, he'd never needed anyone the way he needed Kylie—the one woman who had managed to breech the barrier he'd so carefully erected around his heart.

His next step faltered, his knees buckled. He grabbed a tree limb, but it was not strong enough to hold him and he fell to the soggy ground.

"Hawk!" Kylie knelt by his side. "Jester!"

Her voice sounded a million miles away, even the rain pelting his face no longer stung, and he had no sensation of hot or cold. His body felt light, as if he were floating up from the face of the planet. Was this what it felt like to die? He closed his eyes and darkness consumed him, irrevocably, in its grasp.

***

"Jester, help me get him to his feet." Together they managed to pull Hawk out of the gushing torrent of cold water.

"Neither of us is strong enough to carry him." Jester eyed Kylie. "Put his right arm over your shoulders, I'll take the left. We'll have to drag him. We have to keep moving." He stared at her. "If he's to live, we must find the woman."

Kylie felt warm tears mix with the cold rain. She crouched down on Hawk's left side, while Jester took the other, and on the count of three they stood and pulled him with them. Wet and lifeless, Hawk felt like he weighed a thousand pounds. She didn't care, she would find help. "Let's go, Jester."

She didn't have to tell Jester his friend was dying, she saw it in his eyes. They traipsed around plants and small trees, the branches slapping them in the face. Jester could not wield the machete very well while holding Hawk upright. Her strong warrior's head bobbed as they dragged him through the god-forsaken jungle.

It seemed like time-units, especially now that the moon-cycle had laid its dark blanket over them. The storm only worsened, but lightning served to show them the way. Her body shook from cold and dread. Hawk had to live—she would not allow him to die.

"Look!" Jester pointed straight ahead and a little to the left.

Kylie's eyes focused on a faint light in the distance and she prayed it was the woman's cabin. Right now she did not care who lived there, she planned to demand shelter. They were armed, and she would use whatever means she had at her disposal to care for Hawk. "Hurry, Jester. I don't know how much longer he can last."

Relief spread through her trembling body when they cleared the heavily vegetated jungle and stepped into a clearing in front of the cabin. Hawk suddenly mumbled something loud and incoherent. It sounded like he said he was fine and intended to help her. Her heart raced. She loved him so and wanted to tell him. He was consumed with fever, and his mind was no longer his.

"Jester, stay with him. I'll go to the house."

"No. Hawk wouldn't like that. I can't let you go by your..."

"If it is the woman, you might scare her. I need to do this. Don't argue. Just stay with Hawk." Without another word she ran up the wooden steps of the cottage, her dripping clothes creating a huge puddle on the covered porch. Her heart beat so fast she thought it might jump from her chest of its own volition. She raised her fist and knocked loudly.

She watched the door knob turn, then heard the hinges squeak, before a face appeared in the small opening. It suddenly dawned on her what little they knew about this mystery woman. She could be a willing friend, or chase them off without a thought or care. However, she would not leave until Hawk recovered.

"Who goes there?" a female voice called from inside the house.

"We need help. Please let us in."

"Who is us?" the woman replied.

"My life-mate and a friend." It wasn't a total lie, she told herself. Jester was a friend, and she could not allow herself to be separated from Hawk on a note of propriety.

"And who are you?"

"I'm Kylie, a Researcher from Estra." She saw the door open a bit wider and a stream of light poured over her.

"What kind of help do you need?"

"My life-mate has been bitten by a giant snaktor. He's burning with fever. We just need a place to rest for the moon-cycle. We mean no harm. Please...you must help us. He could die."

Kylie sighed. Her plea was answered. The woman stepped onto the covered porch and looked her up and down. She had a kind face, tired eyes, and a pale complexion. The woman appeared to be about her mother's age, her hair was gray, yet she retained a mature beauty. Her green eyes revealed a kindness she seemed reluctant to show. "Please, I beg you."

"Bring him inside. But don't try anything. I'm armed, and I won't hesitate to kill you."

"I understand. Thank you."

CHAPTER TWENTY-FOUR

Kylie rushed back to Hawk and Jester. She leaned close to Jester. "No funny stuff. The woman says she's armed, and she'll..."

"I heard her. Don't worry. I can behave myself."

She grinned and hoped Jester was right. Their lives could depend on it. "Let's get him up."

It was no easy task getting Hawk to the cabin. His incoherent mumbling continued. At least he was not in a coma, but she did not know if his ranting was a good or bad sign. Hawk was strong, but was he strong enough to fight the snaktor's poison? All she could do was pray.

The door opened as they approached, and she was surprised to see a younger woman holding it open. They entered the warm cabin and quickly shed their backpacks, leaving them in the entryway. "Where do you want him?"

"Follow me," she said.

Kylie studied the girl as she led them through the main living area, down a short hall to a bathing room. She was a couple of annual-cycles younger than her, but the girl's hair was the same shade of red, and her slightly pudgy face was covered in freckles. Kylie judged her the same height as herself, but her build was a bit sturdier, and she carried herself with confidence.

"He needs cooling to slow his fever before you put him to bed." She pointed to the personal room to the left. "And it will do him no good to rest with half the jungle on him."

"You're right."

"How long ago was he bitten?"

"Several time-units."

"You're lucky he's still alive. A smaller man like him..."

Kylie watched the young woman point to Jester and look him up and down before she continued.

"...would have died within the first half-time-unit." She turned her attention back to the injured man. "He's in for a long fight. I'll help my mother prepare some medicine for the fever, and an antidote to fight the poison in his system."

"Thank you." Kylie noticed the questioning look in her eyes. "My name is Kylie. This is my life-mate, Bryce, and our dear friend, Jester."

"I'm Jenna, and my mother's name is Shandra." Jenna eyed Jester for a moment, then turned on the water to fill the tub.

"It's a pleasure to meet you, Jenna." Jester bowed at the waist, his head down for several moments before he lifted his head back up. "We greatly appreciate your hospitality." He smiled. "You're beautiful."

"Jester!" Kylie said curtly, hoping he would not take the compliments any further. "Help me get Haw...Bryce into the tub, please." She took a step, but Jester stood frozen, his mouth gaping open while he stared at Jenna. "Jester, come on."

"Sorry." Jester helped his friend to sit on the small bench by the tub.

Jester gawked at Jenna while she left the room. She snapped her fingers at him. "Over here. Jester?" Finally he turned around to look at her.

"Sorry, I just...aah..."

"I understand. But for now let's get Hawk taken care of. Together they quickly stripped all the wet clothes off Hawk, then placed him in the large, copper bathing tub. Kylie soaped his burning-hot skin, then used the hand sprayer to wash him off. She used a bit cooler water in hopes it would bring his temperature down a bit. Hawk still mumbled things that made no sense.

"I'll get our bags. He'll need dry clothes." Jester turned and walked to the door. "If we have any."

Kylie watched Jester leave, amused by his obvious attraction to Jenna. Great. A crazy man attracted to a total stranger in the middle of the jungle on a strange planet. What next? She hoped Hawk recovered soon, because Hawk was the only person who could control Jester.

She continued to bathe Hawk, his head resting on the high back of the contoured tub. He babbled incessantly about star-fighters and fish. What a combination. She hoped his hallucinations did not become too vivid because he'd be a handful to control should he begin to thrash about.

"Stop or I'll kill you. No! You won't take me alive!" Hawk yelled.

Hawk started fighting her like an enemy. Even in his weakened state, she could not control him. He swung his fist and grazed her jaw. When she tried to subdue him he got in one last lick to her eye. Kylie knew he never meant to hurt her. God only knew who he thought she was, or what threat she presented. Her eye stung and her cheek burned, but not as badly as Hawk's delirious fever.

"Sssh, warrior. You're safe with me. I won't let anyone hurt you."

"Can I trust you?"

Hawk blinked heavily then stared at her. The usual clarity and color of his eyes were missing. Actually his stare passed straight through her, as if she was not really there. He looked, but he didn't see. Her heart sank with an ache beyond explanation for the fierce, virile warrior wanted for crimes beyond description. If anyone saw him now...no, she refused to think about it. "You can trust me with your life." She slipped her arm around his neck.

"I trust no one!"

Before she could say another word, Hawk went limp in her arms. She pulled her arm back and felt the side of his neck. His pulse beat so erratically she feared it might stop. His body was so hot it had warmed the cooler water in the tub. She tried to ignore the possibility of brain damage from such a high fever.

Without warning he slid under the water, bubbles rising to the surface as his head submerged. Quickly she slipped her arms under him and pulled him up. He coughed and sputtered then turned an angry gaze at her.

"You can't drown me you sorry son-of-a..."

"Sssh, Hawk. You're safe with friends." She tugged him higher so his head rested once again on the back of the deep tub. The door opened and Kylie nearly jumped out of her skin. "Jester, you scared me."

"Sorry." Jester closed the door behind him then walked to Kylie. "How's Hawk?"

"He's hallucinating." Kylie scooped water over his hot chest. "I'm so scared he'll..."

"Don't say it." Jester patted Kylie on the back. "Hawk is one tough son-of-a-star-fighter. One hell of a warrior. I've seen him in worse shape than this."

"When?"

"Aah...when the dragon tossed him around like a toy." Jester cleared his throat. "He's recovered from many wounds."

"Has he ever looked this bad?" Hawk suddenly screamed names she'd never heard before and shouted orders to attack immediately. Jester stared at her, his expression grim.

"Truthfully, no. Of course the other times usually involved blood so it's hard to compare." Jester took Kylie's free hand. "He'll recover. You'll see. He'll be fine."

"He has to, Jester. I won't let him die. I can't lose him." Kylie swiped at tears that rolled down her cheeks. She didn't care who saw her crying. She felt as if she'd been ripped in two, and that half of her was missing. Seeing him helpless as a babe made her realize just how much she relied on his advice, counted on his strength, and craved his touch.

"Your love will bring him back. Now let's get him out of this tub and into bed. Jenna said the medicine was almost ready. The sooner he gets it the better."

Kylie stared at Jester. "What kind of medicine?"

"Jenna said her mother is a psychic, a kind of shaman with healing abilities. She's made something to counteract the poison."

"Let's get him dried off and in bed so they can work their magic."

"You really love him, don't you?"

Jester looked even more worried than she felt. "Of course I do. How could I not?"

"You're good for him. He needs you." Jester lowered his head. "I'm glad you're here for him. He's like a brother to me, and I don't want to lose him anymore than you do."

Kylie tilted Jester's jaw up with the tip of her finger. "Listen to me. We're *not* going to lose him. I won't allow that to happen." She heard Jester mumble his usual, "Olly-dolly", but his usual charming enthusiasm seemed to be missing.

"You two have a special bond, and I would never come between you." Kylie knew how much it hurt Jester to see The Hawk like this, because the sight held her stomach in knots as well. "Now, help me get him to bed."

***

Kylie paced beside Hawk's bed, the same as she had for the past two sun-cycles while he lay unconscious. Shandra and Jenna forced medicine down his throat, chanted mystic words, and placed aromatic simmer pots around the room, filling the air with delightful scents they said would help the healing process.

She knelt on the wood floor next to the narrow bed and took his hand in hers. Closing her eyes, she concentrated on his vibratory level. When she'd first tried mental contact with him in that storm on Andor she never thought it would work, but they shared a bond. She had no other choice than to pour all her trust and faith into communicating with him. Being this close to him, she felt him as if she were inside his head. She called his name in her mind and sent peaceful, healing thoughts, and visions of them making love. Anything to calm him, and pull him back to the land of the living.

"Kylie?"

The soft voice made her turn. "Shandra. Come in."

Shandra walked to Kylie and took her hand. "It's time for the spirits to guide him back. You've done all you can, and so have I."

"No, I won't leave him. He needs me. If he wakes and I'm not here..."

"Come, we must talk. He'll sleep longer, this I know."

Kylie followed Shandra out to the porch where Jester and Jenna were seated on a swing suspended from the porch roof. They looked cute sitting there together, which only made her wish Hawk was by her side.

"Kylie," Jester began, "Shandra has been asking me a lot of questions, and I think it's time we told her."

"Jester's right, Kylie. You know I'm psychic." Shandra looked into Kylie's eyes. "I've sensed your quest from the moment I saw you."

"But you were afraid to let us in. You said you'd kill us..."

"I had to be sure. When I heard your voice pleading for help, I knew." Shandra handed Kylie a glass of fruit juice from the tray on the table. "You have need of my services. Am I right?"

"We were told you knew the Vanefca language."

"Who told you?"

"A man from Andor."

"His name. I must know his name," Shandra insisted.

"Redmon." Kylie watched the color drain from the woman's face, her pale green eyes darkened and her bottom lip quivered. "Do you know him?"

"What I know is not important. Did you speak with him personally?"

"No, only my life-mate saw him."

"I see." Shandra took a long drink.

Kylie glanced at Jester for his reaction and found the same shocked look on his face. "Will you help us, Shandra? So much depends on that journal."

"First I must know what this man, Redmon, has to do with all this."

"Nothing, except telling us you could translate a journal written in Vanefca." Kylie wasn't sure how to read the play of emotions on Shandra's face. Even her silver hair seemed to go limp around her face. What had shaken her so badly?

Shandra set her glass down on the table. "I sense this journal is of great importance to you?"

"It contains the cure to Genesis Disorder. It will save the lives of my parents, and thousands of my people. But that all depends on you."

"Where is this journal you speak of?"

"On our ship."

"You will bring it to me."

"It's not safe. You'll have to come with us when Bryce can travel."

"I will not leave my home and my daughter." Shandra turned her gaze to Jenna.

"Shandra," Jester began, "we can't guarantee your safety if we bring the journal to you, but I promise you'll be safe on *The Redemption*." He glanced at Jenna with a smile. "You can bring your daughter with you."

"We will not go." Shandra hurried down the porch steps and walked out of sight.

"My mother will change her mind. She's a stubborn woman at times, but her will to help others is strong."

"I've seen the way she's helped my life-mate." Kylie stood and reached for the handle of the door. "I'd better go check on him."

"Good idea." Jester said as she stepped inside. He turned toward Jenna. "Would you like me to help with the chores?"

Jenna smiled. "Sure. We'll start in the garden."

They walked down the steps and followed the path around back of the house. When they turned the corner, Jester reached for Jenna's hand and suddenly found himself flat on his back on the ground. "What did you do that for?"

"Because you touched me!"

Jester rose to his feet. "I'm sorry. I only wanted to hold your hand."

"You should have asked."

"Where did you learn that move?"

"Did I forget to mention that I'm a twelfth-degree Corel?"

"What's Corel?"

Jenna smiled. "It is the ancient self-defense techniques of the Spectran Monks."

"Monks know that stuff?"

"Absolutely. Would you like to see more?"

Jester nodded. She grabbed his arm, pulled him toward her and he suddenly felt himself flying through the air over her head, landing with a thud on the ground. "Will all your moves put me in this position?" He looked up at Jenna's smiling face.

"Maybe, maybe not, Are you man enough to find out?"

"Only if I can hold your hand without being thrown."

"Deal." Jenna laughed. "All you had to do was ask."

"Silly me!"

***

Nyles paced the length of the small cabin. "How did you arrange all this, Sira?"

"Konar arranged it, you fool. If I had my way, you'd still be in the holding cell on SEA Lab." Sira laughed.

"I don't think so. He needs me."

"You're delusional. All you've done is botch things up by becoming a thief."

Nyles groaned. "Why are we on Konar's ship?"

"He wants us to intercept Saxon and Kylie. He wants the journal, and the woman who can interpret Professor Winn's scribbles."

"What happened to Winn?"

"Poor man had a stroke and died."

Nyles grabbed Sira's wrist. "You killed him, didn't you?" He grinned. "You're the reason his journal is missing."

"It was an accident. Now let me go. If it wasn't for you stealing those damned artifacts, Saxon wouldn't have interfered. Konar said you were an incapable imbecile, and he's right." Sira jerked her hand away. "I should have done Konar a favor and killed you."

"If we worked together we could both be rich. That journal is priceless."

Sira grinned. "You've lost your mind. If you think you can betray Konar, you're sadly mistaken. He'll search the universe for you, and when he finds you, you'll *wish* you were dead."

"You're a gutless whore!"

"Are all your brains in your pants?" Sira grinned when he looked down. "As I thought."

"Didn't know you were capable of thinking, my pet."

Sira landed a blow in Nyles' groin and grinned widely when he doubled over in pain, howling like an animal. "First, I'm not your pet. Second, you *will* follow my orders, or I'll take great pleasure in torturing you slowly."

Nyles straightened and stared at Sira.

"We'll be landing on Spectra in one time-unit. Be ready." Sira turned and left, laughing to herself. Nyles couldn't be trusted, which was why she'd rendered his weapons useless. The slime-worm wouldn't hesitate shooting her in the back, and she had no intention of letting him. Konar said to bring him, but he didn't say how long she had to keep him

234

alive.

***

Hawk's eyes flew open. He studied the simple room until his gaze found Kylie sleeping in a chair next to the bed, her fingers entwined with his. Soft red curls framed her face, her lips were slightly parted, and she never looked more beautiful, or kissable.

He sat up and rested his back against the cool, stone wall. He coughed and cleared his throat, hoping the gesture would wake her, and it did. She opened her eyes as wide as saucers and stared, her mouth dropping open. "You look like you've seen a ghost."

Kylie grabbed his arm. "I think I have." She stood and placed her hand on his forehead. "Your fever is gone. How do you feel?"

"Better now that I've seen you." He watched her blush and the sexy twinkle returned to her brilliant green eyes. "How long have I been out?"

"Five sun-cycles. We didn't think you'd make it for the first three."

"Guess that snaktor was bigger than I thought."

"Maybe you're not as invincible as you thought."

"I survived didn't I?" She grinned at him as if she wanted to hit him. "Come closer, I feel weak." The moment she leaned closer he pulled her to him and kissed the lips he'd missed, and savored the firm fullness of her breasts against him.

She pushed back. "This is no way for a sick man to act."

"How should I act?" She sighed and stared at him with a puzzled look on her face. "Wasn't it you who put images in my mind while I was unconscious?"

"You saw them?"

"They were so real I thought I was making love to you. And the way you said my name still makes my heart beat faster." He smiled when her hand covered her mouth. "I enjoyed it, Amica. There's nothing to be ashamed of. You saved my life by conveying your love." Her cheeks turned bright crimson. "What's wrong with that?"

"I think you misunderstood."

"No, I didn't." He wondered why she seemed so reluctant to admit she loved him. She'd said it in his mind when she thought he was dying, but now she wanted to hide it. Was it because of who he was? That was a subject he did not want to open. Besides, they would be separated soon enough, and he wanted their remaining time together to be enjoyable. "Where's Jester?" he asked to break the silence.

"You're not going to believe this, but Jester has fallen in love with Jenna."

"Who's Jenna?"

"Shandra's daughter." She smiled. "I forgot you haven't really met them yet. Shandra is the woman we came to find."

"I see."

"Not yet you don't, but you will. I'll be right back."

Kylie rushed from the room and Hawk laughed. Jester in love? Not possible. He liked women well enough, but he was not the type to make a real commitment. What woman could put up with his wild antics? No. Kylie had to be mistaken. This he would have to see for himself.

The door opened and in walked a young woman who could pass for Kylie's sister. Long red hair, green eyes, and a sunshine smile. Jester followed behind her, his hand entwined with hers, giving her the *smitten* look Jester accused him of giving Kylie. How a few sun-cycles could change things.

"Boss! It's good to see you've returned to the living." Jester pulled Jenna closer to Hawk. "I want you to meet Jenna. Isn't she gorgeous?"

"Absolutely." He shared a wink with Jester and stifled a laugh when Jenna stomped on his foot and Jester's only reaction was a smile. Kylie was right, the man was a goner. "It's an honor to meet you, Jenna."

"How is my patient?" Shandra asked as she entered the room and approached the opposite side of the bed.

"I owe you my life and sincere thanks for caring for me and my friends."

"Your life-mate insisted. She's a very persuasive woman. You're lucky to have her."

Hawk grinned at the mischievous look on Kylie's face. "I am truly blessed to have Kylie as my life-mate. I have chosen well." How he wished that statement were true.

Shandra smiled. "That is good to hear." She pointed toward Jester and Jenna. "I'm worried about those two."

"I can control Jester." He glanced at his friend. "Has he been a problem?"

"No!" Jenna blurted.

"Not really," Shandra said, shaking her head. "But they've become inseparable. Are you prepared for that?"

"It is a concept I will adjust to should Jenna continue to enjoy his company." Hawk yawned and blinked heavily. He was more tired than he thought.

"I can handle him just fine. Watch," Jenna said, tucking her shoulder toward Jester, flipping him over her back to the hard wood floor.

"Ouch!" Jester complained.

"You said you liked it when I did that, Funny-bone," Jenna said.

"Only when we're in the garden." Jester glanced at Hawk then back at Jenna. "I think we should leave now, Jungle-Flower."

Hawk waved good-by to the overly adoring, way too happy couple. "I think I'm going to be sick."

"I told you that you weren't prepared," Shandra said.

"I tried to warn you too." Kylie smiled.

"I never dreamed he could be so far gone so quickly. What have you two been feeding him?"

Shandra frowned. "He needs no love potion, that's for sure."

Hawk studied Shandra's expression, not quite sure what was running through her mind. "Just say the word, and he will not go near your daughter again."

"I've never seen Jenna happier. Your friend is odd, but my intuition tells me he's an honorable man."

"You have my word on that." Hawk liked Shandra. She seemed honest and fair, along with intuitive.

Kylie smiled. "And mine."

"I'll leave you two alone. Call if you need anything."

Hawk's gaze followed Shandra as she left the room. She was the first person to see Jester so quickly and thoroughly for the man he was, not what he pretended to be. For that he respected the woman.

"Hawk?" Kylie took his hand. "What are you thinking?"

"That I need to get out of this bed." He swung his legs over the edge and placed his feet on the floor. "Wife, get me some clothes. I can't parade around like this."

"I had to tell Shandra we were mated. I was afraid she'd separate us if we weren't bonded according to the church."

"You were worried about propriety?"

"No. Only you." She kissed his cheek and handed him a shirt and a pair of pants."

"Well, Mrs. Saxon, we have to talk to Shandra about the journal." Hawk stood, quickly dressed and walked to the door. He wobbled a bit. Five sun-cycles with no movement or food had left him weak, a feeling he could not accept.

"Hawk," Kylie called, "you're not ready to be walking around like this."

"One more sun-cycle in that bed and I'll never walk again. I need exercise and food, but first I want to speak with Shandra."

"Hope you have more luck than Jester and I had. She said she'd translate the journal only if we brought it to her. She refuses to leave her home."

"We'll see about that."

CHAPTER TWENTY-FIVE

Dinner was wonderful." Hawk rose from the table. "Please, Shandra, walk with me?" He held her chair while she stood. They walked to the front of the room, and Hawk opened the heavy wooden door so Shandra could step outside on the porch. They descended the steps in silence and strolled across the vibrantly green lawn. Hawk purposely waited until they were a good distance from the house. "I'm told you know of our dilemma."

"Nothing has changed. I'll only decipher the journal if you bring it to me."

"What are you afraid of, Shandra?"

She stared at the ground. "There are things you don't understand."

"Then tell me."

"I can tell no one. The secret must die with me."

"Lives are at stake and you have the power to save them." Hawk wasn't a psychic, but he somehow knew her secret held a critical piece to this puzzle. He had to gain her cooperation, and judging by the obstinate look on her face, he was in for a battle. "I don't care about your secrets. We all have them. But you cannot, in good conscience, stand by and let thousands of people die because you don't want to leave your home."

Shandra stopped and stared into Saxon's eyes. "You have secrets as dark as mine, this I know, but I also feel the only life you risk is your own. My secret goes beyond my own life. I cannot leave."

"Neither of our secrets can stand in the way. I will protect you and your daughter. You will both be safe."

"If I leave Spectra, my daughter and I will never be safe again. I care nothing for myself, but I must insure her safety."

"Who are you afraid of, Shandra?" He stared into her pale green eyes and recognized her terror, he'd felt it himself more than once. "If there is someone threatening you, I can take care of him, and you will never be bothered again."

"There will be no violence."

"As you wish." Hawk had to convince her to go willingly. He doubted force would work with Shandra, but her daughter was a different story, Jenna would follow Jester anywhere. "You're a woman of great compassion. I know you want to help."

"On my terms, I will."

A faint rustle in the brush behind them caused Hawk to turn. He saw small branches in the distance sway. They were being watched. "Come," he said, offering his arm to Shandra, escorting her back to the house as if nothing was wrong.

Jester and Jenna stepped off the porch to greet them, and Kylie leaned against the rail with a smile he wanted to kiss. When Shandra stepped onto the deck, he motioned them all inside.

"What's wrong, Boss?"

"Pack up. We're *all* leaving within the time-unit."

"I told you, my daughter and I will not be going with you!"

"The choice is no longer yours." Shandra scowled and he caught a glimpse of Kylie's startled expression since she stood behind the woman.

"If my mother says we're staying, we're staying," Jenna insisted. "I'll fight you if necessary."

"She can do it, too," Jester added with a smile.

Kylie took a step toward Hawk. "Explain yourself."

"We've been followed. Shandra and I were being watched. Whoever is out there will make a move before long." He glanced at Shandra, whose expression verified what he'd just said. "You and your daughter's life are in jeopardy. You're what they're after, Shandra, and they won't hesitate to use Jenna against you."

"I can take care of myself," Jenna said.

Hawk smiled. "I've seen your moves. You're very good, but I'm afraid you're no match for our enemies."

Shandra squared her shoulders. "We will pack."

Jenna and Shandra left the room and Kylie stepped closer to Hawk. "This isn't right, Hawk."

"Do you want your parents to die? Your people?" He took Kylie's hand in his and pulled her close. "We're all pawns in a game we did not start. But it's a game we *will* finish."

"I know. It's just that Shandra and Jenna have been so good to us.

She saved your life and..."

"And now we're going to save hers."

***

Kylie wiped sweat from her brow with her sleeve. Even moon-cycle travel in the humid jungle climate was oppressive. Hawk looked tired. He was not fully recovered, yet he was out here in the blistering heat, hacking his way through the jungle. She hoped they'd find the old path soon so the going would be a bit easier.

Hawk was clever. He'd led them out the back of the house, but made it look as if they were still inside. She laughed when she saw the two dummies he and Jester had made and propped up on the couch in front of the window. From a distance they would be convincing, but looking at pillows with hats and clothes over them had been funny.

Without warning, a red beam of light ripped in front of her and seared off a tree limb to her right. Hawk grabbed her and threw her to the ground.

"Everybody down!" Hawk belly-crawled over to Jester. "Take this," he said, pulling an eradicator from the pack. "Keep moving, but keep low. I'm going after them. Wait for me at the shuttle."

Jester nodded. He knew his friend would protect the women with his life while he searched for the assailants. Whoever they were, they'd expect him to run with the women, which would give him a slight advantage. Shandra, Jenna, Kylie and Jester disappeared into the darkness while he waited and prayed for their safety.

Doubling back, Hawk hoped to approach the attackers from behind. There had only been one shot, which seemed odd. If they wanted to kill them, they would not have stopped shooting. "Damn," he mumbled to himself as plants and branches crunched beneath his feet. A surprise attack in the moon-cycle jungle was next to impossible.

A flicker of light twenty meters in the distance caught his eye. He rushed toward it, but it did not shine again. The enemy was close. He pressed on through the thick, broad-leafed foliage. Whoever shot at Kylie was a dead man! He paused and listened for footsteps. A short distance ahead he heard a crunching sound and began to run, eradicator in hand.

A guide lamp flickered again and he saw their faces. By the Gods! It was Sira and Nyles. They extinguished the small lamp. How in the universe had they escaped SEA Lab? All that mattered now was stopping them before they found Jester and the women. He picked up his pace, more determined than ever to put an end to their miserable existence.

While he chased Sira and Nyles, realization struck. How could he have been so stupid not to see it earlier? The only person they could be working for was Redmon. Redmon was the one who sent him here to find the woman, so Redmon was the only person who knew he had the diary, and that he would be here.

Redmon was not his friend, so it came as no surprise. He'd never trusted the man. Only Redmon could have gotten that rotten duo off SEA Lab to pursue him. Redmon was greedy enough to have engineered the caper, and powerful enough to pull it off. Why he had those two incompetent idiots working for him was another story.

In the clearing ahead, Hawk sighted Sira and Nyles running for their shuttle. He fired and sparks flew when the red beam bounced off the hull. Before he could fire again, they had managed to enter the craft and start the engines. His weapon could not penetrate the metal. They may have successfully escaped this time, but he *would* meet them again.

His hands fisted at his sides as their shuttle rose and zoomed off into space. "This is *not* over. I will destroy you both." It was a promise he meant to keep.

Hawk rolled away from Kylie to catch his breath. "You've worn me out, Amica." He sighed and reached for her naked breast. He smiled when she caught his wrist.

"The Hawk? Worn out? Not possible!" She laughed.

He pulled her close and kissed her neck. Her taut nipple teased his flesh and burnt its imprint into his chest. She felt so good, and he loved her more than life itself, and he wanted to sing it out to the universe. His tongue traced her ear until his lips found her earlobe.

"I thought you said you were worn out."

"I was wrong."

Kylie took his head in her hands and eased him back to gaze into his eyes. "No, you weren't wrong. You hacked your way through the jungle, chased attackers, got *The Redemption* underway, and made mad passionate love to me, all within the last time-unit. By all rights you should still be in bed, recovering from the snaktor bite."

"I am in bed, aren't I?"

"And so you shall stay. I'm going to see Shandra and Jenna. They're probably lost on this big ship, and feeling lonely."

"I could get lonely."

"A sleeping man can't get lonely."

Little did she know how he craved her company, her body, her mind and her soul. She was everything he ever wanted in a woman. She fulfilled his life in ways he could not possibly explain, or understand. He blinked. His eyes felt heavy. Kylie was right, he needed rest. There would be time to ponder their relationship later.

***

While Kylie showered and dressed, a feeling of impending doom invaded her senses. Why? She'd been so happy only a few minutes ago making love to Hawk, satisfied and safe in his arms. Images of the Delphins flashed in her mind. Was this some kind of psychic premonition? So many new and strange things had happened to her in such a short period of time it made her head swim. The least of which was falling in love with The Hawk.

The urge to go to Shandra and comfort her was compelling, yet she did not understand. Why Shandra? Jenna felt like a sister to her, not just as a friend, but in the blood-relative sense. It was a very confusing message to be sure. Her parents were on Estra, and she had no brothers or sisters. It must be wishful thinking to have a sister, and her feelings for Shandra were because she missed her mother.

She would see her parents soon. Hawk said they were five sun-cycles away from Estra. Anxious barely described what she was feeling. It would be a bittersweet arrival. Once they were all safe, Hawk would leave, his job over. Could she convince him to stay? No. Even on Estra he was a wanted man. Would he ask her to go with him? The question scared her. Even worse, she feared he might not ask.

This train of thought was going nowhere. She finished brushing her hair, opened the lav door and tiptoed past Hawk, who slept peacefully on the bed. Just seeing his powerful body half covered made her want him all over again. She felt dizzy under his gaze and lightheaded beneath his touch. A tear rolled down her cheek. What would she do without him?

The door swooshed open, and she turned the light off on her way out. As she headed down the hall she heard Jester yell, then the distinct sound of a thud on the floor. They were at it again.

She smiled when she entered the galley. Jester lay sprawled on the floor, rubbing his head while Jenna stood over him with a satisfied look on her face. They were quite a couple. They might even have a future together, if Jenna didn't kill him first. "Having fun?" Kylie asked when she walked past the two of them to get a drink.

"Ah...yeah. Jenna was teaching me more of those Corel moves she knows," Jester groaned.

Kylie laughed. "I hope you live through your lessons."

"Don't you worry, Kylie," Jenna said, offering Jester a hand up. "I won't hurt him too bad."

She wanted to tell Jenna she would never hurt him if she loved him. Jester seemed to be falling harder for Jenna by the time-unit, and she had never seen him happier. He may be spending a lot of time on the ground, but when he looked up, there was love in his eyes. Love. It certainly did strange things to people.

"I'm going to get even with her," Jester said, brushing off the seat of his pants as he stood. "I'm going to teach her how to use the computer."

"That ought to be interesting." Kylie finished her drink. "I'm going to see Shandra. Please, don't kill each other while I'm gone." She heard them giggle as she made her way to Shandra's cabin. The scramble for the shuttle had been very difficult for Shandra. The woman appeared to be healthy for her age, but it was her soul that remained in a state of torture.

Kylie knocked. Shandra's soft voice invited her inside. The door slid open. She walked toward the older woman and sat next to her on the bed. "How are you feeling?"

"How do you think? Your mate has forced me to leave my home. I may not have left visibly kicking and screaming, but I assure you, that's how I left."

"I'm sorry, Shandra. We never meant you any harm." Kylie touched her arm. "It's just that many lives depend on you."

"I understand your need to help your parents and your people, but you've set an even greater evil into motion."

Kylie saw a lone tear trickle down Shandra's pale face. The woman did not bother to wipe it, she simply stared at the wall in front of her, but the sadness in her voice still lingered on the air. "What do you mean?"

"It's better if you don't know."

"Saxon is a powerful man. He can help you if you let him."

Shandra stood and paced the length of the cabin in silence. Kylie's heart poured out to her, but there was little she could do, especially if Shandra refused to confide in her. Shandra and Jenna were in danger because some greedy person wanted to make money off other people's grief. It wasn't fair. Life wasn't fair. Whatever troubled Shandra was beyond reach until she chose to share the heartache in her soul.

Kylie stood and walked to the door. "If you want to talk, I'm available. I may not be able to change the past, but I can help you face the future." Shandra nodded but her gaze remained fixed on the floor. There was nothing she could do about the demons in Shandra's life.

***

"You bumbling fool!" Sira snapped. "Why did you try to kill the woman?"

Nyles laughed. "Why should you care? I thought you wanted Saxon for yourself. Getting his little whore out of the way should make you happy."

"Saxon will do me no good if I'm dead. And that's exactly what we'll both be if Konar gets wind of this. He said to follow them. We're not to kill anyone until the transcribed journal is safely in our hands."

"And when it is, you're going to hand it over to Konar." Nyles stepped closer to Sira. "Then who will the fool be?" He slipped his arm around her waist and pulled her to him. "*We* could have the power, own the universe. Why give it away?"

Sira stroked Nyles' cheek. "Power without life is useless, my pet. I'm not ready to die. Are you?"

"Who is Konar? I know you know his real identity."

She pushed away. "You don't want to know."

"Of course I do. He's nobody to fear."

Sira laughed. "You get dumber by the time-unit. If I told you who he was, I'd have to kill you."

"And you get bolder. What makes you think I won't kill you?"

"Because deep down, *you* fear Konar as well. Besides, we still need each other."

Nyles grabbed a clump of Sira's hair. "I think you'll change your mind when we have the journal." He grinned and stroked her hair back in place. "We could be happy together, and very rich."

"First we get the journal, then I'll decide. But remember, for now we do it Konar's way. He wants us to follow them, not kill them."

"What makes you so sure Saxon will hand over the journal?"

"I have something he desperately wants. He just doesn't know it yet."

"You have a magnificent body, Sira, but don't overrate yourself."

"I'm not talking about my body, you moron. I have a hologram disk that will clear his name."

"What are you talking about?"

"You're slow, Nyles, very slow. Haven't you figured it out yet?" She shook her head. "Saxon is The Hawk."

"Are you sure?" Sira nodded. "He didn't seem that tough to me."

"Only because he was protecting his identity."

"I had a minor altercation with him by the Delphin pool, and I had the upper hand until Jester and Kylie interrupted us. Hawk was lucky I didn't hurt him worse than I did."

Sira doubled over in laugher.

"You don't believe me?" Nyles pushed her away.

"You're so deluded. Hawk has never lost a fight."

"Except the one that destroyed him, which makes the pot even sweeter, doesn't it, my pet?" Nyles ran his hand up and down Sira's arm. "And once we get what we want, I'll kill the bastard."

"I'll allow you that pleasure. I know how well you two get along, but I want Kylie. The bitch needs to be taught a lesson."

"And I'm sure you're the woman to do it." Nyles kissed Sira's cheek. "And what about Konar?"

Sira's arms threaded around Nyles' neck. "We'll worry about him later." She smiled and trailed her hands down his chest. "Why don't you show me how happy you can make me?"

"Only if you take off that damned ring you so conveniently used last time."

She slipped the gold weapon off her finger and laid it on the table. "This time you will have to prove yourself." She laughed. "Your future wealth depends on your expertise. If you please me better than Konar, we might have a deal."

Nyles grinned. "We'll make splendid partners, of that I'm sure."

***

Kylie searched Hawk's closet for the dress he'd bought her. This would be their last moon-cycle on *The Redemption* and she wanted to surprise him with dinner in his cabin, and a little seduction, Sira style. But where was it?

A duffel bag on the top shelf caught her eye. She grabbed the closest chair, pulled it to the open door and stepped on the seat. Her fingers snagged the leather handles, and she pulled it to the edge. The zipper slid easily. Inside, her hand touched something cold and hard. She lifted the object out, and the shock nearly knocked her off the chair. It was the stolen scepter he said he'd returned. The jewels sparkled in her hands, but her stomach turned upside-down.

She lifted the bag down and looked inside. Her body went numb and a nauseous feeling welled deep within her. Every item reported stolen from SEA Lab was inside his bag. Dear stars, Hawk was the thief! He'd lied to her about returning the artifacts. "I'll take care of them," he'd said. He simply neglected to say how.

The scepter suddenly felt evil. She dropped it back in the bag, zipped it closed and pushed it back where she found it. She replaced the chair then sat on the bed in a state of disbelief. How many other lies had he told? If he lied about the artifacts, he'd certainly lie about murder. She wanted to give him a chance to explain, but it was obvious he could not be trusted.

Traitor, thief, murderer. He was all those things and more. Tears rolled down her cheeks. He'd betrayed her! Lies. Everything about Bryce Saxon was a lie. The only truth she believed was that he was indeed The Hawk. What else could she expect from a man like that. She had to get out of his room. Grabbing her empty bag, she stuffed her few belongings into it and ran to the door. Before she could activate the panel, it slid open and she found Hawk staring at her.

"Where are you going, Amica?" Hawk threw his arms around her and pulled her into his embrace. "I have a very special moon-cycle planned for us." He glanced at the bag in her hand. "What's this?"

"We'll be landing on Estra next sun-cycle, I just...wanted to be ready." If he could lie, so could she, because she had no intention of letting him know what she'd found.

Hawk smiled. "I didn't know you were that anxious to get rid of me."

"Don't be silly." If he only knew how anxious she was. If they were anywhere but on *The Redemption*, she'd be long gone. How would she get through this last moon-cycle? She did not want him to touch her, ever. Panic flowed through her and she fought the urge to run. "I was on my way to see Shandra. I'll be back later."

She rushed out through the open doorway before he had a chance to blink. Why had she given her heart to a traitor? They may never have had a chance together, but to have it end this way was devastating. She wiped tears from her cheek while she walked. No matter how angry she was with Hawk, she had to be careful. He still controlled the mission, the journal, and worst of all, her heart.

CHAPTER TWENTY-SIX

Why had Kylie rushed off so abruptly? She seemed nervous. Was their impending arrival on Estra giving her a case of the jitters? There was no reason why it should. She was anxious to see her parents, and unlike him, had nothing to fear on her home planet.

Was she upset because their time together would be over? Hopefully that was the problem. If that were the case, why did he have the gut feeling he'd just lost her? From the moment they met, he'd sensed her moods, and this one felt darker than he could explain.

The door opened and Jester pushed in a cart laden with dishes, candles, and something that resembled a flower. Jester had an easy smile on his face and an odd twinkle in his eye.

"Here you go, Boss. This should prove to be one special moon-cycle."

"Maybe for you." Hawk crossed his arms over his chest.

"What's wrong?"

"Wish I knew. Kylie flew out of here all upset, and I don't know why."

"She'll be back. She loves you." Jester's hand flew to his mouth. "Oops."

"How would you know that?" Hawk saw a guilty little smile tug the corners of Jester's lips. He knew the man well enough to know what that expression meant. "Spill it, buddy."

"When we both thought the snaktor was getting the better of you, Kylie admitted she loved you, but she made me promise never to tell you." Jester hung his head. "You didn't hear it from me."

"Of course not. With the mood she's in, I doubt she'll ever say it again." He looked into his friend's eyes. "I'll never understand women." He groaned at Jester's choked laugh. "What's so funny?"

"Women, of course. I'll never understand them either. I think Jenna loves me, but I spend so much time on the floor, I doubt I'll ever get her in bed."

"If you know what's good for you, you'll stay on the floor!"

"I don't think so. I've seen the looks on your face, and Kylie's too. I want with Jenna what you have with Kylie."

"I have nothing with Kylie."

"Of course you do."

"You know as well as I do, I cannot permit a woman in my life. Even if Kylie vowed her eternal love, I couldn't put her life in danger. And to travel with me, that's exactly what I'd be doing." He stepped closer to Jester and gave him a firm pat on the back. "And if you want a future with Jenna, we'll have to part company."

"I hadn't considered that option." Jester hung his head. "I don't want that."

"Be happy, my friend. You deserve it. You've been loyal. We're closer than brothers. But there comes a time when a man wants, and needs, his own family. And if you and Jenna love each other, then it's your time."

"I can't handle this. I've got to go. Have fun with Cutie."

Jester left in such a rush he nearly ran his head into the metal door. He hadn't meant to crush Jester's happy little bubble, but it was the truth. Women had no place in the world of a criminal. If he loved Kylie and Jester, he had to let them go. Maybe it was best Kylie turned from him. One more moon-cycle of love was a selfish craving.

Kylie. She was more than he deserved. His life had been nothing but one crime after another. Some more legal than others, but he could not change what he'd become. Kylie was pure joy, full of love and good intentions. She had no place in his world, or his life, but she always had a place in his heart.

***

"What brings you here, Kylie?" Shandra asked. "I heard Jester talking about the special plans your mate has for you before we land on Estra."

"I think you know, he's not my life-mate."

"I suspected, but the love you share is a far stronger bond than any ceremony."

"He broke that bond. He lied, and I cannot forgive his lies."

Shandra took Kylie's hand. "Sometimes lies are necessary, even between lovers."

"No. If he loved me, he would have told me the truth."

"Even if he knew it would hurt you?"

"Yes."

"Trust in Hawk's love. I feel he has good reasons for whatever he'd done."

"No. He never had a reason to lie to me. His life is so full of lies, he doesn't know the truth. I want no part of it. I'm through! Besides," Kylie felt tears burn her eyes before they rolled down her cheek, tears she was powerless to stop. "I can't love Saxon, because I can't give him the children he wants. I'm a genetic outcast, child of scientists...you know what that means!"

"Calm down." Shandra moved to the personal galley and ordered two cups of herbis tea. Once the mugs were full she took them to the table and motioned for Kylie to join her. "Drink this, it will ease your nerves."

Kylie took a seat at the table and sipped her tea. "I'm sorry to burden you with my problems. I should leave." When she started to rise, Shandra's hand pressed against her arm, and her eyes said stay. "I have nowhere to go."

"Stay with me. I think of you like a daughter, Kylie."

"When I look at Jenna, I feel like I'm looking at myself. How could it be we look so much alike?"

"You know what they say, everyone has a double. Maybe Jenna is yours?"

"Have you and Jester finished translating the journal?"

"Almost. I've had problems because of all the technical words, but Jester's been a great help. We only have a few pages left." Shandra smiled. "Jester is quite a man. Underneath that sense of humor is an extremely intelligent, gentle soul. And he is kind of cute."

"Jenna certainly thinks so." Kylie took another drink. "She's just what Jester needs. He's a lonely man."

"So is Saxon."

Shandra's words sliced through her. She knew Shandra was right, but it did not matter. If Hawk was to find happiness, it would be with someone else. As a couple, they were doomed from the beginning, but the knowledge did little to ease the pain that throbbed in her heart. She'd known the rules from sun-cycle one. Keep it casual, nothing more. Hawk had made her violate the one rule she was doomed to obey. He made her love him.

***

Hawk paced the width of the bridge. They were being followed. There had been a ship visible on their scanner from the moment they left Spectran air space. Nyles and Sira. What were they up to? Who did they work for? He wished they'd make a move so he could find out, but it was too dangerous with the women on board. They were after the journal, so they'd make their move soon. They would attack before he entrusted Roloc with the precious book.

How could he deliver Kylie, Shandra, Jenna, and the journal safely without being caught? Security on Estra was tight, especially since he'd allowed Kylie to alert Roloc of their impending arrival. Roloc may be the most powerful scientist on Estra, but he did not control the government, or their methods of security. It would take only one person to recognize him for Bryce Saxon to be history, and The Hawk to be captured.

He had to talk to Redmon. If anyone could arrange safe passage, it would be him. "Beggar, page me if anything happens."

"Yes, Captain."

It was a distance to his private office, a place he had not spent much time in since their return to *The Redemption*. Kylie had kept him too busy, until now. He stepped inside, locked the door, then sat in the big office chair behind his desk. The private com-link stared at him from the center of his desk. His words to Redmon needed to be carefully chosen. The private line was supposed to be secure, but with Sira and Nyles so close on his tail, he was not so sure.

Hawk opened the link and tapped his fingers on the smooth, leather top while he waited. A quick check of his timer said Redmon should be in his quarters. Andor was exactly twenty-four time-units ahead of Estran space-time.

"Hawk? Is that you?"

"Yes, Redmon. We're close to landing on Estra, and I need you to clear security for me. I don't want any problems."

"Done. Anything else?"

"Just make sure I don't get arrested."

"Of course. Have you translated the journal yet?"

"No. The woman is ill. Space travel doesn't agree with her. Roloc will have to wait until she's settled in on Estra before she'll be able to work."

"I see. What's your ETA?"

"Three time-units."

"Good. I'll take care of that security matter right away."

"Thank you. Hawk, out."

Redmon's voice had an edgy, impatient tone. What did he have to be nervous about? He might be worried about his life if The Hawk discovered he was the man Sira and Nyles worked for. This would be a test, and he would know shortly if his hunch was correct. Redmon's only interest should be SEA Lab's security, but he suspected that was only a minute part of a far larger scheme.

At least Redmon seemed to believe his little lie about Shandra. It was the only way he could assure her safety. If anyone knew she'd completely deciphered the journal, her life would be worth absolutely nothing to Sira, Nyles and their employer.

Hawk turned on his desktop vid-screen and accessed CAM. He tapped into the confidential channel Redmon would use to order Bryce Saxon's security clearance. Of course Redmon had no idea he had the capability to tap into Andor's secrets. No one knew except Jester, the man who created the program. He waited impatiently, even though it could take Redmon a time-unit to complete the task, a time-unit he did not intend to waste. He had to see Kylie. He'd been on the bridge with Beggar most of the moon-cycle, and he had no idea if she was as mad as she seemed.

With wide strides, he walked the short distance to his cabin and hesitated outside the door. Should he enter? Would she be there? Hawk shook his head. He'd never had problems with decisions, especially one as simple as entering his own quarters. He touched the pad and the door opened. "Kylie?" The door whooshed closed behind him.

"Where have you been?"

Her voice still held an angry tone. "On the bridge, why?"

"No reason."

He stepped closer and slipped his arm around her waist. When he eased her toward him, she twisted in his grasp and turned away. "What's wrong, Amica?"

"Nothing."

"I'm not a fool. I knew you were upset when you left to see Shandra. Now you turn from me as if you can't stand my touch, yet you say nothing is wrong?"

"You're the Captain, the Chief of Security, *The Hawk*. You figure it out."

"You're the woman who talks to fish, you tell me."

"Why you insensitive slime-eel!" Kylie turned her back to him.

Hawk placed his hands on her shoulders and she immediately tensed as if his gesture revolted her. His grip tightened, and he turned her to face him. "What have I done to make you angry?"

"It no longer matters. We'll be on Estra in a few time-units, and you'll be free of me."

"Is our parting what disturbs you?" Her emerald eyes darkened and her brows tightened. Her gaze looked more like contempt than heartbreak. What happened to cause her to hate him? "Well?"

"It's useless to talk about it. You wouldn't know the truth if it hit you between the eyes!"

"I've never lied to you. I love you." He took a deep breath and let it out slowly. He said it, and he was glad. She had to know how he felt so they could work something out. "Did you hear me, woman, *I...love...you!*" She turned her head to the side, unable to meet his gaze.

"More lies. You'd say anything that suits your needs. You're just like all men. Take what you want and discard the leftovers. Well, I refuse to be your leftovers, Hawk, or Bryce, or Saxon, or whoever you feel like being."

"Tell me what I lied about."

"Captain, Captain. Come to the bridge," the voice on the intercom yelled.

Hawk stepped toward the speaker in the wall and pressed the red, blinking button without taking his eyes off Kylie. "On my way." He dropped his hand. "Are you going to tell me?"

"You have more important things to worry about. Go. Take care of your men and their problems."

"This is not over, Kylie." Her angry glare ripped through him like a dagger. She'd turned against him, and he intended to find out why. He refused to part this way. More to the truth, he refused to part with her at all.

He left and swiftly made his way to the bridge. "Beggar, what's going on?"

"Captain. The ship that's been following us is closing in. They locked on to our frequency a time-unit ago to monitor any messages we send or receive. It's state of the art equipment, even better than ours."

"Slow air speed and do nothing until you hear from me." He turned and ran to his office. What information he found on CAM would determine his next course of action. The door opened and he was in his chair before it closed. He could not believe what he saw on the screen, or the deep sense of betrayal he'd tried to convince himself would not happen.

The message read, "Bryce Saxon, The Hawk, is about to land. Immediate arrest and deportation to Andor is requested, via Andorian ship in the area. All persons traveling in the company of The Hawk are to be returned to Andor with him. Use deadly force if necessary."

Thank the Gods for "Jester the Wizard" or they'd all be dead. He rushed back to the control room, pressed the intercom and announced, "Everyone to the bridge, now!"

"Beggar, prepare to 'drop'. We're going to SEA Lab as fast as this buggy will go."

"Understood, Captain." Beggar cleared his throat. "Do you really wish to maintain Velox-9 when we level?"

"Affirmative."

"But sir, maintaining that speed could rip the ship apart."

"You heard me."

"Yes sir. Maintain Velox-9 after drop."

Hawk strapped in next to Beggar at the control panel and entered complex instructions into the computer system, altering the normal route to Neptus. The crew poured in and took their assigned positions. He didn't turn when Kylie, Shandra, Jenna and Jester arrived. "Jester, secure the women for *'the drop'*."

Out the corner of his eye, he saw Jester strap the women into their respective seats without a word from any of them. Jester knew better than to question his moves, but he suspected there would be protestations from his other passengers. If it were simply his life and that of his crew, he'd land and face the enemy. They'd done it a thousand times over the annual-cycles, but he promised Shandra he'd protect her and Jenna. And, he would never risk the life of the woman he loved.

A sudden rush of desire washed over him just thinking about Kylie. Since he met her he'd had difficulty controlling his lust, and now it was love he could not control. He'd win her back, no matter what it took. She was his. He might be the biggest fool of all time, but he would find a place for them to make a life together. Jester would probably settle down with Jenna on Spectra, his crew could have *The Redemption* and find legal work for a change. Surely there was a planet where he would be safe.

"Drop in ten seconds," Beggar announced.

"All secure." Hawk silently counted down each second as it ticked away. He prayed the ship Sira and Nyles were on was at least one annual-cycle older than *The Redemption*, the first ship built to travel Velox speeds. It was their only hope if they were to reach SEA Lab first.

"Two...one...drop"

Hawk's stomach lurched into his throat, and he struggled for breath. The human body never got used to defying time, space and gravity all at once. It felt as if his head would explode and every muscle would snap from the tension. The maneuver was always the longest moments of his life.

The true miracle was that they could survive. He never suspected this sun-cycle would turn so dire, and necessitate another dangerous move. None of them ever fully adjusted to the jump, nor would they. But it was the only maneuver that would save their lives.

The ship leveled, lurched and kicked into top speed. He'd never pushed their speed this hard before, but there was a first time for everything. If they could reach SEA Lab before Nyles and Sira, *The Redemption* would be worth every credit he'd paid for her; she was a *lady* to be proud of.

He unbuckled and stood to confront the inquiring faces all looking to him for an explanation. They might as well know, there were no more secrets, and they were all on the flight of their lives. All three women had the "green around the gills" appearance. At least they would all rest for a while, and he could have some peace to ponder his next move.

"What is the meaning of this?" Kylie demanded, throwing her harness free, standing to face Hawk.

Hawk held up his hand to silence her further protests. "Have a seat, Researcher Beryl, and I *will* tell you." He wanted to smile as she plopped back down, since she reminded him of Jester when he was mad.

He took a very deep breath. "We are returning to SEA Lab. We were about to walk into a trap on Estra, and I decided to make our stand on SEA Lab. It will be easier to control the situation there. You have six sun-cycles to rest before we arrive." He knew his men understood perfectly, but the women looked as if they wanted to kill him with their bare fists, even though they bit their tongues. "Beggar, you're in charge, Jester, come with me."

As he walked past Kylie her mouth opened as if she were about to speak, but she closed it just as fast. He'd deal with her later.

"Boss," Jester said, securing Hawk's office door behind him. "What's going on?"

"Redmon betrayed us. Sira and Nyles are working for him." Hawk raked his fingers through his hair. "He ordered all of us to be arrested and sent to Andor upon arrival on Estra."

"That doesn't surprise me. I've never trusted him." Jester sat on the chair in front of Hawk's desk. "But we've fought bigger odds."

"Not with women. And not with the journal. If we fail to deliver it, thousands could die. And..."

"I see what you mean. So, what's the plan?"

"Is the transcription complete?" Jester nodded, but he wasn't sure if it was good news or bad. "I want you to duplicate Winn's writing and create another journal in Vanefca, but fill it with misinformation. Make it convincing."

"I like it—I like it a lot." Jester smiled.

"You'll need Shandra's expertise, but don't tell her what you're doing."

"She already knows I've entered the journal into the computer. I'll tell her I need a few more words to make the program run. She'll help. She doesn't ever want to translate again. I'll convince her this is the only way to insure her request."

"Good. Keep Kylie, Jenna and the men out of this. The less they know, the safer they are." Hawk exhaled loudly. "Make a duplicate chip of the real journal, then hide them both."

"Gotcha, Boss. It'll take me a awhile." He laughed. "Who will entertain Jenna??"

"I have a feeling Kylie will have plenty of spare time."

"You still haven't ironed out your differences?"

"I'm on my way to see her now. But I'll tell you, I don't understand what's got her upset. She said I lied to her."

"That's funny, considering she's the first person, outside of the crew, you've ever confided in."

"Honesty gets you nowhere."

"Well, give it the old *'Academy try'*."

"Yeah. That really got me far on Andor." Hawk groaned. "It damned near got me killed."

***

Kylie sat in the chair, back stiff, eyes focused on the door. He'd be here any minute, and he'd better be able to explain, although she'd probably only hear more lies. Hawk was damn good at them, but she was no longer the innocent, gullible woman she once was. She was past worrying about making him angry. What a joke. He was taking them, and the journal, wherever he pleased. She was no more in control of her situation than Shandra was.

Hawk had forced Shandra to come with them, and now look where they were. Stuck on a battleship with the most wanted criminal in the galaxy. That little secret, she'd kept from Shandra. It was difficult to admit she'd been foolish enough to believe his lies, and impossible to explain why she'd fallen in love with him.

The door opened and she stared at the large, powerful physique of the man who once had her trust, and he'd stolen her innocence in the process. Another mistake she had a lifetime to regret, but one look at his tempting body and she knew good and well why she'd shared his bed. His long dark hair lay recklessly across his shoulders, his blue eyes set with determination, and his square jaw planted firmly for battle. The sight of him sent desire spiraling through her body, settling between her legs. She silently cursed herself for being so weak.

His white shirt was open part way and his dark chest hair peeked at her, inviting her touch. His tight black leather pants revealed all too much of his masculinity and she had a sudden desire to run before she threw herself at him. Warrior was written all over him, and she found that strength as appealing now as when she first laid eyes on him. "I'll require my own cabin for the remainder of our trip." It seemed odd, but he had no reaction to her request.

"There are two empty cabins, take your pick. Anything else?"

How could he be so cold? His voice was flat and emotionless, the same tone he used when he greeted her for the first time on SEA Lab. She remembered all too well how guarded and indifferent he could be. "The journal," she looked him in the eye, "what are your intentions?"

"Why don't you tell me? You seem to have made up your mind about what kind of man I am." He crossed his arms over his chest. "You talked to Roloc during our flight. Maybe it was you who set the trap to have me arrested."

"Maybe I should have, but I didn't." His gaze penetrated through her and she shifted, all too aware of his potent presence. "Why would I betray you?"

"Why not? You're the one who wants the cure. I'm sure you'd stoop as low as necessary to obtain it. Is that why you slept with me? To guarantee your success?"

Anger welled in her chest, and every muscle in her body tightened. Did he really think that little of her? "Maybe. Maybe I *am* the spy you accused me of being."

He just stared at her, his eyes focused and angry, but he refused to speak. "What are you going to do with me? Put me in the holding cell? I'm already familiar with it." He did not move a muscle, and that annoyed her more than if he lashed out. "I'm sure it was you who told Beggar to lock me up while you were gone. You couldn't have me interfering with your diabolical plans, could you?"

She'd seen his temper before, but it suddenly seemed as if he no longer possessed one since he seemed completely unaffected by anything she'd said. "I suppose Sira is waiting for you on SEA Lab. I'm sure she'll please you far better than I ever did." With an assessing eye, she waited for the slightest flicker of reaction, but saw none. No wonder he'd earned such a reputation.

"Are you through?"

"Quite."

"Then kindly find your way to the cabin down the hall."

"Gladly...Captain." She grabbed her bag, squared her shoulders and marched passed him like she was happy to leave. Pain gripped her soul when his musky, masculine scent followed her into the hall, and she cursed under her breath for even noticing.

He was the enemy. Had he forgotten she possessed the knowledge to destroy him? He'd made a mistake, and it was up to her to turn him in when they arrived on SEA Lab. Could she surrender a man who held her heart in his hands? A man who had possessed her body? If he did not give the journal to the Estran scientists, he left her with no choice. Even if he did, it was her obligation as an Estran citizen, to report the whereabouts of a wanted criminal. But she knew in her heart she could never betray the man she loved. May the Gods forgive her, but she did love him.

***

Hawk threw himself on the bed. It had been a long, sleepless mooncycle and an even longer early sun-cycle. How ironic to discover that nothing in his life had changed. His motto was to trust no one but his crew, and he never should have violated his own rule. Kylie could turn him in, but without her, he had nothing. Besides, Redmon knew, and he was a greater threat than Kylie could ever hope to be.

Kylie. Just the sound of her name was painful. He'd lost her forever. Their sun-cycles together had been numbered from the start, but deep down in his soul, he'd foolishly believed that somehow, someway, they could stay together. He missed her loving touch, her sweet scent, and the warmth of her body next to his.

"Smitten, lovesick fool," he mumbled. He'd stepped over the line where Kylie was concerned, but he could not roll back the hands of time, not even for her. Kylie's wrath was what he deserved. He'd tried to hide from the inevitable, tried to believe he was innocent, and tried to believe himself free to love Kylie. *Tried* was no longer good enough.

It was better he failed Kylie now than attempt a life with her, only to fail her later. She was better off without him. Kylie needed a man she could trust, who would always be there for her, a man that was safe. All of which he was not. He would always love her, he could not stop, but he could make sure he hurt her no more.

He intended to give her all the space she needed. He would make sure the cure stayed in the proper hands. Then he'd leave so she could find the happiness she deserved. That was all he could do for her, all he ever could have done. He had to make her believe he never loved her, that he truly was The Hawk, the contemptible man of legend.

All the cutting accusations he made toward Kylie hurt him even more than her, but he had to drive her away, for her own good. It would serve no purpose to win her back. Why make the situation worse than it already was? He'd been called a heartless monster most of his life so he might as well live up to his reputation.

His eyes were heavy, and the thought of sleep was a welcome relief to the ache in his chest that threatened to consume his very soul. He would never forgive himself for causing Kylie such pain. He still did not know what had inspired her angry wrath, but it no longer mattered. She'd given him the perfect opportunity to save her even more heartache, and he'd taken that opportunity to help her. Their separation had been written in the stars long ago, and he accepted his fate. Loving her forever in his mind.

CHAPTER TWENTY-SEVEN

"Sira!" Konar yelled into the com. Where was she? "Sira!"

"Yes."

"What in the universe is going on? You should have landed on Estra by now. I've heard nothing."

"For some reason Hawk...he aah...well..."

"Just tell me!"

"He's disappeared. We can't find his ship on our screen. It's as if he dropped out of space."

"Knowing Hawk, that's exactly what he did." Konar slammed his fist on the table. "What were you doing when he disappeared?"

"I was...taking a shower."

"I'll kill you for letting him get away!" Konar wracked his brain. What would The Hawk do? Where would he go? There was only one place he would go if his guess was right. He knew Hawk and he had to take the risk. "Head for SEA Lab. I'll meet you there."

"You're coming to Neptus?"

"What's wrong, Sira? Are you warming someone else's bed?"

"Of course not, Konar. I would never betray you."

"Betray me and you'll die." He broke the link. "You'll die anyway, you two-timing bitch!"

***

"Kylie? Are you in there?"

Kylie knew it was Shandra. She opened the door and greeted the older woman. "Come in." With the sleeve of her jumpsuit she wiped tears from her cheeks.

"It's not good to stay in your room like this. Come to the galley with me and have dinner."

"I'm not hungry."

"Your heart is in pain, and I want to help." Shandra touched Kylie's shoulder. "You're shivering."

"It's just nerves. I always shiver when I'm upset."

"Talk to me, Kylie. It helps to talk about it."

"What's there to say? I fell in love with a murderer, a thief, and a liar."

"What's this nonsense about murder?" Shandra asked.

"Bryce Saxon, the man you nursed back to health is *The Hawk*. Have you heard of him?"

"Even on *my* mountain I've heard rumors of The Hawk."

"They're more than rumors. He murdered a woman, committed treason, and..."

"Kylie, you can't believe that. What did *he* tell you?"

"*He* denied everything. More lies."

"Listen to me, child. I saw the love you shared when he was at death's door. I saw into his soul, as well as you did. There was no dark shadow surrounding him. He's good, Kylie, you must believe that."

"I can't."

"You mean you won't. What are you afraid of? Look inside yourself. The answers are there. Search for them. Let your heart guide your decisions." Shandra took Kylie's hand and led her to the door. "Don't hide like this. We will have dinner together. Then you can return to your room."

Kylie nodded and let Shandra lead her to the galley. Her stomach growled at the aroma of food, but she really had no desire to eat. She took a seat at the large round table in the middle of the room.

Her heart skipped a beat when she heard Hawk's voice in the hall. Dear stars, he was walking toward her. She glanced up at his face in time to see his smile fade. The smile was for Jester who entered the room behind him with Jenna in tow. Would he ever smile at her again? She missed that sexy little grin he gave her when he thought no one could see, and the touch of his hand on her waist, his lips on hers, his...

"Good moon-cycle, Shandra," Hawk greeted. "Kylie." He took a seat at the table. "Mind if I join you?"

"Of course not, Captain," Shandra replied.

Kylie forced a grin. "It's your ship."

"So it is."

"And a mighty fine ship she is." Jester smiled at Jenna then glanced at Hawk. "I've never seen a ship that can do what *The Redemption* can. That drop was sheer poetry." He turned to Jenna. "Don't you think so, my little Jungle-Flower?"

"Absolutely, Funny-Bone."

"You two stop that mushy stuff," Shandra said, placing a plate of food in front of Kylie. "Eat this. You'll feel better."

Kylie picked up her fork and pushed food around on the plate. It looked good, and smelled good, but with Hawk sitting across from her, her stomach turned into a knot, and she knew if she took one bite it would come right back up.

"Are you still feeling space-sick from *'the drop'*?" Hawk asked.

"I'm fine." She protested a little more than she'd meant to, but he had a way of getting under her skin even when he seemed concerned about her. It was probably just a ploy to aggravate her. Well, she'd prove to him it was not working. She took a bite and forced herself to swallow. The food slid down in a giant lump and settled in her throat. She coughed several times, but she was still choking.

"Let me get you a drink," Hawk offered.

How dare he insinuate she was not capable. She pushed from the table and walked to the galley computer in front of Hawk. Without warning, her legs began to shake and she grabbed the counter, fighting the faint feeling.

Strong hands settled on her waist. Hawk held her steady, which did little to settle her stomach. Her head began to spin, her knees buckled, and she prepared to meet the floor.

Hawk whisked her into his arms. "I think you'd better rest."

Her arm had no place else to go except around his neck, but in the process, her fingers tangled in his long, loose hair. He glanced at her, and she could have sworn he was about to smile.

"I'll take her to her room."

Shandra stood. "I'll help you."

"No. Finish your dinner. I'll stay with her until you're through."

"All right," Shandra replied.

By the Gods! She didn't want to be alone with him. His pity was not necessary. He began to walk, and she felt his heart beat faster against her, and his breathing quickened. Did it mean he still cared? Did he want her? No. It was her twisted mind doing its usual wishful thinking. He'd made himself clear about his intentions toward her. The man was incapable of honest emotions.

He carried her into her cabin and laid her on the bed, but made no move to leave like she wanted him to. Hawk never did what she wanted.

His penetrating blue eyes made her body start to shiver once again, and a warmth settled between her legs. Damn him for making her want him.

Hawk leaned over the bed and braced a hand on each side of her. "I'm not leaving until you kiss me."

***

Hawk hardened while her green eyes danced over his body. This may be the second biggest mistake of his life, but he had to know if she hated him as much as she claimed. Or did he just want to taste her sweetness one last time? So much for backing away and being her savior.

"I will *not* kiss you."

"But you will." He lowered his head and pressed his lips to hers. She refused to open her mouth so he teased her pursed lips with his tongue, pushing for entry on every pass. Kylie was being stubborn, but that was no surprise. He'd provoked her, and it was that very stubbornness that brought them to this impasse.

He felt her body tremble the same as he had many times before whenever she was scared or nervous. Holding her and comforting her had worked in the past, but he doubted it would have any effect now. He pressed harder with his tongue, hoping she'd give in to his seduction. His body had betrayed him the moment he saw her in the galley, and when he lifted her in his arms, all control fled. He wanted to be inside her, to claim her—to love her.

A few more nibbles on her lips and he lifted his head. He thought for a moment she wanted to surrender, but she'd held her ground. If she hated him she'd have kissed him just to get him to leave, but she'd resisted, so he had to believe she feared losing control if she kissed him deeply.

He backed away from the bed, turned the back of the chair toward her and straddled it. He would not let her off that easy. There was a kiss he still intended to get from her. He hoped Shandra took all moon-cycle to finish her dinner, or use that psychic ability of hers to know not to intrude.

Kylie would break. She'd talk to him if he stared at her long enough. He was worried. She'd not eaten, and her eyes were red, her lids swollen. He caused those tears. At least he wanted to believe her present state was because of him and not sickness over *'the drop'*. "Would you like a pill to ease your stomach?"

"There's nothing wrong with my stomach."

He grinned. "Of course not, that's why you almost passed out in the galley."

"Why don't you just go and have your dinner."

"You can't get rid of me that easily." From the sound of her voice, she was becoming even more upset. That was not what he wanted. Why had he thought he could mend all wounds with a kiss? He was an even bigger fool than he gave himself credit for. With Kylie it had been one mistake after another. She had Shandra, Jenna and Jester to watch over her, and she'd made it crystal clear she had no need of him. He should ignore her, yet he could not. "I'm not leaving until you tell me what I lied about." Her eyes narrowed at his demand.

"The artifacts. You stole them. I found them in your room."

"I see. And what am I going to do with them?"

"Sell them, of course. The Gwadra coins alone are worth enough to keep you the rest of your life, let alone the chalice and scepter. Now you have the journal and Shandra. You have it all."

"So I do." Hawk stood and paced beside the bed. He doubted she'd believe anything he said in his defense, so he might as well let her revel in her assumptions. She'd be better off believing he was the thief than thinking they had a future together.

"If you turn over the journal to Estra, I'm sure I can arrange a handsome payment."

"Do you really believe your planet can pay me what I want?"

"How much do you want?"

Hawk grinned. He wanted his freedom. He wanted her. Neither of which was possible. Her eyes revealed contempt and pain, something he'd wanted to avoid but always knew would happen. He walked to the door. "I'll see if Shandra is finished."

"How much?" she yelled.

His hand touched the control pad. When the door slid open he stepped into the hall and glanced back. Kylie laid on the bed, her searing gaze burning a hole in his heart. He'd hurt her and there was no going back. His past would haunt him till the sun-cycle he died, and he would love Kylie even longer.

"Don't you dare leave, you, you..."

"Scoundrel? Bastard? Mercenary? Killer? Call me what you like. Estra can't give me what I want." He turned and left without a backward glance. Estra would have their cure. Kylie's parents and all her people would be saved from Genesis Disorder, and he would live out his sun-cycles in misery without her.

Kylie would be free to find a man who loved her, and he'd continue to live the life of a criminal because clearing his name meant nothing without Kylie. At least she'd be safe. The high price of love would be her hatred, a price that would save her life...even if it cost him his.

***

"Boss?" Jester entered Hawk's office. "I've finished the duplicate journals. Where do you want them?"

Hawk took the two books from Jester. "We'll plant one in my office on SEA Lab. I'll keep one with me. The real journal will be put in the secret compartment inside the control panel in the bridge."

"I like it. And don't forget, there's also a copy in the computer under a password no one could ever figure out." Jester sat and crossed his legs. "I still wish we could send it to Estra's computer and be done with it, but I'm as sure as you are that it would be intercepted."

"And don't forget, we want the man behind all this misery." Hawk raked his fingers through his hair. "Should anything happen to me, make sure the original journal is delivered to Estra." He noted Jester's concerned expression. "We'll see just how smart our enemies are. With a little luck, they'll steal the fakes and leave. Then we can leave the women safely on SEA Lab and chase them. I don't want anything to happen to them."

"When have we ever been lucky?" Jester shook his head. "I don't want anything to happen to them either, Boss. "Nyles and Sira, and God knows who else, will come to SEA Lab. How are we gong to protect the women?"

"At least on Neptus we'll see them coming. They'll be safe. We have Throm and the other guards."

"I'm not questioning your plan. I'm just worried."

"About Jenna?"

"About Kylie, Shandra, and yes, Jenna. I've come to...aah...care about her, you know?"

"All too well, my friend." Hawk leaned back in his chair. "I fear we've both fallen into the worst trap of all."

"What's that?"

"Love." Hawk picked up a pen and drew lines on a piece of paper that began to duplicate the pyramid shape of SEA Lab. He heard Jester groan and felt like joining him.

"I'm not in love, Boss."

"What would you call it? Lust?"

"No. It's more like...like..."

"Face it, we've both fallen head over heels for two of the most beautiful, stubborn, redheads in the galaxy. If I didn't know better, they could be sisters." Hawk rubbed his chin, realizing he should have shaved. "We brought them with us, and put them in danger. Now that's something to be proud of."

"It's not so bad. They could be in danger without us, you know."

"I believe that would make Kylie extremely happy right about now."

"She'll forgive you. I know she will."

"I don't want her to." Hawk held up his hand to silence Jester's protest. "When this is over, I want you and Jenna to find happiness together." He smiled. "After seeing the way she throws you around, I think you've found a perfect mate."

"I could stop her anytime I choose, but I kind of like it."

"And so does she. You're a lucky man. Enjoy her, love her, protect her."

"What will you do?"

"What I've always done." The scowl on Jester's face was more than he could handle. "Don't look at me like that. Of course I'll miss you. More than I'd like to admit. In fact, I'll probably curse you every sun-cycle for messing up my computer systems."

"When will we arrive on Neptus?"

Jester's voice sounded overly emotional and he knew why his friend had changed the subject. "In a few time-units. But I'm going to SEA Lab alone."

"No! That's suicide."

"It's the only way. It'll be up to you and Beggar to deliver the cure to Estra and return Shandra and Jenna to their home. From there, you're on your own."

"I'm not going to leave you on SEA Lab to die!"

"I'm a dead man no matter what. Have been for annual-cycles. I've just been postponing the inevitable."

"What's happened to you? I've never heard you talk like this before. And don't tell me it's love, because that story doesn't hold any more water than the dead zone on Andor!"

Hawk raked his fingers through his hair. "I'm tired. Tired of running, and not having a normal life."

Jester moaned. "I've seen you depressed before, but this takes the prize. If it's Kylie you want, fight for her. You've never run from a fight in your life."

"I'm not running now." Hawk stood and began to pace the small area behind his desk. "There's no way I'm going to drag you, the women, or the rest of the crew into this. I work best alone, you know that."

"Just let *me* go with you. I'll set up vid-cams and monitor them from your office. *The Redemption* can hover close for back-up." Jester walked around the desk and laid his hand on Hawk's shoulder to stop him. "We've always worked together. This is no different. I've always had your back. You know that."

Hawk grinned. "You know how to get to me."

"That's why you keep me around. Now, what's the plan?"

"A trap, but we don't want to endanger anyone on SEA Lab. Sira and Nyles are no more than four time-units behind us."

"Let's start now. I'll call Throm and feel him out."

"Do it."

Jester picked up the con-line and waited.

"Throm here."

"It's Jester. What's going on down there?"

"It's been insane! Roloc is here, Redmon is on his way as well as three high priests from Spectra. I've heard every story under the three suns. What in the universe is going on?"

"What have you heard?" Jester asked as Hawk paced.

"Roloc is furious. He's demanded to speak with Researcher Beryl, who obviously left with you and Saxon. Redmon insists that Saxon is The Hawk, and if he returns I'm to arrest him immediately, and you as well."

Hawk nodded at Jester.

"Throm, what is your assessment of the situation?"

"You mean, do I believe Redmon?" Throm cleared his throat. "I don't know what to believe. Saxon is a good man, and I don't want to make up my mind until I speak with him."

"Throm, this is Saxon. We will arrive shortly. Tell no one."

"Sir, I can't send a sub for you. I'm being watched."

"No problem. Meet us in my office."

"Yes, sir."

Hawk closed the link. "Throm will help us, I have no doubt. He was never the type to jump to conclusions without sufficient evidence."

"That's why you put him in charge." Jester stood. "How are you going to keep the women on the ship?"

"We won't tell them we've leaving. Go fill Beggar in. Tell him as far as the women are concerned, we haven't arrived and that you and I are in conference and are not to be disturbed. Better yet, I'll tell Kylie myself."

"Olly-dolly, you're the boss."

* * *

Kylie pushed the food around on her plate. Shandra was acting like a mother, insisting she take care of herself and eat. Food was the last thing on her mind. She'd worried about her parents, the cure, and Hawk. What was he up to? She had not seen his face for the last two sun-cycles. Was he planning the great escape to a distant planet where he could sell the artifacts and hold the cure for ransom?

His face flashed in her mind. She'd never admit it to anyone, but she missed him terribly. Love was hard to admit even to herself. His caress, his kisses, the feel of his body, and the masculine scent of his skin was all too fresh in her memory. So was his betrayal, his lies, his crimes.

"Kylie, are you all right?" Shandra asked.

"Fine."

"She misses Saxon, Mother. Let her be." Jenna patted Kylie's hand. "It'll work out. You'll see."

"It's too late for..." Kylie stopped speaking when The Hawk entered the galley. He looked as if he had not slept in several sun-cycles. His hair lay wild on his shoulders, his jaw tilted high with an arrogant air of forcefulness. He was up to something.

"Good-sun-cycle, ladies," he greeted.

"Good-sun-cycle, Captain," Jenna answered.

"We'll arrive on Neptus in about thirty time-units. Until then, Jester and I will be in conference. I want no interruptions. Is that clear?"

Kylie stood. "Why don't you just address your request to me? I'm the one you don't want to see. Right, Captain?"

A chill ran down her spine when his blue eyes narrowed and a scowl creased his lips. She waited for him to deny her words, but he silently turned and headed toward his office. Her heart raced as anger mixed with desire. Just the sight of him stirred her longing. What would it take to get him out of her thoughts?

She could never forgive his blatant deceptions. How could she have put her faith and trust in a man who admitted he was a criminal? Damn him to Diabolus! He'd stolen her heart and her virginity. No. That was not true. He took nothing. She'd offered herself to him willingly, and if she were honest, she'd do it again.

It was apparent Roloc sent the wrong person for the job. He never should have insisted she accomplish the impossible. If it had not been for her personal, selfish interests, things might be vastly different. Roloc told her to be objective. She should have listened.

Had that loss of objectivity cost her Hawk? Did she really want to give him up? She'd always prided herself on being logical, but she had not given Hawk a chance to explain. There could be a thousand reasons why he possessed the artifacts.

He was headed back to SEA Lab. If he wanted to escape with the cure and all the riches, he would have headed for Cryon, or some other remote planet to peddle his wares. Whatever his plan, she owed him the opportunity to account for his actions.

Dear stars, had she made the worst mistake of her life? Evidence was not always what it seemed. He had said as much about his murder charge. People were always quick to believe the worst. Was it a trap she'd fallen into as well, or was Hawk guilty as charged?

Kylie stood. "I'm going to see Saxon."

Jenna grabbed her hand and pulled her down to the chair. "I don't think that's a good idea."

"I don't care what he said. I've got to talk to him, now."

"Kylie," Shandra began, "what's so important that it can't wait?"

"I may have been wrong. I have to find out."

"Your change of heart is a good sign, but Hawk has much on his mind right now."

"Mother's right. I can't even talk to Jester when he's with Saxon." Jenna laughed. "Even my little Funny-Bone gets angry if I disturb him when he's in conference. Give them a little time, then we'll both go see them together. Okay?"

"Maybe you're right. What's a few more time-units?" Kylie stepped toward the door, noting the concern on Shandra's face. "It's all right. I think I'll go take a shower. I promise to wait for Jenna."

"I'm not sure either of you has any business disturbing those two, but I'll leave it up to you," Shandra said.

"I think Saxon will want to hear what I have to say."

"You may be right, my dear, but be careful. Jenna, you keep her out of trouble." Shandra followed the two girls out of the galley. "Promise me?"

"I promise."

Kylie stopped in front of her door. "Shandra, You have nothing to worry about." She turned toward Jenna. "Stop by in two time-units. That should be long enough." She watched Jenna's eyes sparkle and she knew it was due to the thought of seeing Jester.

"Sure. They can't live without us, and we need to remind them." Jenna giggled. "That is what you're going to tell him, isn't it?"

"Absolutely." Kylie smiled. "I wish I had a sister like you."

Shandra smiled. "That would be double trouble."

"Indeed it would." Kylie entered her room and headed for the lav. This moon-cycle she could have Hawk back in her bed. If she had not been so stupid in the first place, they would still be together. He said they'd arrive in thirty time-units. That was not long enough, but she planned to spend every moment in his arms and create memories to savor.

She owed Hawk an apology. Jumping to conclusions had been costly, and she vowed never to let that happen again. He'd said to trust him, and she failed. He had protected her and Estra's interest from sun-cycle one, and she repaid him with mistrust and accusations. Could he ever forgive her? She'd see to it he did, and then she planned to help him clear his name.

CHAPTER TWENTY-EIGHT

"Throm," Hawk extended his hand across his desk when the security officer entered his office on SEA Lab.

"Chief Saxon, how did you get here?" he asked while he shook Hawk's hand.

"I have my ways."

"The same way you left, and I know better than to ask."

"Please, have a seat." Hawk pointed to the chair next to Jester's in front of the desk. "Who has arrived since I left?"

"As I said, Roloc is here. He's busy in the lab. Redmon is to arrive within the time-unit." Throm lowered his head. "I'm sorry to inform you that Nyles and Sira escaped."

"They'll be here within the time-unit as well. And don't blame yourself. You did your job well. Sira is a clever spy." Hawk crossed his arms over his chest and leaned back. "I need to know where your loyalty lies, Throm."

"I'm here to do a job. Duty is where my loyalty lies.'"

"That's an honorable answer, but you know what I want to hear." He studied Throm's eyes, but the man did not waver. He'd know immediately if Throm lied. "Well?"

"Redmon contacted me. He told me you were The Hawk, and if you returned I was to arrest you and turn you over to him when he arrived. He asked about Professor Winn's journal and offered me a handsome sum to turn it over to him."

"And?" Hawk glanced at Jester who sat silently observing Throm.

"I trust no man who offers me credits in the amount Redmon spoke of. I told him I'd consider his proposal, but I have no intentions of accepting."

"Are you willing to work with us?" Hawk asked.

"That depends on your motives." Throm shifted in his chair.

"I intend to deliver the cure to Estra and stop anyone who gets in the way. No credits. No applause. Do you understand?"

Throm nodded. "I'll be happy to work with you."

"Even if I am The Hawk?"

"I've heard the stories, and to be honest, they bother me. But, I trust you. I have family on Estra, and I'd do anything to keep them alive and well."

"Good." Hawk glanced at Jester. "Bring us three cups of koffa. We have plans to make."

"Sure, Boss."

"When Redmon arrives he's to find me in the holding cell. He must believe you're on his side. When Sira and Nyles show up, and trust me they will, play along with their little games. They aren't the real threat, Redmon is, and he'll make his move as soon as he arrives. I don't want any of the people on SEA Lab involved in this. Someone could get killed. We'll stage the final show-down in the Delphin room."

"That's good, no one has used that room since you left. All research stopped without Winn and his journal."

Jester straightened. "How is that possible? Surely all that information was in the lab computers."

"After you left, I was called to the lab. Those scientists were ready to kill someone. It seems when they entered their password to access the material, everything had been permanently erased. Computers aren't my specialty, but someone sabotaged them."

"It had to be Sira."

"I'll call a meeting with all the security officers. They'll make sure no one wanders into that area. In fact, the Delphins haven't been seen since Researcher Beryl left."

"Good. Keep all personnel away from level two. Don't alarm your men, just tell them to keep everyone away. They're not to make a move without checking with you first."

"Yes, Chief Saxon. Good to have you back, sir." Throm saluted.

"Thanks for the show of respect, but I want you to treat me as if you hate me when Redmon arrives. After you meet with your men, Jester will fill you in on what you need to do."

"I'll be back shortly." Throm turned on his heel and left the office.

"Boss, I have a funny feeling something is wrong."

"Don't tell me you're turning psychic too."

"Don't knock it till you've tried it." Jester stood, walked to the vid-screen in the wall and turned it on. "At least the hidden vid-cams are working."

The private com-link sounded and Hawk answered. "Yes."

"Captain, thought you'd like to know the ship that was following us will reach SEA Lab in two time-units."

"Thanks, Beggar. Notify me at once if any other ships approach." Hawk closed the link. "You heard him. We have little time to prepare."

"Let's do it."

***

Ready?" Jenna asked when Kylie stepped into the hall.

"More than ready." She followed Jenna to Hawk's office, and they both stopped and stared at the thick metal door. Kylie raised her hand and knocked loudly. "It's Kylie and Jenna." She waited, tapping her foot. Nothing. "Why do I think they're not here?"

"I have the same feeling, but where are they?"

"We've been tricked. Follow me." Kylie led Jenna to the bridge. "Beggar, where are we?"

"We're getting close to Neptus."

"How long?" Kylie asked, noticing Beggar shift in his chair, an uneasy look on his weathered face.

"Twenty–eight time-units."

"And where is our Captain?"

"In conference with orders not to be disturbed."

"I see. Of course, I won't disturb him." She turned toward Jenna. "Let's leave them to do their jobs."

Jenna walked out of the room first, Kylie on her heels, not stopping until they were alone in the galley. "What's up your sleeve, Kylie?"

"Hawk and Jester have gone to SEA Lab."

"How could they, we're not even there yet."

"I know Hawk and his crew. Do you remember when we walked into the bridge just before we executed 'the drop'?" She watched Jenna nod. "Saxon said he wanted to maintain Velox-9, which means we would have arrived two time-units ago." Kylie grabbed Jenna's arm. "Come on."

Kylie led Jenna to the shuttle bay, and they both stopped short when they found Shandra standing beside the four-man craft. The two man shuttle was gone.

"Mother, what are you doing here?"

"I'm psychic, remember? And the two of you will not go without

273

me."

"Then get in, we're leaving." Kylie opened the hatch and gestured for Jenna and Shandra to step inside. Before her foot touched the shuttle someone grabbed her from behind. She wiggled in his arms enough to see his face. Beggar. She should have known she'd tipped him off in the bridge. "Let me go!"

"Hawk told me to guard you with my life, and that's exactly what I'm doing. You will not leave *The Redemption*."

Kylie kicked at his shins as hard as she could, but only provoked a moan. She threw her elbows, but it had little effect since he held her off the ground. Just as he spun her, Jenna performed a series of moves she'd never seen. In a flash, Beggar released his hold. Her feet hit the metal floor and Beggar slumped on the deck. "Jenna. Thank the stars."

"He won't bother anyone for a while," Jenna said, dusting the palms of her hands together.

"You must teach me that...stuff you know."

"Corel?" Jenna smiled. "I'd be happy to, but not right now. We don't want our friend here to wake up." She helped her mother into the shuttle and followed behind.

Kylie took the pilot's seat. "Buckle up." She fastened the harness over her shoulders then flipped four switches.

"You know how to pilot this thing?" Jenna helped Shandra strap in.

"Yeah, but my landings aren't always the best." Her mind recounted her first crash landing in the Agor Sea. This time there would not be a malfunction in the steering mechanism. She powered up and released the bay doors, then headed into space. Sure enough, Neptus lay like a big green ball below them, its three suns cresting the horizon as dawn broke on the watery planet.

"It's beautiful," Shandra remarked.

"Sure is." Jenna laid a hand on Kylie's shoulder. "How are we going to get into SEA Lab?"

"There should be three breath helmets in back. See if you can find them."

Jenna moved to the back of the craft and looked around. She held up one clear bubble. "Is this it?"

"Where are the other two?"

"There's only one."

"Hawk and Jester must have taken them. How good a swimmer are you, Jenna?"

"I used to dive for pearls without equipment."

"Good. Shandra, you'll wear the helmet. Jenna and I will take you down." Kylie leveled off the shuttle and surveyed the great expanse of glistening green ocean for the landing pad. A speck in the distance caught her eye and she headed for the tiny point.

Soon the small spot took shape and Kylie sighed as she slowed for landing. She fought memories of impacting the water and sinking to the bottom.

"Kylie, you're shaking. What's wrong?" Jenna asked.

"I'll be fine. Prepare for landing." The large landing area came at her with blinding speed. Kylie reversed the throttle to put the shuttle in a hover mode and eased it down until it settled with a thud on the thick, metal platform above the sea. She let out the breath she'd been holding and wiped beads of sweat from her forehead.

"Kylie," Shandra whispered.

She turned to face the older woman. "What is it?"

"I sense terrible danger. Evil awaits us."

"What exactly do you see?" Jenna asked her mother.

"What I see isn't as important as our ability to change it. Please, you must be careful, or..."

Kylie laid a hand on Shandra's arm. "I understand. We'll take care of you."

"It's not me I'm worried about, it's you and Saxon."

Her heart raced, but Kylie forced herself to stand. "Jenna, keep a close eye on your mother. I trust her instincts. This will be dangerous, are you sure you still want to go?" Both women nodded. "Okay. Let's go."

Jenna opened the hatch and stepped out on the platform, offering Shandra a guiding hand. The two women huddled together in the early sun-cycle light, and she suddenly missed her own mother. She could only hope she was doing the right thing.

Kylie secured the helmet on Shandra. "Just breathe naturally. Don't panic, we'll be with you. Jenna will take your right and I'll take your left. We'll guide you down."

"How deep do we have to go?" Jenna asked.

"About forty feet. It won't be easy without a helmet."

"No problem," Jenna confirmed.

"Jump on three. One...two...thr..." The cold water grabbed her, the shock nearly sucking the air out of her lungs. She began to kick, pulling Shandra and guiding Jenna. They had to hurry since she and Jenna held only one breath of air to sustain them.

The currents made every stroke with her one free arm more difficult. Pressure bore down, her ears rang and her head felt like it might explode. She kicked harder and pulled the water with her right hand, but progress was slow. The salty water stung her eyes, and she had a terrible urge to gasp for air.

Something brushed her hand and she heard a message in her mind to "hold on". Mia. Thank the heavens. She grabbed Mia's dorsal fin and allowed the mammal to pull all three of them toward the entrance to the Delphin pool. Images from Mia played in her mind's eye.

Mia seemed to be telling her the same thing as Shandra. Evil and death were the recurring theme of the Delphin's thoughts as they passed through the opening in the side of the pyramid she knew so well. They surfaced and Kylie filled her lungs with life-giving air. Mia guided them to the belly-slide.

Jenna took a deep breath. "Wow! What a ride!"

Kylie lifted the breathing helmet off Shandra. "That was Mia, a Delphin I've been working with. She's a real sweetheart."

"I'll say. She saved us." Jenna stood on the submerged platform. "I hate to admit I was struggling back there."

"It isn't the first time Mia has saved my life." Kylie stood and sat on the edge of the pool.

"Where do you think Jester is?" Jenna asked.

"Now girls, you must promise me you'll be careful. We don't know what to expect." Shandra shook her head. "I need to rest. I'm afraid I'm not as young and fit as you two."

Kylie helped Shandra out of the pool. "Jenna, help me get her to my cabin." Shandra trembled beneath her grasp while they made their way to the lift. She was grateful to find the conveyance empty when they stepped inside, and happier still when the doors opened to a vacant hallway. They hurried to the cabin she'd shared with Hawk. Jenna took Shandra to the bunk and Kylie stared at the familiar surroundings.

Memories of waking after her accident and seeing Hawk for the first time seemed like another lifetime now. He was simply Saxon then, a man who intrigued her. Now he was The Hawk, the man she loved.

"Jenna." She waited for her to turn and motioned her to join her in the lav so Shandra could not hear. She handed Jenna a towel. "I'm going to find Saxon. It's too dangerous for Shandra to roam the halls, someone is bound to see her. Promise me you'll stay with her."

"What about Jester? I want to find him."

"I'll find him and send him here. Don't leave this cabin, no matter what. Okay?"

"Hurry, Kylie. I don't like the feelings I'm getting."

"Do you have your mother's abilities?"

"Sometimes, but this is more an educated guess. We're in big trouble here, and I don't mean Saxon and Jester."

Kylie dried herself with a towel. "I have the same feeling, that's why it's so important to keep Shandra here."

Jenna gave Kylie a quick hug. "Hurry."

***

Everything was set. Jester was editing the vid of him in the holding cell to make sure it would fool Redmon if he checked up on him from the office, after he'd visited The Hawk in person. He knew the man well and hoped he'd follow his usual routine.

All that remained was the arrival of the players. Hawk leaned his head against the back of the chair. He could not remember the last time he'd slept. If he were lucky, he could catch one time-unit before his *guests* intruded into his life.

The moment he closed his eyes visions of Kylie flooded his mind. Her perky red hair, sexy green eyes, and a body that could send him over the edge just looking at her, but it was more than that. He loved that part of her he could not see, the part deep within he could only sense.

Kylie was safe on *The Redemption*, hating him as she should. If all went well, she would have her cure and be back on Estra within a week. Then he could be on his way, free of her spell, free of the pain that seeing her caused.

He jerked upright at the sound of a knock. Quietly he moved to the door and pressed his body against the wall, ready to grab whoever entered. The door whooshed open and he grabbed the intruder. His heart raced as a familiar scent invaded his senses. She felt good and he hated what he had to do.

Hawk pushed her away and secured the door. "What are you doing here?"

"I had to see you."

"You see me. Now go back to the ship where you belong."

"I belong with you." Kylie grabbed Hawk's hand when he turned away.

He pulled free of her grasp. "You belong with your people, not me."

"I was wrong not to give you a chance to explain. Hawk, please, don't turn from me."

"Researcher Beryl, wrong?" Hawk returned to his chair and sat behind his desk. "I'll arrange for your immediate return."

"No you won't. I was assigned to SEA Lab the same as you, and I'm going to stay."

"Sira, Nyles and Redmon are on their way. When they arrive it isn't going to be pretty. I can't guarantee your safety."

"I'm not asking you to." Kylie shook her head and stared at the floor. "You intended to return the artifacts all along, didn't you?"

She looked up and met his gaze, and his heart melted. He knew what it took for her to come. "Maybe."

"Don't play games, Hawk, and don't push me away." She stepped toward him and put her arms around his neck. "You may fool your men with this tough-guy image, but underneath this cold exterior is a man with a heart. Now, tell me the truth."

Hawk reached up, grabbed her hands and guided them to her side. "Been studying Sira's techniques?" She wrenched free and turned her back. His attempts to distance himself from her were only making matters worse. He stepped closer, pressed his chest to her back and rested his hands on the swell of her hips. "I'm sorry, Amica."

She stiffened beneath his touch. Desire coursed through every vein in his body. It was wrong to want her, but it was worse to hurt her with words he did not mean. He turned her to face him.

"I had the artifacts for safe keeping." He traced the outline of her jaw with his fingertip. "I have all the credits a man could ever want, and I earned every last one of them." He bent and brushed her lips with his, afraid to kiss her for fear of not being able to stop.

"That wasn't so hard, was it?"

"I must admit, it's easier when you give me a chance."

Kylie reached up and stroked the stubble on his cheeks. "I love you." She smiled. "I'll give you a chance for more than confession."

"I don't think..." Before he could finish, her mouth covered his, her tongue seeking, her breasts pressing against his chest. How could he resist such temptation? She kissed him deeply, passionately, just the way he'd dreamed of. But most important, she said the words he'd prayed she say again. Her body was hot against his, and her kiss inspired the response he knew he could not satisfy.

With regret he ended the kiss and eased his head back. "I love you, Amica, and if I had the time I'd show you how much."

"Oh Hawk, I've really made a mess of things."

"No more than I have." He wiped a tear from her cheek with his finger.

"I don't think you understand. I brought Jenna and Shandra with me."

"You what?"

"Chief Saxon," Throm's voice called over the com. "Sira and Nyles have just arrived.

Hawk stepped toward the vid-screen that showed the Delphin room and watched. Sira and Nyles were right on schedule and acting in character. He felt the warmth of Kylie's body behind him. He reached back and grabbed her hand. "You might as well know, Roloc is here."

"I want to see him."

"There will be plenty of time when this is over. First we deal with the enemy, then friends, then I deal with you." How he wanted to make love to her this moment, to forget the battle ahead, and the obstacles that stood in the way of a lifetime of happiness with the woman he loved.

"Hawk, look! What in the universe are they doing?"

CHAPTER TWENTY-NINE

Nyles removed his diving gear and dropped it on the floor of the ready room by the Delphin pool. "Did you see that? He attacked me!"

"The Delphins don't like you any better than people do."

"Funny, Sira." He picked up a towel from the shelf and wiped his face. "What's it going to be? Have you made your decision yet?"

"Konar is only one time-unit behind us. If we can get the journal and escape before he arrives, I'm with you."

"Your loyalty is so reassuring. And if we can't? What then?"

"What do you think? I'll do what I have to. All the credits in the universe won't do me a bit of good if I'm dead."

"You're scared." Nyles grinned. "I should have known you're a coward."

"And I suppose you're going to protect me against Hawk and Konar? Sure, Nyles. I've seen you in action. I must say, you're rather pathetic."

Nyles grabbed Sira around the waist and jerked her to him. "That's not what you said last moon-cycle."

"Never mistake sex for business." Sira reached behind her and drew her weapon.

"Going to shoot me?"

"You are incredibly stupid. I don't need to waste my time. I'm quite sure Hawk will take care of you."

"You're so sentimental, Sira, dear. I'd watch my back if I were you."

"You think I underestimate you?"

"We'll see soon enough." Nyles shoved her away.

Sira snickered. "I don't need you!" She pulled a vid-disk from her pocket, then held it in the air. "As long as I have this."

"And what is that?"

"Insurance."

Nyles stepped toward her. "Let me see it."

She pointed her weapon at him and backed toward the edge of the pool. "I swear, I'll kill you."

In a flash Nyles lifted his arm knocking hers back, the weapon flying into the salty water behind Sira. He grabbed for the disk, but she held it behind her, over the pool, out of his reach. "Give it to me, bitch!"

"Never!"

The water rippled and gushed when a Delphin leapt into the air, grabbed the disk from Sira's outstretched hand, then disappeared from the pool, out into the depths of the sea.

Sira screamed at the top of her lungs.

"Was that something important, my love?"

She kicked Nyles in the groin then stomped past him toward the lift. "You have no idea!"

Nyles groaned and ran after her. He grabbed her arm while she waited. "Tell me about that disk. You have nothing to lose now that it's fish food."

"That disk means life or death to Hawk, and a lot of credits to me. Hawk would pay anything to get his hands on it."

"Let me guess, you stole it from Redmon and it shows Hawk killing Lissa. And it's a hologram disk that cannot be duplicated." Nyles grinned widely. "Redmon will kill you slow and painfully for betraying him."

"Why didn't you drown on your way here!"

"You're getting testy, Sira." He gripped her arm tighter. "Now, tell Nyles all about that disk."

"Over my dead body."

"That could easily be arranged."

***

Hawk watched the screen and shook his head. "It's good to see Sira and Nyles getting along so well, however, I wonder what's on that disk."

"She said it meant life or death to you. It must be the evidence you've been looking for."

"I've seen the vid that convicted me. If that's what she had, it's of no value to me." He turned toward Kylie. "Where are Jenna and Shandra?"

"In our cabin." *Our cabin*? She'd always thought of it as Saxon's cabin, but suddenly *our* had a nice ring to it. She studied Hawk's worried expression, even though his demeanor was unusually calm.

"They're not safe there. Redmon will search there first."

Hawk ran his fingers through his lose hair and stared at her. She could not stop the tears that welled in her eyes, yet his gaze raked her from head to foot. "I'm sorry, I wasn't thinking. I just wanted to see you and explain." She looked him in the eyes. "Or should I say apologize?"

Hawk walked toward her, put his arms around her and pulled her close. "It's all right, Amica. I'll take care of it."

His beautiful, blue eyes gave her confidence, eased her apprehension, but his embrace said he wanted her. Her hands found his shoulders and toyed in his silky black hair.

"Captain," Throm's voice called over the com, "I just received word Redmon has landed. We're sending a sub for him now."

Hawk rushed to the desk. "Throm, meet me at the holding cell." He walked back to Kylie. "I have to go. I'll send Throm for you, Jenna and Shandra. He'll take you to a safe place, where I want you to stay until this is over. Promise me, Amica, that you won't come after me. I can't fight Sira, Nyles and Redmon *and* worry about you."

"I promise. I'll stay where Throm puts me."

He bent his head and kissed her. She felt his anxiety, but most of all, he sent her his tenderness and love. This was not the kiss of a murderer, it was the compassionate man she'd surrendered to. He tasted sweet and masculine. She savored his scent and his touch, never wanting to let go. Her body tingled and she desired him more than she thought possible.

Emptiness overwhelmed her when he ended the kiss and pulled his lips from hers. "Hawk, please, come back to me." His eyes darkened with emotion before he turned and walked to the door. He smiled over his shoulder as he left, and she forced herself to smile back.

The door slid closed behind him and she never felt more alone. "Be careful," she whispered, knowing he could not hear her. She walked to the small couch and all but fell onto the soft cushions, unable to see through her tears. Whatever Hawk's plans were, she'd support him. He'd told her repeatedly to trust him, and it was past time she gave him the trust he'd earned.

She closed her eyes and prayed nothing would happen to him. If anyone could deliver the cure to Estra it was The Hawk. She was sure the cure was safe on *The Redemption*. Hawk would never risk bringing it here.

The quiet whoosh of the door announced Throm's arrival. She hated to open her eyes and face reality, but she'd promised him.

"Get up, Bitch!"

All thoughts instantly fled at the all too familiar sound of Sira's evil voice. Kylie opened her eyes and stared at the dark-haired woman who stood before her. Sira's wet hair clung to her skin, most of her usually heavy make-up was gone, and what was left lay in streaks under her eyes and on her cheeks. Her soggy plain uniform made her look like just another crew member rather than the well-manicured vixen she'd first met.

"I said, get up!"

Kylie stood and faced her nemesis who held a weapon aimed at her chest. "Going to kill me, Sira? Would that make you feel better?"

"Don't tempt me."

"I thought Hawk was the only one who could tempt you." Kylie noticed Sira's hand begin to shake. "Too bad you had to settle for Nyles. He isn't even second best." She laughed when Sira snarled at her. So, the woman had a weak spot where men were concerned.

"I have the man I want. Konar is more man than Hawk could ever think of being."

"Konar?"

"Surely you've heard of him?"

"If you're referring to the man who kills women and children and steals everything he can get his hands on, then yes, I've heard of him." Kylie smiled. "I suppose he suits you, Sira. You couldn't find anyone other than a slime-snake to take you to bed."

"You're jealous."

"Hardly." Kylie swallowed hard. She couldn't let Sira think her revelations bothered her, although her words had shocked her down to her boots. "Even Konar's reputation can't compare to Hawk's."

"You don't know, do you?" Sira laughed. "Maybe I should have said, Redmon. Would that clear things up for you?" She stepped closer. "Konar and Redmon are one and the same. I'm surprised you and the almighty Hawk haven't discovered that little secret."

The shock of Sira's words washed over her. She pulled on Saxon's strength. He had taught her well without even trying. If she could maintain indifference, and make Sira crazy enough, she might be able to get the weapon away from her. "We suspected." Kylie smiled. "But thanks for confirming it. Too bad you'll never know what you missed with Hawk."

"I know all I need to know. Now, start walking."

Sira shoved the weapon into her ribs to prod her forward. The woman meant business, and she knew Sira would do anything to get what she wanted. The door opened and she stepped into the hall.

"Walk." Sira shoved the weapon in Kylie's back. "And make it fast."

She had no choice but to follow Sira's directions. Her chance would come, and she'd take great pleasure wiping the smug grin off the hateful woman's face. She may not be a trained spy like Sira, but she needed no special training to enjoy pulling the woman's hair out by the roots.

***

"Mother, what's wrong?"

Shandra placed her fingertips on her temples. "Thoughts keep invading my mind. I can't figure out who is…. Wait! It's the Delphins."

"Kylie told me she communicated with them, but why would they call to you?"

"Danger, suffering, evil. I see them with something flat and round. They're calling to Kylie…she's…."

"What? What's happened to Kylie? Do you see Jester or Hawk?"

"Just Kylie in the clutches of evil. We have to help her."

"She insisted we wait here in her cabin. Jenna placed her arm around her mother's shoulders. "You're shaking."

"Kylie needs our help. We have to go to her."

"I can't go back on my word." Jenna glanced at the timer on her wrist. "We'll give her a few more minutes."

Shandra stood and began to pace, wringing her hands. "I'm afraid, Jenna."

"Kylie will be fine. She has Hawk and Jester to watch out for her."

"You don't understand."

"Of course I do. Hawk is a professional." Jenna watched her mother shake her head. "He's the best in the universe at what he does. Everyone knows that, whether they believe him innocent or guilty."

"That's not what I'm worried about."

"For stars sake, just tell me what it is."

"There's things I haven't told you. Things about my past. Things that may shock you. Things that may cause you to hate me."

"Things, what things?"

Shandra stopped pacing. "I pray you'll never know, but I want you to be prepared in case I'm forced to reveal my past."

Jenna laughed. "I can't believe you've kept deep, dark secrets from me."

"I had just cause."

The smile disappeared from Jenna's face. "Tell me, mother."

"It's too painful. Lives will be destroyed."

"You're scaring me." Jenna checked her timer. "I'm worried about Kylie too, but what could your past have to do with all this?"

"I'm sorry I brought it up." Shandra sat beside her daughter on the bunk. "I know you're fond of Kylie, and I'm glad the two of you have found a friendship. You've never had friends. I've forced you to be a recluse because of my gift...and my past."

Jenna took her mother's hand in hers. "I've enjoyed making friends with Kylie. She's like the sister I never had, but I've never blamed you for anything. I love you, and I understand why we've had to live apart from other people." She wiped a tear from her mother's cheek.

"Oh, Jenna. I'm so happy to hear you say that. Please," Shandra looked into her daughter's eyes, "hold on to that feeling."

***

Throm saluted the man who approached, blocking his path to Saxon's cabin.

"Where is he?" Redmon exhaled loudly. "Hawk, where is he?"

"Follow me, sir." Throm led the way to the holding cell on the level below. He stopped in front of the one-way, impenetrable glass wall and kicked it once with his boot.

Redmon peered inside and grinned. "Well done, Officer Throm."

"Thank you, sir."

Hawk heard Throm's boot hit the bottom of the door, their signal Redmon was watching and listening. He jumped from the bunk and rushed toward them, beating his fists against the glass. "Let me out of here! Throm, you traitor! I'll kill you for this!"

He stomped to the bunk, threw the mattress across the room, then picked up the pillow and shredded it. Screaming at the top of his lungs, he ran back to the window and beat on the glass repeatedly.

"Redmon! Help me. Get me out of here!"

"There's nothing I can do for a traitor." Redmon turned and stepped away from Hawk.

He kicked the glass wall as hard as he could. "So, you've turned your back on me as well!"

"I wouldn't help you for all the credits in the galaxy." Redmon looked at Throm. "Let's go. We have better things to do."

Hawk turned and walked to the back corner, leaned against the back wall, then folded his arms across his chest and stared as if he could see the devil himself.

Throm kicked the door one last time and Hawk relaxed. After that performance he should take Kylie's suggestion and join the theater, but then, all operatives received extensive training for just such occasions.

He gave them a few moments, then reached in his pocket for the small electronic device Jester had devised to release the lock. Throm and Redmon were probably on their way to his cabin for a search, then Throm would take Redmon to his office so he could discover the fake journal. Kylie, Jenna and Shandra should be safe in the storeroom where he'd told Throm to take them, but he had to see for himself. First he had to secure some protection.

After a check of the corridor, he ran for the slide pole across from the lift to avoid being spotted. He didn't need further complications now. He grabbed the pole with his hands, wrapped one leg around it and made his descent, stopping half-way to make sure the area was empty. Throm had done a good job busying the security crew, he'd yet to see one of them, in fact he'd seen no one. Hawk made his way past offices, wondering where everyone had gone.

It was unusually quiet for this time of sun-cycle. He slipped into the armory, secured the door behind him, then stepped over to the weapons cabinet. The glass doors had been pried open, and a quick inventory revealed two pieces missing. Sira and Nyles. He continued around the room, but everything else seemed in order.

Footsteps echoed in the corridor outside and he ducked behind a large crate. Peering around the edge, he saw Jester enter and walk to the cabinet. He quietly crept up behind him. "Looking for something?" An unexpected laugh escaped when Jester nearly jumped out of his sandals, both hands shaking as he clutched the front of his pink flowered shirt.

"You gave me a heart attack!" Jester turned around.

"What are you doing here?" Hawk smiled. "You know you can't hit a target unless it walked into your fazer."

"Yeah, well." Jester stared at the ground. "I passed Throm in the hall. He said he did not have time to explain, but he was on his way to get Kylie, Jenna and Shandra as you ordered. When I heard that, I decided I needed a weapon. We have to protect them."

"Easy. We can't afford to think with our hearts."

"But Boss, they're our women!"

"I know. They're fine." Hawk reached into the cabinet and removed two fazers. "Here." He handed one to Jester and tucked one in his belt, then pulled a cutter from the drawer and slipped it into his boot.

A glance at Jester's expression caused his blood to run cold. He'd never known his friend to be so upset or emotional in his life. Jester's hands were shaking, and he was babbling to himself about Jenna and *bad vibes*.

"Get a grip on yourself." Hawk patted Jester on the shoulder. "I've never seen you like this."

"I've never been in love before." Jester stared into Hawk's eyes. "How can you be so calm?"

"You've seen battle with me before, this is no different."

"But it is. The women we love are...are..."

"You know the drill as well as I do. Don't think with your emotions no matter what happens, or how tempted you are. It's another mission, that's all."

Jester squared his shoulders. "You can't mean that."

"Not a word, but that's how we do it. Are you with me?"

"Yeah, Boss."

"Promise me you won't fire that thing unless it's absolutely necessary. We don't want to risk--"

"I know. Just scare them."

Jester wasn't faring well at all. Sweat beaded on his forehead and he kept wiping his palms on his pants. His friend had stood at his side many times and never let him down—this time would be no different. "Is the vid you edited in place?"

"I ah...forgot about it when I ran into Throm," Jester admitted.

"You'd better get it planted before Redmon gets to the office."

"Right, but what about Jenna and Kylie?"

"I told Throm to take them to the storeroom. They'll be safe there."

"You're sure?"

Hawk inhaled deeply and stared at his lovesick friend.

"Okay, okay, I'm going."

Hawk watched Jester leave. He felt the same uneasiness as his friend. Nothing about this mission was going as planned, and he suspected that would not change. He could easily handle Sira and Nyles, but with Redmon involved it was sure to take an ugly twist.

First he'd make sure the women were safe, then he'd have his showdown with Redmon. Ever since Redmon saved his neck all those annual-cycles ago, he'd suspected the man had an ulterior motive. He never trusted him. Redmon did nothing without expecting payment in full. Every instinct said Redmon was in this mess up to his eyeballs.

***

"It's about time, Sira." Nyles turned toward her. "Where's Saxon and the journal?"

"I couldn't find him. But with the bait we have here," she nudged Kylie with the fazer, "he's sure to show up."

Nyles groaned. "You'd better hope so because I overheard two guards talking about Redmon."

"He's here?"

Kylie laughed. "What's the matter, Sira? Think he deserted you? You should be so lucky." She saw Sira's hand coming toward her face and braced herself for the blow. Pain shot through her and she gritted her teeth, refusing to give Sira the satisfaction of a reaction. "Feel better now?" Sira's hand raised again but Nyles grabbed her wrist.

"It's hard to catch a fish with dead bait, my dear."

Sira jerked her arm out of Nyles' grip. "Stay out of this, Nyles."

Nyles ran his fingers down the side of Kylie's cheek. "Why don't you let me take care of her?"

Sira shoved Kylie from behind and she found herself pressed against Nyles' chest. His cheap cologne gagged her, or was it because his arms wrapped around her, and he groaned like a mudhog in heat? Sira and Nyles truly deserved each other.

"Take her Nyles. Do what you want."

"Is that jealousy in your voice, my pet?"

"Go tie her up or something. Just get her out of my face." Sira spotted a large cloth bag on the deck and picked it up. She looked inside and smiled. "My, my. What do we have here?"

Nyles shoved Kylie toward the wall. "Stay put." He walked to Sira and yanked the bag from her hand. "You have your insurance, I have mine. Obviously you failed to find Hawk and the journal. However, I will not be leaving empty- handed."

"When did you steal these artifacts, Nyles?"

"While you were failing miserably at your job."

"My job?"

Kylie inched her way along the wall, around the portable vid screens toward the door that led to the research lab. Her gaze remained on Sira and Nyles. They were so busy arguing they did not see her hand find the button. The door groaned as it slid open and she ran inside.

"Go get her, you fool!" Sira yelled.

Nyles' footsteps sounded heavily behind her. She willed herself to run faster, but she could not get out of the lab. She turned, picked up a glass beaker and threw it at him. Damn! He ducked and laughed at her.

"It's no use, Kylie. But if you want to play games, I'd be happy to oblige. You're a very tempting woman. The chase only excites me more."

"You're sick. Why don't you save your perverted acts for Sira."

"She doesn't appreciate me like you do, my sweet."

Kylie had a sinking feeling in the pit of her stomach. It looked like she was stuck. Her hand searched the counter top for something to use as a weapon.

Nyles stepped toward her. "Make it easy on yourself."

"I'd rather die first." She eased open a drawer behind her back and her fingers found a sharp object and wrapped themselves around the handle.

"That could be arranged, but I'd much rather have you alive."

The moment he reached for her, she slashed at him and cut the top of his hand. She ran across the room, but looked back and saw the damage the dissecting cutter had done. Blood gushed down over Nyles' fingers and splattered on the tile floor. All color drained from his shocked face. He hurried toward her, and she hoped he'd pass out before he reached her.

"I'll kill you, bitch!"

***

Jester finished installing the vid program he'd made of Hawk in the holding cell. He checked the desk drawer to be sure the second fake journal was hidden under a stack of papers, then slammed it shut.

When he turned to leave, the door slid open and a large man stepped into the room. "Redmon."

"Jester. Just the man I was looking for." Redmon walked to the vid screens and switched them on. "I see Hawk isn't happy with his accommodations." He smiled. "He really shouldn't have torn his bed up like that." With a groan Redmon turned to stare at Jester. "But, it won't be long before he's executed."

Jester's hands fisted at his side. "I wouldn't know." He stepped around the desk. "Cut to the chase, Redmon. What do you want?"

"Winn's journal."

"I don't have it."

"You know where it is."

"Hawk has it."

"I don't think so." Redmon moved to Jester's side. "You know I can hurt you."

"Yeah, but it won't gain you a thing."

"Really?" Redmon lunged at Jester, grabbed his little finger and bent it back until it snapped. "That's one, you have nine more."

"It's good to see you've kept up on your math skills."

Redmon reared back, then shoved his fist into Jester's stomach just as hard as he could. The little pigor squealed just as he expected he would. "What's the matter? Can't decide which hurts most, your finger or your gut?" He laughed. "Open those drawers and show me what you've hidden there."

"Hawk doesn't like me messing with his desk."

Jester stepped to the side to avoid him, but he was not quick enough. One good, hard punch in the chest sent the little runt backwards. He hit the wall hard enough to lose his breath. Jester's painful groan was music to his ears. "I've never liked you. You're a weakling, and I hate weaklings!" He tightened his fist and rammed it into Jester's ribs and smiled. "You're a puny, simple-minded fool." With one swift blow to Jester's face, he knocked the man to the floor.

Redmon pulled out the middle drawer and it crashed to the floor. He continued riffling through the side drawers until his hand found a book beneath a stack of papers.

Jester forced a laugh.

"Shut up, fool." Redmon threw papers at Jester, then his hand wrapped around the leather-bound journal. He opened it and scanned the contents. "Don't know where it is, huh?"

"So shoot me."

"I will, but I intend to do it in front of Hawk. I'm sure he'd like to be there to say his good-byes."

"That's downright sporting of you."

Jester cringed at him when he slapped him across his face. "It's good to know you have a sense of humor. I'll take great pleasure silencing you. Now get up and let's go."

"Where? You havin' a party?"

"Yeah. Now move!"

***

"Kylie? Jenna?" Hawk searched the storage room from top to bottom. Something had gone wrong. Throm would have brought them here if he could. Redmon. It had to be him. He turned and ran. The vid-screens in his office would be the quickest way to find her. Jester had all the pertinent areas covered, and he could not blindly walk into a trap if he was to save the women.

Anguish burned in his chest while he raced to the lift. It was his fault. He wished he could have kept Kylie, Jenna and Shandra out of this. They were innocent victims in a game that was between him and Redmon. He knew Redmon would use them against him, he expected no less from a man who placed no value on human life. Exactly why he'd left them safe on *The Redemption*. Women.

The door whooshed open and he ran to the screens. They were already on. Redmon had been here. The scattered papers on the floor proved Redmon had found the fake journal. At least that part of the plan had worked. His eyes were drawn to a pink button on the floor, along with a few drops of blood. By the Gods! He'd done something to Jester.

One screen showed Nyles' empty quarters, the other his deserted cabin. The last screen focused on Jester's room, which showed no one. He flipped to the Delphin room and his jaw dropped. Redmon was just entering with a fazer in Jester's back. Sira was screaming for Nyles who must be in the lab with Kylie from the sounds of her muted, yet audible protests.

Instinctively his hand touched the fazer tucked in his belt, then he felt for the journal inside his shirt. He hoped it would work, everyone's life depended on it. The two people he loved were in the hands of the enemy and it was up to him to save them. He'd faced worse odds before, but never more important ones.

CHAPTER THIRTY

Kylie heard Sira yelling for Nyles. Then a deep, authoritative voice bellowed, "Join us, now!"

"If you value your life, you'll do it," Nyles said.

She looked toward the entrance and saw a large, powerful man silhouetted in the doorway. It had to be Redmon, he fit Hawk's description perfectly. He motioned with the fazer in his hand for her to come.

"Nyles, bring the woman."

"Yes sir."

A shiver of disgust coursed down her spine when Nyles grabbed her hand and dragged her toward the Delphin room. His sticky blood dripped on her and she cringed. Not from the feel or sight of the blood, but because she had not cut him enough to stop him.

"Tie her up," Redmon ordered.

Redmon held his fazer on her while Nyles went to the ready room. He returned a moment later and bound her wrists together behind her back with a diving strap. Before he left her, he wiped his bloodied hand on her sleeve and gave her a sinister, *get-even* grin.

Where was Hawk? Had Redmon killed him? Her heart raced and her body felt numb. When Nyles stepped away, she leaned against the cold metal wall and followed its contour to the floor. Hawk was fine, she felt it in her soul, as sure as she knew he'd save her.

A moan from the opposite end of the pool caught her attention and she saw something pink move. She blinked back tears and focused. Jester! The urge to run to him was strong, but not prudent. What had they done to him? Relief spread through her when he sat up and leaned against the bulkhead.

Sira walked up to Jester and kicked him in the thigh. "Still want to flirt with me, *little man*?"

Jester looked up at Sira's face, grabbed her ankle and pulled her foot from underneath her. She landed with a thump on her backside. "I loathe the sun-cycle I even thought about it."

She slapped his face, picked up the fazer from the ground behind her and stood. "You're a dead man."

Kylie watched in horror as she leveled her weapon between Jester's eyes at point blank range. She screamed Hawk's name in her mind. If there was any connection between them, she prayed he would hear her as before. *Hawk, come to the Delphin room. They're going to kill Jester!* She repeated the words several times, picturing Hawk's face, concentrating on his mind, trying to plant her thoughts into his.

Was that an answer she heard in her head? No, it wasn't Hawk, it was Mia. She glanced at the water and saw the Delphin surface quietly and glide to a stop on the belly-slide. Mia studied her with that smiley grin and gave several high-pitched clicks.

Help me, Mia. Call Hawk, find help. Had she lost her mind asking a Delphin for help? Probably, but she had nothing to lose at the moment. She looked up in time to witness Redmon take the fazer away from Sira and throw it into the water. Mia dove after the object and sent her a message that conveyed evil and death. Even a Delphin knew what could harm them.

Redmon shoved Sira away from Jester. "Don't interfere again. I have plans for him."

"Don't be angry, Konar."

Kylie caught her breath when she saw Jester's eyes widen at the mention of Konar's name, obviously shaken. It was strange to see him so serious and quiet. Her heart went out to him, and she thought of Jenna and Shandra. Thank the stars they were safe. She relaxed until Redmon angrily picked up a cloth sack.

"What do we have here, Nyles?"

"Why ask me?"

"Your stench is all over the bag and its stolen contents." Redmon stepped closer to Nyles. "Trying to pull a fast one on me?"

"Of course not, I..."

"You're a liar and a thief." Redmon gritted his teeth.

"We're all thieves here, aren't we?"

"I steal nothing!" He grabbed Nyles by the front of his uniform. "I take what I want."

Sira stepped between the two men. "This is no time to fight amongst ourselves."

"Fine, Sira," Redmon said, turning to face her. "I won't fight with you, I'll just kill you."

"Me? Why Konar?"

"Because you're a whore who betrayed me."

"I never betrayed you."

Redmon grabbed Nyles by the throat and squeezed. "Well, Nyles, how about it. Did you sleep with Sira?"

Kylie wasn't sure who to root for. Actually she hoped all three of them would kill each other. Her gaze met Jester's and she almost laughed at the grin on his face. He seemed to be enjoying their disagreements as much as she was.

Nyles squirmed. "I...ah..."

Redmon applied more pressure. "Tell me or I'll finish you off."

"Yes!" Nyles fell to his knees when Konar released him.

"Konar," Sira said while she stepped closer to him. "Nyles is lying, the same as he was about the artifacts."

Redmon shoved Nyles away then backhanded Sira. She fell to the floor, hitting her head. "You betrayed me, whore, and still have the audacity to deny it!"

Kylie watched Sira's head move from side to side. She gasped in horror when Redmon knelt beside Sira, picked up her head in his hands and slammed it back down against the hard surface. When he pulled back blood dripped from his fingertips. She'd wished Sira dead on more than one occasion, but the reality of seeing her lifeless form on the floor was not as satisfying as she thought it would be.

The water rippled and she saw Mia pop up in the middle of the pool. *Evil, death.* Two words that were more than obvious. Then Mia implanted the image of something round and flat, with the message *the end.* What in the universe was Mia trying to tell her?

***

Hawk had seen enough. There was no logical plan for dealing with the insane trio. He could not take the lift because the door opened into the main area in front of the Delphin pool. As he ran from the office to the slide-pole, he thought he heard Kylie calling him in his mind. His connection to her grew stronger with each passing sun-cycle, but at this moment he heard her clearly.

He grabbed the pole and shimmied up. Voices drifted toward him. Nyles and Redmon were arguing. Good, maybe they'd be too caught up in their own drama to notice him.

"Was it necessary to kill her?" Nyles asked.

"She's not dead." Nyles knelt beside Sira and touched the side of her neck. "Why don't you fight a man instead of a defenseless woman?"

Redmon tipped his head back and roared.

Hawk took advantage of the situation and entered the room. He pulled the fazer from his belt and pointed it at the two men's backs.

"First of all, Sira is far from defenseless, and the only man in this room that I intend to fight, is the one standing behind me." Redmon chuckled. "Good of you to join us, Hawk." He turned. "I've been waiting for you. Didn't want to kill your idiotic friend until you arrived."

"You won't be killing anyone, Redmon."

"Please, Hawk. Call me Konar."

Hawk grinned. "I think traitor fits you better."

"You were my brightest student, but far too trusting. You made it too easy for me."

"Easy to drug me, kill that woman and frame me?" Hawk stepped closer. It felt good to say the words he'd been thinking for annual-cycles. It mattered not if Redmon had a fazer in his hand. If it was his time to die, so be it, but he'd take Redmon with him.

"You think I'm responsible?" Redmon laughed.

"I don't *think*, I *know*." He watched Redmon's free hand fist at his side, and he clenched his teeth like he always did when he didn't like the turn of events.

"You have no proof."

"I don't need proof."

"It certainly took you long enough to figure it out."

Hawk shook his head and glanced toward Kylie. Her beautiful features were marred by fear, but otherwise she was unharmed. Jester on the other hand did *not* look as good, but he was still alive.

Redmon waved the fazer in small circles in front of him. "You think you know, but you don't understand a damn thing!"

"Then tell me, Redmon, or should I say Konar?" He held his weapon steady and noticed Redmon begin to sweat.

"I set you up, you've got that part right. I needed a patsy for my crimes, and another criminal to occupy Andor's resources, someone they could chase to get the heat off Konar. I knew you'd be good at evading capture, you always proved your expertise in escape."

"So I did, and I will again."

"Not this time Hawk." Redmon turned his head toward Nyles. "Get the woman."

"Leave her out of this. It's me you want. It's always been me, hasn't it?" Hawk watched the right side of the man's face twitch, he was definitely getting to him. "You couldn't stand it when your student surpassed his mentor, could you?" Hawk laughed. "Never could settle for second best. It's not in you."

"And what do you know of me?"

Hawk's attention was drawn to Kylie when Nyles jerked her to her feet and began to push her toward them. He could not allow Redmon to get his hands on her. "Kylie!" He'd yelled loudly to distract his enemy. It worked. Redmon turned his head and he quickly made his move. He threw his fazer to Jester, then threw himself at Redmon.

The sound of Redmon's weapon splashing into the Delphin pool was music to his ears. Redmon's fist made contact with his jaw and pain shot through him. He landed several good hits of his own, gratified by Redmon's low, painful growl in response. Rolling away from the edge of the pool, he got the upper hand after several more blows and jumped to his feet. When Redmon tried to stand, Hawk spun once and landed a swift kick with his boot to the man's head.

Redmon fell motionless to the deck. This was his opportunity to check on Kylie. He turned and found Nyles with a fazer pressed to Kylie's head. Nyles was one pathetic human.

"I'll kill her, I swear I will."

"Don't listen to him Hawk, save yourself and Jester."

"Brave little thing, isn't she? She's also the only person who wants you to survive." Nyles laughed while he took several steps back, pulling Kylie with him.

"Way too brave for the likes of you." Hawk took steady steps toward Nyles. "Let her go."

"You'd like that, wouldn't you?"

A loud splash drew Nyles' attention. Hawk reached forward, knocked the weapon from Nyles' hand and jerked him away from Kylie. She fell to the floor when Nyles clung to her for support. With one strong jerk he pulled his enemy to him, applied pressure to his neck and the man wilted to the floor.

He ran to Kylie, untied her wrists and held her close. "Amica," he whispered in her ear.

"Oh, Hawk. I knew you'd come." She pressed her lips to his.

She tasted sweet through her salty tears, and he longed to have her alone, to satisfy her, to love her. Reluctantly he pulled back. "Amica, I love you, but this..."

"Hawk!" she screamed.

He turned in time to avoid the full thrust of Redmon's advance, but a cutter slashed the front of his shirt, and left a surface cut on his chest that started to bleed. His fist drove Redmon back long enough for him to pull his own blade from his boot. Redmon regained his footing, pulled a hidden phazer from him and fired.

Hawk dodged Redmon's shot. Thank the Gods the blood that trickled down his forehead had gone into his eyes, inhibiting his aim. A few more blue streaks of fazer fire came at him, but were not close enough to hit him. He'd never known Redmon to miss a target, but he was thankful he had.

Nyles and Jester started to shoot it out, but he did not have time to worry about them. Redmon ran toward him, lunged, and they both fell to the floor. Redmon was an able opponent, always had been. They struggled, muscle against muscle, matching wits with every practiced move.

When he heard Kylie's scream, he rolled on top of Redmon in time to see Sira attack her from behind. The two women became instantly engrossed in physical battle. Jester and Nyles remained locked in a dangerous laser battle. Thank the Gods they were both lousy shots.

Redmon took advantage of his distraction, knocked the cutter from his hand and now levered a blade against his throat. Cold steal scraped his skin, and warm blood trickled down his neck. He grabbed Redmon's wrist and pushed back in a battle of strength. If he lost this battle, he'd pay with his life.

The fingers of his left hand found Redmon's eyes and dug in. After a loud scream, Redmon rolled off, his hands covering the damage. Hawk jumped to his feet and ran toward Kylie and Sira who were holding tight to each other's hair. Just as Hawk was about to separate them he was hit from behind.

Pain seared through his head. His vision blurred, then all movement stopped. It was as if time stood still. He turned and tried to focus on Redmon's face, but his features grew blurry, then turned dark. The room grew fuzzy and spun in circles, and that's when his legs wobbled and gave way. His body hit the floor.

***

"Hawk!" Kylie screamed and shoved Sira away from her. The evil woman was wounded and bleeding from Redmon's abuse. She lay unmoving on the cement and Kylie ran toward Hawk. He lay unconscious on the floor and her heart raced so fast she could not catch her breath. She knelt at his side, terror. "Hawk, talk to me. Hawk!"

She felt her hair being yanked from behind and had no choice but to rise with it. Sira had already pulled out chunks, but she'd gotten her fair share as well. Only this time it was a man's strength that pulled her up.

"He's not as good as you thought, is he?"

The very tone of Redmon's voice made her shiver. She finally realized what the Delphins had been trying to tell her. It was Redmon they feared, Redmon whom they compared with evil, war and destruction. They had been sending her messages since she arrived, but it took direct contact with Redmon before she *felt* what they had been saying.

"You're coming with me." Redmon jerked her closer to his side.

"Leave her alone. You don't need her." Sira rose to her feet and staggered toward Redmon. "Take me, my love. We'll leave here and go to your retreat. Everything we need is there."

Redmon turned to face Sira. "You conniving whore. I wouldn't take you anywhere. You betrayed me and slept with Nyles! You don't deserve to live."

He shoved Kylie to the floor, pulled a cutter from his belt and thrust it between Sira's ribs and laughed as she sank to the floor in a pool of blood.

Kylie stared in horror. Her legs shook and she fell to her knees. The woman may not have had any redeeming qualities, but this..." Blue fazer beams sparked off the metal walls and she turned toward Jester. Nyles still hid behind a support beam, firing in Jester's direction at regular intervals. Thank the Gods his shots missed and only burned holes in everything that was not made of metal.

"Get up," Redmon ordered.

"You're an animal! I hate you." She stood, unable to comprehend how Redmon could look so pleased with himself for taking a life. "How many lives have you destroyed?"

Redmon snickered.

Kylie's skin crawled when he took her arm and pulled her toward the lift. Where was he taking her? Sira lay dead on the floor, Hawk was unconscious, and Jester and Nyles were still trying to kill each other. Even worse, not one person would know where she'd gone, or who took her.

"Hold it right there."

She spun at the sound of Hawk's voice. The front of his shirt lay open, and blood dripped from a red line across his chest where Redmon's cutter had done its damage. Her mind reached out to him, but his anger was so strong and violent she could not get past it to reach him. He had plenty of reason to hate Redmon, they all did, but Hawk's revulsion for the man, and his need for revenge had completely consumed him.

"So, the fearless warrior comes to life to save his damsel in distress.

How endearing. Too bad you two will never be together." He held his cutter to her throat. "She is a striking woman."

Hawk held up the journal. "I believe this is what you want."

Kylie's hand flew to her mouth. How could Hawk give away the cure like this? Surely he had a plan. She had to trust him.

"Let her go and it's yours."

Redmon eased toward Hawk, the cutter firm against Kylie's throat. "Let her go."

"I think this is another trick." Redmon took a few steps backward.

"What's the matter? Don't trust me?"

The lift door opened and Shandra and Jenna stood like statues, their gazes frozen. They stepped into the room and Kylie felt her mind touched. Was it Shandra, or Mia? It was difficult to tell, but the look on Shandra's face was fierce, and she'd never seen her look stronger.

"Let her go, Redmon," Shandra said.

"You!"

Shandra took several steps forward. "Your past always has a way of coming back to haunt you, doesn't it?"

"You're no threat to me." Redmon pressed the blade tighter against Kylie's throat.

"I've seen into your soul. You're a threat to every living being in the universe, and I'll not let you leave SEA Lab alive."

"Oh, my dear, I don't think you understand. I will be the *only* one to leave here alive." Redmon backed away as Shandra stepped toward him. "I'll kill Kylie if you take one step closer."

"I wonder, Redmon, if even *you* could kill your own daughter?"

Kylie felt her eyes widen and Redmon's grip faltered. She slipped from his grasp and ran to Hawk, who shared her shocked reaction. He put his arm around her and held her tight.

"My daughter is dead."

"Look closely. She's very much alive." Shandra smiled. "I told you she was dead and gave her to the newlywed couple from Estra who stumbled into my home the sun-cycle after Kylie was born. I refused to let you get your hands on her and use her in your sinister crimes."

"I should have killed you the sun-cycle you told me you were pregnant and wanted me to life-mate with you."

"Instead you ran like the coward you are."

Kylie screamed when Redmon grabbed Shandra by the throat. Hawk moved with lightning speed to break apart the quarreling couple. Shock gripped her and she began to shake. Jenna wrapped warm arms around her. Jenna--her sister.

***

Hawk rammed Redmon with his shoulder and shoved his fist into the man's stomach. When Redmon bent his head, Hawk punched the man square in the mouth. He heard Redmon's teeth slam together, satisfied when one fell to the deck. The moment Redmon staggered back to wipe his mouth with his sleeve, Hawk extended his leg, spun and landed a crushing blow to the man's head.

Redmon fell to the ground and groaned, but Hawk roughly pulled him to his feet. He intended to enjoy every moment of revenge, every ounce of sweat, every drop of blood. Redmon could not suffer enough for all the misery he caused, and it was not just a personal issue. He'd seen destruction and carnage on other planets caused by none other than, Konar. He may not have known Redmon was Konar then, but he had hated the name longer than he could remember.

First Hawk's left fist, then his right made contact with Redmon's face. Blood oozed from a cut over his left eye and more drops fell from the socket where his right front tooth had been. Hawk had no sympathy. The man had destroyed planets and taken so many lives he'd lost count. Redmon's last mistake was threatening the people *he* loved.

Redmon fell and pulled Hawk down with him. They rolled, fists pounding, each blow harder than the one before. He heard Kylie gasp, and the fazer fire ceased. Out the corner of his eye he saw Jenna attack Nyles, and a moment later she flipped the stupid man through the air. Jester now had his opportunity and attacked Nyles like the warrior she knew him to be.

Hawk's hands clasped around Redmon's throat as they rolled closer to the edge of the Delphin pool. Redmon seemed to gain strength, but he'd seen it before when a man was about to die. He would take great pleasure snuffing out Redmon's miserable life. His grip tightened and he watched Redmon's eyes glass over as he gasped for air.

Redmon rolled over him and tried to break free, instead, they both fell into the cold seawater that instantly engulfed them. He'd never let go of the evil man's neck. They sank slowly toward the bottom of the pool. Redmon's arms let loose of his and he watched bubbles escape from his nose and mouth. Was he really dead? Just when that thought crossed his mind, Redmon reached for his throat with a death grip. Suddenly Redmon was ripped from his grasp, each of his arms in a Delphin's mouth. He watched in total amazement while two Delphins whisked Redmon through the exit door into the wide open sea.

Hawk swam to the surface and gasped for air, spitting half the Agor sea from his mouth. Water splashed in his face. He wiped his eyes with his hands and when he opened them, Kylie's emerald gaze sparkled at him. "Amica."

She jumped onto the belly-slide and threw her arms around his neck. He could swear he heard her crying as he eased her back. "Are those tears I see?"

"Just water," she said, sniffling.

"That's what I thought."

Kylie laughed. "You're all wet."

"As I have been since we met." He lowered his head and kissed the tip of her nose. If he kissed her lips he'd never stop. He would make love to her right here in the Delphin pool in front of her mother, her sister, his best friend, and Nyles, if Jenna and Jester hadn't killed him.

"Boss! Boss! Are you all right?"

"Fine. How about you? Did you actually hit your target?"

"Jenna gave me a hand and *we* took care of Nyles. He's over there," Jester said, pointing toward the back corner.

Hawk stood on the belly-slide and laughed. Nyles was lying on his stomach, his wrists tied to his ankles behind him so tight he rocked back and forth like a child's hobby horse with each breath. His mouth had been taped shut, but he still squealed like a pigor. "I can see the two of you make quite a team."

"As do you two." Shandra stepped from behind Jenna and Jester.

"As we should." Hawk glanced at Kylie, wiped wet hair from her eyes and groaned. If only they were alone. He called for two of his men to take Nyles to the holding cell. This time the man wouldn't get out. There was still one thing he had to do. He had to see Redmon's dead body

Kylie's hands flew to her temples. "Hawk! Mia's in trouble, she's telling me she's in pain. We have to help her."

"Jester, bring us helmets." He turned to Kylie when his friend ran to the ready room. "We'll help her. We owe her that much."

"She's in extreme pain." Kylie looked into Hawk's eyes. "You don't think Redmon hurt her do you? I saw Mia and Artus swim off with him, but..."

"Don't jump to conclusions. We'll find her."

"Here, Boss," Jester said, his voice echoing inside the helmet on his head, handing two to Hawk.

"What the...?" Jester and Jenna jumped into the water, ignoring his question.

"I'm going with my sister," Jenna said when her head popped up above the surface.

Jester laughed. "I can't trust you two alone."

Kylie donned her helmet and disappeared. Hawk studied her figure under the water, heading toward the exit. He secured the clear bubble over his head and followed Jester and Jenna. "Hawk, I can't see her. I...feel her pain."

He swam to Kylie's side and took her hand. His heart lurched in his chest when she doubled over in pain. "Are you all right, Amica?"

"Yes, it's just so intense. Help me find her."

He took Kylie's hand and pulled her through the water, around rocks and sea plants. "Are we going in the right direction?"

"Yes. Hurry."

"Boss, over there!" Jester pointed to their right.

"Look, Kylie!" Hawk turned her by the shoulders. "There's Artus, Mia's mate, I'm sure she's close."

"Take me to him."

Hawk swam holding Kylie to his side. It felt good to be close to her, but it would feel better to have her in his bed. What if it were the last time? The thought was more than he could bear. How could he leave the woman he loved? She'd be safe with Redmon gone, and a new family to watch over her, but would she ever forgive him?

"Kylie!" Jenna blurted, pointing to a circle of Delphins.

"It's Mia!" Jester stopped beside Jenna and pointed.

"She's still in pain, I can feel it."

Hawk tightened his hold around Kylie's waist. "But she's with her family. Look, they're all swimming in circles around her. Why would they do that?"

"Oh, Hawk, I know what's wrong!"

Hawk stared through the clear bubble at Kylie's face and watched deep concern turn to exuberant joy. What had caused such a change? "I don't understand."

"Her family is circling in celebration. They're protecting her while she...there it is!"

He turned and witnessed a miracle in progress. Mia was giving birth! They all watched in silence as Mia's young emerged from her body, tail first, into the green waters of the Agor Sea. "I've never seen anything so beautiful." He smiled, but nothing compared to Kylie's proud smile.

"I should have guessed." Kylie threw her arms around Hawk's neck. "Listen, Hawk. Do you hear that?"

"The whistling sounds?"

"Yes. They're excited and communicating their congratulations to Mia and Artus. Isn't it wonderful?"

He heard the motherly tone of Kylie's voice and it pierced through his heart. She did not have to say she wanted children of her own, it was written all over her face. Since Shandra was her mother, she'd be able to have the children she longed for. But not with him. He couldn't risk her life, or the life of a child.

"Hawk? What's wrong?"

"Nothing." He couldn't let her know what he was thinking. The ugly truth of his past would separate them soon enough. Redmon may be dead, but he still needed proof to prove his innocence to the Andorian government. "Can you communicate with the Delphins and get one of them to take me to Redmon's body?"

"I'll try." Kylie closed her eyes and took a deep breath.

Small fish scurried back and forth while Kylie tried to link with the mammals. He saw Mia and her offspring swim to the surface with several of the others. How he wished he could have a family, roots, and his precious Amica by his side.

"He's coming. Grab his dorsal fin. He'll take you," she said, opening her eyes.

"Who's he?"

"One of Artus' friends. Artus wanted to come, but he does not want to be separated from his new son during the bonding process."

"I understand." He glanced behind him and saw his ride close the space between them. "Jester, Jenna, take Kylie back to SEA Lab." Just then the Delphin swam by and he grabbed his dorsal fin and held on. Bubbles bounced off the clear helmet and water flowed over him while the Delphin pulled him toward the bottomless crevice on the other side of the lab.

If that's where they took Redmon, it was a fitting burial. The Delphin took him just low enough to see Redmon's body, still slowly sinking from sight into the dark oblivion. The one man who could have cleared his name was gone—along with all hope for a future.

CHAPTER THIRTY-ONE

"Jester, would you mind leaving us alone for a minute?" Jenna watched him nod. "Thanks."

"Mother," Jenna called, "join us."

Kylie smiled when Shandra walked toward them and stopped at the edge of the pool. It was hard to comprehend the woman was her mother. So many questions floated through her mind she had no idea where to begin, or if she should.

"You both must hate me." Shandra looked first to one daughter, then the other.

"I could never hate you, Mother, and I think I understand you better than anyone." Jenna picked up her mother's hand and held it.

"And you, Kylie?"

What could she say? So much had happened she did not know how she felt at the moment. The people she'd always known as parents were suffering from Genesis Disorder, yet all she could think about was her real mother that now stood before her. It was hard to get a grip on her emotions when tears threatened to spill.

"Redmon, your father, is, or should I say *was*, an evil man. He hurt me deeply all those annual-cycles ago." Shandra looked into her daughter's eyes. "When I first met him, I did not see him as evil. He was handsome, intelligent and loving. He courted me for several months, lavishing me with gifts and gentlemanly attention.

"One moon-cycle we made love, and I thought I had found the man of my dreams, the man I would spend my life with. I knew he was from Andor and worked for the government, but I foolishly assumed he'd take me with him when his assignment on Spectra was over."

Kylie listened with interest, and her heart went out to Shandra. This had to be difficult for her, and Jenna as well. Their lives would change forever because of this revelation.

"Then one sun-cycle he left. I was young and foolish. I honestly believed he'd take me with him. He'd promised he would, but I was wrong. Six months later he returned a changed man. He was greedy, and I saw and felt the blood on his hands. Suddenly he claimed he loved me, but I knew he wanted my psychic powers, not me or my child.

"He said he hoped his child inherited my ability, and talked about all the things that would be possible if he had the foresight of two psychics behind him. I couldn't allow him to use you, Kylie."

"Mother, you're shaking. Sit down." Jenna led her to a bench along the wall.

Shandra sat in the center, Kylie to her left and Jenna to her right. This time Kylie picked up Shandra's hand and held it. "Please, continue." She glanced at Jenna who nodded approvingly.

"I don't know what changed him, or if he'd always been that way. I'd never seen that side of him. Love can be blind, even for a psychic." Shandra glanced first at one daughter, then the other. "I was relieved he only had a few weeks to spend on Spectra, and when he left, I vowed he'd never see his child."

"Didn't he check on you?" Jenna asked.

"That's when I moved to the mountain where I live now. Away from the scrutiny of my village, to where I hoped Redmon would not find me."

"I can certainly understand that." Kylie studied her mother's face. She forced a grin, but she knew how hard this was for her.

"The sun-cycle after you were born, two scientists from Estra found my cabin while exploring the mountain. I offered them moon-cycle lodging. When they saw you, Kylie, they were spellbound. I'd never seen two people who wanted a child as much as they did. They explained they were life-mated, but could never have children of their own because their genetic codes had been altered during scientific experimentation."

Jenna picked up her mother's right hand and gave it a little squeeze. "It's all right, Mother."

"I knew Redmon would return looking for you, so I did what I had to do to keep you safe."

"You made a wise choice. My parents are wonderful people who love me unconditionally. I've had a good life with them on Estra."

"Oh, Kylie, you'll never know how I regretted giving you up. How I've worried about you, and wondered how you were being raised. But I see I made a good choice." Shandra bowed her head. "I love you, Kylie. You're my daughter."

"You know, Mother," Jenna began, "I've always wanted a sister, and now I have Kylie."

"Jenna, promise me something." Kylie looked her sister in the eyes. "Anything."

"That we can fight and play like sisters. I never had anyone to fight with, or play with." Kylie laughed. "I suppose we're a bit too old to play, but..."

"You're never too old to play!" Jenna said as she rose and stepped in front of Kylie then pulled her to her feet. "Come on, Sis, let's go find Jester."

"Take Shandra. I'd like a moment alone."

***

Hawk stared into the bottomless crevice. Light from the surface reflected off Redmon's body lying over a protruding rock twenty feet down. Even in death evil remained on his face.

The Delphin that brought him circled above then dove into the crevice. He nudged the body with his nose until Redmon was in the open space, sinking slowly out of sight, deeper and deeper to his watery grave.

With Redmon gone, he'd never be able to prove the truth. Redmon killed Lissa and set him up, but who would believe Redmon's dying confession? Without cold hard evidence, he was in the same position he'd been in for the past five annual-cycles, a man wanted for execution.

He turned and swam back to SEA Lab. Would Kylie be waiting for him? He'd know soon enough, he thought while he entered the pool and surfaced on the belly-slide.

"Thought you decided to become a Delphin yourself," Kylie said.

"I've spent all the time I care to in the water."

"What did you find?"

"Redmon." The expression on Kylie's face confused him. She looked happy and sad all at the same time. "Is everything all right?"

"It couldn't be better."

Hawk stood, removed his helmet and tossed it on the deck. "Come here and kiss me." He watched her perplexed expression turn to a seductive smile. "Now, woman, I can't wait any longer."

Kylie threw herself at him and they both fell under the water. Her lips found his and their tongues entwined while they floated to the surface. Salt never tasted sweeter. He pulled back. "I think we'd better get to the cabin as fast as we can."

"Should I ask why?"

"You *know* why." Hawk picked her up in his arms and stepped up onto the deck. He stared into her emerald eyes. "Any objections?" Her coy, little girl look made him laugh and caused him to walk faster toward the lift. He didn't even care about the trail of water they left behind. "I love you, Kylie Beryl."

***

Kylie lay sated in Hawk's arms. She'd never felt so loved in her life. His every caress spoke the truth of his words, and she savored every touch. She smiled as her head rose and fell gently on his shoulder with each breath he took. He'd dosed off, and rightly so, after his artful, non-stop lovemaking.

She glanced at the clock on the wall. They'd been entranced in each other's arms for over four time-units. Not long enough. He'd loved her as if it were the last time. She desperately wanted to shake the feeling she'd never see him again, but the sensation remained far too real, and too final.

Visions popped into her mind. The Delphins. She closed her eyes and concentrated on their message. It was Mia, and she projected the image of something small, round and flat, sending the words, "The End". Could it be they found Sira's disk? She had to know. It just might be Hawk's redemption.

Slipping out of his grasp she quickly dressed and rushed to the Delphin room. She walked to the edge of the belly-slide and knelt. "I'm here, Mia." She waited, then called again.

The water in the center of the pool rippled and she smiled. Three Delphins broke the surface. Mother, father and baby. It was a sight that warmed her heart. Two bottlenoses peered at her as they slid to a stop. "Where's Mia?"

Under the surface she saw Mia leave the pool, but Artus and baby remained in front of her. Moments passed before Mia's shadow was visible below the surface. Artus clicked and flapped his tail, and baby mimicked his actions.

Mia slid to a stop and proudly presented her with the missing vid-disk. She took it from her and patted her on the back. "Well done, girl. And your baby is beautiful." Both Mia and Artus let out several high-pitched clicks then swam away with their young. "Thank you, my special friends." she whispered.

Kylie ran to the portable vid-screen against the wall. Shivers coursed through her. She remembered her attempt to hide behind this vid-tower to escape Nyles, but that was not what bothered her. It was the dread of what she might see.

When she opened the square case there were two disks inside. One marked hologram-final, and one marked vid-final. She slipped the vid-final disk into the play-tower. Hawk's image covered the screen in living color. The vid was so real she felt as if she were there. He stepped aside and she saw a beautiful woman in the bed, a woman who held her arms out to Hawk and begged him to make love to her.

A gasp escaped her throat when she watched the man she loved, rip off his clothes to have sex with another woman. Tears rolled down her cheeks and she closed her eyes, the sounds of their lovemaking ripping her very soul apart. She could not watch, the lovers' grunts and groans said it all.

The sounds ceased and she opened her eyes in time to see Hawk straddle the woman and raise his cutter high in the air. He laughed, then plunged the dagger into her heart! Kylie stopped the vid and ran. She had to get away, she had to think. This was not possible. Her foot slipped and she fell hard against the cold floor. She just laid there and sobbed.

Hawk was indeed a murderer. She'd seen it with her own eyes. He'd warned her, but somehow she'd always thought it was impossible for him to harm a woman. The terrified look in Lissa's eyes played in her mind. How could he kill her? She wanted to hate him, but he'd told her the truth, whether she wanted to believe it or not. She couldn't love a man who was guilty of murder. But she did.

She wiped her nose on her sleeve, but tears poured from her eyes. Devastated did not even come close to the way she felt. She wanted Hawk, she hated him. She loved him, she loathed him. Why did Mia bring her the vid if it was only going to bring her misery?

She heard the lift doors open and the sound of boot-heels echoed through the room. Opening her eyes she turned to see Hawk looming over her. He bent down and pulled her to her feet.

"What's wrong, Amica?"

"The vid," she blurted, slumping in his arms. She felt his strength and shivered. "Let me go."

"No." He cradled her in his arms, carried her to the bench and eased her down. "Tell me what you saw."

"You...ki...killed Lissa."

"I never kept that a secret. I told you all I knew based on what the vid showed." He brushed hair from her eyes and tears from her cheeks. "I'm sorry you had to see that, but it makes what I have to say easier."

Kylie felt as if her heart were in her throat and it beat so hard she heard each throb as it pounded in her ears. "I'm leaving, Kylie, and I won't be back. I can't offer you a life of peace and prosperity when I'm wanted for execution and being chased all over the galaxy. You deserve better. Someone who can..."

"Stop! I don't want to hear any more." She looked into his dark blue eyes and shared his pain. "Don't leave me, Hawk. I can forgive you. I'll help you clear your name."

"That's not possible. You saw the vid yourself. The evidence is clear, and nothing can change it."

"Hey Boss!" Jester called, hurrying toward Hawk with Jenna in tow. "We've been looking all over for you. We wanted you to be the first to know." He paused and gazed into Jenna's eyes. "Jenna has agreed to be my life-mate."

"And we thought we could have a double ceremony. What do you think, Sis?"

Kylie turned her back, tears burning her eyes and rolling down her cheeks. She's lost the man she loved. Forever. What could she say to her sister who had just found happiness?

"Kylie and I are happy for you, but there will be no double ceremony. I'm leaving immediately."

Jester shook his head. "But...you have to stay. You love Kylie, and she loves you. Anyone can see that."

"As true as that is, it can never be. Now if you'll excuse me I need to summon Beggar."

Pain seared through Kylie's head and she screamed. It had never hurt so bad. Mia was adamant about her message and sent her thoughts with such intensity she had to hold her head in her hands. If it got any worse her head would surely explode.

She looked up and saw Hawk start toward her, but he hesitated. His love was strong, but so was his resolve to leave. *The end, the end, the end*, Mia screamed in her mind. Did Mia know Hawk was leaving and this was the end for them? Or was Mia simply reading her anguish? Whatever it was she wished she'd stop so the pain would cease.

"Kylie," Jenna said running to her sister. "What's happening?"

"Mia keeps saying, 'The end, the end'. I don't know what she means."

Jester stepped closer to Hawk. "Tell me what's going on here."

"Kylie saw the vid."

"Where you killed Lissa?" Jester watched Hawk nod. "But she loves you. Isn't that all that matters?"

"I wish it were."

"Jester," Jenna said walking up behind him. "Kylie's head still hurts. She says Mia keeps saying, 'the end, the end'. Do you know what it means?"

"I might." He grabbed Jenna's hand and pulled her to the screen and turned it on. "Don't trust what you're about to see. I always felt this vid was created, but I never could prove it because I never had it. Redmon turned it over to the high echelon in the government immediately."

Jester watched what he'd seen before while Hawk walked away. "I sure hope they can work this out. I don't want to be the only one taking the big step." He smiled at Jenna.

Jenna slapped Jester across the arm. "What are you trying to say, Funny-Bone?"

"Nothing, Jungle-Flower."

"Kylie?" Hawk tilted her chin up with his finger. "I'm leaving now." A tear fell on his hand. "I never meant to hurt you. I'd hoped to find the evidence to clear me, so we could--"

She gazed into his eyes and felt as if a dagger had been thrust into her heart rather than Lissa's. Hawk was a part of her, no matter what he'd done. "How can you leave?"

Hawk knelt in front of her and wrapped his arms around her. "It's the hardest thing I've ever had to do, Amica. I have no choice. I will not put you in harms' way again. What happened here will repeat itself. Redmon was not, is not, the only man who wants me dead."

"I don't care, Hawk. Take me with you. We'll deliver the cure together." Kylie pressed her lips to his, tasting her own tears. His masculine scent mixed with the salty air, and she knew she'd remember this moment for eternity.

"Hawk!" Jester yelled. "There's a second disk. A hologram disk."

"Now you want to see me kill Lissa in a more real presentation?" Hawk shook his head and started to walk away.

Jester slipped the hologram disk into the special player slot.

Everyone froze when a life-sized bedroom appeared in the center of the floor. A communal gasp sounded when Redmon entered the picture and slipped into bed with Sira, who wore a blond wig. They proceded to have sex exactly the same as in the other vid.

When the love act was over, they watched Sira and Redmon get out of bed. For a moment the vid was void of people, then Redmon appeared carrying a motionless Lissa. He laid her in the center of the bed, then he straddled her, raised his right arm in the air, his fingers curled around Hawk's cutter. Redmon plunged the dagger into Lissa's chest, and blood spurted everywhere when he pulled the weapon back out.

It was obvious he'd hit an artery because the entire area quickly became covered in blood. Redmon then hopped out of bed and out of the picture. He returned with an unconscious Hawk over his shoulder, and struggled to dump Hawk's naked body next to Lissa's on the bed. From the back, Redmon resembled Hawk. Then Sira entered the picture wearing nothing but a thin robe and the blonde wig.

They discussed how to "fix" the vid by inserting Hawk for Redmon, and Lissa for Sira. Redmon gave Sira specific orders on how to destroy the hologram original disk when the special tech was finished. Then Redmon laid his hands on Lissa's bloody body and proceeded to smear blood all over Hawk. He had no scruples at all, no regard for human life.

"I knew it!" Jester yelled. "Hologram disks are easy to doctor and convert into a regular vid, but the hologram itself cannot be changed. By the Gods!"

"Mia. That's what she was trying to tell me. To watch the hologram disk because it meant "the end" to Hawk's situation!" Kylie turned to face Hawk. "You never saw this disk. You only saw the one that was created to frame you." Loud clicks caught their attention and they all turned to see Mia, baby and Artus doing back flips in the water, landing with big splashes.

Kylie ran to the edge of the pool. "Mia. Thank you, thank you." In her mind she heard, "Be happy." She felt Hawk's strong arms scoop her up off the ground. "What are you doing?"

"Hanging on to you, just in case you wanted to join Mia in a celebration. I've spent all the time swimming I plan to." He bent his head and placed a kiss on the tip of her nose. "Jester?"

"Yea, Boss?"

"Arrange that double ceremony you talked about. And make it fast."

Kylie watched Jester and Jenna rush from the room. "Are you sure this is what you want?"

"Yes, my love. I've wanted you from the moment I laid eyes on you. I want you now and forever."

Hawk's lips closed over hers, and he kissed her with all the passion of the universe, she knew she had finally found what she'd searched for her entire life. Everlasting love with a man who cherished her, who would die for her, a man she would die to protect, a man she would love forever and beyond.

ABOUT THE AUTHOR

Born in Michigan, raised in California, Kathleen is now a twenty-seven year resident of Missouri, living in the beautiful Ozarks. She lives with her husband of forty-six years and her dog, an Akita named Bandit. Her son, daughter-in-law, and three fantastic grandchildren live close and keep her life busy.

Writing is Kathleen's passion, which she became serious about when she first moved to Missouri in 1987. Always a fan of sci-fi and romance, she loves combining the two elements into stories of *love and adventure in another time and place*.

OTHER TITLES BY kATHLEEN gARNSEY

Now Available at Amazon & B&N in Paperback or e-book.

To be re-released soon:

Warrior's Link
Secret of the Kiah

New work in progress—*The Traveler*